What Divides

A Children of the Pines Novel

Book Two

By
Kelly Schweiger

Copyright © 2026 by Kelly Schweiger

All rights reserved.

No part of this publication may be reproduced, distributed, or transmitted in any form or by any means, including photocopying, recording, or other electronic or mechanical methods, without the prior written permission of the publisher, except as permitted by U.S. copyright law. For permission requests, contact Kelly Schweiger.

The story, all names, characters, and incidents portrayed in this production are fictitious. No identification with actual persons (living or deceased), places, buildings, and products is intended or should be inferred.

First edition 2026

Acknowledgements

I am forever grateful for all of the love and encouragement of the people who kept believing in this book and in me, on the hard days. To my family, both by blood and by bond: thank you for your strength, your stories, and your endless supply of patience. Thank you for sharing your knowledge and the small bits of your personality that found their way into my characters.

I especially want to thank my husband for standing by me and loving me through all my adventures, projects, and endless chaos. I love you forever, and ever, amen

Most of all, thank you, dear reader, for walking this path with me. Thank you for loving these characters as much as I do. Thank you for coming back, again and again, to read the stories that live in my head. I'm so glad you're here.

Contents

Act 1

Chapter One

Alignment

The heat came early that year.

Franklin felt it before he saw it, the weight of it pressing through the cabin walls before sunrise, thick and unmoving. By the time he stepped onto the porch, the sky over the ridge was already pale, the air holding that damp June heaviness that promised thunderstorms later but delivered nothing yet.

He stood there a moment, rolling his left shoulder where the old injury liked to remind him it still lived. The pines were motionless. Not a whisper of wind. Even the birds sounded lazy, their calls half-hearted and spaced too far apart, like they couldn't be bothered to finish a thought.

Boone was at the wagon, tightening the rear strap with more force than necessary. Cole stood at the wheel, one boot propped on the spoke, testing the iron rim with the toe of his other foot.

"Axle's holding," Cole said without looking up.

Franklin nodded. "It held last week."

Boone grunted. "Last week isn't this week."

They didn't say more than that. Didn't need to. The three of them had worn the words down to nubs over the last few months, talked everything through until silence became its own kind of shorthand. Franklin watched Boone yank the leather strap and knew it wasn't the strap that bothered him. It was Beth. She'd been up half the night with the baby goat that had refused to nurse, and Boone carried her tiredness like it was his own fault.

Gin came down the path from the cabin she shared with Hunter, Morales, and Kosinski, rifle already slung, braid tight against her neck. She didn't greet them. She scanned. The road. The tree line. The rise past the south trail. The habit of it had settled into all of them, that restless sweep of the eyes that looked like caution but was really just living.

Two months ago they'd voted for daylight.

Now they traveled in rotation.

Franklin, Boone, and Cole took turns leading the Market wagon. Gin went every time. Jo went once a week, to sell herbs and honey and to "keep an eye on things," though she would never call it that. Gus rarely went to Market except to help unload in the morning, too many people.

Today was Franklin's turn.

He lifted the crate of jars and slid it into place beside the sacks of cornmeal. The glass clinked, warm already from sitting in the kitchen overnight. Blackberry preserves. Jo's recipe, Mary's hands. The two women had spent three days in the summer kitchen last week, faces flushed over the copper pots, arms stained purple to the elbow. Ian had been underfoot the whole time, sneaking tastes until Mary threatened him with a wooden spoon against his knuckles. He'd grinned. The boy had his grandfather's grin, the kind that made punishment feel like a waste of breath.

Boone checked the strap again. Cole climbed up to the bench seat and settled there with the easy patience of a man who'd spent half his life waiting on other people to be ready.

Behind them, the Lodge was waking. A door banged. Someone laughed. Chickens protested the morning. Franklin caught the smell of woodsmoke and coffee substitute, that roasted chicory blend his mother brewed dark enough to strip paint.

Lily and Fiona came down the path together, heads bent close, the way they always had. Fiona's braid had come loose near the nape of her neck. Lily reached without thinking and tightened it, fingers quick and practiced. Fiona kept talking the whole time, hands moving, sketching some shape in the air that only the two of them understood.

"Inseparable," Boone muttered.

Franklin almost smiled.

Almost.

He caught himself the way he always did, right at the edge of it, where the warmth met the worry. Lily was thirteen now. Old enough to notice things. Old enough to ask questions he couldn't answer. She'd started writing in her journal again, filling pages in that careful handwriting that looked nothing like his own rough scrawl. He didn't know what she wrote about. Didn't ask. Some things a father held loosely on purpose.

"You planning to stand there all morning, or you want to get to the Market before the good spots fill up?" Cole smirked at his younger brother.

Cole's voice carried no heat. Just fact. Franklin grabbed the rifle from where he'd leaned it against the porch rail and swung up beside his brother. The bench seat groaned under their combined weight.

Gin appeared at the tailgate and climbed in without a word. She positioned herself facing backward, rifle across her knees, eyes already on the road behind them.

Boone slapped the side of the wagon twice. "Bring back salt if they've got it."

"If," Franklin said.

"If," Boone agreed.

The road to the school had grown soft with June growth. Ferns leaned into the path, brushing the wagon wheels with a whisper that sounded almost deliberate. The pines smelled sharper in the heat, sap thickening in the bark until the air tasted like resin on the back of his tongue.

Franklin counted without meaning to.

Vendors' wagons ahead. Three.

Two from the west road. He recognized the Meyers' gray draft horse and the Potters' patched canvas cover, the one with the blue corner that had been sewn and resewn until it looked like a quilt square.

One he didn't recognize. A flatbed, clean lines, no visible markings. Good condition. Too good.

He noted it and let it settle.

Cole noticed it too. Franklin could tell by the way his brother's hands shifted on his knees, not tense, just awake.

When the school clearing came into view, the Market was already forming. Tables up. Cloths spread. Water drawn from the pump, the handle still swinging from someone's recent effort. Kids chased each other between the stalls. A dog slept in a patch of sun near the old flagpole. It looked the same.

It never looked different.

That was the trick of it. Sameness could lull you. Franklin had learned that in Fallujah, where the marketplace had looked the same every morning until the morning it didn't.

The Harbingers were there first.

Two women at the south edge of the field arranged bundles of dried herbs in neat rows, spaced with a precision that had nothing to do with salesmanship and everything to do with discipline. A man knelt beside a leather roll, stitching methodically, head bent, movements precise. His hands never paused. Never wandered. Their children stood near the fence line, not drifting, not running.

Waiting.

Franklin had seen kids wait like that exactly once before. Boot camp families at Lejeune, the ones who'd been raised inside the rhythm of orders. Children who understood that stillness was a posture, not a state.

Lily saw them before Fiona did.

Franklin watched the recognition cross her face. Not excitement, not relief. Recognition. A nod exchanged across the distance. Subtle. The kind of greeting that belonged between people who'd already established terms.

His stomach tightened a fraction.

Fiona followed her gaze. "They're early."

"They're organized," Lily said.

It wasn't defensive.

It was factual.

Franklin filed that away too. The tone. The certainty. The way his daughter's voice carried no judgment in either direction, just observation delivered with the flatness of someone reporting weather.

He stepped down from the wagon, boots finding packed earth. "Unload first," he said evenly.

Lily nodded and moved toward the crates without argument. Fiona followed, reaching for the sack of cornmeal with both arms. The two girls worked shoulder to shoulder, passing jars between them with the easy choreography of cousins who'd spent their whole lives in tandem.

Gin was already scanning the perimeter. She'd dropped from the tailgate the moment the wagon stopped and positioned herself at the northeast corner, where the old playground equipment rusted in a stand of goldenrod. From there she could see the road, the tree line, and both entrances to the field.

Franklin moved past her, carrying the second crate.

"Attendance looks lighter," he said quietly.

Gin didn't look at him. "They're self-organizing."

He knew what that meant.

Fewer wandering conversations between stalls. Fewer of the loose, aimless clusters that had marked the early Market days, when people drifted because drifting was all they had. Now the Harbingers kept to their section. The families from the west road kept to theirs. The school families held the center. Lines drawn in grass and habit.

More internal cohesion.

He set the crate down on the table and straightened. Across the field, one of the Harbinger women looked up from her herbs and met his eyes. She held the gaze for a beat, then returned to her work.

He didn't like the way that felt.

The sun climbed past the tree line and sat on the field like a hand pressing down. No breeze. The well bucket groaned on its rope each time someone hauled it up, the sound carrying across the stalls in the still air. Water sloshed over the rim and darkened the dirt in circles that dried almost as fast as they formed.

Children who'd been running earlier now sat in the shade of the old school's overhang, legs stretched out, dust caked to their shins in pale stripes where sweat had run. A boy Franklin didn't recognize fanned himself with a torn sheet of cardboard. Two girls shared a cup of water, passing it back and forth without speaking.

The Market had settled into its midmorning rhythm. Slower. Quieter. Conversations held closer to tables, voices lower, as if the heat had weight and sound had to push through it.

Deb was carrying a basket of early greens toward the central table when she paused.

Nothing dramatic. Just paused.

She set the basket down on the edge of the nearest stall, pressed a hand lightly against her stomach, and drew a careful breath. Her eyes went unfocused for a half second. The world tilted, only slightly, like stepping off a rock you thought was steady.

"You all right?" Ellie asked, passing her with a jar of preserves balanced against her hip.

"Fine." Deb's hand dropped from her stomach. "Must've eaten something."

She hadn't.

She'd woken before dawn with a sour taste coating the back of her tongue and a wave of nausea she blamed on last night's rabbit stew. She'd stood at the basin in the gray light longer than usual, gripping the edge, waiting for it to pass. Splashing cold water on her face. Breathing through her nose.

It had passed. Mostly.

She was forty-three.

Menopause, she'd told herself weeks ago when her cycle had skipped yet again. It was time. Her mother had started early. These things ran in families. She hadn't counted days. Hadn't tracked anything. There were too many other things to track. Firewood. Water levels. Seed stores. Whether the fence on the north side would hold another season.

She straightened and lifted the basket again. Smiled at Ellie. Moved toward the table with steady steps.

Across the field, Jo sat on the bench near the old flagpole, Odin resting at her feet. Her cane leaned against her knee. Her hands were still in her lap.

She watched Deb set the greens down and arrange them.

Just watched.

The well rope sang its tired note again, and water darkened the stones at its base. Franklin shifted the crate of preserves to his other arm and angled toward the central table, but something snagged his attention. Not a sound. A stillness.

Near the well, Lily and Fiona stood with two Harbinger girls. Ruth's age, maybe a little older. Their hair was braided tight against their scalps, identical parts, identical ribbon. One of them held a small cloth pouch cinched at the top with twine. She loosened the drawstring and tipped a few seeds into her palm, dark against the pink of her skin, and pointed at them one by one.

"We sort by cycle alignment," the girl said. Her voice was careful. Practiced. Like someone who'd explained it before and knew the words by heart. "Moon phase and soil temperature together. Each seed goes in during the window that matches its growth pattern to the lunar pull."

Fiona frowned. A single crease between her brows. "We just plant by frost dates."

The Harbinger girl smiled. Not unkind. Patient in a way that looked older than her face. "That's one way."

Lily tilted her head. Her notebook was tucked under her arm, pencil behind her ear. She studied the seeds in the girl's hand the way she studied everything. Like she was already writing it down somewhere behind her eyes.

"It makes sense to plan in patterns," Lily said. Quiet. Thoughtful. No challenge in it.

Franklin heard it as he walked past with the crate of jars.

Plan in patterns.

He set the crate down harder than necessary. Glass rattled against glass. Ellie glanced up from across the table but said nothing.

He straightened. Looked at his daughter. She was still listening, still watching those seeds, her weight shifted to one hip the way her mother stood when she was thinking. Thirteen years old and she already had Mary's patience and his stubbornness woven together so tight you couldn't pull them apart.

A few stalls over, Cole leaned against a post with his arms crossed. His jaw worked once. A Harbinger boy, maybe fifteen, had walked to the edge of the Market boundary and adjusted one of the line stakes. Just reached down and shifted it. Two inches, maybe three. Pressed it back into the dirt with his boot heel like it belonged there.

Cole muttered under his breath. Low enough that only Franklin caught it.

"They like to drift."

Franklin exhaled through his nose. He watched the boy walk back to his family's stall without looking at anyone. No defiance in it. No hesitation either.

Behind him, Lily turned slightly. Not toward Cole. Not toward Franklin. Toward the space between them, the way someone speaks into a room rather than at a person.

"They stay inside their structure." Her voice didn't rise. Didn't sharpen. "We're the ones who move."

Silence stretched for half a breath. The well rope creaked. Someone's child laughed in the distance, and the sound dissolved in the heat.

No one challenged her.

She hadn't sounded angry.

She'd sounded conversational, but certain.

Fiona laughed lightly, the kind that broke tension without dismissing it, and nudged Lily's shoulder with her own. "You've been listening."

Lily shrugged. One shoulder. "Everyone says they want order, don't they?"

The Harbinger girl with the seed pouch watched Lily for a moment longer than was comfortable, then pulled the drawstring closed and tucked the pouch into her apron.

Franklin felt something settle low in his gut. Heavy and quiet. Like a stone dropped into a deep well where you never hear it hit bottom.

Not rebellion.

Alignment.

He hated that word.

He picked the crate back up. Gentler this time. Carried it to the table without looking at Lily again, because if he did, he'd see Mary in her face, and he'd see himself, and he'd see the thing he couldn't name yet. The pull his daughter felt toward structure that wasn't theirs. Toward a logic that sounded clean and moved like water into every crack you left open.

He set the jars down. Lined them up. Kept his hands busy.

By noon the Market had found its rhythm. Trade passed cleanly. Jars moved one direction, dried herbs the other. Smoked venison for soap. Soap for candle wicks. A woman from the Bradshaw family traded six fresh eggs for a spool of linen thread and walked away satisfied. No raised voices. No children crossing the fence line without permission.

The Harbinger stalls stayed neat. Their people spoke when spoken to and smiled when it was expected. They weighed fair and didn't haggle past the first offer. Franklin noticed that. Everyone noticed that. It was the kind of behavior that made you want to trust someone and made you wonder why you couldn't.

The sun climbed until shadows shrank to almost nothing and the air pressed down like a wool blanket left too close to the stove. Flies found the preserves. Children found the shade. The Market slowed the way rivers slow in wide spots, spreading thin, losing urgency.

Deb sat against the school wall where the bricks still held morning cool. Her basket of greens rested beside her, half traded, the remainder wilting in the heat. She pulled her knees up. Dropped them. Shifted. Couldn't find a position that settled the low ache in her back or the faint greasy roll that kept washing through her stomach.

She started counting.

April. March. February.

Her fingers pressed against her thigh, one month per finger, the way her mother had taught her when she was fifteen and too embarrassed to write it down.

She stopped.

No.

That couldn't be right.

She tried again. Slower this time. Tracking weeks instead of months. She anchored to the last frost, early April, because she remembered hanging laundry the morning it came and her back had ached then too. She'd bled that week. She was sure of it. Almost sure.

After that, nothing.

Her stomach rolled. Not the sharp heave of sickness. Something lower. Deeper. Like her body shifting to make room for a conversation she hadn't agreed to have.

Forty-three.

Marcus was fifty-six.

Too old, she thought. She pressed the heel of her hand against her forehead. Sweat slicked her hairline.

We're too old.

She pressed her palm flat against her abdomen. Not searching. Not confirming. Just trying to quiet something that might not even be there. Her fingers spread wide across the worn cotton of her shirt. Beneath it, her skin was warm. Her pulse beat in places she didn't usually feel it.

Could be the heat. Could be the rabbit stew. Could be a hundred things that happened to a woman's body when the world stopped offering easy answers and the stress sat in your bones like weather.

Could be.

A shadow fell across her legs.

Jo stepped into the shade beside her and leaned her cane against the brick. She lowered herself with the careful, measured grace of someone whose joints demanded negotiation for every movement. She settled. Smoothed her skirt over her knees. Looked out at the Market like she'd come over to watch the trading and nothing more.

"Heat's heavy today," Jo said mildly.

Deb nodded. Her hand stayed where it was for one beat too long before she moved it to her lap. "Feels different."

Jo's eyes rested on her. A second longer than necessary. They dropped to Deb's hands, then back up. The kind of glance that measured without weighing. That saw without staring.

"Drink water," Jo said. "Before you decide what it is."

Deb gave a brittle little laugh. Short. The kind that came out sideways when the real sound wanted to be something else entirely. "It's nothing."

Jo didn't answer. She sat with her hands folded over the top of her cane, her face turned toward the sun, her silence as deliberate as a closed door that still left the light on underneath.

The Market thinned the way it always did. Families finished their trades, gathered their unsold goods, lingered over final conversations that served as much as currency as anything on the tables. Wagons creaked to life. Horses stamped. The slow dissolution of a temporary town.

The Harbinger children gathered without being called.

No mother's voice carried across the yard. No father whistled or waved an arm. The children simply stopped what they were doing and moved toward their wagon. Together. Quiet. The two girls Lily and Fiona had spoken with earlier fell into step beside the boy Cole had noticed at the boundary stake. They walked with their hands at their sides and their chins level. Not fearful. Not robotic. Just certain, the way water is certain about which direction to flow.

Lily watched them.

Just a second too long.

Fiona tugged her sleeve. "We're packing up."

"Coming," Lily said.

She didn't look ashamed. She didn't look conflicted, eyes darting sideways the way a child does when she's been caught admiring something her parents have warned her about. She looked thoughtful. Her gaze held on those children a moment longer, then released them cleanly, the way a person sets down a book she fully intends to pick up again.

Franklin saw it.

He was stacking the last of the empty crates into the wagon bed and his hands kept moving, kept working, but his chest went still. The expression on Lily's face was one he recognized. He'd worn it himself, years ago, the first time a drill instructor explained how discipline wasn't punishment but architecture. How structure could hold a man together when everything around him was falling apart. He'd been nineteen. Hungry for something that made sense.

Lily was thirteen.

He set the final crate down harder than he needed to. Gin glanced at him from across the wagon. Franklin shook his head. Not now.

The ride home unspooled slow and green. Gin rode ahead on the mare, rifle across his thighs, scanning the tree line out of habit rather than alarm. Franklin held the reins loose. The horse knew the way. Behind him in the wagon bed, Lily and Fiona sat close, knees touching as always, their shoulders pressed together like two pages of the same open book. They spoke softly, heads bent, their voices low enough that the rattle of the wheels over packed earth swallowed most of the words.

Franklin caught fragments. Torn pieces carried forward on still air.

"...fear makes people exaggerate..."

"...not everyone is against us..."

"...structure isn't control..."

Fiona hesitated once. Franklin heard it in the gap between words, the slight intake of breath before she spoke. "Do you think they're right about that?"

Lily's voice was calm. Measured. Too measured for thirteen. "I think people say something's dangerous when they don't understand it."

Franklin kept his eyes on the road.

The trees passed in steady green walls on either side. June sunlight filtered through the canopy in sharp beams that striped the wagon bed, painting the girls in alternating bands of gold and shadow. A thrush sang from somewhere deep in the understory. The horse's hooves beat a patient rhythm against the dirt.

He had voted for daylight. He had stood in that room across from his brothers and his father and believed that patience was strength. That watching was wiser than acting. That the Harbingers would reveal themselves in time if the Callahans just held steady and kept their eyes open.

Now patience was sitting behind him on the wagon bed, wearing his daughter's face.

When the Lodge came into view, the main building rising solid and weathered above the meadow, heat shimmering over the tall grass like something breathing, Franklin felt something he hadn't allowed himself since the collapse.

Not fear. Not yet.

But the quiet recognition that waiting might have a cost. That every day they spent observing was a day the Harbingers spent planting. Not seeds in soil. Ideas in children.

And for the first time, he wasn't sure who would pay for it.

The wagon rolled to a stop and the girls jumped down, the planks rocking under their feet before going still. Mary was already on the porch, wiping her hands on a flour sack towel, watching them come up the slope.

"How was it?" she asked.

"Hot," Boone answered from somewhere behind Franklin.

Franklin climbed down and reached back into the wagon bed for the small pouch of salt. "Sparse."

Mary came off the last porch step to meet him. He pressed the pouch into her hand and her fingers brushed his, and she didn't look at the salt first. She looked at him.

"Sparse how?"

He hesitated half a second too long.

She noticed. He saw it in the slight stillness that came over her face, the way her expression didn't change so much as settle, the way a pond settles after a stone breaks its surface.

They'd been married long enough that silence had textures.

"Them," he said quietly.

Mary's eyes moved past him to where Lily and Fiona were dragging a crate toward the porch steps, still bent toward each other, still talking in that low, private register they'd carried home from the Market like something they didn't want to lose to the open air.

"She said something?" Mary asked.

Franklin nodded once. "Not wrong. Just certain."

Mary turned the salt pouch over in her hands, not looking at it. "She's always been certain."

"That's what worries me."

She didn't argue. She didn't make a face or wave it off with the towel. She stepped closer and laid her hand flat against the center of his chest, right where his shirt clung damp to his skin, and held it there.

"We raised her to think," she said. "We didn't raise her to agree."

He exhaled. The breath had been sitting in him since the ride home, since the tree line, since Lily's face.

"Thinking can drift off course," he said.

Mary's thumb pressed once, firm, against his sternum.

"Fear can drift as well."

He met her eyes.

Green. Steady. A little tired at the edges from a long morning of her own.

Not dismissal. Not denial.

Partnership.

Behind them, the screen door banged open and Ruth came barreling out with Ian at her heels, both of them already talking at once, Ruth demanding to know if he'd brought anything sweet, Ian grabbing a fistful of Franklin's shirt before he'd even turned around. Boone's younger two rounded the side of the house at a dead run, Rowan shouting something about the chickens and Fiona dropping her side of the crate to holler back.

The porch erupted.

Mary's hand dropped from his chest and she turned toward the noise the way a captain turns toward a squall, calm and already assessing.

"Rowan, what did I say about running near the garden beds?" she called.

"We watch," Franklin said quietly. Low enough that only she caught it.

Mary paused, one hand on the screen door, and glanced back at him.

"Together," she said.

He nodded.

That word settled better than patience ever had. Heavier than patience, too. More honest about what it asked of a person. Patience was something a man did alone, grinding it out quietly behind his own ribs. Watching together meant two sets of eyes, two read on what they saw, someone to catch you when you started mistaking your fear for truth.

He picked Ian up off his feet and the boy shrieked with laughter and the sound of it cut straight through everything. Franklin held him a moment, solid and squirming and real.

Chapter Two

Counting Backward

She dressed quietly, pulling her skirt down over her hips in the dark, not lighting the candle. Marcus hadn't stirred. She watched him for a moment, the grey shape of him in the dimness, the slow rise and fall of his chest. Fourteen months they'd been sharing this bed. Fourteen months of something she hadn't expected and still hadn't fully named.

She needed air.

The cabin door opened without noise. She'd oiled the hinges herself in May, a small private satisfaction. The porch boards were damp with dew, and the sky had just begun its first pale confession in the east, more grey than light, the tree line a dark ragged edge against it.

She sat on the step.

Pressed her hand to her middle again.

Still nothing. Just the familiar weight of her own body, her own organs, the soft roundness. Nothing different. Nothing that spoke.

That doesn't mean anything, she told herself.

It didn't.

She counted again.

April. The frost. She was certain about April. She'd been cramping and irritable and Marcus had made the mistake of asking if she was all right in that careful tone men use when they already know the answer, and she'd told him she was fine in a way that meant the opposite and he'd been wise enough to pour her tea and say nothing else.

After that, though?

She pressed her fingers against her lips.

After that there'd been nothing she could point to. No anchor. The summer had come on fast and her body had been doing what it pleased for years now, cycling in and out of sense, skipping months, doubling back. She'd assumed. She'd been reasonable about it.

Maybe she'd been too reasonable.

The birds had started up somewhere past the tree line, that first tentative volley before they committed to morning. She listened to them without hearing them.

Forty-three years old.

Her body had been through things. Hard things. The years had changed it in ways she'd catalogued and accepted one by one like debts come due.

She hadn't accounted for this.

If this was even a this.

She pressed both palms flat on her knees and made herself breathe.

She needed Jo.

The thought came before she'd given it permission. Clean and simple and inconvenient as a splinter. Jo, who watched without pressing. Jo, who knew things about bodies and remedies and the long silences between what a woman suspected and what she said out loud.

Deb hadn't told anyone about the nausea. Not Marcus, who would go still and careful in a way that would undo her. Not the rest of them who wandered through the Lodge with their casual certainty, their familiar sorrows, their settled positions in the order of it all

A sound shifted behind her, soft and internal, the cabin settling or Marcus turning, and she went still on the step like a deer gauging threat.

Nothing.

She let out her breath slow.

The sky was going pink now at the edge, the colour seeping up through the grey in that wordless way dawn had of arriving before anyone agreed it was ready.

She sat with her hands in her lap and looked at it.

She needed to talk to Jo.

She didn't know how to start.

The dew had soaked through her skirt by the time she heard the door of the lodge open and Jo stepped out with Odin.

Jo came out the way she always did, unhurried, as though she'd been awake for some time already and the world outside had simply caught up to her. She carried nothing. Just stepped off her porch in her bare feet and walked toward the garden with her eyes on the sky.

Deb watched her.

Jo stopped at the garden gate, hand on the post, and looked over.

"You're up early." Not a question. Not quite an observation either. Something in between.

"Couldn't sleep." Deb pushed herself off the step. Her knees ached, which was new this summer. One more thing she'd filed away and not spoken aloud.

Jo waited while she crossed the yard. The grass was long between the cabins, beaded with dew. She stopped at the gate beside Jo and looked at the garden rows instead of at her.

"Something's been eating the bean tips," she said.

"Rabbit. Got under the wire again." Jo crouched and pressed two fingers into the soil. "Ground's drying fast this week."

Deb nodded.

They stood there a moment in the way that old friends sometimes could, the silence not demanding anything.

Then Jo straightened and looked at her with those steady eyes that took in everything and gave back only what was earned.

"You going to tell me what's kept you on that step since before light?"

Deb's throat tightened. She'd had words ready. Reasonable words, clinical and brief, the kind that kept a thing from becoming too large to carry.

They didn't come.

"I've missed two months." Her voice came out flat. "Maybe three."

Jo didn't move. Didn't blink, didn't fill the space with reassurance or alarm, just held the weight of it there between them in the morning air.

"I thought it was the change," Deb said. "I've been waiting on it. Expected it."

"But?"

Deb pressed her hand briefly to her stomach, then let it drop. "I don't know. I feel different than I did before. When it was just the skipping."

Jo looped her arm through Deb's, "Let's walk up to the clinic."

The light was grey and thin when Deb finally stopped pretending sleep was coming back.

Behind her, the mattress creaked.

"You sick?"

Marcus's voice carried the rough edges of sleep but underneath it he was already sharp. He had always woken that way, like a match struck in the dark.

"Just my stomach," she said. Too fast.

He pushed up on one elbow. "You eat something bad?"

She kept her eyes on the ceiling. The plank boards above her had a long knot in the wood she'd memorised over the past weeks.

"No."

The word came out smaller than she meant it to.

Silence stretched between them, slow and full.

Marcus swung his feet to the floor. He didn't reach for her. He stood back a step, hands on his hips, studying her the way he studied a fence line he suspected was failing. Not assuming collapse. Not ignoring the lean.

"Deb."

She closed her eyes.

June. May. April.

She tried to remember the last time she'd actually marked it. The kitchen calendar still hung on the wall, but half those squares were scratched through with weather notes and market days and supply tallies. There hadn't been room for anything else.

"I think I miscounted," she said.

"Miscounted what?"

She turned then.

The look on his face almost made her laugh. Not fear. Not the brittle edge of panic. Just confusion. Honest, practical confusion. The look of a man confronted with something that had no field manual.

"Weeks," she said. "I miscounted weeks."

He stared at her. Then something shifted behind his eyes and his chin dropped slightly.

"Weeks since what?"

She sat up and pulled the quilt into her lap, more for something to do with her hands than for warmth.

"Since my last cycle."

The room went very still. Outside, a bird started up somewhere in the pines. One of the goats bleated twice from the lower pen.

Marcus sat back down on the edge of the mattress. He didn't look at her right away. He looked at the floor, which was his version of thinking, she'd come to understand. The man processed with his eyes on the ground.

"How many weeks?" he said finally.

"Eleven." She paused. "Twelve, maybe. I honestly am not sure."

His head came up.

"Deb." Her name in his mouth again, but different now. Quieter. "That's not miscounting."

"I know that."

"Have you talked to Jo?"

"Yesterday morning." She smoothed a crease in the quilt. "She walked me up to the clinic."

"And?"

She looked at him then, really looked, watching his face the way she would watch the sky before weather. He was fifty-six years old and had spent the better part of his adult life in places where the ground could kill you. She had watched him absorb hard news before and hold it without flinching.

But this was something else entirely.

"We used one of the last test strips," she said. "The ones Mary had put back."

He nodded slowly. "And?"

The bird in the pines had gone quiet.

"Positive." She said it plainly, the way she tried to say hard things. "Two strips. Both positive."

Marcus didn't speak. He reached over and took her hand where it rested on the quilt, not squeezing, just holding it the way a man holds something he isn't sure yet whether to call fragile.

The grey morning light crept across the floor between them.

"Alright," he said. Just that.

She studied his face. "Alright? That's all?"

He rubbed his thumb across her knuckles. "Give me a minute."

They stood amid shadows, the room pregnant with silence. Each, in their own way, counting unspoken costs. Marcus's hand went to his jaw, feeling the familiar roughness there, as if it could anchor his thoughts.

"Are you okay?" His voice gentle.

Deb swallowed. Her own voice felt foreign. "I don't know what I think."

A lie.

She knew precisely what she feared. The futility of starting anew. Age, creeping up faster perhaps than she'd let herself notice. Forty-three. The stone of that number lodged in her throat, immovable.

Marcus, watching her with the careful attention of a tracker, made his move. Slow. Varied steps approaching something delicate. His hands found her shoulders. Steady and warm. The familiar weight of reality in a world that often felt tilted.

"You know, " he spoke quietly, like morning rain on a tin roof, "we'll handle it."

She offered a laugh, brittle, breaking before it was full-grown. "Handle it?"

His gaze held steady. He didn't even blink. "Yes."

She shook her head, vision swimming with something that wasn't entirely tears. "I don't want to start over."

So there it was. She let the words hang between them. Exhaustion, not fear, drove them, filled with the heavy possibility of losing all she'd built, all she'd finally begun to understand.

He heard it. Recognized the weariness that too often walked hand-in-hand with determination. "You wouldn't be starting over," he said, his voice that solid ground returning.

"Marcus."

"You wouldn't," he repeated.

His hand drifted down, covering her own where it rested over her stomach. Familiar contact, grounding them both in this shared uncertainty.

"You'd be adding," he said.

His words were more than comfort. They were conviction. He angled her chin upward gently. The touch brought her to meet the weight of his gaze, where weariness and something akin to hope mingled. His face spoke of battles fought and won, of times endured rather than conquered. Of wisdom past pain.

The room held its breath, seeming to shrink around them. The simplicity of his words gnawed at the edges of her fear, the truth hollowing out space she couldn't yet call hope. Not yet. But maybe soon.

And in the pause between heartbeats, she touched the edges of possibility. Understanding sank roots into the soil of her stubborn will. Maybe it wasn't starting over. Maybe it was simply a continuation.

"Can we really do it, at our age?"

The question escaped before she could catch it. She felt its weight the moment it left her lips.

Marcus didn't flinch. Didn't glance away or drum up some practiced reassurance. His eyes stayed fixed on her, steady and clear.

"At our age." He repeated it quietly, rolling the words like a smooth stone turned in a palm.

The smallest half-smile crossed his face. Not gentle. Not easy. Something older than that.

"I'm fifty-six, Deb. I'm already tired."

That pulled something loose in her chest.

He wasn't reaching back toward youth or painting this rosy. No comfort softened his voice. He wasn't pretending the road looked short. He was standing square in the middle of the same hard ground she stood on, feet planted, eyes open.

Her breath came out in pieces.

"What if something's wrong?" she whispered.

The words barely made it across her lips.

That was the real thing. Not the grey at her temples or the ache in her knees come cold mornings. Not the sleepless nights or the labor of it. The fear lived somewhere older and darker than all of that.

No clinic. No ultrasound. No specialist to read the results and offer odds. No tests. Jo was brilliant and steady and worth more than most doctors Deb had ever known, but there were limits now that couldn't be wished away. The world had stripped away its safety nets and left only the fall.

Marcus didn't answer.

He leaned forward instead, pressing his forehead against hers. Solid. Warm. Unhurried.

"We are together. We will take care of each other, we will face whatever comes."

Her eyes fell shut.

He didn't move away. Didn't reach for words to fill the hollow space she'd cracked open between them. Didn't promise her anything that wasn't his to promise. He simply remained. A fixture. A wall against the wind.

After a long moment, he pulled back enough to look at her.

"Then we count forward," he said.

She blinked.

"Forward?"

"If you're going to count, count forward." A slight tilt of his chin. "See where it puts you."

She turned that over. No sentiment in it. No flourish. Just the plain geometry of a man who had navigated worse terrain by refusing to look backward at the ground he'd already lost.

The logic of it reached her in a way comfort wouldn't have. It moved through her ribs and settled somewhere below her sternum.

She let her hand fall from her stomach.

The nausea hadn't vanished. It still pooled low and insistent, a tide that came and went without asking permission. But something in its character had shifted. Less like alarm. More like proof.

Outside the single window, the ridge had begun to lighten. Pale gold crept along the treeline, slow and deliberate, the way summer mornings here always arrived. The kind of heat that started polite before it meant business.

Marcus squeezed her shoulders once. A brief, solid pressure. Then he stepped back, reaching for his boots.

"I'll get the water," he said.

She watched him cross to the door. Tall still. Broad still. The years had settled into his frame without breaking it, the way weight settles into old timber. He moved a fraction slower than he had fourteen months ago. She noticed, because she noticed everything about him.

Too old, she thought again.

And then she began the count. Properly this time. Weeks stacked against weeks. Months built from those. A number at the end of it that didn't make her stop.

She let it land.

And she didn't look away.

Chapter Three

Terms

Lily turned the pencil over in her fingers.

The yard was loud again. Ian had given up the slingshot argument and was now chasing one of the barn cats through the long grass, arms wide and utterly useless. Ruth stood with her hands on her hips, watching him with the expression of someone twice her age.

Fiona was still waiting.

"You think they're dangerous," Lily said.

"I think they're careful in a way that makes me nervous." Fiona pulled her knees to her chest. "There's a difference."

Lily looked out past the fence line, toward the thin thread of smoke still rising from the school chimney. Whoever kept that fire going kept it precise. Same hour. Same column. Never ragged, never too much.

She'd noticed that three weeks running.

"Gran watches them," Lily said. "She doesn't say much. But she watches."

"Gran watches everything."

"Not like that."

Fiona was quiet for a moment. A concession of sorts.

The screen door swung open and Mary stepped out, drying her hands on a cloth tucked into her apron string. She scanned the yard the way mothers scan yards, cataloguing without appearing to. Ian. Ruth. Lily and Fiona on the rail. Her eyes moved on.

"Either of you seen Dad?"

"Barn," Lily said.

Mary nodded and went back inside.

Fiona leaned her chin on her knees. "You're keeping notes on them."

It wasn't a question.

Lily didn't answer right away.

The pencil tapped once against the closed cover of the notebook.

"I keep notes on everything," she said.

"Lily."

The way Fiona said her name. Flat. Even. No heat to it, just weight.

Lily turned and looked at her cousin full on. Fiona's face caught the last of the evening light, and she looked younger than fifteen and older at the same time.

"You're the one who taught me to look closely," Lily said. "You draw everything you see. You don't look away from anything."

"Drawing something isn't the same as getting closer to it."

Lily considered that.

Down at the fence, Hunter set down his water barrel and said something to Quinn that made Quinn laugh, a short, startled sound like he hadn't expected it. Quinn braced his forearm against the post where his hand used to be, steadying the barrel with his body instead. He didn't pause. He didn't grimace.

He just adjusted and kept moving.

Something about it settled in Lily's chest like a slow-struck chord.

That was the Lodge. The whole shape of it. You lost something, you found another way. You didn't build a system around the loss. You carried it and kept going.

She opened the notebook again.

Beneath the word Order, she wrote more.

At what cost.

"I'm not getting closer to them," she said quietly. "I'm trying to understand what they want."

Fiona looked at the notebook, then at Lily. "And if what they want isn't bad?"

"Then we'll know that."

"And if it is?"

Lily took the pencil and slid it along the spine of the notebook.

The smoke from the school chimney had thinned to almost nothing now. The fire was either dying or banked low, carefully managed so it would last through the night without waste.

Not one ember beyond what was needed.

She thought about that.

"Then we'll know that too," she said.

Fiona didn't move from the rail.

The cicadas filled the silence between them, relentless, and Lily stood with the notebook pressed against her ribs and watched the tree line go dark at its edges.

"They're not wrong about structure," Lily said finally.

"Structure isn't the same as control," Fiona shot back.

"They didn't say control."

"They don't have to."

Silence.

Lily watched a moth drift toward the porch lantern. It circled twice and pulled away.

"When something falls apart," she said slowly, "isn't it smarter to build it back in a way that doesn't fall again?"

Fiona crossed her arms.

"We did."

Lily shook her head.

"We rebuilt what we had."

Fiona stared at her.

"That's not the same thing."

Lily felt the shift then. Not dramatic. Not explosive. Just a small, invisible line drawn where there hadn't been one before. Like the first hairline crack in autumn ice. You couldn't unsee it once you noticed it.

"You think they're better?" Fiona asked.

"I think they're different."

"That's not what I asked."

Lily stood, sliding her notebook under her arm.

"I don't think better is the right word."

Fiona's voice dropped.

"It sounds like you do."

Lily looked at her cousin. Fiona's jaw was set, her chin lifted a fraction. Not angry, not yet. Hurt, maybe. Or something adjacent to it, the particular sting of feeling like the ground had shifted under your feet and you hadn't seen it coming.

Lily understood that feeling. She just couldn't let it make her stop thinking.

"I love this place," she said quietly. "I love every single person in it."

Fiona said nothing.

"That's why I'm asking the questions."

Down in the yard, Ruth had caught Ian by the back of his shirt and was steering him toward the porch steps with the practiced firmness of someone who had done it a hundred times. Ian protested. Ruth ignored him entirely.

Lily watched them for a moment.

"If something is coming," she said, "I want to understand it before it gets here."

Fiona uncrossed her arms, but her shoulders stayed tight.

"And if you understand it and still end up on the wrong side of it?"

Lily didn't answer.

The lantern flame bent sideways in a breath of warm wind, then straightened itself again.

Mary's voice carried across the yard, firm and unhurried.

"Girls. Chores."

Fiona pushed off the rail and moved down the steps without a word, her braid swinging once across her shoulder. She didn't look back.

Lily stayed.

Her hand rested on the porch post, the wood warm from a full day of sun, and she watched Fiona cross the yard toward Ruth and Ian. Watched her cousin scoop Ian up from behind, making him shriek and kick his bare feet. Watched the familiar ease of it, the way Fiona slid back into the fabric of the family like she'd never left it, effortless and whole.

Lily looked south.

The road disappeared into the trees where the ridge dipped, and past that, out beyond what she could see, Little Bear Lake sat still and cold even in summer. She knew the Harbingers' property well enough now. She'd heard enough. The staked boundary lines, the measured rows, the children who sat with their hands folded and stood when elders entered a room.

She tried to name what she felt.

A question. Like pressing her thumb to a bruise just to see if it still hurt.

The Harbingers organized what others left loose. Even Dad had noticed that.

She couldn't stop turning them over in her mind the way Gran turned a river stone in her palm, looking at every facet before deciding whether to keep it or put it back.

That was the part that sat wrong.

Not the Harbingers themselves. Not what they believed or how they kept their children quiet and their stakes plumb and their voices low.

The part that sat wrong was how much she wanted to understand it, and how little that want had to do with fear.

Fear she could work with. Fear meant danger, and danger meant distance.

But curiosity meant she'd walk toward a thing. It meant she'd lean in.

Fiona knew that about her. That's why her cousin had walked away without looking back.

She glanced toward the lower pasture and caught sight of Edwin near the fence line, shoulders bent over a repair that didn't need much fixing. He worked harder than necessary lately. Quieter too.

He never looked toward the south.

Lily wondered why.

With a small shake of her head, she let go of the post and followed.

Chapter Four

What He Saw

Edwin set the pliers down and pressed his palm against his thigh, rubbing the red line the grip had left behind.

Rosa held up her clover chain. It was lopsided, one end heavier than the other, and she studied it with the gravity of someone evaluating real craftsmanship.

"Do you think it's long enough?"

"For what?"

"For a crown."

He glanced at it. "If you've got a small head."

She gave him a look that belonged on someone three times her age and went back to braiding.

The afternoon had gone yellow and thick, the kind of summer heat that pressed down without relief. A pair of swallows cut fast and low across the pasture and disappeared into the treeline. He watched them go.

He did not look south.

"She went down near the Harbingers," Rosa said. Casual as weather.

Edwin's hands went still.

"Who told you that?"

"Nobody. " She pulled a fresh clover stem from the grass beside her knee and slipped it into the chain. “I saw she wrote about watching them from the woods.”

He didn't say anything right away. He picked the pliers back up, turned them in his hands, and set them down again.

"You didn't tell Gran?"

"Lily's like my sister."

He understood that. He didn't love that he understood it, but he did.

Up on the porch, Marisol shifted. She'd pulled one knee up to her chest and rested her chin on it, still watching. She'd heard every word. She always did, and she never reacted until she'd finished deciding how she felt about something.

"What did she say about it?" he asked.

"Nothing." Rosa tied off the chain with a careful knot. "She just came in and washed her hands and sat down like she'd only been outside."

Which meant Lily had thought it through ahead of time. The hand washing, the sitting down, the ordinary face. Lily planned things the way Edwin planned radio schedules, timing and precision and backup positions if the signal broke down.

He should've expected it.

He’d once repeated one of their ideas aloud, thinking it sounded reasonable. The silence that followed had never quite left him.

The way Jo's gaze had turned sharp still stayed with him too—not mad. Not blaming. Just taking measure.

He'd sworn off ever being weighed like that again.

He stood up and pressed his boot against the fence post. The wire held. It had been holding fine all along.

"Rosa." He kept his voice level. "If she goes again, you come find me."

Rosa tilted her head. "Are they bad?"

He had no clean answer for that, so he didn't offer one.

Rosa was still watching him, the clover crown finished and draped across her knee.

He picked up the bucket.

"Just come find me," he said again.

She nodded, satisfied enough, and went back to studying her work.

Edwin walked toward the barn, but his feet slowed before he reached the big doors. He stood in the shadow of the overhang and set the bucket down. The swallows were gone now. The pasture sat empty and bright.

He hesitated.

The memory came the way memories do when they've been waiting; quiet, and patient, and exactly where he'd left them.

He'd gone too close once. Close enough that he could see through the gaps in the young birch stand, close enough that sound carried.

The Harbinger place sat quiet in the late afternoon. Their gardens were straight as ruled lines, their paths swept clean despite the summer dust that coated everything else within a mile.

A younger girl had been carrying a basket of jarred goods across the yard. He put her at seven, maybe eight. She'd caught a toe on a root knuckle pushing up through the packed dirt and went forward hard. The basket hit the ground before she did. One jar broke clean, the wet sound of it loud in the still air.

He'd braced for the shout.

It never came.

The woman beside her crouched, unhurried. Her voice reached him through the birch screen, level as creek water on a flat stretch.

"You disrupted the pattern."

The girl's spine pulled itself straight. Whatever had been on her face smoothed away. No reddening. No welling up.

"I misaligned," the girl said back.

That was all. The woman straightened. The girl began collecting the unbroken jars.

Edwin had stood very still.

Then the longhouse door opened, and a man came through it. He hadn't called out. He hadn't raised a hand or made a sound that Edwin could detect. He'd simply appeared in the doorway.

Every child in the yard stood up at the same moment.

Not one by one. Not rippling outward from nearest to farthest. Together. Like something had passed through the ground beneath them.

Hands folded at the front. Eyes down. They faced the man and waited.

He walked past them without acknowledgement and disappeared around the side of the building.

They sat back down when he was out of sight.

Same silence. Same smooth movements. Not one of them looked at another.

Edwin had backed away slowly, watching his own feet so the leaves wouldn't give him away. He'd put a quarter mile between himself and that birch stand before he'd let himself breathe at a normal pace.

He wasn't afraid of the Harbingers.

What he'd felt was colder than fear.

Fear was honest. Fear told you something was wrong and pushed you to act.

This was something that had no name yet, and the not-naming of it was what kept him up some nights with the shortwave pressed close and the static filling in for thought.

He picked the bucket back up and pushed into the barn.

Rosa ducked through the barn door sideways, careful not to knock the clover crown loose from her head. She settled it with both hands, then picked up right where she'd left off, as if the walk across the yard had been nothing more than a breath between sentences.

"I don't think they are good people," she said. "Because Gin looks mad when she sees them."

Edwin hung the bucket on its hook and turned that over quietly. Rosa noticed things the way birds noticed weather, without effort, without knowing how significant the noticing was.

"Gin doesn't look mad," he said. "She looks careful."

"That's not the same thing."

He almost smiled. "No. It's not."

Rosa climbed onto a hay bale and sat with her legs swinging, the crown tilting slightly to the left. She didn't fix it. She was already somewhere else in her thinking.

Edwin moved toward the stall nearest the door and checked the water level in the trough. He wasn't really looking at it. He was running a quiet inventory in his head the way he did when something needed sorting and he hadn't found the right shelf for it yet.

He thought of Zeke. Thought of the way the old man laughed, wide open and without reservation, the kind of laugh that had nothing to prove. Thought of how Zeke had clapped him on the back one afternoon after

Edwin helped wrestle a fence rail back into plumb, the old man's gnarled hand landing between his shoulder blades like he'd always belonged to that particular patch of ground.

Then he thought of the wagon that had come back without Zeke in it.

He was pulling loose hay from a clump matted against the gate when he caught Lily through the gap in the barn doors. She stood on the lodge porch, not doing anything in particular. Not moving toward any chore or person. Just standing there the way you stand when your body is in one place and your head has already left for another.

She was looking south.

Edwin straightened.

He watched her for a count of five. She didn't shift her weight. Didn't look away. The afternoon light sat flat and yellow across the yard and she was still as a fence post in it, her chin tilted just enough.

South was the Harbinger place.

Something moved low in his chest. Not the hot flare of anger and not the hollow ache of jealousy. Something quieter and more familiar. Something he'd felt the first time he'd pressed the headphones against his ears and heard voices coming out of the dark.

Recognition.

He understood what that pull felt like. The want to know. The itch of a question that nobody around you had thought to ask yet. Curiosity didn't announce itself with noise. It just leaned, steady and patient, until you followed.

He knew how that went.

He also knew it didn't care what it walked you into.

Rosa said something behind him about whether goats could wear crowns, and he answered without turning around, something half-formed and agreeable that satisfied her enough.

He wiped both hands down the front of his pants, the hay dust coming off in a pale smear.

Lily still hadn't moved.

Edwin walked toward the barn door.

He didn't call her name.

Not yet.

Chapter Five

Between

Fiona understood Lily's moods the way others understood weather.

Not because Lily made a show of things but because she didn't.

Lily changed quietly.

And when she changed, the world around her changed too.

They were working peas on the porch when Fiona sensed it again — that faint pulling back. Not in her body. Not where you could point to it. Just in the way Lily's words came a breath slower than they once had.

"You heading down to the lower pasture again?" Fiona asked, eyes down.

"Maybe."

"Maybe's not really an answer."

Lily snapped a pea into the tin bowl. "I just need to see something."

"From the tree line?"

Lily's fingers stopped moving.

Fiona kept her gaze on her lap.

"I wasn't sneaking around," Lily said.

"Didn't say you were."

Quiet settled between them.

Fiona set a pod down against her knee and stripped it slow, the peas dropping one by one into the tin. The sound filled the silence between them the way small things do when larger things go unsaid.

"But you were watching," Fiona said.

Lily didn't answer right away. She picked up another pod and split it with her thumbnail.

"There's a girl," Lily said finally. "Maybe twelve. She carries a bucket to their fence line every morning, same time, same path. She never looks up."

"That's not strange. I don't look up when I'm carrying water."

"You would if there was anything worth looking at."

Fiona turned that over. She wanted to argue with it, but she couldn't find the angle.

"I am pretty sure Gran knows you've been going out there," she said instead.

Lily's jaw tightened, just slightly. "How?"

"She knows your footprints...and she's Gran"

A long pause. A blackbird called from somewhere near the garden and then went quiet.

"I'm not going to their door," Lily said. "I'm not talking to anybody. I just want to understand what we're actually looking at."

"Your Dad says leave it alone."

"My Dad says a lot of things."

"He's usually right."

Silence spilled into the space between them.

Lily turned her face toward the yard.

Franklin dropped the rope coil off his shoulder and crouched beside the barn door, working at something near the latch. His back was to them. But he hadn't moved on.

Fiona stayed standing.

The porch felt smaller than it had ten minutes ago.

"He's going to say something," Fiona said quietly.

"Then let him."

"Lily."

"I'm not doing anything wrong." Lily set the bowl on the rail and straightened. "I'm thinking. That's all. And thinking about something isn't the same as agreeing with it."

"It's starting to sound like agreeing."

Lily's chin lifted, just slightly. Not defiant. Something more careful than that.

"You ever read about cults?" she asked.

Fiona blinked.

"What does that have to do with anything?"

“Because just yelling about something doesn’t mean you’re right." Lily turned to face her fully now, voice low and steady. "If you don't understand why people go, you can't just call them brainwashed. That doesn't fix anything."

"Maybe scared is the right thing to sound."

"Scared doesn't convince anybody."

Fiona pressed her lips together.

Across the yard, Franklin stood. He slung the rope back over his shoulder and moved toward the second barn without a word, his boots raising small puffs of dry dirt with each step.

He still didn't call out.

But Fiona had watched her uncle long enough to know the difference between a man walking away and a man choosing his moment.

"I'm not hiding." Lily picked the bowl back up. "I'm just not announcing it either."

"There is no difference when it comes to your parents."

Lily's fingers wrapped around the bowl rim.

"Gran thinks before she decides. The adults don't always agree."

"Gran doesn't go to the Harbinger fence line without telling anyone, either."

"I'm not doing anything wrong," The word came out flat and final. "I'm watching."

The blackbird called again from near the garden.

Fiona looked out across the yard. Franklin had disappeared into the second barn. The doors were still open, and she could hear the faint sounds of him moving around inside.

She sat back down.

"Why does it matter to you so much?" she asked.

It was the real question. The one under all the others.

Lily was quiet for a moment.

"Because everybody's already decided what they are," she said. "Dad. Boone. Edwin. They looked once and they're done. But that girl with the bucket doesn't look like a threat. She looks like she's been told exactly how to walk and exactly where to go and she does it and nobody thinks to ask her what she wants."

"Or she's exactly where she wants to be."

"Maybe." Lily met her eyes. "That's kind of the point."

Fiona pulled the bowl back toward herself and picked up the last of the pods.

The rhythm of the work settled between them again, quieter now and less comfortable.

Inside the second barn, something metal rang against the floor and Franklin's voice came low, talking to himself the way he did when something needed fixing.

Neither of them said anything else.

But Fiona kept listening.

And she was fairly certain Lily knew it.

Franklin kept his eyes forward as he crossed the last stretch of yard toward the shed.

He heard the pitch of it more than the words. Fiona's voice carrying a note of something urgent. Lily's measured and unmoved beneath it.

That measured quality was the thing that stayed with him.

Ruth had his temper. Ian had Mary's warmth. Lily had something harder to name. A stillness that could be wisdom or could be the beginning of a very costly mistake, and the distance between those two things was not always visible from the outside.

He set his hand on the shed door without opening it.

Behind him, the porch had gone quiet.

He didn't look back.

Mary had said together, and she'd meant it the way she meant most things. With precision. Together meant he didn't pull Lily off that porch by the collar of her stubbornness. Together meant he didn't pretend he hadn't heard.

Together meant patience, which had never fit him quite right, the way a good coat fits a man with shoulders too wide for it.

He pulled the door open and stepped into the shade.

He'd talk to Mary tonight.

Fiona set the bowl on the kitchen table harder than she meant to.

Jo looked up from the counter where she stood pressing dried lavender into a small tin, her fingers moving slow and careful the way they did when her knuckles were bad. She read Fiona's face the way she read her favorite novel.

"Peas need shelling or they need company?"

"Shelling." Fiona pulled out a chair and sat.

Jo slid the tin aside and lowered herself into the seat across from her granddaughter, reaching for a fistful of pods without being asked. The two of them worked in silence for a moment, the snap and patter of peas hitting the bowl filling the kitchen.

"She went near their fence line." Fiona said it to the bowl.

Jo didn't rush.

"The Harbinger place."

"Yes ma'am."

Another pod opened. Three peas, clean and bright.

"She tell you that herself?"

"Just now. Didn't deny it." Fiona's thumb split a pod down its spine. "She said she didn't cross. Like that's the whole answer."

"Maybe to her it is."

Fiona looked up, frowning. "Gran."

"I'm not defending it." Jo's voice was even, no edge, no comfort. Just the plain shape of the thing. "I'm saying Lily has always drawn her own lines. Same as you do. They're just not always in the same place."

"She kept it from me."

There it was again. The same sentence, but this time it sat in the room differently.

Jo set down a pod and looked at her granddaughter. Really looked at her. The tightness around Fiona's eyes, the way her jaw sat a little forward.

"That's the part that stings," Jo said.

Fiona didn't answer, which was answer enough.

"She said she didn't know what she thought yet." Fiona's voice came out smaller than she wanted it to. "She always tells me when she's thinking. That's what we do. That's always what we've done."

Jo was quiet for a long moment. Outside the window, a woodpecker started up somewhere in the tree line. A steady, knocking rhythm.

"You two have been side by side since you were small enough to fit in the same feed bucket." Jo picked up another pod. "There's going to come a day when she thinks something through without you first. Doesn't mean she's gone."

"What if she goes?"

Not to another house. Not down the south road.

Jo heard what Fiona meant.

"Then you be the thing worth coming back to," she said.

Fiona's hands stilled over the bowl.

Jo reached across the table and tapped the back of Fiona's wrist once, lightly, the way she might tap a fence post to check if it was still solid.

"You're not losing her. She's just moving around in her own head a little. Let her." Jo pulled her hand back and reached for another pod. "The worst thing you could do right now is make her feel like thinking costs her something important. You."

Fiona turned a pea between her fingers.

"I'm not trying to stop her from thinking."

"No. But you're a little scared of where the thinking leads."

The woodpecker went quiet.

Fiona looked at the bowl, at the small green pile growing between them.

"Aren't you?" she asked.

Jo considered the question with the same honest weight she gave everything.

"Yes," she said. "I am."

She picked up the next pod, split it clean, and said nothing more.

Chapter Six

Open Ground

Franklin heard them from the seat of the wagon.

Not the words. Just the shape of the conversation. The flat, careful way Lily spoke and the sharper edge under Fiona's voice.

He didn't turn around.

Boone pulled up alongside him, close enough to speak low.

"How long have they been set up there?"

Franklin handed the reins to Gin, who had appeared at the wheel without being asked. He climbed down and looked toward the south edge of the clearing.

"Week at least." He watched a Harbinger man lift a bundle of herbs from a crate and set it on the table with the kind of precision that looked practiced. "Maybe two."

"Cole know?"

"Cole's got eyes."

Boone crossed his arms. "That's not a no."

The Harbinger table was neat. Everything on it placed just so. No haggling, no rough piles, no personality in the arrangement. Just goods, set out the way you'd set out an argument. Methodical. Pre-decided.

A woman moved behind the table in a pale dress, her head covered with a simple cloth. She didn't call out her wares or catch anyone's eye. She just waited.

Franklin had watched Marine recruiters work like that. Let the silence do the pulling.

Cole appeared at his shoulder.

"Moved up about thirty feet from last week," Cole said, not looking at Franklin when he said it. His gaze was on the table, on the woman, on the two men standing quiet and useful at each end. "Didn't ask, didn't announce. Just showed up in a different spot."

"Anyone say anything?"

"Patrice Holden went over and bought a bundle of chamomile." Cole finally looked at his brother. "Smiled at them like they'd always been there."

Franklin watched the Harbinger woman accept a jar of apple butter from an older man he recognized from the Whitmore place. She nodded once. Didn't smile. Set the jar beneath the table with the same careful motion.

"They're not pushing," Franklin said.

"No," Cole agreed. "They're not."

That was worse, and both of them knew it without saying so.

Behind them, Lily and Fiona had gone quiet.

Franklin glanced back once. Lily stood at the edge of the crowd with her arms at her sides, watching the Harbinger table. Still as a bird dog on point.

Fiona watched Lily.

Edwin kept his eyes on the girl as he lifted Rosa down from the wagon board. Rosa landed with a small grunt and immediately reached for his hand.

He let her take it.

He didn't know her name yet, but he'd watched her enough to know the way she moved. Deliberate. Like every step was a considered thing. Like the ground beneath her feet required permission.

She crossed the open space between the well and the Lodge kids without hesitation, and that bothered Edwin more than anything else. No awkwardness. No tentative glance back toward the Harbinger table for approval. Just steady forward motion.

Rosa tugged his hand. "Who's that?"

"Don't know yet."

"She's pretty."

"Hush."

Fiona had seen it coming in pieces. The shift of weight. The separation from the group. The clean, purposeful walk. She felt the small hairs on her arms lift, though the morning was already warm and growing warmer.

The girl stopped a comfortable distance away. Not too close. Not so far that it read as uncertainty.

"Morning," she said.

Her voice was softer than Fiona expected. Not timid. Just soft, the way water is soft when it moves without rushing.

Lily answered without hesitation.

"Morning."

"I'm Willow."

Lily held the girl's gaze a beat, then offered her name in return. Fiona heard herself give hers too, almost without deciding to.

Willow looked between them both. There was nothing sharp in her expression, nothing calculating that Fiona could point to. Just a quiet, patient openness that felt too settled for a girl her age.

"You trade here every week?" Lily asked.

"When we're permitted." Willow glanced once at the Harbinger table, then back. Not a check for approval. Just an acknowledgment that the table existed. "We don't always come to market. It depends on what's needed."

"What's needed by who?"

"The whole." Willow said it simply, like the answer was the shape of water. "What we have extra of, what others need. It balances."

Fiona watched Lily absorb this with the particular stillness that meant she was storing it somewhere.

Edwin had drifted closer without realizing it. Rosa swung their joined hands, oblivious, looking at a cat sleeping under a nearby wagon. He stopped at the edge of easy earshot, close enough to hear if Lily gave him reason.

Willow turned her eyes toward him. Not startled. Not wary.

"You're with them," she said. Not a question.

"Yeah." Edwin kept his voice flat.

Rosa looked up at Willow with the frank appraisal only a five-year-old could manage without consequence.

"Your dress is nice."

Willow glanced down at the pale grey dress, plain as a field stone. The corner of her mouth moved.

"Thank you."

"Mine has a strawberry on it." Rosa pulled the front of her shirt out to display the faded print. "Gran sewed it."

"She sounds handy."

"She's Gran," Rosa said, as though that explained everything, which to Rosa it did.

Fiona cut a look at Lily. Lily was still watching Willow, reading her the way she read everything. Slow and careful, like a page she wasn't sure she trusted but couldn't set down.

Willow seemed content to be read.

That was the part that unsettled Fiona most of all. The girl had the kind of stillness that came from practice. From being told, over and over, that patience was a virtue worth sharpening until it didn't feel like waiting anymore.

It felt like knowing.

Willow's gaze drifted to the sacks of peas beside their wagon. "You grow those here?"

"Yes," Fiona said. "North field."

Willow's head canted slightly. "We've been shifting our planting schedules."

Lily's curiosity stirred.

"How?"

Fiona caught it as it happened. That pivot. That draw.

Willow's smile came measured, neither broad nor empty. Just controlled.

"Spacing. And timing."

"According to what?" Lily pressed.

"According to patterns."

The word hung there.

Edwin sensed it from ten paces off.

He moved nearer without even realizing it.

"Patterns shift," he said casually.

Willow angled toward him. No startled motion. No downcast gaze.

"They do," she allowed. "When the old patterns fail."

It carried no challenge.

It sounded like discussion.

That made it more troubling.

Rosa pressed closer against Edwin's leg.

Fiona crossed her arms.

Willow said simply, “We look at what’s failing.”

Franklin crossed the clearing at half-pace when he spotted the group.

Lily. Fiona. Edwin. A Harbinger girl.

He didn't quicken his stride. He didn't shout.

He shifted direction.

Gin had noticed it as well.

She didn't draw nearer. She only observed.

Lily knelt beside one of the sacks and lifted a pea, turning it over between her fingers.

"What if it's not broken?" she asked. "What if it just needs fine-tuning?"

Willow's attention sharpened—not with hostility. With thought.

"Then you fine-tune it."

Fiona felt something constrict in her chest.

The exchange was too easy.

Too simple.

Beyond Willow, two Harbinger boys drifted in. Not encircling. Not cutting off exits. Just tightening the radius.

Edwin noticed it as well.

"Market's for bartering and trading," he said. "Not remaking the world."

Willow's focus shifted to him.

"Everything remakes the world," she said softly.

Franklin arrived then.

"Morning," he said calmly.

Willow stepped back half a pace.

Not in fear.

In acknowledgment.

"Morning," she replied.

Franklin nodded once. "You folks settling in all right down south?"

"Yes, sir."

The "sir" landed wrong.

Too formal. Too smooth.

"We've found clarity," she added.

Fiona felt Lily go very still beside her.

Clarity.

Franklin held her gaze a beat longer than was comfortable.

"Good," he said. "Clarity's useful."

He looked down at Lily.

"Unload those sacks, Lil."

It wasn't a rebuke.

It wasn't dismissal.

It was direction.

Lily hesitated.

Just long enough to be noticed.

Then she set the pea down on top of the sack and straightened, brushing her palms against her trousers.

Fiona moved first, grabbing the nearest sack by its folded top and hauling it toward the table. Edwin fell in beside her without being asked, lifting two at once.

The Harbinger boys didn't move.

Willow watched Lily with an expression Fiona couldn't name. Not smug. Not wounded. Something settled and patient, like a woman watching a season turn.

Franklin crouched beside the wagon wheel and checked the pin, turning it twice. His back was to Willow. That was deliberate.

"You plant the north field in rye this year?" he asked, without looking up.

Willow answered without pause. "Winter wheat, mostly. Some rye along the edge."

"Smart." He stood. "Wind off the ridge'll dry out rye something terrible come August."

"Our teacher accounted for that."

Franklin dusted his hands on his thighs. "That so."

Not a question.

Willow absorbed it the same way she absorbed everything. Quietly. Completely.

One of the Harbinger boys shifted. Franklin's gaze moved to him without haste, held there for exactly one second, then returned to the wagon.

The boy went still.

Lily had both hands on a sack now, dragging it across the ground. Fiona watched her from the corner of her eye. Lily's jaw was set. Not angry. Thinking. Chewing on something she hadn't swallowed yet.

Willow looked at her again.

"You should visit sometime," she said. The words were directed at Lily, clear and unhurried. "Our teacher explains things well."

Fiona's grip tightened on the sack she carried.

Franklin answered before Lily could.

"We keep to our own place." His tone hadn't shifted. Still even. Still mild. "Busy time of year."

"Of course." Willow dipped her chin. "The offer stands."

She turned then, smooth and unhurried, and the two boys followed without a word or a glance back. The three of them moved toward the Harbinger table as though they had simply completed a task and were returning to the next one.

Franklin watched them for a moment.

Then he lifted a sack from Lily's hands, set it on the table with a thud, and said nothing.

Fiona exhaled.

Edwin set his two sacks down and rolled his shoulders. "Friendly," he muttered, just low enough.

"Mm." Franklin's eyes tracked the Harbinger table from across the clearing. Willow had already returned to her place beside the woman at the front. She didn't look back.

Lily stood at the edge of the table.

She was watching Willow too.

Franklin put his hand briefly on top of Lily's head, the way he had when she was six. She didn't pull away from it. Didn't lean into it either.

He let his hand drop.

"Come help me with the preserves," he said.

She came.

Franklin walked toward the crates of jams and jellies.

"Market's for trade," he said. "Not philosophy."

"Yes, sir." Lily fell into step beside him.

The words were respectful.

But something in them felt measured. Precise. Like she'd chosen them carefully from a longer sentence and set the rest aside.

Franklin's chest tightened.

He lifted a jar of blackberry preserves and set it on the table without looking at her.

Across the clearing, Willow stood with the Mayhew family, her head tilted in that particular way, listening. Mrs. Mayhew nodded at something she said. Her husband nodded too, half a second later.

The well rope creaked as someone drew water.

A burst of laughter rolled from Boone's direction, loud and easy, the kind that carried across a yard without trying.

Market continued.

But something had shifted beneath it, the way a floorboard shifts before it gives. Nothing visible. Just a new give underfoot.

Franklin kept his hands busy.

For the first time the Harbingers hadn't waited to be approached.

They'd stepped into the open ground first.

Chapter Seven

Heat

The sun hung high and brutal by the time Deb conceded she ought to have remained home.

She hadn't desired to.

Market was ordinary. Market was evidence they were still upright.

Marcus had accompanied her without being asked.

He hadn't mentioned it was due to the nausea. Hadn't mentioned it was because she'd clutched the kitchen counter that morning and turned white as cream.

He simply grabbed his hat and said, "I'll come along."

He disliked crowds.

He disliked even more the notion of her standing in one without him.

The heat bore down on the clearing like a palm.

Deb moved more slowly than usual, jar of honey tucked beneath one arm, her other hand settling briefly against the small of her back. She convinced herself it was the sun. Convinced herself it was because it was summer.

Marcus observed everything.

"You're sweating too much," he muttered.

"It's hot out Marcus."

She waved him off and moved toward the shade near the well.

The two women spoke in that measured, unhurried way the Harbingers all seemed to share, as though their words had been weighed before leaving their mouths.

"...productive members," one of them was saying. "We all contribute where we're strongest. The Teacher says clarity removes confusion."

Mrs. Mayhew stood across the herb table, her grey head tilted. Listening.

Deb slowed near the well, not meaning to eavesdrop. The shade was there. She stepped into it.

Productive. Clarity.

The words worked their way under her skin. Quiet. Insistent.

"And the older ones?" Mrs. Mayhew asked.

"We support what strengthens the whole," the woman replied. Her voice held no malice. That was the unsettling part. "We don't burden the pattern."

Burden.

For the first time, the word felt personal.

Deb stood holding a jar of honey and thought about the morning. The way she'd gripped the counter. The way Marcus hadn't said a word about it, just set his hat on his head and followed her out the door. She thought about the weeks she'd been counting backward, and about how she was only beginning to count forward.

Her stomach rolled.

Not the nausea she'd come to expect before breakfast. Something colder.

Marcus was watching her.

She knew his gaze before she turned to meet it. He had that stillness about him that could pass for casual but never quite was. Even here, even in the middle of a Summer market with children threading between the stalls and someone's dog barking itself hoarse near the wagon line, he was tracking.

Her hand tightened around the honey jar.

Her shoulders dropped a half inch. The trees at the clearing's edge blurred at their tops. She felt like there was cotton in her ears.

"Deb."

She heard it. Couldn't answer.

The jar slipped.

His hand closed around it before it reached the ground.

Her knees went. Not dramatically. Not the way it happened in old stories, with a gasp and outstretched arms. Just a quiet folding, like a candle flame pinched between two fingers.

Marcus went down with her.

One arm caught her shoulders. The other braced the back of her head before it could find the dirt. He turned her into his chest, and she felt the solidity of him from far away, real and steady and unmovable, while the clearing tipped and righted itself in slow increments.

"I've got you."

Three words. The same three he'd said in a dozen hard moments.

She heard him call out. He used the tone he'd spent thirty years perfecting, the one that moved people without alarming them.

"Need some water and some room."

Doc pushed through from the far side of the tables, sleeves already rolled.

“Get her in the shade,” Doc said calmly. “Marcus, lift from under her arms. Not the shoulders.”

Marcus didn't argue.

He carried her toward the schoolhouse door, boots grinding dirt.

Inside it was cooler. Not cool.

Doc pressed fingers to Deb's wrist, then her neck

Jo's voice cut through the rest, close already, moving fast despite the cane.

"Give her air, give her air." Jo said to the crowd, "Back up."

She's breathing fine."

"She's not waking up."

"She will."

Marcus crouched beside her, one hand gripping hers too tight.

"Deb."

Her eyelids fluttered.

The room steadied in pieces.

She became aware first of Marcus's voice, then of the smell of old chalk and wood dust, then of Doc's familiar, unhurried presence.

"I'm fine," she managed.

"You were on the ground." Marcus looked down at her, jaw tight, the honey jar still in his free hand.

"I noticed. Oh Marcus, I dropped the honey," she murmured.

"You didn't," Marcus said. "I've got it."

Doc's mouth twitched.

"Of course that's what you're worried about."

Jo was beside them, Odin pressing his broad head between Marcus's arm and Deb's shoulder, warm and heavy and smelling of dog and summer grass.

Deb looked up at her.

Jo's expression didn't alarm her. It settled her. The way a plumb line settles a crooked wall. Steady and reading and already thinking three moves ahead.

"Breathe," Jo said quietly.

Deb breathed.

Doc shifted Deb upright and passed her a tin cup.

"Little sips."

She complied.

Marcus stood like a man bracing for another strike.

Doc studied them both.

"You've had nausea," he said quietly.

Deb went rigid. Marcus's eyes cut to her.

"It's only the heat."

Doc lifted one eyebrow.

"At your age, heat doesn't generally knock you flat unless there's more going on."

Quiet.

Marcus's attention moved between them.

"What more?"

Doc settled back against the wall, crossing his arms loosely.

"Deb," he said softly. "Are you pregnant?"

Marcus went still.

Deb shut her eyes.

"Doc."

"When was your last cycle?"

The room waited.

"February," she murmured.

Marcus stared.

"That can't be...February? That means... four months?"

"I assumed it was finishing," she said, sharper than she meant. "I assumed it was done."

Doc showed no surprise.

No alarm either.

Just a single slow nod.

"Well," he said. "Appears it's not."

Marcus's eyes widened. He opened his mouth to speak but nothing came.

Doc's expression softened.

"Forty-three isn't ancient, Deb."

"It's not young."

"No," Doc agreed. "But it's not ancient."

Marcus dragged a hand down his face.

"You sure?"

"As sure as I can be without modern miracles." Doc shrugged lightly. "We'll keep an eye on you. Extra rest. More water. No lifting anything heavier than a stubborn chicken."

Deb let out a weak laugh despite herself.

Marcus didn't.

"What are the risks?" he asked.

Doc met his gaze evenly.

"Same as any pregnancy. Slightly higher chance of complications. Slightly higher chance of chromosomal issues."

Deb's breath caught.

Doc held up a hand.

"Slightly," he repeated. "Not guaranteed. Not doomed. Just statistics."

Marcus swallowed.

"We can handle statistics."

Doc smiled faintly.

"I thought you might say that."

Deb looked between them.

The world felt different now. Rearranged.

Doc stood.

"Sit here a few minutes. Then you can walk out together like nothing happened. No drama."

Marcus nodded.

When Doc stepped outside, Marcus leaned closer.

"We're too old," Deb whispered.

He shook his head once.

"We're still here."

That was his answer.

They sat in the cool of the schoolroom for several minutes. Neither spoke. Outside, the market carried on, voices threading through the open window, the occasional clatter of a crate or a child's bright laughter rising above the general hum.

Deb kept her hands folded in her lap, studying them. The knuckles. The small scar on her right thumb from a canning accident over the winter. These were the hands of a woman who had already built a life, already buried parts of it, already rebuilt what the world had taken.

Marcus sat close enough that his shoulder pressed against hers.

He didn't speak. Didn't need to.

He breathed.

Deb exhaled.

"Jo and Doc are the only two that know."

Marcus almost smiled.

"She won't say anything until you are ready. Doc is a doctor so he can't.""

Deb turned her head, studying his profile. The clean line of his jaw, the grey at his temples, the way he carried a room's weight without ever reaching for it. He had come into her life, so unexpected.

She had not planned for any of this.

She hadn't planned the world ending either.

"What do we tell the family?" she asked.

Marcus considered that.

"The truth."

"Gus is going to be insufferable."

"Gus is always insufferable."

"He's going to take full credit somehow."

"He takes credit for the weather," Marcus said. "This won't be different."

That drew a real laugh from her, quiet and low, and it loosened something in her chest. The tight coil of dread that had lived behind her sternum for weeks shifted and she felt, not relief exactly, but space. Room enough to breathe without bracing.

She pressed a palm to her middle.

Nothing showed. Nothing would, not yet. But she held her hand there anyway, deliberate.

Marcus watched her do it.

He reached over and covered her hand with his own without a word, his palm broad and warm.

Outside, the market noise rose and fell. Somebody's goat bleated with what sounded like genuine complaint. A woman called to her children.

Deb looked at the window.

"All right," she said quietly.

She straightened her spine, rolled her shoulders back.

"No drama."

Edwin stayed close to the steps once the gathering scattered.

He hadn't planned to listen.

But he'd caught enough.

Productive.

Burden.

Pattern.

Sound traveled.

Father Tom stood by the well, sleeves pushed back, hands wet from hauling buckets. He studied folks the way others studied clouds.

Edwin walked over without weighing it much.

"Father?"

Tom glanced up.

"Something on your mind, Edwin?"

Edwin wavered.

He left out Lily's name.

He left out Willow's too.

He skipped past the word cult.

Instead he offered:

"Their voices sound rehearsed."

Father Tom kept quiet.

"At Market," Edwin went on. "Those Harbinger children. They speak like someone drilled the answers into them. Like only one reply fits."

Tom's attention focused.

"Does that trouble you?"

Edwin gave a small nod.

"And Lily's been studying them from the treeline."

He stopped there.

Father Tom absorbed that quietly.

"Children test fences," he said after a moment. "Sometimes by leaning on them. Sometimes by stepping over."

"I don't think she's stepped."

"Yet?"

Edwin didn't answer.

Father Tom rested a hand briefly on Edwin's shoulder.

"Keep your eyes open," he said.

Edwin nodded.

Tom looked out across the clearing where Lily stood beside Franklin, head bent toward him. The girl held a jar loosely at her side, listening to her father with the particular stillness of someone who was holding something back.

"Yes," Father Tom murmured to himself. "Something is shifting."

He didn't say it loudly.

He didn't need to.

Edwin studied Lily too. She wasn't sulking. She wasn't arguing. That was almost worse.

Rosa appeared at Edwin's elbow, a new daisy crown wilting in the heat, tugging his sleeve without a word.

He let her pull him away.

But he kept his eyes on Lily until the wagon blocked his view.

Chapter Eight

What is Carried

The wagon wheels found every rut on the north road.

Lily sat near the back, notebook balanced on her knee, pretending to review the figures Franklin had asked her to tally. Pea sacks traded. Honey exchanged. Two jars short of what they'd expected.

She liked numbers. Numbers stayed put.

The wagon jolted over a shallow washout and something shifted against her hip.

Not hard. Just there.

She frowned and slid a hand into the pocket of her skirt.

Paper.

Small. Folded once.

Her pulse skipped.

She hadn't put paper there.

Careful not to draw attention, she kept her face angled toward the road and eased it out beneath the cover of her notebook.

The fold was clean. Deliberate.

No name on the outside.

She waited.

Franklin and Boone were discussing fence posts up front. Cole laughed at something Gin muttered under her breath. Rosa was asleep against Edwin's shoulder.

No one was looking at her.

Lily unfolded it.

Three words.

When you're ready.

Below that, smaller.

South treeline. Dusk.

No signature. No symbol. Nothing dramatic.

The paper didn't shake in her hand.

She folded it again the same way it had been folded before and slid it between the back cover and last page of her notebook.

Her face didn't change.

But her thoughts did.

She didn't look south.

She didn't need to.

The lodge came into view around the long bend, amber light catching the upper windows and the garden fence where Jo's bean poles stood in their patient rows.

Lily jumped down before the wagon fully stopped.

"Numbers?" Franklin called after her.

"On the board by morning." She didn't break stride.

She crossed the yard, passed the porch, nodded to Mary who stood in the doorway wiping her hands on a towel. She took the stairs without rushing. Closed her door without slamming it.

Sat on the edge of her bed.

The notebook lay in her lap, and for a long moment she just held it. Outside, she could hear Ian's shriek of delight at something, Ruth's voice cutting in with sharp older-sister authority. The creak of the wagon as it rolled toward the barn. Boone's deep voice carrying through the window glass.

All of it exactly what it was supposed to be.

She pulled the note out and read it a second time. Not because the words were complicated. Because she wanted to be certain she understood what she was deciding, even now, before she had decided anything at all.

When you're ready.

Not come tonight. Not we need to talk. Not you should know something.

Just that.

Patient. Even-handed. The way Willow spoke.

Lily set the note flat on the quilt beside her and pressed two fingers against it.

She was thirteen years old. She kept her own tally of what she noticed in the world. She understood that her father's worry came from love and that love was not always the same thing as being right.

She also understood that if she went, she could not pretend afterward that she hadn't chosen to.

Through the floorboards came the soft sound of the kitchen fire being stoked. Jo's cane, slow and certain across the stone floor.

Lily folded the note a third time, smaller now, and tucked it into the spine of the notebook.

She picked up her pencil.

She started on the tallies.

The fainting had been noticed.

People had asked about her.

"Heat'll get you."

"Sun's no joke this time of year."

"Drink more water, Deb."

No one pried. No one pressed.

That was Lodge custom. You offered help. You didn't force confession.

Deb appreciated that more than she could say.

Dinner was loud in the way summer made it loud. Longer tables, doors propped open, air drifting through the great room in slow, uneven currents. Gus had already claimed a chair near the center, settled in like a man who intended to preside over the whole evening whether anyone asked him to or not.

Gunny came in late, dust on his boots from the south fence line. He pulled his hat off at the door and caught Deb's eye as he passed.

"You upright?" Low, easy. No drama in it.

"For now."

"That'll do."

Doc and Rita were up for dinner and they both chuckled at Gunny.

Marcus stayed closer than usual. Not hovering. Just nearer than he needed to be.

Jo watched all of it from her usual seat, Odin heavy against her boot, his eyes half-closed but missing nothing. Same as his owner.

Plates filled. Bread passed hand to hand. Someone argued mildly about seed spacing. Blessedly, stubbornly normal.

Deb waited until the second round of stew. She caught Marcus's eye.

He gave the smallest nod.

She rose to her feet.

The chatter faded but lingered in the air.

"Before Gus decides to let loose something big that's not his to share," she said with calm resolve, "Marcus and I have news."

Gus froze mid-reach for the bread basket.

"I don't announce—"

"You do," half the table chimed in together.

Laughter broke out.

It steadied her nerves.

She placed her hand gently on the table.

"I fainted today... because I'm pregnant."

Silence settled over them.

Not shocked. Not frantic.

Just heavy.

Marcus stood at her side.

Doc leaned back in his chair, his face unreadable but alert.

Gunny blinked slowly.

Gus set the bread down with care.

"Well," he said after a moment, "that explains the glow."

Deb rolled her eyes despite herself.

Franklin's gaze flickered instinctively to Marcus.

Marcus met his look.

No apologies. Just truth.

“We’re about four months along,” Deb added. “We think.”

Mary's hand went to her mouth.

Boone let out a low whistle.

Rita crossed herself automatically.

"Marcus you are fifty-six," Gus muttered, calculating out loud. "You don't believe in retiring, do you?"

"Gus," Jo said mildly.

He stopped.

Then grinned.

"Well," he said, raising his cup. "Guess the Lodge isn't done expanding."

The tension eased.

Questions came, but careful ones.

"You feeling all right?" Jo reached across the table and pressed Deb's wrist.

"What do you need?" Beth asked, already thinking.

Doc lifted his cup in quiet confirmation when someone asked if he was watching over things.

Boone leaned toward Franklin.

"Did you know?"

Franklin shook his head once.

Boone let out a soft breath and reached for the salt.

Gunny said nothing for a long moment, then raised his cup with the rest of them.

Ruth pressed close to Mary and tugged her sleeve.

"What's pregnant mean again?"

Fiona pressed her lips together.

Ian looked up from his plate.

"Is Aunt Deb getting fat?"

"Ian." Mary pulled him in by the shoulder and whispered something in his ear that turned his ears red.

Deb laughed.

It was the first full laugh she'd had all day, and it loosened something inside her she hadn't known was wound tight.

Marcus reached for her hand under the table, said nothing, and she let him hold it.

The conversation shifted around them, the way it always did at a full Lodge table, one thread pulling into another. Beth mentioned the goat was eating again. Gus started in about whether the walapini greenhouse would be finished soon. Jo refilled cups with the efficiency of a woman who had been feeding large rooms her whole life, Odin following her path in a long arc and settling again near the hearth.

Normal.

Blessedly, stubbornly normal.

Lily sat at the far end of the table.

Her hands had been slow to move, her mind somewhere else, when Gus made his toast, and the moment had passed by the time she caught up to it.

She watched Deb now.

Not Deb's face, not the tears that had threatened at the corners of her eyes and then retreated. Not Marcus, whose stillness held an entire conversation in it.

Lily watched Deb's hand.

The way it had moved, without thought, from the table's edge to rest against her own middle. Curved and quiet. An old instinct, maybe, or a new one finding its shape.

Something pulled beneath Lily's ribs.

She knew the word for it.

Across the noise and the candlelight and Ruth's follow-up questions and Ian's red ears, Willow's voice surfaced clean and unbidden, the way certain things did when Lily wasn't guarding against them.

Productive.

Burden.

Pattern.

She had written those words in the notebook beside her plate. Not because she agreed with them. Because Willow had said them like they were obvious. Like they were the same word.

She looked again at Deb's hand.

At Marcus watching Deb with that steady, unwavering look on his face.

At Jo, who was refilling Deb's cup with both hands because the pitcher was heavy and her knuckles were swollen and she did it anyway.

None of that fit the pattern Willow described.

Lily pressed her fingers to the notebook cover.

Closed it a little tighter where it rested beside her plate.

No one noticed.

Edwin was watching Father Tom, who had gone very quiet.

Father Tom sat with both hands wrapped around his cup, his gaze somewhere past the candles. His expression had shifted the moment

Deb mentioned the word statistics. Not dramatically. Just a small closing behind his eyes, the way a window shuts before a storm.

Gunny leaned back in his chair, studying Marcus.

"Statistics?" he asked.

Marcus gave a single nod.

"We can handle statistics."

Gunny held his gaze a moment longer.

Then nodded once in return.

"That's right."

It was a brief exchange, clipped and plain, but Lily caught the weight of it. Two men who had both spent long years staring down unfavorable odds, agreeing in the particular language men like them used. Not comfort. Recognition.

Jo rose slowly, leaning on her cane.

She didn't make a speech.

She simply walked around the table and placed her hand on Deb's shoulder.

"You are not a burden," she said softly.

It wasn't addressed to anyone.

But it landed in the center of the room.

Deb swallowed.

Marcus's jaw tightened.

The fire popped. Ian had fallen asleep against Mary's arm without anyone noticing, his fork still loosely held in his fist. Ruth sat straight and uncharacteristically still, reading the room the way children do when they understand something large has passed through, even without knowing its name.

Gus looked at the table. His broad hand opened and closed once against the wood, the way it did when he was keeping something quiet inside himself.

Across the table, Lily felt something pull in opposite directions inside her.

Willow's words had a shape to them. Clean and certain. A vocabulary for what contributed and what didn't.

But Jo's hand on Deb's shoulder had a shape too.

And Gunny's single nod.

And Marcus, sitting stone-still beside the woman he loved, absorbing the word statistics the way a man takes a punch he saw coming.

None of it fit into columns.

She did not look south.

But she thought about dusk.

Chapter Nine

The Weight of It

Morning came early at the Lodge.

Not because anyone rushed it.

Because summer had its own momentum. The sun climbed before most people finished their first cup of coffee, and by the time the dew burned off the grass there were already chores half done and arguments about seed spacing underway.

Lily stood at the board in the main room with a piece of chalk between her fingers.

Peas: 11 sacks traded. Honey: 7 jars. Salt: 3 bricks remaining.

Numbers.

Numbers were clean.

Numbers stayed where you put them.

Behind her, the kitchen moved in its usual rhythm. Beth and Mary were talking quietly over the bread dough. Someone had left the door open to the porch and the smell of warm hay drifted in from the barn.

Jo's cane tapped once against the floor as she crossed the room.

"Your tallies right?" she asked.

Lily didn't turn.

"They match the sacks."

Jo grunted approval and continued toward the stove.

Normal.

The notebook sat open on the table beside Lily's elbow.

The note was still inside it.

She had not taken it out again.

She knew exactly where it was.

That was enough.

Through the open door, she could hear Ian arguing with Ruth about whether the barn cat had kittens or was just fat. Ruth's voice carried the particular authority of a nine-year-old who considered herself an expert on most things. Ian made a sound that was somewhere between protest and acceptance.

Lily added a line beneath the salt entry.

Preserves: 22 jars remaining. 9 traded.

She heard her father's boots on the porch steps before she saw him. Franklin came through the door with a hay stem caught in his collar and a look on his face that meant he'd already done two hours of work and was calculating a third.

He stopped beside her. Studied the board.

"Preserves look low," he said.

"We traded nine yesterday."

"Your mom or Gran putting up more this week?"

"Mom said Thursday."

Franklin nodded. His eyes moved across the column of figures without hurry. Then he looked at the notebook.

Not at the note inside it.

He couldn't see the note inside it.

Lily kept her chalk against the board.

"Good work," he said, and moved toward the kitchen.

She wrote nothing for a moment.

Then added a small line at the bottom of the column, neat and even, and set the chalk down.

Outside, Jake and Max were wrestling in the dust beside the wagon shed, their voices rising and falling in the particular chaos boys produced when neither one intended to lose.

Max went down first.

Jake whooped in victory and then immediately offered a hand to pull him up.

Max took it.

"Cheater," he said.

"Better," Jake corrected.

They circled each other again.

Jake stopped suddenly.

Inside the open doorway he could see Lily at the board.

She wasn't writing anymore.

Just standing there.

Still.

Max followed his gaze.

"What?"

Jake shrugged.

"Nothing."

They went back to shoving each other.

But Jake noticed something else a little later.

Lily closed her notebook faster than usual when Fiona walked in.

Not guilty.

Just quick.

Jake stored that away without thinking much about it.

That was what he did.

He noticed things.

Like the way Edwin always checked the tree line before he spoke, even when he was only talking about weather.

Like the way Father Tom's fingers went still on his Bible when someone mentioned the Harbingers.

Like the way Marcus touched Deb's elbow when she was tired, not to steady her, just to remind her he was there.

Jake had been noticing things his whole life and nobody had ever told him it was useful. His mother used to say he was too quiet for a boy his age. His father, before everything, used to say Jake had eyes like a barn cat. Always watching. Always waiting.

He didn't know if that was a compliment.

He'd decided it was.

Max tackled him from the side and they went down together in a cloud of dry dirt, arms tangled, both of them laughing too hard to continue.

"That's cheating," Jake said.

"That's better," Max said.

Jake shoved him off and lay on his back for a moment, staring up at the summer sky. It was that particular shade of blue that only showed up in summer, deep and clean, like the world had rinsed itself overnight.

He sat up.

Lily had moved away from the board. She was crossing toward the stairs now, notebook tucked under her arm, chin level and steady.

Fiona stood at the table, one hand resting on the chalk tray, watching her go.

Fiona didn't call after her.

That was the part Jake filed away most carefully.

Because Fiona called after everybody.

She was the kind of person who filled silences before they had a chance to settle. She and Lily had always moved like two parts of the same machine, one talking while the other thought, one reaching while the other pulled back.

But this morning Fiona just watched the stairs and said nothing.

Max stood and brushed dust from his knees.

"You hungry?"

"Always," Jake said.

They headed toward the porch, the argument about the wrestling match already dissolving into something about whether biscuits were better with honey or without.

Jake climbed the steps and held the screen door for Max.

Through the main room, he caught a last glimpse of Lily's notebook on the bottom stair. She'd set it down for a moment to adjust something in her boot.

She picked it back up immediately.

Held it the same as always.

But Jake had noticed the way her palm pressed flat against the cover before she lifted it.

Like she was keeping something in.

Or keeping something from getting out.

He went inside.

Deb moved slower now.

Not dramatically slower.

Just enough that Marcus found himself shortening his stride without thinking about it.

She was already on the porch when he came around from the barn, a basket between her feet and a bowl in her lap.

"You're supposed to rest," he said.

"This is resting."

"You've shelled two buckets."

Deb didn't look up. "That's barely a start."

Marcus leaned against the porch rail.

The yard spread out easy in front of them, children drifting in loose orbits between the garden fence and the barn.

Lily sat under the big maple with a book open across her knees.

Deb watched them a long moment.

"They'll grow up fast," she said, quiet.

Marcus followed her gaze.

"They always do."

Deb rested a hand against her stomach. Didn't seem to notice she'd done it.

Marcus noticed.

He didn't say anything.

After a moment he said, "Doc wants you drinking more water."

"Doc needs to drink more water."

"Doc isn't pregnant."

She shot him a look. He didn't apologize.

Deb smiled despite herself. "You're hovering."

"I'm observing."

"That's a nicer word for it."

Marcus didn't deny it.

Deb set a handful of pods into the bowl and reached for another fistful from the basket.

The snap of each shell was crisp and clean in the morning quiet, a sound that had always steadied her. She'd shelled peas as a girl in her grandmother's kitchen, and the motion lived in her hands now the way familiar things did, without thought, without effort.

Marcus crossed his arms over the rail and watched the yard.

Jake wound up and threw a stick. It clipped the fence post and he turned to Max with an expression of pure satisfaction. Max was already hunting for a better stick.

"She's been out there an hour," Marcus said, meaning Lily.

Deb glanced toward the maple. Lily hadn't turned a page in some time.

"She's thinking," Deb said.

"What about?"

Deb shelled another pod. "Whatever thirteen-year-old girls think about when they're pretending to read."

Marcus was quiet a moment.

"Franklin's worried."

"Franklin should talk to her."

"He has."

"Then he should do it again." Deb dropped a pea that missed the bowl and rolled across the porch boards. She didn't reach for it. "Talking once doesn't count as talking."

Marcus retrieved it without being asked and set it on the rail.

She looked up at him.

He looked back at her with that expression she'd come to know, the one that was somehow both patient and immovable, the face of a man who had waited out worse things than silence.

She reached for the water jug sitting beside the rocker.

His expression shifted slightly, not quite a smile.

"Don't," she said.

"I didn't say anything."

"You were about to."

She drank. It was lukewarm and tasted faintly of the cedar bucket, and she drank more of it than she intended to. She set the jug back down with more force than necessary.

Lily turned a page.

Deb watched her for a moment, this girl who sat so still under the maple that a sparrow had landed three feet from her boot and didn't seem troubled by her presence.

"She reminds me of you," Deb said.

Marcus looked at Lily.

"That's not a compliment," Deb added.

"I know," he said.

Neither of them disagreed with it.

The air cooled slowly as the sun dropped behind the western ridge.

Dinner smells drifted out of the kitchen.

The Lodge settled into evening the way it always did — not suddenly, but by degrees.

Lily sat on the edge of the porch steps with her notebook in her lap.

The note remained inside.

She had not unfolded it again.

Three words were not complicated.

When you're ready.

She closed the notebook and rested her palms on the cover.

Across the yard, Jake was watching her again.

Not openly.

Just the way boys watched things they didn't yet understand.

Jake saw Lily close her notebook and rise to her feet.

She rolled her shoulders the way a person does when they've sat too long. Then she headed toward the garden.

Nothing to read into that.

He turned back to the game, but paused suddenly.

Lily had disappeared past the bean poles.

"You going to throw or what," Max complained.

Jake let Max win the next three throws without argument.

Max didn't notice. He was too busy celebrating each one, arms wide, chin up, the kind of victory that only existed when nobody was keeping real score.

Jake kept his eyes on the bean poles.

The garden had gone quiet.

That wasn't unusual. People disappeared in there all the time.

Ten minutes passed. Jake set down his stick.

"Where are you going?" Max asked.

"Nowhere."

"You're going somewhere."

"I'll be back."

Max scowled at the fence post like it had offended him and wound up for another throw.

Jake crossed the yard slowly, hands in his pockets, the way he'd seen Edwin move when Edwin didn't want anyone to know where he was headed. Not sneaking. Just walking with no particular hurry, which was different.

He passed the bean poles.

The garden ran long here, the rows tight and orderly, the smell of warm soil and something leafy and sharp. He moved between the rows without stepping on anything.

At the south end of the garden, the ground dropped away toward the lower pasture.

A deer trail ran along the fence line.

Jake knew it well.

He and Max had followed it half a dozen times looking for signs of the fox that kept raiding the chicken run. It ran south along the fence and then curved east into the tree line, and if you followed it far enough, it put you up on the ridge that looked down over the old logging road.

The old logging road that ran past the Little Bear Lake.

He stood at the garden's edge.

The trail was empty.

He looked back toward the lodge. The porch was clear. A lamp had come on in the kitchen window, warm and amber against the fading light. The fiddle had found its tune, something slow and untroubled drifting out through the screen door.

He looked south again.

The tree line stood dark and still.

Jake was ten years old. He understood more than people gave him credit for, and less than he thought he did. Somewhere in the gap between those two things was where most of his trouble started.

He understood that Lily had been watching that tree line for days.

He understood that the Harbinger girl had given her something at market, because he'd seen the way Lily's hand moved at her hip on the wagon ride home, fingers pressing flat against something that wasn't there before.

He understood that his uncle Franklin had eyes that went quiet in a particular way when he was worried, and that those eyes had followed Lily across the yard more than once this week.

What he didn't understand was what any of it added up to.

Behind him, the screen door opened. Boots crossed the porch. He heard Clare's voice calling something toward the barn, the words too soft to catch at this distance.

Jake stood between the garden and the tree line with the evening pressing down around him. He could see Lily, standing near the treeline, far down the trail.

The trail curved south and disappeared into shadow.

He stepped onto the trail. Then stopped.

Not tonight. He needed a plan.

Chapter Ten

The Treeline

July held the heat long after sunset.

Even in the shade of the trees the air felt thick, carrying the smell of warm pine and lake water rising from the low ground beyond the ridge. The insects had started their evening chorus, a steady thrum that filled the quiet spaces between sounds.

Lily crossed the yard without hurry.

The Lodge windows glowed behind her, lanternlight spilling across the porch boards. Someone inside had started the fiddle again. The tune drifted out through the open screen door, slow and familiar.

Normal.

She kept walking.

The garden rows brushed softly against her skirt as she passed the bean poles. The path narrowed where the deer trail began, bending south along the fence before dipping toward the ridge.

She didn't look back.

Not because she was afraid someone would see.

Because she had already decided.

The trail curved south and the trees pressed close on both sides, branches knotting overhead until the last pale light of evening became something fractured and dim. The ground softened underfoot, damp leaves matted thick over the dark earth.

Lily slowed when she heard the voices.

Not conversation. Something more deliberate. A cadence to it, like the sound of people who chose each word before they released it.

The trail opened at the ridge and she stopped.

The camp lay below her in the shallow bowl near Little Bear Lake. She had watched it from the tree line before, from a safe distance with the familiar world at her back. Down here the scale of it changed. The cabins stood in a clean arc around the longhouse, their walls raw timber, each door facing the center of the clearing. The longhouse itself sat low and wide with a sod roof and a single lantern burning at its entrance.

A cookfire smoldered near the water. Smoke climbed straight into the still air, perfectly vertical, undisturbed. Two women worked at the wash basins, lifting and wringing without speaking, their rhythm matching without effort.

Children moved between the cabins carrying split wood.

Small armloads. Careful steps.

Not a single one ran.

Lily watched a girl of maybe seven cross the clearing with a bundle pressed against her chest. The child's eyes tracked forward. No stumbling. No looking sideways at something that caught her interest. She set the wood down beside the longhouse entrance and turned back without being told.

Lily descended the last yards of the trail.

No one called out. No one raised a hand or changed their pace. One of the women at the wash basins glanced up and returned to her work without expression.

Then Willow came away from the basins, drying her hands on the front of her skirt.

"You came."

Lily stopped a few feet from her.

"You left a note."

"We left an invitation." Willow's voice held no correction in it, just the flat certainty of a distinction that mattered to her.

"That's the same thing."

Willow tilted her head slightly, a small, unhurried movement.

"Not here."

Lily looked past her toward the clearing. The child with the wood had already made a second trip. One of the women said something low to the other and they both shifted to a new basin without pause or discussion.

"What is it here, then?"

Willow considered the question as though it deserved that.

"A note tells you to come. An invitation says the choice belongs to you." She glanced toward the longhouse, then back. "If you had stayed home tonight, no one would have followed you to ask why."

Lily let that settle.

She thought of Fiona on the porch. Thought of Jake watching her from across the yard with that careful look he had picked up from her father. She thought of her own notebook tucked beneath her mattress and the tallies on the supply board and the way she had stood at that board this morning and felt the shape of numbers as a kind of order she could trust.

She looked at the arc of cabins. The straight smoke. The children with their careful feet.

"What do you want from me?"

Willow didn't hesitate.

"Nothing yet."

Lily glanced around the clearing again.

A boy about Edwin's age carried a crate toward the longhouse door. When he reached it he stopped and waited.

The door opened.

A woman stepped out and spoke quietly to him.

The boy nodded, adjusted the crate in his arms, and continued inside.

He had waited without being told.

Lily noticed.

"Do you all live here?" she asked.

"Most of us."

"And the others?"

"They come when they're ready."

Lily watched a group of younger children seated near the fire. One of the older girls was reading aloud from a small book, her voice steady and measured.

But when Lily stepped closer she saw something that prickled at her.

The girl read a short passage. Then closed the book. The children repeated the words back to her.

Not laughing. Not questioning. Just repeating.

"Is that a lesson?" Lily asked.

Willow nodded. "We study every evening."

"What are you reading?"

"Selected writings."

"From who?"

"Our teacher."

"Only him?"

Willow seemed mildly surprised by the question. "He explains things clearly."

"That's not what I asked."

Willow didn't answer right away.

Lily glanced back toward the book.

The older girl had already moved to the next passage, her voice steady as river current, never pausing to check whether the children were keeping up. They were. Every one of them.

None spoke unless a finger pointed their way.

"Do you have other books?" Lily asked.

"Some."

"What kind?"

"The ones that matter."

Lily studied her. "That's not really an answer."

"It is here."

Something settled cold in Lily's chest. Not fear exactly. Something with more teeth than that.

Lily looked at her. Really looked at her.

Willow's face was open, her posture easy, nothing in her expression suggesting she knew she'd said something worth pushing back on. That was the part that unsettled Lily most. Not cruelty. Not pressure. Just certainty, the kind that had been handed to someone so young and so early that it had grown right into the bone.

Lily glanced back at the children by the fire.

The older girl pointed to a small boy in the second row. He repeated the passage without hesitation, word for word, inflection matching the girl's own. When he finished he looked straight ahead again.

No one praised him.

No one needed to.

"At home," Lily said, "my gran lets me read whatever I find."

"And what have you found?"

"Enough to know I don't know everything."

Something moved briefly behind Willow's eyes. Not disagreement. More like curiosity about a strange animal.

"That sounds exhausting," Willow said.

"It is," Lily admitted. "But it's mine."

The fire crackled and a log shifted, sending up a brief column of sparks. One of the smaller children flinched. The older girl kept reading without looking up.

Lily watched the boy who had flinched settle himself back into stillness. His face went smooth again, the way a pond surface closed over after a stone.

She thought of Ian back at the lodge, who hollered at moths and chased the barn cat and asked fourteen questions before breakfast and didn't wait to be pointed at before he spoke.

"Who decides when someone understands truth?" Lily asked.

"Our teacher."

"And before him, who decided?"

Willow tilted her head slightly.

"That's a question people ask when they are still at the beginning."

Lily turned that over.

"Maybe," she said. "Or maybe it's the most important question and nobody here is allowed to ask it anymore."

Willow didn't answer.

But she didn't look away either.

They stood there in the firelight, the sound of repeated words rising and falling behind them in steady, measured waves, the children's voices blending into something that almost sounded like prayer.

Almost.

Lily gripped her notebook tighter.

Lily watched the children again, their voices carrying the lesson across the clearing in careful, measured turns.

One boy stumbled on a word.

The girl beside him corrected him. Quiet. Even.

He started again from the beginning.

Nobody laughed.

Nobody helped.

They just waited.

The clearing had gone still around them. Not the easy stillness of a summer afternoon. Something tighter than that.

"Do you ever disagree with him?" Lily asked.

Willow blinked. "Why would we?"

No hesitation. No flicker of doubt behind it. Just the answer, smooth and immediate.

A chill moved through Lily despite the warmth pressing down on the clearing.

The longhouse door swung open.

A man stepped out, pausing to speak to someone still inside before he turned and moved into the evening light. Unhurried. Deliberate.

Every person in the clearing shifted. Not stopping what they were doing. Not bowing. Just... adjusting. Like a room drawing itself upright.

It was subtle enough that you might have missed it.

Lily didn't miss it.

"That's him," Willow said quietly.

Lily watched the man cross the clearing.

No one interrupted him. No one called out. People simply made space without looking like they were making space, the way water parts around a stone.

He paused beside the herb table and spoke briefly to one of the women. She nodded once. The exchange lasted only a moment, but the woman straightened after he moved on, her hands returning to her work with new precision. She saw him raise his head and look into the dark trees for a long pause. Then he moved on.

Lily couldn't hear the words.

But she felt the way the clearing held itself. Like a room full of people pretending not to listen.

"He's your teacher?" Lily said.

Willow nodded. "He helps people see clearly."

Lily thought about the boy starting his recitation over from the beginning. About the books arranged on the table inside the longhouse, their spines uniform, their pages chosen by someone else. About the boy who had waited at the door without being told to wait.

The air felt tighter than it had a moment ago.

"I should go," Lily said.

Willow didn't move to stop her.

Lily held Willow's gaze for a beat, then turned toward the trail.

The ridge was steeper going up than she remembered it being on the way down. She kept her eyes on the ground in front of her, stepping over exposed roots, hands brushing the low pine boughs as they leaned across the path.

Behind her, the lesson resumed.

The girl's voice lifted into the evening air, steady and practiced, reading from whatever page had been selected for her. A pause. Then the children's voices together.

Choice can be confusing.

Lily's foot caught on a root. She steadied herself against a birch trunk.

Freedom without understanding.

She climbed faster without meaning to.

Our teacher guides us.

When she crested the ridge she stopped, turning back without meaning to.

From up here the camp looked different. The lantern glow from the longhouse cast a warm amber light across the arc of cabins, and the fire at the center burned low and steady.

It looked peaceful.

Orderly.

Beautiful, even. The kind of scene she might have written about in her notebook, before she understood what she was looking at.

But the words were still moving through her chest, settling somewhere below her ribs.

Choice can be confusing.

She thought about Willow's face when she'd asked about disagreement. The complete absence of conflict in it. Not the look of someone who had wrestled with a question and landed on an answer. The look of someone for whom the question had never been asked.

Lily turned away quickly and started back toward the Lodge.

The tree line swallowed the camp's light within a few steps. The path ahead showed itself only by the difference between shadow and deeper shadow. She moved through it by feel, by memory, by the sound of a fiddle still drifting faint and familiar from the direction of home.

The music grew clearer as she descended.

She kept her notebook pressed against her ribs with one arm, and she did not look back again.

Jake lay flat in the brush twenty yards from the trail.

Pine needles pressed into his forearms. A root dug into his ribs. He hadn't moved for so long, that a moth had landed on his wrist and stayed there, unconcerned.

He had followed farther than he meant to.

The camp sat below the ridge in a neat, quiet arc. Lantern light caught the faces of the children seated in rows by the fire. They were still in a way that kids weren't still. Not tired still. Not bored still. Something else.

Jake had watched them repeat the words together and felt his skin prickle.

He'd seen Lily walk straight into the middle of it without hesitating, like she belonged there, like she'd been thinking about it for a long time. And he supposed she had.

When the man came out of the longhouse the whole clearing changed. Jake couldn't explain it better than that. People didn't scatter or go quiet. They just adjusted themselves without seeming to. The way the barn cats did when Odin walked in.

When the man stopped and looked toward the trees where Jake lay, his stomach turned over.

He stayed flat and still and waited.

When Lily finally climbed back up the ridge, the fading light caught her face just long enough. She wasn't crying. Wasn't scared exactly. The shape of her face was the same but wrong. The look behind her eyes was working something out that wasn't finished yet.

She passed him on the trail close enough he could have touched her.

He let her go.

Then he slipped out of the brush and fell in behind her, keeping to the soft edge of the path where his footsteps were silent. Far enough back she wouldn't hear. Close enough nothing else would reach her first.

The Lodge lights showed first through the gaps in the pines. Then the garden fence. Then the glow of the porch lantern, warm and constant.

Lily crossed into the yard without looking back.

Jake stopped at the tree line.

He turned once and looked toward the ridge. The camp was invisible from here, swallowed by dark and distance. But he knew exactly where it was now.

Jake looked once more toward the ridge.

Then he turned toward the Lodge. He had to beat her home.

He knew he was going back to that camp though.

Chapter Eleven

Something Wrong With Quiet

The fiddle had switched to a faster tune by the time Lily reached the edge of the yard. She knew it was her dad playing. She could always tell.

The Lodge glowed warm in the summer dark. Lantern light spilled across the porch and through the great room windows. Someone laughed inside. A chair scraped the floor.

Normal sounds.

Lily stepped through the garden gate and crossed the yard.

Jake saw her immediately.. He had cut across the field once she was in sight of the lodge and found Max peeling bark off of some good whittling sticks.

He sat on the wagon tongue beside Max and began whittling a stick down into something that vaguely resembled a spear. The knife went still in his hand.

Lily didn't walk like herself.

She walked like someone who had forgotten where her feet were supposed to go.

Max noticed Jake stop carving.

"What?"

Jake didn't answer.

Lily passed the barn and headed for the porch. The lantern light caught her face for just a moment.

Jake felt something pull tight in his stomach.

She didn't look scared.

Just wrong.

Like she'd seen something that had nowhere to land.

Max squinted toward the house.

"Why's she look like that?"

Jake folded the knife shut and shoved it into his pocket.

"Dunno."

But he did.

Or at least he knew where she'd been.

Inside the Lodge the fiddle hit a bright note and the room broke open with laughter.

Lily climbed the porch steps.

Jo sat in her chair by the door with Odin stretched across her feet. The old dog lifted his head as Lily passed.

Jo's eyes followed her.

"Evening," Jo said.

Lily stopped.

"Evening."

Her voice sounded normal.

Too normal.

Jo studied her for half a heartbeat longer than most people would have. Then she nodded once and turned back toward the music.

Lily stepped inside.

Jake watched the door close behind her.

Max nudged him with his elbow.

"You gonna tell me what's going on?"

Jake hopped down from the wagon.

"Nothing's going on."

"You're a terrible liar."

Jake ignored that and walked toward the barn instead of the porch.

Max followed, because Max always followed.

The barn smelled like hay and leather and warm animals settling in for the night. A lantern hung from a nail near the door, throwing long shadows across the stalls.

Jake leaned against the fence rail and stared out toward the south tree line.

Max waited.

Finally he said, "Did she go down there?"

Jake didn't answer straight away.

The ridge was invisible from here. But he knew exactly where it was.

"Maybe."

Max's eyes widened.

"You followed her?"

"Sort of."

"What's it like?"

Jake thought about the clearing. The rows of children. The way no one spoke unless they were supposed to. The way the whole place shifted when the man stepped out of the longhouse. The way his eyes seemed to know he was watching.

"Quiet," he said finally.

Max snorted. "Lots of places are quiet."

Jake shook his head. "No."

He picked up a loose piece of straw and twisted it between his fingers.

"They call him Teacher."

"Who?"

"The guy running it."

Max wrinkled his nose. "That's dumb."

"Maybe."

He hesitated, then added quietly, "But the grown-ups called him something else."

Max leaned closer. "Like what?"

Jake lowered his voice. "Oracle."

Max blinked. "That sounds like a wizard."

Jake looked back toward the tree line. "Yeah." He tossed the straw aside. "Kind of does."

"Do you think he has magic?"

Jake didn't smile. "No."

"What then?"

Jake pushed away from the rail. "I think he knows stuff."

Max followed him toward the door. "Like what?"

"Like when someone's watching."

Max stopped. "You mean like you?"

Jake didn't answer.

The music inside the Lodge had slowed. Someone was singing now, a low easy voice that drifted out across the yard like smoke. She thought it might be Clare.

Lily stood at the well pump beside the kitchen door, working the handle harder than she needed to. The metal clanked sharp with every stroke.

Jake watched her a moment, then cut past the wagon toward the porch.

Max jogged to keep up. "Where are you going?"

Jake didn't look at him. "Bed."

"You're not tired."

Jake stopped at the bottom of the porch steps. "No."

Max waited.

Jake dropped his voice. "I just need to check on something tomorrow."

"Check on what?"

Jake glanced once toward the dark ridge beyond the treeline.

"That place."

Max went still. "You're going back?"

Jake climbed the steps. "Maybe."

Max stood in the yard watching him. "Jake."

Jake had his hand on the door. "What?"

Max scratched the back of his neck, the way he always did when he was working up to something. "If he really is a wizard..."

Jake waited.

"...maybe don't let him see you."

Jake thought about the way the man had stopped outside the longhouse. The way the clearing had seemed to tighten around him. The way his eyes had moved to the ridge, just once, half a second too long.

Jake swallowed.

"Yeah," he said quietly. "I know."

The camp waited in the dark beyond the trees.

Chapter Twelve

The Listener

The clearing had gone quiet again.

Not silent. The night insects still hummed along the lakeshore, and somewhere out in the dark a frog called from the reeds. But the steady rhythm of the evening lesson had ended. The children had been sent to their cabins, their footsteps fading one by one into the soft dark.

The Oracle sat alone on the low step outside the longhouse.

The lantern beside the door burned steady, its flame unmoving in the still air.

He liked this hour best. When the camp settled. When voices dropped away and the shape of the place revealed itself again.

The cabins stood where they were meant to stand. The paths between them had worn smooth under careful feet. Even the wood stacked beside the fire ring sat in neat rows, each piece set down with quiet intention.

Order was not something you forced on people.

It was something they learned to want.

He rested his hands loosely on his knees and watched the lantern light stretch across the clearing.

Inside the longhouse, Devotion moved quietly among the tables, gathering the lesson books and stacking them in their proper places. She did not hurry.

No one here hurried.

The world had ended because everyone had hurried. Because everyone had believed their own thoughts were as valuable as the next person's. That had been the great lie. The rot that worked its way through everything long before the lights went out.

The Oracle closed his eyes and let the sounds of the night settle around him.

Footsteps crossed the clearing toward him.

Ash stopped a few paces short.

"The children are settled," he said.

The Oracle opened his eyes.

Ash held his usual posture, the one the others had slowly learned to imitate. Hands easy at his sides. Shoulders dropped. No urgency in him, just presence.

"Good," the Oracle said.

Ash dipped his chin once.

He didn't move to leave.

The Oracle tilted his head.

"Something else."

A beat passed.

"Girl came down off the ridge tonight."

The Oracle said nothing for a moment. The fire popped somewhere behind them.

"Yes," he said.

Ash's stillness broke, just slightly. "You saw her?"

"No."

The Oracle's eyes drifted toward the dark treeline beyond the cabins, where the ridge swallowed the last of the stars.

"But the woods were listening."

Ash looked out that direction, jaw tightening. "You want us to send somebody up tomorrow?"

The Oracle let the question sit.

People always reached for action the moment something unsettled them. As if movement were the same as wisdom.

"No," he said.

Ash waited.

The Oracle's gaze drifted back toward the longhouse door where Devotion was finishing her work.

"She came because she was curious."

Ash said nothing.

"Curiosity," the Oracle continued, "is rarely dangerous on its own."

Ash's frown came slow and small.

"What about the one watching from the trees?"

The Oracle's mouth curved just slightly.

"You heard him too?"

Ash shifted his weight from one foot to the other.

"Branches moved."

The Oracle nodded once.

"A boy, I think."

"How do you know?"

He gestured loosely toward the line of cabins.

"Children breathe differently when they're trying to stay quiet."

Something close to a smile crossed Ash's face and was gone.

"What do you want done about it?"

"Nothing."

Ash studied him the way a man studies weather he doesn't trust.

"Nothing?"

The Oracle leaned back against the rough timber beside the door, easy and unhurried, like a man who had already seen how this would go.

"The Lodge children are already watching us," he said. "That means the work has begun."

Ash glanced toward the ridge again.

“You think they’ll come?”

“They already have.”

The Oracle let his gaze drift back toward the clearing, and the image came without being called, the way certain things do when they have already settled somewhere deeper than memory. The girl standing at the edge of the lesson circle, still as creek water on a windless morning. Not hanging back the way a frightened child does, weight shifted toward retreat, eyes already looking for the door. She had been rooted. Present. Her face turned toward the circle with something quiet and deliberate working behind her eyes.

Not fear.

Thought.

He had seen fear often enough to know the difference. Fear flinches. Fear watches the hands and the exits. What she had carried in her expression was the other thing, rarer and worth more, the look of a mind turning something over slowly, testing the weight of it, unwilling to set it down until it made sense. That kind of attention was not taught. It was either in a person or it wasn't.

That was the more interesting kind.

"Some will come out of curiosity," he continued.

"Some will come because they are lonely."

"And some will come because they want to understand."

Ash nodded slowly.

"And the boy?"

The Oracle looked toward the tree line one more time.

The woods had gone still again.

"If he comes back," the Oracle said calmly, "we'll let him watch."

Ash raised an eyebrow, the question sitting somewhere between doubt and genuine curiosity.

"You're not worried about any of it?"

The Oracle smiled, slow and certain, the way a man smiles when he's already lived through the version of the story where things go wrong.

"Children are how the future learns to change its mind," he said. "Always have been."

He rose slowly from the step, joints protesting with the stubbornness of bones that had spent too many years close to the ground, and moved inside the longhouse without another word, letting the doorway swallow him whole.

Ash lingered outside a moment longer, hands loose at his sides, eyes tracing the familiar line of the ridge as the last of the evening light bled out from behind it. The clearing held that particular quiet that came just after conversation, when the air hadn't quite decided what to do with itself yet.

The lantern flame guttered once as a faint breeze finally stirred through the clearing, threading between the posts and brushing the tall grass flat for just a breath before settling again.

He looked toward the tree line.

The trees showed nothing. No movement, no suggestion that anything stood between them watching. Just bark and branch and the deep, patient dark.

But the feeling stayed with him anyway, low and persistent, settled somewhere beneath his ribs where unease lives when it doesn't want to be argued with. It wasn't fear exactly. It was something older than fear.

The woods had not stopped listening.

They had simply learned how to be quieter about it.

Chapter Thirteen

The Noise of Joy

Deb had barely cleared the threshold of the great room when the ambush began.

"Don't let her escape!"

Mary cut across the room and caught her gently by the elbow before she could even set down the basket she was carrying.

"What—?" Deb laughed, startled. "What on earth is happening?"

Judith came out of the hallway with a wooden crate hugged against her chest. Ellie followed close behind, cradling something bundled in a faded blue blanket. Clare appeared in the kitchen doorway with a box balanced on her hip, wearing the kind of smile that meant she'd been in on this for a while.

Beth shut the front door with her foot and leaned back against it, arms folded, grinning like she'd just won something.

"You're not going to get out of this," she said.

Deb looked from face to face, completely at a loss.

"Out of what, exactly?"

Mary lifted the basket from her hands and set it aside without ceremony.

"Sit down," she said.

Marcus had been leaning against the mantle, half-listening to whatever Gunny was grumbling about, when the commotion pulled his attention across the room. He straightened, taking in the scene with the measured calm of a man who'd learned long ago to read a situation before stepping into it.

"What'd she do?"

Beth swung a finger in his direction without even looking at him.

"Stay out of it."

Gunny's chuckle was low and private, the kind a man keeps mostly to himself.

Marcus lifted both hands, palms out.

"Not my circus."

They steered Deb toward the long table, and someone pulled a chair out for her with the no-nonsense efficiency of women who had already decided how this was going to go. Deb sat, slowly, the way a person does when they're not sure whether to be touched or suspicious.

She looked around at all of them.

"Alright," she said. "Somebody better start talking before I convince myself I'm in trouble."

Judith set the crate down on the table with a solid thunk.

Inside lay folded baby clothes.

Tiny shirts. Little socks. A pair of knitted booties so small they'd disappear in Deb's palm.

Deb stared at them.

"Oh."

Clare set her box beside Judith's and lifted the lid.

More clothes. Blankets. A stuffed rabbit with one ear noticeably longer than the other.

Ellie laid a blue bundle down with care.

"Saved that blanket from when Rowan was born," she said. "Figured it had one more round left in it."

Deb's eyes moved slowly over the table.

"I... you didn't have to do all this—"

Beth snorted.

"Yes we did."

Mary held up a pair of tiny knitted mittens.

"My mother made these for Lily," she said. "Three babies have worn them already."

Judith grinned.

"Four after this one."

The room filled with voices layered over each other, warm and unhurried.

"That one was Luke's."

"Rowan chewed on that blanket for a solid six months."

Clare lifted a small pair of leather shoes.

"Gemma's first pair."

Deb reached out slowly and picked up one of the tiny shirts. Her throat tightened before she was ready for it.

"I don't even know what babies need," she admitted quietly.

Ellie rested a hand on her shoulder.

"That's what you've got us for."

Across the room, Marcus leaned against the mantel, watching it all with an expression caught somewhere between amusement and low-grade alarm.

Gunny nudged him with an elbow.

"You look like a man who just realised he's outnumbered."

Marcus exhaled slowly.

"I already am."

Gunny grinned.

"Just wait."

Outside, the noise spilled through the open windows.

Jake paused near the wagon and glanced back toward the Lodge.

Laughter carried across the yard.

Max came jogging through the grass, skidding to a stop beside him.

"What's going on in there?"

Jake shrugged. "Baby stuff."

Max wrinkled his nose. "That sounds boring."

Jake didn't answer. Through the window he could make out movement inside. Women passing things across the table. Deb cradling something tiny in her hands while Mary talked beside her, gesturing with both arms.

Everyone was looking inside.

Nobody was looking out.

Max followed his gaze. "You're thinking about it again."

Jake bent down and pulled the small pack from beneath the wagon seat where he'd tucked it that morning. Just a few things. A heel of bread. His canteen. His pocketknife.

Max's voice dropped. "You're really going."

Jake slung the pack over one shoulder. "Just to look."

"That's what you said yesterday."

Jake didn't argue.

He glanced once more toward the Lodge. Someone had picked the fiddle back up inside, the notes threading out through the screen.

Max shifted on his feet. "What if they catch you?"

"They won't."

"How do you know?"

Jake looked toward the dark tree line at the far edge of the field. "I'm small."

Max frowned. "That's not a plan."

Jake smiled, just barely. "It's part of one."

Max kicked at the dirt. "You're going to get in trouble."

"Probably."

"You want me to tell someone?"

"No."

Max looked miserable about the whole thing.

Jake hesitated, then crouched down so they were eye to eye. "If I'm not back by dessert tonight," he said quietly, "tell Gus."

Max blinked. "Why Gus?"

"He listens."

Max nodded slowly, filing the words away even though he wasn't entirely sure what to do with them.

Inside, someone cheered loud enough to rattle the windows.

Jake stood. "I'll be back before that anyway."

Max watched him start across the field. "Jake?"

Jake turned.

Max scratched the back of his neck. "If the wizard sees you..." He paused. "...maybe run faster than last time."

Jake snorted. "Good plan."

He turned and walked toward the tree line.

Inside the Lodge, Lily slipped out the kitchen door while no one was looking, easing it shut behind her so the latch barely clicked.

The laughter in the great room had swelled to a roar. Beth's voice carried clean through the walls, sharp and animated, building toward the punchline of some story about Boone going pale as a sheet and folding like a bad hand of cards right there in the delivery room when Rowan came into the world. The howling that followed rattled the windows. Someone, probably Gran, let out that high wheeze of a laugh she got when something truly caught her off guard, and that only made the rest of them laugh harder.

Lily stood on the back stoop for just a moment, breathing in the warm summer evening. The air smelled of cut grass and pine resin and the faint ghost of baking still drifting from the kitchen behind her. Fireflies blinked low along the tree line. The sky above the ridge had gone the color of peach skin at the horizon, deepening to violet higher up.

She crossed the yard quietly, her worn canvas shoes whispering through the grass, her notebook tucked under one arm. The sounds of the Lodge softened with each step, the laughter growing muffled, then distant, then just a low warm hum she could feel more than hear.

The trees received her without ceremony. The path up toward the ridge was familiar enough that her feet found it without much thought. Birch trunks glowed faintly in the dusk. A thrush somewhere overhead sang three clean notes and went quiet.

She was so caught up in whatever was unfolding in her head, some opening line she had been turning over all through supper, that she never thought to look down at the path in front of her.

She didn't notice the small set of footprints already pressed into the soft earth, toes pointed uphill, heading exactly where she was headed.

And somewhere above the ridge, Jake sat on his favorite flat rock with his knees pulled to his chest, watching the last of the light.

Chapter Fourteen

The Edge of the Circle

Jake waited until the Lodge lights disappeared behind the ridge.

The woods felt different at night.

Not darker, exactly. Just deeper. The trees seemed to hold their breath the way they never did in daylight, like the whole forest was listening for something it hadn't heard yet.

He moved carefully along the deer trail he knew best, placing his feet where the ground was firm and dry.

The ridge climbed slowly beneath him.

When he reached the flat rock he liked to sit on during the day, he crouched and looked out through the canopy toward the clearing below Little Bear Lake.

The Harbinger camp glowed with lantern light.

Not much of it. Just enough.

People moved between the cabins in slow, quiet lines. Jake watched for a long time.

Nobody shouted. Nobody laughed. Nobody ran.

Even from up here, something about the place pulled at him the wrong way. Not dangerous, maybe. Just wrong in a way he couldn't name yet.

He dropped down from the rock and worked his way lower along the ridge. The trees grew thicker there, young pines and scrub brush packed tight enough to swallow a person whole, if that person knew how to move through them.

Jake did.

He crept downslope until the longhouse came into view. It sat at the center of the clearing like the hub of a wheel, the cabins fanning out around it in careful, deliberate rows.

Even the woodpile was stacked with a kind of precision that made his skin prickle.

Jake frowned.

Who stacked wood like that?

He crouched behind the fallen log and studied the clearing.

Children moved between the cabins with water buckets. Two older boys stacked split wood beside the fire pit. A woman worked a packed dirt path with a branch broom, raising little puffs of dust with each stroke.

Nobody spoke. Not even the kids.

The tight feeling in Jake's stomach came back.

He shifted for a better angle.

A door opened on the longhouse and a man stepped out. Jake had seen him once before, standing in the lesson circle the day Lily had gone down into the clearing. Even at this distance the man looked calm. Not big. Not loud. Just steady in a way that was hard to explain.

The man paused beside the doorway and let his gaze move slowly across the clearing.

Jake pressed himself flat against the earth.

After a moment the man turned and said something quiet to the nearest guard. Jake couldn't catch the words. The guard gave a single nod and walked toward the cabins.

The man stayed where he was.

Watching.

Jake stayed perfectly still.

A mosquito landed on his wrist. He let it.

The man eventually stepped back inside the longhouse.

Jake let out a slow breath through his nose.

The clearing settled back into its strange, unhurried rhythm. Children lugged buckets. Lanterns threw soft light against the log walls. A woman worked a laundry line, shaking out clothes with practiced snaps.

He stayed another ten minutes. Then twenty.

What struck him most was what wasn't there. No one walked the tree line. No one checked the ridge. These people moved like it had never occurred to them someone might be watching.

A small spark of confidence settled in his chest.

Maybe this wasn't going to be as hard as he'd feared.

He eased backward through the brush and started up the ridge, careful with his footing on the loose shale. When he reached the flat rock, he stopped and looked back one last time.

The lanterns below burned like scattered embers through the trees. The longhouse sat quiet at the center of it all.

Jake smiled to himself. He had the layout now. That was enough.

He turned toward the Lodge and started down the trail.

Behind him, the lantern outside the longhouse door guttered once in the night breeze. And in the clearing below, the Oracle stepped back outside and turned his eyes slowly toward the ridge.

Chapter Fifteen

The Shape of Obedience

Lily reached the ridge just as the last of the daylight slipped behind the trees.

Below, the clearing near Little Bear Lake had already begun to glow with lantern light.

She crouched behind the familiar fallen log and opened her notebook without really thinking about it. The habit had followed her up the hill the way breathing did. Words had been turning over in her mind all afternoon while the Lodge roared with laughter and baby blankets and stories she'd heard a dozen times before.

She hadn't written any of them down.

Not yet.

The clearing moved in slow, deliberate patterns below her. Children crossed between the cabins carrying buckets. Two boys stacked wood beside the fire pit with careful, identical movements, each log placed exactly where the last one had been.

Near the longhouse, a group of younger children sat cross-legged in a half circle.

Lily leaned forward slightly.

No one spoke.

The silence down there was different from the quiet of the woods around her. The forest quiet was alive with small noises, insects, leaves shifting, birds settling for the night. The quiet below was arranged. Shaped by something she couldn't explain.

A door opened on the longhouse.

The man they called Teacher stepped outside.

That tightening came again, low in her chest, the same one she'd carried home with her the last time she'd watched him. She pressed her notebook against her knees and stayed very still.

He wasn't loud. He didn't raise his voice.

But the clearing changed the moment he appeared.

Children straightened. Women lowered their heads slightly.

Teacher stepped into the open space before the circle.

"Good evening."

The children answered as one.

"Good evening, Teacher."

Their voices rose in unison, perfectly even, like something practiced until it had no edges left.

Lily blinked.

Teacher folded his hands loosely behind his back and looked slowly around the group.

“Today we talk about freedom.”

Lily turned the word over in her mind the way you'd turn a stone with your boot, looking for what was underneath.

Freedom.

She pressed her pencil to the page and waited. Freedom sounded like a good subject.

"The old world believed freedom meant doing whatever you wished." Teacher's voice was calm, almost gentle. He let the words settle before continuing. "That belief destroyed it."

Her pencil stopped moving.

He walked the edge of the circle slowly, his eyes passing from one child to the next like a man taking inventory.

"True freedom comes from understanding your place."

The children murmured it back to him.

"Understanding your place."

Lily wrote the words down, but her hand felt strange doing it.

"When each person understands where they belong, there is no confusion." He paused beside one of the smaller boys. "No argument." He moved on. "No conflict."

The boy stared at the ground, shoulders drawn in, still as a post sunk deep in frozen earth.

"No suffering."

Around her, heads nodded.

Lily looked down at her notebook. Back at the Lodge, Her Dad and Boone had nearly come to blows over fence placement two days ago.Gran and Marcus disagreed about everything — irrigation ditches, coffee beans, you name it, loudly and often and with considerable feeling.

But nobody at the Lodge ever looked like that boy.

Like they were waiting for permission to breathe.

Teacher wrapped up the lesson a few minutes later.

The children rose together, bowed their heads briefly, then drifted back toward the cabins in loose clusters. The clearing came alive again with quiet movement.

But the strange stillness underneath it all didn't leave.

Lily watched a girl climb the longhouse steps carrying a stack of thin books against her chest. Teacher said something to her, too low to carry across the clearing. The girl held the stack out. He took it, worked through each volume one by one, then separated two from the rest and handed them back.

The girl nodded once and walked away without a word.

Teacher carried the two books inside.

Lily's frown deepened.

A moment later Devotion appeared and gathered the children again.

"Reading hour," she said, her voice the same flat calm it always was.

They lined up outside the longhouse without being told twice. Lily leaned forward from her spot at the tree line, trying to get a clear view.

The books came out one at a time. Same thin cover. Same color. Same careful hand delivering each one.

Lily's pencil scratched across the page.

All the same book.

She watched one of the younger boys open his copy. He held it like something fragile, something borrowed. No one compared pages. No one whispered to a neighbor. They simply read, heads bowed, hands still.

Then the girl with the bucket reappeared at the edge of the clearing. The handle cut into her fingers with the weight of it. She didn't shift her feet. Didn't set it down. Didn't let her eyes wander.

She just waited.

Teacher came back outside. The girl stepped forward immediately and passed the bucket over. Only then did her grip finally ease.

Lily's stomach turned.

That wasn't normal.

She closed the notebook slowly.

From that distance, the clearing looked peaceful. Orderly. Quiet.

But the longer she watched, the more it felt like the air down there had been pressed flat. Like a place where the wind had simply forgotten to blow.

Lily stood and brushed the pine needles from her knees. She took one last look at the camp below, then turned and started back toward the Lodge.

She never noticed the faint track in the dirt beside the trail. Small boot prints. The same ones that had passed this way not long before her.

Inside the longhouse, the Oracle went still. One of the books lay open in his hand, but he wasn't reading anymore.

He turned his head.

Toward the ridge.

Toward the place where the wind still moved through the trees.

Chapter Sixteen

Feathers in the Yard

The morning started quiet.

Not the strange, flattened quiet Lily had felt on the ridge the night before. This was the ordinary kind that belonged to the Lodge in the early hours, when mist still clung low over the pasture and the only real sounds were the creak of the pump handle and the soft thud of kindling being split somewhere close.

Rowan carried the grain bucket under one arm and nudged the chicken yard gate open with her boot.

The hens were already awake and already opinionated about it.

They clustered toward her in a loud, complaining mass of feathers and sharp beaks.

"Yeah, yeah." Rowan scattered the grain in a wide arc. "You'd think nobody fed you yesterday."

Behind her, the barn door groaned open and Donovan stepped out, pulling a shirt over his head as he walked.

"You're late," he said.

"I'm not late. You're early."

Declan appeared a moment later, still rubbing sleep from his eyes.

"You two arguing before breakfast now?" he asked.

"Every day," Donovan said.

Rowan rolled her eyes and leaned over the coop door to top off the water pan.

Across the yard, Fiona and Lily were walking back from the garden rows with two baskets of cucumbers. The vines had finally started producing faster than they could eat them.

Clare had already announced that meant pickling day.

Again.

Lily adjusted the basket resting on her hip and stole a glance at the woods, a motion she couldn't shake.

It wasn't her intention to dwell on the ridge once more.

Yet, there it was.

The children had huddled in a perfect circle last night — hands clasped, backs erect.

Listening.

Reading.

Waiting.

No whispers.

No fidgeting.

No laughter.

She struggled to recall if any of them had even smiled.

The answer weighed heavily in her gut.

None had.

The sharp scream of a chicken tore across the yard.

Rowan's head snapped up.

Another scream followed. Then a burst of frantic wingbeats.

"Fox!" Rowan shouted.

The chicken yard erupted into turmoil.

Feathers swirled as the flock scattered, a red streak darting beneath the coop, emerging on the other side with a hen tightly gripped in its jaws.

Rowan dropped the grain bucket and leaped over the fence.

"Hey!" she called out, snatching the first thing she could find — a length of fence rail propped against the coop.

The fox shot to the side, dragging the screeching hen across the dirt.

Donovan was already sprinting, with Declan right on his heels.

"Cut it off!" Donovan shouted.

Rowan swung the rail with all her might.

The fox turned just in time, the rail crashing into the ground hard enough to rattle her shoulders.

Feathers scattered in all directions. The hen broke loose and dashed underneath the coop.

The fox spun, teeth flashing.

For a moment it looked straight at Rowan. Bloody saliva dripped from its jaws, a single feather stuck in the fur of it's muzzle.

Then it darted toward the far corner of the yard.

Declan vaulted the gate and tried to block it, but the fox slipped past him like water.

Marcus's rifle cracked from the porch.

The shot tore into the dirt a foot behind the fox.

The animal vanished through the fence line and into the trees.

Silence dropped over the yard.

For about three seconds.

Then the screaming started.

Rowan bent at the waist, hands resting on her knees, panting.

"Well," Declan finally remarked, "that certainly roused everyone."

Rowan straightened, shooting him a fierce glare.

"You could have done something sooner."

"I did my part."

"You just stood there!"

"I was blocking the exit."

"You missed the exit."

Donovan picked up the fallen rail, setting it back against the coop.

"It's gone now," he said. "Just relax."

Rowan placed her hands on her hips defiantly.

"I was handling it."

Declan snickered.

"You nearly got bit."

"I almost *hit* it."

"You're smaller," Donovan replied with a simple shrug. "It's different."

Rowan fixed him with a hard stare.

"Excuse me?"

"You're smaller," he said again, this time with patience. "Leave that kind of stuff to us."

Something shifted in Rowan's expression.

Not anger—something sharper.

"Hello," she said flatly. "Yes, I am a little smaller than you. Hello... I'm a girl."

The twins blinked in surprise.

Declan looked genuinely perplexed.

"...yeah?"

Donovan shrugged.

"We know that."

Rowan threw her hands up in exasperation.

"No... you really don't!"

The twins exchanged looks.

Donovan frowned slightly.

"Rowan, you climb trees faster than we do."

"You beat Declan in a race last week," Declan chimed in.

"You got kidnapped and gave the bad guys a real hard time."

"And you broke your dad's nose that one time."

"That was an accident."

"Still counts."

Rowan pressed her fingers to her temples in frustration.

"That's not the point."

From the garden path, Fiona's laughter rang out.

Lily, however, remained silent.

She observed Rowan standing in a yard of squawking chickens, dirt smudged on her knees, hair spilling from its braid.

Alive.

Annoyed.

Arguing.

The Lodge behind them was stirring with life now.

The kitchen door creaked open.

Clare's voice floated across the yard.

"Why are there feathers everywhere?"

Rowan directed her hand toward the woods.

"Fox."

Clare let out a sigh.

"Of course."

Lily glanced back one last time toward the tree line.

Toward the ridge.

Toward the spot where the Harbinger children had sat so quietly the night before.

Not laughing.

Not running.

Not chasing anything.

Just waiting.

She adjusted the cucumber basket on her hip and followed Fiona into the kitchen.

Behind her, Rowan was still in the thick of it with the twins.

And for the first time since the night before, Lily felt a gentle release in her chest.

Because whatever the Lodge might be—

At least the children here still knew how to fill the air with noise.

Chapter Seventeen

The Quiet Between Storms

By late afternoon, the Lodge had settled into its familiar rhythm that after a noisy morning.

The chickens had quieted at last.

Most of them, anyway.

Deb sat on the porch swing, Luke nestled against her shoulder. The baby's tiny fist clutched a loose handful of Marcus's beard, while Marcus did his best to remain still.

"If he pulls that," Deb warned lightly, "you'll wish you hadn't."

Marcus kept his gaze steady.

"I'm aware."

Luke let out a contemplative hum and tugged harder.

Marcus flinched.

Deb grinned.

"I could always set him down."

Marcus shook his head slowly.

"No sudden movements."

Luke gurgled.

Then drooled directly onto Marcus's beard.

Deb chuckled.

Marcus briefly closed his eyes.

"This child," he proclaimed with a hint of dignity, "is trying to drown me."

Deb adjusted Luke, seated him between them on the swing.

The one-year-old immediately began exploring the buttons on Marcus's shirt.

For a few moments, silence enveloped them.

The afternoon air carried the scent of freshly cut grass and vinegar from the kitchen, where Clare and Mary had begun their first round of pickling of the day.

Someone was hammering in the barn.

Rowan's voice drifted across the yard, still embroiled in the argument about the fox.

Suddenly, Luke leaned forward and slapped both hands on Marcus's knee.

Marcus looked down, startled.

"He's surprisingly strong."

Deb crossed her arms over her belly, observing the two of them, smiling.

The smile slowly faded from her face.

Marcus caught the change.

"What's wrong?"

It wasn't a question, more an observation.

Deb hesitated.

Then she replied softly, "Marcus... we're actually doing this."

He met her gaze.

"Yes."

"I mean, really doing this."

Marcus stole a glance at Luke again, who was fixated on trying to munch on his own foot.

Deb rubbed her hands together nervously.

"I'm forty-three, and Doc said geriatric. Geriatric, Marcus!"

Marcus pondered her words with a curl of his lip.

"You were forty-three yesterday, too."

"That doesn't really help."

He nodded, conceding, "Fair point."

Deb rested a hand on her stomach.

"I never thought about having babies," she confessed. "Not really. I always figured that part of life just... wasn't meant to be for me."

Marcus leaned back against the post, the weight of her words settling in.

"Same here."

Deb turned to look at him, surprised.

"You?"

He shrugged slightly. "I was mostly busy trying to stay alive."

Luke squealed with delight and toppled sideways into Marcus's leg.

Without thinking, Marcus caught him.

For a moment, the three of them basked in the warmth of the afternoon light.

Eventually, Deb voiced the quiet fear between them. "What if we don't know what we're doing?"

Marcus contemplated her question with seriousness.

Marcus looked across the yard where Rowan was now demonstrating to Donovan and Declan exactly how she had almost hit the fox.

The twins were arguing back.

Clare came out of the kitchen holding a jar.

Franklin walked past carrying a coil of wire.

Jo sat in the shade with Odin stretched across her feet.

Marcus nodded toward the yard.

"I suspect," he said calmly, "we will have help."

Luke burped loudly.

Deb laughed again.

The tension loosened just a little.

Marcus adjusted the baby in his arms.

Luke grabbed his beard again.

Marcus sighed.

"Yes," he said. "We are definitely going to need help."

Chapter Eighteen

Watching

Jake had never been one for sitting still.

Most folks at the Lodge knew that well.

Franklin said it was because he had too much energy and not enough patience. Boone, on the other hand, claimed it was simply because Jake was ten years old, and ten-year-olds were meant to bounce around like squirrels.

Jake preferred Boone's explanation.

Still, there were times when staying put had its perks.

Especially when nobody knew you were there.

He lay flat on his belly behind a low tangle of blueberry bushes at the tree line, gazing down at the clearing.

The Harbinger camp looked different in daylight.

Cabins stood in tidy rows around the clearing. Smoke drifted lazily from cooking fires. Women moved between the buildings, baskets and buckets in hand, their steps steady and unhurried.

Children were working too.

That caught Jake off guard.

At the Lodge, kids were always working—feeding animals, hauling water, picking vegetables, stacking wood. There was no slacking off for long.

But this was different.

The Harbinger children weren't bustling about like kids with chores.

They moved like...

Jake squinted.

Like soldiers.

Two boys hauled a stack of wood across the clearing. When one piece slipped, neither chuckled nor teased.

They just picked it back up and kept moving.

A group of younger kids walked by with baskets of berries.

No one ran.

No one pushed.

No one threw a fistful or ate any.

Jake frowned.

At the Lodge, someone would have taken a berry to the head by now.

He shifted and rested his chin on his hands.

Close to the longhouse, several older kids lounged in a loose half-circle.

One of the Harbinger women stood among them.

"Teacher says we must practice listening," she said in a steady voice.

The children nodded.

Not a single groan was heard.

Jake blinked.

If that had been said to Rowan or Declan, there'd have been at least three complaints and likely a ruckus.

The woman pointed to a boy.

"What did Teacher say about freedom?"

The boy responded right away.

"Freedom comes from understanding your place."

The woman nodded.

"Good."

Jake picked up a small stick and twirled it between his fingers.

They sure used that word a lot.

Teacher.

Jake had heard the adults call him something different.

Oracle.

Max had said it felt like something from a fairy tale.

Jake wasn't so sure.

Wizards in stories pulled off tricks.

This man didn't seem like he needed any tricks at all.

Everything around him already did what he wanted.

Jake shifted onto his side.

Not too far off, two girls were sweeping the dirt between cabins with brooms made from stiff branches.

One of them cast a glance at the other.

For a fleeting moment, Jake thought they might share a whisper.

Or a laugh.

But they didn't.

They just continued sweeping.

A peculiar prickle ran along the back of Jake's neck.

It wasn't so much fear as it was something unsettling.

Kids were meant to laugh.

Even when they needed to be quiet. Even in church.

He'd caught Edwin stifling a snort during Father Tom's sermons more than a few times.

Jake pushed himself up slowly.

He'd seen enough for now.

The Lodge wasn't far off.

The path wound through the trees before dipping back into the meadow behind the barns.

He moved quietly, just like Boone had taught him while checking the rabbit snares.

Step.

Pause.

Listen.

As the Lodge's roof broke the tree line, voices drifted over the yard like a summer breeze.

Jo settled in a shady spot beside the garden fence, Odin sprawled comfortably across her boots. With practiced hands, she shelled peas into a bowl that rested on her knee.

Jake slowed his pace, feeling her watchful gaze.

Jo had a knack for sensing things, often before the words left anyone's lips.

"There you are," she greeted, raising her eyes. "Been lending a hand to Franklin?"

Jake hesitated.

"Sort of," he finally replied.

Jo tipped a handful of pods into the bowl, assessing him with a knowing look.

"'Sort of' sounds like half trouble," she remarked, her tone light but her eyes sharp.

Jake shifted on his feet.

"I went up by the ridge," he admitted, his voice barely above a whisper.

Jo's hands stilled.

"Did you now."

He nodded.

"Just looking around, exploring."

Odin perked up, sniffing the air, sensing the tension.

Jo remained quiet, waiting.

Jake opened his mouth.

Then closed it again.

The words were there. He could have shared how the other kids moved in the eerie silence, how laughter had vanished like shadows at dusk. But a knot tightened in his gut. Sharing would spark action. If the grown-ups knew, they'd rush to investigate, and the Harbingers would slip back into their shadows, whatever they were up to would remain a mystery—leaving Jake in the dark.

"Nothing much," he finally shrugged.

Jo scrutinized him for another heartbeat before returning her attention to the peas.

"Well," she said, a calmness in her voice, "if you're going to be spying, you ought to eat first."

Jake blinked, about to protest.

"I wasn't—"

Jo quirked an eyebrow, silencing him with that simple gesture.

Her lips curled slightly as she handed him the bowl.

"Take these to Clare before Odin makes them his lunch."

Jake took the bowl, almost without thinking.

As he made his way toward the kitchen, his mind raced. Just watching—his duty as one of the younger ones. Someone needed to keep an eye on things, and if the adults were occupied...

Jake felt the idea settle in his chest. He could manage for a little while.

Behind him, Jo continued to observe as he stepped through the kitchen door, Odin resting his chin back on her boot.

Silence enveloped her as she stayed vigilant, the wind whispering off the ridge carrying an undercurrent of hushed voices. Jo had learned, through years of knowing this land, to listen when the woods began to murmur.

Chapter Nineteen

Closer

Jake waited a full two days before returning.

Not out of fear.

Mostly.

And because Franklin had roped him into mending the fence along the north pasture, while Boone decided if Jake was old enough to roam around on his own, he was certainly old enough to haul posts.

By the time they finished, his arms felt like overcooked noodles.

Yet still.

The ridge kept tugging at his thoughts. He couldn't get it out of his head.

So the next afternoon, while most of the Lodge was busy cutting hay in the lower field, Jake slipped back into the woods.

This time, he moved slower.

Boone always said the woods would let you know when you were being foolish if you paid attention long enough.

Jake took that to mean staying quiet and moving slow.

The blueberry bushes were just as he had left them.

He crouched behind them, peering into the clearing.

From this vantage point, the camp appeared nearly peaceful.

Smoke curled from the cooking fires.

A few women busied themselves near the longhouse, spreading out something on a cloth to dry.

Children moved between cabins, carrying buckets and small bundles of wood.

Always working. Never smiling.

Jake scanned the clearing with care.

He was searching for the Teacher.

Instead, he spotted the guards.

Three loomed at the edge of the camp where the trees began.

They were different from the women and children. There were not a lot of men in the camp besides the Teacher.

They stood poised, heads moving slowly as they surveyed the boundaries of the clearing.

A shiver ran down Jake's spine.

Those men reminded him of Marcus when he assessed a dangerous situation.

Or Gunny.

One adjusted his stance slightly.

Jake went still.

The man was tall and broad-shouldered, with dark hair pulled back at the nape of his neck.

His gaze wasn't on the cabins.

It was fixed on the woods.

Lowering his head, Jake kept only his eyes above the bushes.

The man moved a few steps closer to the trees.

Jake held his breath.

For a long moment, everything remained still.

Then a voice called from the center of the clearing.

"Ash!"

The guard turned his head.

"Coming."

He strode back toward the longhouse.

Jake exhaled slowly.

Ash.

That name lingered in his thoughts.

The Teacher stepped outside moments later.

From this distance, Jake watched the crowd shift when the man arrived.

Children stood a bit taller.

Women paused in their tasks.

The teacher raised a hand casually.

Not a wave.

Just... a simple acknowledgment.

The clearing calmed.

A cluster of children gathered around him.

"Teacher," one of them whispered.

The teacher nodded in response.

"We will practice reading today."

Jake leaned in slightly.

The familiar thin books were handed out one by one.

Each child received the same one.

Jake frowned.

He had seen Lily's notebooks.

And the shelves of books at the Lodge.

None of them matched.

The kids were always swapping them.

Debating about stories.

The teacher continued.

"Freedom comes from understanding your place."

The children echoed the words.

In unison.

Jake shifted a bit.

A twig snapped beneath his elbow.

The sound was faint.

Barely louder than a squirrel.

But Ash's head whipped around instantly.

Jake's heart raced in his chest.

Ash took two deliberate steps toward the trees.

Jake crouched down fully into the bushes.

The leaves brushed against his cheek.

He held his breath.

He stayed still.

For a moment, the woods fell silent.

Jake could hear the faint crunch of Ash's boots at the edge of the clearing.

Another step.

Closer.

Jake squeezed his eyes shut.

Then a shout came from the longhouse.

"Ash! We need the water barrels moved!"

Ash stopped.

Jake tensed.

Seconds stretched out long and thin, each one pulling at his chest like a splinter worked the wrong direction. He counted them without meaning to. One. Two. Three.

Finally the footsteps turned away.

Jake stayed where he was for a long time after that.

Even when the clearing noise returned. Even when the children started reading again, their voices rising in that careful unison that made the back of his neck prickle.

When he finally crawled backward through the brush and stood up, his shirt was damp with sweat. His knees ached from the ground. He pressed himself against the bark of a birch tree, waited another full breath, and then moved.

The ridge didn't feel as safe anymore.

Not after that.

He kept low through the first stretch of trees, placing each foot like Boone had shown him. Heel first. Slow, though his brain screamed for him to run. Slow, let the ground decide. The forest thinned where the deer trail curved north, and Jake straightened, breathing through his nose, listening for anything behind him.

Nothing but wind through the pines.

Still. He moved faster.

By the time he reached the flat rock above the south meadow, the Lodge's roofline appeared through the canopy, amber light beginning to gather in the upper windows as the afternoon softened. Jake stopped there and pressed a hand to his ribs. His pulse hammered.

Another thought pushed through the fear.

Ash had almost caught him. Almost.

Which meant the guards were watching the woods. Which meant the woods mattered to them. And if the woods mattered to them, then they worried about what was in those woods.

Which meant that was exactly where Jake needed to be.

He turned the thought over carefully, the way he'd seen Marcus examine a map. Patient. Deliberate.

He needed to be smarter about it next time. Lower. Quieter. A different spot maybe. He needed to stay still longer than felt reasonable. Boone always said that the deer didn't move early because they were scared. They moved early because something had taught them to.

Jake let out a slow breath and descended the last of the ridge.

The meadow grass came up to his waist, still warm from the afternoon sun. He pushed through it toward the barns, already composing the look he'd wear when he walked through the yard. Casual. Unhurried. Like he'd been checking the south fence the way Franklin had asked him to three days ago and only just gotten around to it.

He was good at composing looks.

Max always said so.

He quickened his pace toward home.

Behind him, in the clearing below, Ash paused again at the edge of the trees.

He looked up toward the ridge. Toward the place where the bushes had shifted. The light was going gold now, angling through the canopy and catching the dust still settling on the far side of those blueberry bushes.

Ash stood without moving for a long moment.

His eyes tracked the tree line the way a man tracks a waterline on a flood plain. Methodical. Patient.

He didn't see the boy.

The gap in the brush told him little. A deer. A branch dropping in the wind. Any number of small, ordinary things.

But Ash had been a careful man long before Oracle had given him reason to be.

He turned back toward the longhouse.

Next time, he intended to find out what...or who was out there.

Chapter Twenty

The Water Path

Jake didn't return the next day.

That was part of the plan.

Or at least that's what he told himself.

Boone always said the woods caught on to patterns quicker than folks did. If you tread the same path at the same hour every day, sooner or later something would be waiting for you there.

Jake figured that applied to guards too.

So he waited.

He helped Rowan gather eggs.

He carried cucumbers from the garden until Clare claimed the Lodge would overflow with pickles.

He even spent half the morning hauling water from the pump to the kitchen barrels.

That part sparked an idea.

The Harbinger kids were always hauling water.

He'd spotted them both times from the ridge.

Buckets. Pails.

Always heading the same way.

Which meant the water had to be somewhere beyond the camp.

Jake finished placing the last bucket beside the kitchen door and wiped his hands on his pants.

Nobody paid much attention when kids carried water.

That was just how things went.

The path down to the creek started behind the south meadow.

Jake had walked it countless times.

Today, he took it slower.

He followed the deer trail where it dipped through the brush and crossed the shallow stream before climbing the ridge toward the Harbinger clearing.

The water ran clear over smooth stones, quiet except for the soft murmur of the current against the banks.

Jake crouched beside it for a moment, pretending to watch the minnows flitting through the shadows.

Then he noticed the footprints.

Small ones.

Many of them.

The mud along the bank was flattened where buckets had been rested.

Jake's heart quickened.

He traced the trail with his eyes.

The prints climbed the slope on the far side of the stream.

Straight toward the Harbinger camp.

There it was. Plain as day. The water path.

Kids hauling buckets wouldn't raise any eyebrows.

Kids trailing down the path wouldn't look out of place.

Jake rose slowly.

This time, he didn't venture all the way to the ridge.

He moved just a short way up the trail and paused.

From this spot, he could faintly hear the clearing.

Voices.

The scrape of wood.

The steady cadence of labor.

Jake turned back toward the Lodge before anyone showed up.

The plan was still taking shape in his mind, like one of Franklin's maps when he'd spread them out on the table, studying them for a stretch before speaking.

But the outline was clear.

It made sense.

That evening, across the yard, Edwin watched as Jake clambered down from the barn loft.

Jake landed the last few feet with a thud and dusted off his hands as if nothing in the world weighed on him.

That was precisely why Edwin found it hard to believe.

Jake had been unusually quiet the past couple of days.

Too quiet.

Edwin leaned against the fence by the mule pen, keeping his gaze fixed on him for another moment.

Then he turned and made his way toward the cabins at the edge of the trees.

When he arrived, Gin was perched on the porch rail, sharpening a knife.

Fergus lay sprawled in the dirt nearby, softly snoring. He could hear Morales and Kosinski playing a game of cards inside.

Gin looked up.

"What's got you sneaking around like a raccoon?"

Edwin shrugged.

"I'm not sneaking."

Gin snorted.

"Kid, I used to track folks for a living. You stomp quieter than most, but you still stomp."

Edwin kicked at a pebble on the ground.

"I think Jake's up to something."

Gin stopped, the whetstone hanging halfway down the blade.

"Up to something how?"

Edwin hesitated.

"I don't know."

Gin held his silence.

Edwin rubbed the back of his neck.

"He's been going up toward the ridge."

Gin's eyes narrowed just a bit.

"How do you know that?"

Edwin shrugged again.

"I saw him yesterday."

Gin slid the knife back into its sheath.

"And you're just telling me this now because..."

Edwin glanced across the yard.

Lily was helping Clare carry jars into the kitchen while Max trailed after them, attempting to sneak a pickle.

Edwin lowered his voice.

"Because Lily's been going up there too."

Gin was quiet for a moment, mulling it over.

Fergus lifted his head slightly and thumped his tail once against the ground.

Edwin shifted his weight.

"I think someone ought to watch over them."

Gin followed his gaze across the yard.

Jake was arguing with Rowan about the fox making a return.

Max lingered close by like a shadow.

Gin let out a slow breath.

"Alright," she replied.

Edwin blinked in surprise.

"That's it?"

"For now."

"You're not gonna tell Franklin?"

Gin shook her head.

"Not just yet."

Edwin frowned.

"Why not?"

Gin stood and stretched.

"Because kids wander," she explained. "And sometimes if you jump on a problem too soon, it grows into something larger."

She stepped off the porch.

"But I'll keep an eye on them."

Edwin nodded slowly.

Across the yard, Max finally snatched a pickle.

Jake laughed and gave him a light shove.

Max shoved back.

For a moment, they appeared like any two boys in the world.

Gin watched them a little longer.

Then her gaze shifted toward the ridge.

And the trees beyond.

The woods were silent.

Too silent.

CHAPTER TWENTY-ONE

THE FIRST STEP

Jake waited until the sun began its descent behind the ridge.

That was the time when most people at the Lodge got caught up with their supper and evening tasks. Buckets clanged. Doors creaked open and shut. There was always someone calling for another to wash up.

A perfect moment to slip away.

Jake edged past the barn and into the trees, hoping no one saw him go.

At least, he hoped no one had noticed.

The path to the creek felt different, now that he knew what is was.

Not just a deer trail.

Not merely a shortcut.

A path.

Used.

Important.

He crept down the slope and crouched beside the water.

The creek ran low this time of year, the stones warmed by the afternoon light. Minnows darted as his shadow brushed the surface.

Jake barely noticed them.

He was listening.

For voices. For footsteps.

For the splash of water in buckets.

It came a few moments later.

Two girls emerged from the trees on the far side of the creek, each with a metal pail in hand. They seemed around Lily's age, maybe a touch younger. Jake crouched behind a fallen log, watching intently.

The girls were silent, not even exchanging words with one another, even though they were alone. They filled their buckets with care, lifting them together as water sloshed over the sides, yet still, no words passed between them.

Jake frowned. Back at the Lodge, someone would have made a fuss by now—splashed water or tried to push the other in.

The girls turned toward the trail leading up the hill. Jake waited until they'd passed before making his move. He slipped across the creek, keeping his distance but close enough to see their path.

The trail rose steadily through the trees, and he paused every few yards to stop, listen, then move again.

Reaching the top where the trees thinned, Jake halted just shy of the clearing. The sounds of camp drifted to him—voices, the chopping of wood, the creak of wagon wheels. The girls stepped into the open, and no one questioned them or even looked surprised. They set their buckets beside a long wooden trough at the edge of the clearing.

Jake leaned forward, the anticipation pulling him closer.

From this vantage, he could see more of the camp than ever before.

Children were huddled in a circle by the longhouse.

Reading.

The same worn books.

Always the same.

A boy around Jake's age stood nearby, cradling a basket.

Their eyes met when the girls arrived.

Time stilled.

Jake froze in place.

The boy offered no smile.

No frown, either.

He regarded Jake like one might regard a fence post.

As if its purpose was a mystery to him.

Jake slowly raised a hand.

Just a little.

The boy tilted his head in curiosity.

Then turned away.

A knot formed in Jake's stomach.

It wasn't the neglect that stung.

It was worse.

The notion of a return wave hadn't even entered the boy's mind.

A voice drifted through the clearing.

"Children."

The Teacher stood at the longhouse door.

The kids straightened at once.

Even the boy with the basket.

"Bring the water."

The girls lifted their buckets, carrying them forward.

The boy followed suit.

Jake remained rooted in place.

Breathing slowly.

Watching.

Up close, the camp lost its sense of peace.

It felt...

tight, constrained.

Like everything within had been drawn tight and secured.

A shape shifted at the far edge of the clearing.

Jake's gaze snapped to it.

Ash.

The guard emerged from the space between two cabins, scanning the treeline.

Jake sank down into a bush beside the path.

Ash's gaze swept slowly over the woods.

Left.

Right.

Up the ridge.

Jake pressed his face into the dirt. Seconds ticked by.

Then Ash turned away.

Jake remained still for a long stretch.

When he finally crept back down the trail toward the creek, his heart raced faster than before.

But fear wasn't what he felt.

Not really.

He was deep in thought. The water path had worked. No one had stopped the girls. No questions had been asked. No one even glanced twice.

Jake crouched beside the creek once more, studying the muddy footprints.

Kids came here daily.

Morning.

Evening.

Sometimes alone.

Sometimes in pairs.

A plan began to take shape in his mind.

If he carried a bucket...

He could walk right in.

A smile crept onto Jake's face.

He turned toward the Lodge and made his way back through the trees.

Behind him, at the edge of the clearing, Ash paused once more.

He gazed at the water trail.

The branches still swayed slightly where someone had passed.

Ash frowned for just a moment.

Then he turned back toward the camp.

Next time, he resolved, he would walk that trail himself.

Chapter Twenty-Two

The Bucket

Jake didn't try the plan the next day because that would have been stupid.

Even he knew that.

Instead he watched.

For two days he paid attention to things he'd never cared about before.

What the Harbinger kids wore.

How they walked. Where they carried the buckets.

He noticed the clothes first.

Not the colors. The sameness. The boys wore loose shirts with plain trousers.

Everything soft and pale like it had been washed too many times.

Nothing bright.

Nothing patched in funny shapes the way Rowan fixed things.

Nothing with pockets full of marbles or nails or bits of string.

Just clothes.

Simple.

Quiet.

Jake looked down at himself.

His shirt had three different repairs on the sleeves and one crooked patch on the shoulder where Clare had fixed a tear.

Rowan said it made him look like a scarecrow.

Which meant it definitely wouldn't work.

So that afternoon Jake did something he almost never did.

He folded his shirt. Carefully.

Then he borrowed another one.

The spare shirts hung on a peg in the wash shed for anyone who needed one.

This one was plain.

Soft.

No patches.

Jake pulled it on and studied himself in the small mirror nailed beside the door.

Better.

Still not perfect.

But closer.

He rubbed dirt off the knees of his pants and smoothed his hair down flat with wet fingers.

Then he found a bucket.

The metal one felt cold in his hands.

Jake stood there for a moment, holding it.

His stomach fluttered.

This was the part where he could still stop.

He didn't.

The woods lay still as he approached the creek.

Late afternoon sunlight filtered through the branches in long, golden rays.

Jake crouched by the water, filling the bucket halfway.

Too full would slosh.

Too empty would look strange.

He lifted it with care. The weight tugged at his arms.

Good. Real.

Jake made his way up the water path.

One step at a time. Not sneaking. Not hiding.

Just walking like the other kids did.

As the trees thinned at the edge of the clearing, his heart began to race.

He pushed himself not to slow.

Two girls were already there, filling their buckets.

They looked up as he emerged from the trees.

Neither offered a smile.

One nodded once and Jake returned the nod.

Silence hung between them.

They carried their buckets toward the camp.

Jake trailed behind. Just another kid with a bucket.

The clearing opened around him. Smoke drifted from cooking fires.

Children moved between the cabins with armfuls of wood and baskets of vegetables.

Everything quiet.

Everything in order.

No shouting.

No chasing.

No running.

No laughter.

Jake felt a knot tighten in his chest.

At the Lodge, someone would have tripped him by now.

Or tried to.

The girls placed their buckets by the wooden trough.

Jake followed suit.

The water sloshed softly.

Still, nobody spoke.

A boy roughly his age strolled by, clutching a stack of thin books.

He glanced at Jake, then he continued on his way.

Jake scanned his surroundings. No one seemed taken aback by his presence.

No one inquired where he had come from. It was as if he had always belonged to the camp.

That notion felt off. Deeply off.

Near the longhouse, a group of younger children sat in a circle.

Reading aloud, together. Their voices moved in unison.

Slow.

Steady.

As if they were one voice speaking.

Jake took a small step back toward the clearing's edge.

That's when he spotted Ash.

The guard stood by a wagon, arms crossed, observing the camp.

Not shifting much. Just watching.

Jake lowered his gaze.

He picked up one of the empty buckets next to the trough and carried it toward the path once more.

Just another kid getting water.

The same girls were already making their way down the trail.

Jake trailed after them into the trees.

Only when the clearing faded behind the branches did he finally exhale.

His hands trembled.

Not from fear, but from excitement.

It had worked.

He had walked right into the camp and no one had stopped him.

No one had asked his name or had even glanced twice.

Jake grinned.

If he could do it once—

He could do it again.

And next time...

He'd stay longer.

Chapter Twenty-Three

Shadows and Secrets

Jake tossed and turned that night.

Not out of fear.

It was more that his mind wouldn't settle down.

Each time he shut his eyes the camp came back.

The stillness.

Kids reading.

No laughter.

Even their steps were careful.

As if they were trying not to anger the ground beneath them.

Jake turned over, tugging the blanket snug against his shoulder.

Morning light began to filter through the window.

Outside, he could hear someone already chopping wood.

Most likely Boone.

Jake swung his legs off the bed before anyone could start searching for him.

If he got up early enough, no one would suspect a thing.

That was the plan.

Max noticed.

Not right away.

He was accustomed to Jake wandering off now and then. That was just the way of things at the Lodge. But lately, Jake had been disappearing in the same silent manner.

Quietly.

Quickly.

Like he was trying to avoid being noticed.

Max perched on the fence rail, observing as Jake dragged a bucket across the yard toward the pump.

"Why you carrying that?" Max called out.

Jake shrugged.

"Because it's empty, duh."

"That's not what I meant."

Jake began pumping the handle, filling the bucket. Water sloshed over the rim.

Max scrutinized him.

"You've been going to the ridge."

Jake paused for just a heartbeat.

Then he lifted the bucket and kept walking.

Max jumped down from the fence and trailed after him.

"You're sneaking around," Max remarked.

"I am not."

"You are."

Jake poured the water into the kitchen barrel and set the bucket aside.

Max leaned in closer.

"What you doing?"

Jake wiped his hands on his pants.

"Nothing."

Max narrowed his eyes at him.

"You're a terrible liar."

Jake nudged him gently.

"Go bother someone else."

Max grinned.

"No."

Gin was halfway across the yard when Edwin caught up.

"Still keeping an eye on them?" he asked in a low voice.

Gin didn't pause.

"Always."

Edwin kicked a stone ahead of him.

"I think Jake's up to something."

Gin looked down at him.

"Something like what?"

Edwin shrugged.

"Not sure yet."

Gin followed his gaze to the trees.

The ridge lay dark against the afternoon sky.

"You'll let me know if you find out?" she asked.

Edwin nodded.

Gin briefly rested a hand on his shoulder.

"That's a good instinct," she said.

Then she continued on her way.

Later that evening Max found Jake sitting behind the barn sharpening a stick with his pocketknife.

Max sat beside him.

"You're doing it again," he said.

Jake didn't look up.

"Doing what?"

"Thinking."

Jake kept shaving curls of wood from the stick. Max watched him for a minute.

"You going back tomorrow?"

Jake stopped.

Slowly. He looked at Max and raised an eyebrow.

Max grinned.

"I knew it."

Jake sighed.

"You gotta stop following me around."

"Nope."

Jake stared at him.

Max's grin faded slightly.

"You ain't doing something dumb, are you?"

Jake hesitated. Just long enough.

Max leaned closer.

"You are."

Jake shoved the knife into the dirt beside him.

"I'm helping."

"Helping who?"

Jake glanced toward the house.

Where Franklin's voice drifted faintly through the open window.

Max's eyes widened.

"You're spying for Franklin, aren't you?"

Jake said nothing.

Max sat back slowly.

For once he didn't grin.

"You're gonna get caught."

Jake picked up the stick again.

"Not if I'm careful."

Max didn't answer. But when Jake stood up and headed toward the house, Max followed a few steps behind. Like a shadow.

Because if Jake was doing something dangerous, Max wasn't letting him do it alone.

Chapter Twenty-Four

The Quiet Camp

Jake waited three days before going back.

Not because he wanted to.

But because he figured if he went daily, someone would catch on.

Even if that someone was just Max.

The waiting gnawed at him the most.

Each time he passed the ridge, an urge tugged at him. Like there was something up there he needed to figure out.

By the third day he couldn't stand it anymore.

He grabbed the same metal bucket from behind the wash shed.

Nobody asked why.

Kids carried buckets all the time.

That was the nice thing about chores.

They made a good excuse.

The creek flowed a bit lower than before.

The stones warmed beneath Jake's boots as he filled the bucket halfway.

Not too much.

Not too little.

Just like the other kids.

He retraced the water path.

Slow and steady.

Just another kid handling a chore.

When the clearing appeared before him, nothing seemed changed.

Smoke drifted from cookfires.

Children moved quietly between the cabins.

No shouting. No running. No games.

That part still nagged at him.

At the Lodge, someone was always running, or yelling, or getting tackled by another.

Here, they moved as if in church.

Jake set his bucket beside the trough.

Nobody paid him any mind.

It felt odd.

He grabbed another empty bucket and started back toward the trail.

Halfway there, a voice called from behind.

"You are new."

Jake halted. A boy stood a few paces away. The same boy from earlier.

The one with the books. He held one now, thin and worn.

Jake shrugged, "Just helping."

The boy tilted his head slightly.

"Helping who?"

Jake hadn't thought that far.

"The Teacher," he replied after a moment.

The boy regarded him for a second.

Then he nodded.

"That is good."

Jake waited.

Usually, when someone spoke to you, they followed with more.

But the boy remained silent, holding the book. Finally, Jake pointed at it.

"What are you reading?"

The boy turned the cover slightly to show him.

No pictures, just words. A lot of them.

"Lessons," the boy said.

Jake frowned.

"That doesn't look fun."

The boy blinked.

"Fun?"

Jake shifted his weight.

"Yeah. Like stories."

The boy's expression turned puzzled.

"We do not read stories."

"Why not?"

The boy shrugged a little.

"They are not useful."

A strange chill crawled up the back of Jake's neck.

"Children."

Jake turned.

Teacher was near the longhouse.

The kids nearby stopped what they were doing almost instantly.

Even the boy beside Jake.

“The evening lesson will start soon,” Teacher said calmly.

The boy nodded toward Jake.

“You should come.”

Jake shook his head.

“I’ve got water to carry.”

The boy accepted that without question.

"Very well.”

Jake lifted the empty bucket again and walked toward the trail.

Halfway across the clearing, he heard someone speak behind him.

“Teacher.”

A guard’s voice.

Jake didn’t turn but slowed just enough to listen.

“Yes, Ash?”

“There are tracks along the water path.”

Jake tightened his grip on the bucket handle.

“Animal?” Teacher asked.

Ash paused.

“I’m not certain, but I do not believe so.”

Teacher didn’t sound worried.

“Keep an eye on the path.”

“Yes.”

Jake kept walking.

Steady.

Just another kid with a bucket.

When he reached the trees, he didn’t look back.

He waited until the camp was swallowed by the branches before releasing the breath he'd been holding.

His heart raced.

Yet a smile crept back to his face.

He had spoken to one of them.

Strolled through the whole camp.

And no one had questioned him.

Jake adjusted the bucket in his hand and stepped onto the trail.

Next time—

He might even join one of their lessons.

Because the more he observed—

The more he sensed something was amiss there.

And if the adults were going to uncover it—

Someone had to bring them the truth.

Jake just didn't yet grasp how perilous that truth would be.

Chapter Twenty-Five

The Things We Notice

The Lodge kitchen was filled with the tang of vinegar and dill.

Clare had named it a pickle day, which meant that every available space in the room was taken up by something green, ready to turn sour. Cucumbers in baskets. Cucumbers in bowls. Cucumbers heaped in the sink as if they'd tried to flee the garden.

Lily was at the long table, knife and cutting board in hand, slicing them into spears while Fiona filled jars.

"You're cutting them crooked again," Fiona remarked.

"They'll taste the same, crooked or not."

"That's not the point."

Lily slid the next spear into the bowl.

"Pretty sure it is," she shot back.

Across the table, Ruth was arranging garlic cloves in a tidy stack, humming to herself.

From another room came the thud of wood being split.

"Dad's going to take down the whole forest," Fiona mumbled.

"Better than Donovan and Declan trying to lend a hand, those two are dangerous," Lily replied.

Fiona let out a snort.

Outside the open window, a voice called out.

Another voice answered.

Then came the unmistakable sound of two boys bickering.

Lily halted, knife poised mid-cut on another cucumber.

"Is that Jake?" Fiona asked.

"Most likely."

"They're always at it, lately."

Lily wiped the blade on a towel and resumed cutting, but her ears were tuned in.

Max trudged into the yard, gripping a bucket as if it had wronged him deeply.

Jake walked alongside him, more composed, yet quickening his pace.

"You're going again," Max stated.

Jake shrugged.

"I carry water every day."

"Not to the ridge."

Jake remained silent.

Max sent a stone skittering across the dirt with a kick.

"You said you'd wait."

"I did wait."

"Not long enough."

Jake switched the bucket to his other hand.

"You don't even know where I'm headed."

Max crossed his arms.

"Yes, I do."

Jake exhaled.

"Max."

"You're going up there again."

Jake halted.

For a moment, he seemed ready to argue.

Instead, he crouched to meet Max's gaze.

"I'm being careful," he said softly.

"That's what people say before they do something dumb."

Jake offered a slight smile.

"You sound like Gin."

Max didn't return the smile.

"That place gives me the creeps."

Jake studied him for a heartbeat.

"You haven't even set foot there."

"Don't need to."

Jake stood tall again.

"Go help Ellie before she realizes you're missing."

Max remained rooted to the spot.

"Jake."

Jake continued on his way.

Edwin leaned against the fence by the mule pen, taking in the whole conversation without pretending to fix anything this time.

He simply watched.

Jake made his way toward the wash shed.

Max stayed back in the yard, not following, which surprised Edwin since Max usually trailed Jake everywhere, especially lately.

Instead, Max kicked a stone hard, sending it skittering.

Edwin pushed off the fence. "You alright?"

Max shrugged, keeping his gaze low. "He's being stupid."

Edwin turned his eyes to the trees, following Max's sight. The ridge stood quiet in the afternoon light.

"You mean Jake?" he asked.

Max nodded.

Edwin waited in silence, and eventually, Max met his gaze. "You ever notice those Harbinger kids?"

A tightness settled in Edwin's stomach. "What about them?"

"They don't laugh."

Edwin kept quiet, letting the words hang in the air.

Max squinted toward the ridge. "They just carry buckets and walk like... like old folks."

Edwin rubbed the back of his neck. "Maybe that's just who they are."

Max shook his head fiercely. "That ain't how real kids act."

Gin picked up on it later.

Not the chat.

Just the pattern.

Jake had begun hauling water more frequently.

Buckets in the morning.

Buckets in the afternoon.

Sometimes he'd make two or three trips.

That alone didn't mean much.

The well was right there, and with so many people, they always needed water. Gin leaned against the porch post, observing him cross the yard again. Bucket in hand.

Heading towards the trees.

Max lingered near the garden fence, watching him go. Edwin watched too.

Gin's eyes narrowed slightly.

Morales joined her on the porch, wiping his hands on a rag.

"What's on your mind?" he asked.

Gin nodded towards the yard.

"Kids."

Morales snorted.

"That's a recipe for trouble."

Gin didn't chuckle.

Jake vanished into the trees.Max remained where he stood.

That part stuck with her. Gin pushed away from the porch.

"Hey, Morales."

"Yeah?"

"Tomorrow, I think I'll take a walk."

Morales glanced towards the ridge.

"Need company?"

Gin shook her head.

"Not yet."

She watched the trees for another moment.

Then turned back toward the house.

Inside the kitchen, someone dropped a jar, and Clare called out about slippery hands.

Normal sounds.

Normal day.

Gin just hadn't realized yet how close the trouble already was.

Chapter Twenty-Six

The Lesson

Jake waited until the afternoon chores had everyone busy again.

That seemed to be the safest time.

People moved around more than usual. Doors opened and shut. Buckets clanged. Someone was always calling for someone else. It was easier to disappear into the middle of all that noise.

Max noticed him pick up the bucket. Max always noticed.

"You going again?" he said flatly.

Jake didn't answer.

"You said you were just looking," Max added.

Jake shifted the bucket in his hands.

"I am."

Max scrunched his face and shook his head.

"That's not what it looks like."

Jake crouched so they were eye level.

"I'm careful," he said quietly.

Max stared at him. Jake saw the worry in his friend's eyes.

"That place ain't right."

Jake didn't argue.

Because Max wasn't wrong. That was exactly why he had to keep going.

He stood again and started toward the trees. Max didn't follow this time.

Jake felt that absence all the way to the ridge.

The creek was quieter than before.

A pair of Harbinger kids were already filling their buckets when Jake reached it.

They nodded when they saw him.

Just like last time.

No smiles.

No questions.

Jake nodded back.

They carried the buckets up the trail and Jake followed behind them.

Just another kid with water.

The clearing looked almost peaceful when he stepped out of the trees.

Children moved slowly between the cabins.

A group of younger ones sat on the ground near the longhouse, books in their laps.

Reading.

Always reading.

Jake set his bucket beside the trough.

Nobody stopped him. Nobody even looked surprised.

He stood there longer this time.

Watching.

Waiting.

A bell chimed from somewhere near the longhouse.

It wasn't loud.

Yet every child in the clearing ceased their play instantly.

Jake felt the stillness settle over the camp like a blanket.

The Teacher appeared on the porch.

"Children."

The word was quiet too.

But all heads turned.

"Gather."

They moved swiftly.

Silently.

Jake lingered where he was.

He knew he should go.

But no one seemed to notice him, so he remained.

Watching.

The children formed a circle in the dirt by the porch.

Books rested open in their laps.

The Teacher stood in the center.

"Today we'll continue our lesson about the old world," he said in a steady voice.

Jake edged closer to the circle's perimeter.

Near enough to listen.

Not close enough to draw attention.

Hopefully.

"Freedom," Teacher remarked, "was the lie that brought about their downfall."

The children echoed the words in unison.

Jake felt the phrase slither over his skin.

Teacher gave a slight nod.

"What is freedom?"

A small girl piped up.

"Chaos."

"And chaos leads to?"

"Pain."

Teacher smiled faintly.

"Right."

Jake gulped.

At the Lodge, freedom was casting lines in the creek, scaling the ridge, or getting scolded for leaving muddy footprints across the kitchen floor.

It didn't lead to chaos. At least, not the bad kind.

The teacher moved steadily around the circle.

"In the old world, children believed they could choose their own path."

The kids sat still, listening.

"That belief tore families apart. It ruined nations. It shattered truth."

A knot formed in Jake's stomach.

He thought of Rowan clashing with Donovan.

Of Max shadowing his every move.

Of Lily sneaking away to observe the camp.

None of that seemed like ruin.

It felt... normal.

The teacher fell silent.

The clearing returned to quiet.

Then, a voice cut through from the edge of the camp.

"Ash."

Jake went rigid.

Ash stood at the trail leading to the creek, his gaze fixed on the trees.

Not on the children. Not on the teacher.

Just the path.

Jake gradually glanced down, grabbing the empty bucket next to him.

His fingers felt stiff around the handle.

Just another kid fetching water.

Ash took a few steps forward.

Jake willed himself to remain calm and move slow and steady.

Step.

Step.

Step.

He finally reached the edge of the clearing.

The trees loomed just a few paces ahead.

Ash spoke up from behind him once more.

"There are more tracks."

Jake continued on.

Slow.

Steady.

The branches enveloped him. Only upon reaching the creek did he feel like he could breathe again. His hands trembled. His breathing was coming in gasps.

Yet, he smiled.

He had managed to remain for the entire lesson.

No one had interrupted him.

No one had even inquired about his name.

Jake hoisted the bucket once more and made his way down the trail.

Next time...

He might linger even longer.

And that was the moment the woods stopped feeling like protection—and started feeling like something that might not let him leave.

Chapter Twenty-Seven

The Empty Chair

The Lodge kitchen was filled with the scents of onions, wood smoke, and venison fat.

Clare stood by the big stove, stirring a pot that could feed an army. The long wooden spoon moved slowly through the thickening stew, sweat beading along her hairline.

"Needs salt," she murmured.

Jo glanced up from the table where she was slicing carrots.

"It always needs salt when you're cooking."

Clare snorted.

"Zeke never complained."

Jo paused at the mention of Zeke.

"Zeke ate anything that wasn't nailed down."

"That's not the same thing."

At the far end of the table, Edwin sat with a whetstone, carefully working the edge of a small knife as Gus had taught him. The steady scrape of steel against stone mixed with the bubbling stew.

Marisol stood on a chair beside him, pouring honey from a clay jar into a smaller container.

"Don't spill it," Edwin said without glancing up.

"I'm not spilling it."

"You always spill it."

"I do not."

Leah leaned against the counter, arms crossed.

"What's that for anyway?"

Marisol capped the jar.

"For Buck."

The room fell silent.

Jo and Clare exchanged a look.

"When are you giving that to him?" Clare asked gently.

Marisol shrugged.

"I already did."

Edwin paused sharpening.

"You did?"

"Last week."

"You didn't tell anyone."

Marisol looked puzzled.

"I put it on his porch."

Leah frowned.

"Did he take it?"

Marisol hesitated.

"I don't know."

Jo set the knife down.

"Have any of you seen Buck this week?"

The kids shook their heads.

Edwin spoke up.

"I saw Flora by the tree line yesterday."

"That mule wanders," Leah said.

"Yeah," Edwin replied, "but Buck wasn't with her."

Clare stirred the stew again.

"He's hunting."

"That's what everyone keeps saying," Leah replied.

Jo wiped her hands on a towel.

"Sometimes folks need a little quiet."

Edwin frowned.

"Did Buck move away?"

Clare looked over.

"No, sweetie."

"Then where is he?"

No one replied immediately.

The front door creaked open, and Gus stepped in with Marcus behind him.

Heat and sunlight followed them.

"You smell that?" Marcus asked Gus with a grin.

Clare pointed the spoon at her Uncle.

"Not until you wash your hands."

Marcus grinned and headed for the sink.

Gus took off his hat.

"What's the meeting about?"

Marisol held up the honey jar.

"I brought Buck some honey."

Gus regarded it for a moment.

"Did he like it?"

Marisol's shoulders sagged.

"I don't know."

Once again, the room fell quiet.

Marcus dried his hands.

"Haven't seen him around much," he said.

"No," Jo replied softly.

Gus leaned against the doorframe.

"How long's it been?"

Clare answered without looking up.

"Three months."

No one needed to ask, since when.

Edwin returned to sharpening his knife, moving slower this time.

"They used to funny stories after dinner."

Marcus smiled faintly.

"Tall ones."

"The best ones," Edwin agreed.

Gus looked around the kitchen.

At the stew.

At the kids.

At the empty seat at the end of the table where Buck usually sat.

Then he grabbed his hat again.

Marcus noticed.

"Where you headed?"

Gus opened the door.

"To go fetch a stubborn old man."

Marcus grabbed his own hat.

"I'll come with."

Outside, cicadas screamed in the summer heat as the two men started down the path toward Buck and Zeke's cabin.

The August air was heavy and thick enough to chew.

Marcus wiped the sweat from his brow as he trailed Gus down the narrow path to the cabin. Cicadas buzzed in the trees, loud and relentless, just as summer always was in the mountains.

"Think he's around?" Marcus asked.

Gus nodded toward the ground.

"Tracks."

Marcus glanced down.

Boot prints. Fresh enough to hold their shape in the dust.

Next to them were the distinct imprints of mule hooves.

"Flora," Marcus said.

"Yep."

They pushed through the trees until the cabin came into view.

The little place sat still in the clearing. Smoke curled lazily from the stovepipe.

A gray shape lifted its head from the porch.

Sandy.

The old dog wagged her tail twice when she spotted them.

Marcus felt a familiar ache in his chest.

Zeke's dog.

Now Buck's.

"Hey girl," Marcus said softly.

Sandy sniffed his hand, then glanced past him toward the trail.

Still waiting.

Gus noticed too but remained silent.

He knocked once as he nudged the door open.

Buck was at the table.

Unshaven, with hollow eyes, a mug of coffee cradled in his hands.

An empty chair waited across from him.

Marcus had seen Zeke sit there countless times.

Buck looked up.

“Doors are usually closed for a reason.”

Gus stepped inside anyway.

“You gonna shoot us?”

Buck shrugged.

“Thought about it.”

Marcus pulled out a chair and settled in.

The cabin still bore the mark of two men living there.

Two beds.

Two rifles on the wall.

Two coffee mugs hanging above the stove.

Yet only one man breathed.

“You've been hunting,” Marcus said.

Buck nodded.

“Game’s thick this year.”

“You ain’t bringing any of it back.”

“Nope.”

“Folks are noticing.”

Buck took a sip of coffee.

“Folks got plenty of other things to notice.”

A hush fell over the cabin.

Outside, Flora shifted her weight and the leather harness creaked.

Gus surveyed the room.

Zeke’s coat still hung by the door.

His old hat rested on the peg above it.

The sight caught Gus's breath for a moment.

Marcus noticed but chose silence.

"You planning to live out here now?" Marcus asked.

Buck stared deep into his mug.

"Been thinking about it."

"That so."

"Yep."

"That thinking get you anywhere?"

Buck met his gaze.

"You come here to lecture me, son?"

"No," Marcus said.

"Then what."

Gus chimed in.

"You're disappearing. You, my friend, are missed."

Buck scoffed.

"I'm sitting right here."

"You ain't," Gus countered.

Buck's jaw tightened.

Marcus leaned in.

"We Callahans gave you plenty of space."

Buck remained silent.

"Three months of space," Marcus pressed.

Still no response.

"Folks brought food."

"You sent it back."

Buck turned his gaze away.

Outside, Sandy let out a soft whine.

Buck's gaze flicked to the door without thought.

"Dog's still waiting," Gus murmured.

Buck kept silent.

"She'll stand out there half the morning, staring down that trail I bet," Gus added.

Buck's voice came out gravelly.

"Yep."

Silence settled around them.

Then Buck pushed his chair back, the scrape of wood breaking the stillness.

"I watched him walk out that door," he said.

No one interjected.

Outside, Sandy let out a soft whine.

"He promised he'd be back by evening."

Buck rubbed his face, frustration etched in every line.

"That was three months ago."

Marcus nodded, understanding.

"We know."

Buck shook his head, disbelief flickering in his eyes.

"You don't."

Gus stepped closer, a warning in his stance.

"Careful."

Buck met his gaze, anger igniting like a flame.

"You knew him thirty years."

Gus remained steadfast, unyielding.

"And?"

Buck gestured around the cabin, a weighty gesture.

"I lived with him. I hunted with him. I heard his damn stories every night. I listened to his awful snores and his sadness about EmmaJean."

Buck's voice faltered, thick with emotion.

"I watched him walk out that door."

Gus nodded slowly, a shared sorrow passing between them.

"Yeah."

Buck blinked, surprised by the acknowledgment.

Gus pulled out the chair beside him and sat down.

"Think that year didn't count?" Gus asked.

Buck fell silent, grappling with the truth.

"That man didn't share a roof with folks he didn't respect."

Buck swallowed hard, the tension easing slightly from his shoulders.

"You earned that," Gus said, his voice steady.

"But don't think," he continued softly, "that you're the only one carrying him."

Buck turned to him, their bond palpable.

Gus nodded toward the empty chair.

"I've been sitting across from that seat in my mind for thirty years."

The words landed, heavy and profound.

Buck stared at the table, lost in thought.

"I keep thinking maybe he's still out there," he murmured.

Marcus leaned in, his tone gentle. "Maybe he is."

Buck's jaw tightened. "Or maybe he's just bones now, and we haven't found him yet."

Outside, Sandy barked—a short, sharp sound that cut through the silence.

Buck closed his eyes. "She waits for him," he admitted.

Gus nodded. "Dogs do that."

Buck let out a quiet laugh. "I talk to her more than I talk to folks these days."

A faint smile crossed Marcus's face. "Marisol left honey on your porch last week."

Buck's gaze shot up. "What?"

"A little clay jar," Marcus explained.

Buck frowned, having missed it. "She thought you might be sick," Marcus added softly.

Buck rubbed the back of his neck, the weight of worry settling deeper. "The kids been asking about you," Marcus continued.

Buck sighed, the air heavy. "Edwin said he is waiting for you to show him how to tie your fancy lures. Ian said the mountain man who tells stories just vanished."

That struck a chord with Marcus.

Buck shook his head. "Didn't disappear."

"Feels that way," Marcus replied, his gaze distant.

Buck looked around the cabin.

First the chair.

Then the coat.

Finally, the hat.

He rose to his feet.

"You done hiding?" Gus inquired.

Buck paused to consider.

"Maybe."

Marcus gestured towards the door.

"Dinner's venison stew."

Buck lifted an eyebrow.

"Who's the cook?"

"Clare."

Buck snatched up his hat.

"Well hell," he murmured. "Someone oughta keep an eye on that. I may need to supervise."

Marcus chuckled.

Buck glanced once more at the empty chair.

"Don't get comfortable," he muttered under his breath before he walked out the door.

Outside, Sandy stood wagging her tail.

Buck knelt to scratch her ears.

"Come on, girl."

Sandy moved toward Buck.

Her tail thumped once.

Like she'd been waiting for this.

Flora snorted as he untied her lead rope.

The three men set off down the trail toward the Lodge.

Sandy trotted ahead of them down the trail, nose high, like she already knew where they were headed.

For the first time since Zeke disappeared, Buck didn't walk the trail alone.

Chapter Twenty-Eight

A Seat at the Table

The Lodge smelled like supper.

Venison stew bubbled on the stove, and the long table was laden with bowls, bread, and worn tin cups. The evening air flowed through the open windows, bringing in the last traces of daylight and the steady song of cicadas.

At the end of the table, Edwin fiddled with a length of fishing line, trying to replicate the knot Buck had taught him over the winter.

It wasn't going well.

"You wrapped it wrong," Leah said briskly.

"I did not."

"You did."

Edwin scowled at the knot.

"It looked easier when Buck did it."

Leah shrugged.

"That's because Buck actually knows how."

Jo brought the pot of stew to the table and set it down.

"He'll show you again," she said.

Edwin looked up, eager.

"When?"

Jo paused just a beat.

"When he comes around."

Outside, the sound of boots crunching on gravel reached the porch.

Leah glanced toward the door.

"That might be now."

The door swung open.

Gus stepped in first, removing his hat and wiping sweat from his brow.

Marcus followed closely behind.

"Smells like supper," Marcus remarked.

Clare aimed a wooden spoon at him.

"You wash your hands yet?"

Marcus grinned.

"I sure did."

"You said that last time." Clare laughed as she threw a dishcloth at him.

Then Buck entered the room.

For a moment, silence enveloped them.

Buck looked thinner. His beard had grown uneven and his eyes carried the dull exhaustion of a man who hadn't slept much.

But he was there.

Sandy padded in behind him, settling by the door as if she had found her place once more.

Marisol was the first to move.

She slid off her chair and made a beeline for Buck.

No second thoughts. No fanfare. Just the unwavering certainty of a child.

"I brought you honey," she said simply, her voice small and steady. She wrapped her small arms around his waist and looked up at him.

Buck raised an eyebrow.

"You did?"

With a nod, she replied, "Last week."

Buck rubbed the back of his neck, a shadow of embarrassment passing over his face.

"I must have missed it."

Marisol looked at him for a moment, weighing whether to give him the benefit of the doubt. Then she extended the small clay jar she'd been saving.

"This one's fresh."

Buck accepted it gently, as if it might shatter.

"Well now," he murmured, "Thank you."

Marisol nodded once and returned to her seat, as if that settled everything.

Edwin leaned in, his curiosity piqued.

"Buck, you gotta show me that fishing lure knot again."

Buck glanced at the tangled line in the boy's grasp.

"That mess?"

Edwin scowled, folding his arms stubbornly.

"It's not a mess."

Buck sighed and pulled out a chair.

"Son, that's a bird's nest."

Leah stifled a laugh.

"Told you."

Buck settled in and took the line from Edwin's grasp.

"You wrap it here," he instructed, his fingers moving deliberately for the boy to follow. "Then back through."

Edwin watched intently.

"Oh."

"That's it?"

"That's it."

Edwin's face lit up with a grin.

"I almost had it."

Buck offered a weary half-smile.

"Almost counts for horseshoes."

"And hand grenades." Gunny mumbled to himself, earning a sharp look from Jo.

Jo had been watching quietly from the stove. She carried a bowl of stew over and set it in front of Buck. Holding a spoon out to him she gave him a look.

"You look like you haven't eaten a proper meal in a while."

Buck nodded.

"That obvious?"

"A little."

He picked up the spoon but paused before taking a bite.

Jo studied him the way she studied storms on the horizon.

"You sleeping?" she asked quietly.

Buck shrugged.

"Some."

Jo didn't look convinced.

"You look worn down, Buck."

Buck finally took a bite of stew.

His shoulders dropped slightly. A smile of pleasure flashing across his face.

"That's good," he sighed.

Clare smirked from the stove.

"I know how to cook venison."

Buck nodded slowly.

"Maybe you do at that."

The table filled with the sounds of eating.

For the first time in weeks, Buck sat where he belonged.

Across the table from him, the chair where Zeke used to sit remained empty.

Buck noticed.

His gaze lingered there a moment.

Then Edwin spoke again.

"You gonna tell a story tonight?"

Buck blinked.

"Story?"

"The one about the bear and the outhouse."

Leah groaned.

"That story's gross."

"That's why it's good," Edwin said.

Buck leaned back in the chair. He put his hands behind his head, elbows sticking out wide. For a moment he looked like the old Buck again.

"Alright," he said with a small nod.

"But only if someone pours me more coffee."

Marcus slid the pot toward him.

"Welcome back," Marcus said quietly.

Buck gave a small nod.

Jake rose and slipped over to the pegs by the door, lifted his pack and checked the straps before setting it back.

Then he stepped onto the porch and looked out into the darkness.

Jo watched him from the kitchen window.

Something about the way he stood there made her uneasy. She made a note to check on him in the morning.

And as night settled across the pines, beyond the dark line of trees, something was already beginning to move.

Chapter Twenty-Nine

The Quiet

Morning came the way it usually did now.

Work came first, then conversation.

Clare threw open the kitchen windows, letting the heat escape before it settled in for the day. The scent of fresh bread wafted out into the yard, mingling with the sharpness of pine and the warm sweetness of hay stacked near the barn.

Lucy dashed barefoot across the grass, a wooden spoon held in one hand like a scepter.

"Queen Lucy!" she declared.

Rosa glanced up from where she and Marisol were braiding clover stems.

"You're not a queen," Rosa replied plainly. "Queens wear shoes."

Lucy paused, thought it over, then tossed the spoon aside and dashed toward the porch steps.

Jake caught her just before she tripped over the bottom board.

"Mind your step, Your Majesty," he teased.

Lucy giggled as he lifted her effortlessly, settling her against his shoulder.

"You smell like the woods," she said, nuzzling his shirt.

"That's because I've been in the woods," Jake answered.

Lucy wrapped her arms around his neck, holding on a moment longer than usual.

Jake didn't hurry her. He squeezed back.

From across the yard, Max noticed.

Max noticed most things these days.

Eventually, Jake set Lucy back down, giving her a spin before letting her run to the others. She stumbled toward Rosa and Marisol, who were now in a debate about whether a clover crown required symmetry to truly count.

Jake leaned against the porch post, watching them for a spell.

Rosa's brow furrowed in concentration as she threaded another stem into the chain. Marisol worked slowly, careful and patient, her small fingers steady even as the stems twisted.

Jake smiled, caught off guard.

"Hey," Rosa said suddenly, noticing him.

"What?"

"Why are you staring?"

Jake shrugged.

"Just thinking."

Rosa narrowed her eyes, skeptical.

"About what?"

"Important things."

That seemed to satisfy her.

Max approached, moving quietly like he had been lately.

Jake noticed him and straightened slightly.

"What's up?" he asked.

Max kicked at the dirt near the porch step.

"You're heading up the ridge again."

Jake paused for just a heartbeat.

Not long enough for most folks to catch on.

But enough for Max.

Jake leaned against the porch post.

"Maybe."

Max nodded once, as if he had seen that coming.

"It's about Lily. Isn't it?"

Jake stayed silent.

Across the yard, Lily was aiding Fiona in carrying a basket of green beans toward the kitchen.

Jake watched her for a beat before responding.

"You shouldn't worry about grownup troubles."

Max shrugged.

"You're looking out for Franklin."

Jake glanced down. Then back up at him.

Max met his gaze with steady eyes.

At nine years old, he already held more understanding than anyone should have asked of him.

Jake sighed.

"Just keeping an eye on things," he said. "He can't be everywhere. None of them can. They didn't have to take us into their family. But..."

Jake shrugged.

Max nodded again.

Then he spoke softly:

"Be careful."

Jake returned a crooked grin.

"Always am."

Max didn't return the smile.

Edwin noticed Jake making his way toward the trail. Sandy lifted her head as Jake passed, watching him a moment before settling again.

Edwin stood near the barn door, wrestling with a stubborn knot in a piece of twine when Jake crossed the edge of the yard.

Not sneaking.

Not rushing.

Just walking.

Edwin straightened up slowly.

Toward the ridge.

"Hey... headed that way again, huh," he called.

Jake turned partway.

"Just stretching my legs."

Edwin slid the pliers into his belt.

"That ridge gets crowded these days."

Jake chuckled softly.

"Didn't notice."

Edwin kept his gaze on him for a moment longer.

Then he nodded once.

"Sure."

Jake tipped two fingers in a casual salute and continued toward the tree line.

Edwin stayed put, but he watched until the woods enveloped him.

Gin spotted the tracks just beyond the water path.

They weren't fresh.

But not old, either.

Frequent.

She knelt by the narrow strip of soft earth, examining the marks in silence.

Boot prints. Same size. Same direction.

Again and again.

Someone was using this trail often.

She traced the edge of one print with her fingers, gauging its depth.

Then she stood.

Franklin appeared up the path moments later, a coil of rope slung over one shoulder.

Gin nodded to the ground.

"See that?"

Franklin crouched down.

Studied the prints.

"Kids?" he inquired.

Gin shook her head, then nodded slightly.

"Small, but feels too consistent for kids," Gin said. "Could be a small adult though."

Franklin rose.

Neither voiced the name that lingered in their minds.

Gin wiped the dirt from her hands.

"Kids make patterns," she said softly.

Franklin looked at her.

"Adults miss them."

They started back toward the Lodge in silence.

Market day brought heat and dust. The soft murmur of trade floated through the heavy air of the schoolyard.

Jo sat near the pump, with Odin sprawled at her feet, exchanging quiet words with a woman whose child clung to her skirt.

Her cane rested against the bench beside her.

The woman nodded repeatedly as Jo spoke, the tension in her face gradually easing.

Across the field, two Harbinger women worked in silence at their table, arranging small cakes of harsh soap.

One of them glanced over at Jo.

"Is that her?" she asked softly.

The other woman kept her gaze down.

"Yes."

"The healer."

"The one they listen to."

They observed as another person approached Jo, politely waiting for the first conversation to finish.

The second woman's hands continued tying bundles.

"Influence spreads faster through kindness than command," she remarked.

The first woman nodded.

"Does the Oracle know?"

A brief silence followed.

"Yes."

Deb was halfway across the Lodge yard when the nausea hit again.

She stopped beside the garden fence and pressed one hand against the post until the moment passed.

Marcus noticed immediately.

"You alright?"

Deb nodded quickly.

"Just the heat."

Marcus didn't argue.

He simply stepped closer, resting one hand lightly at the small of her back until her breathing steadied.

"We'll slow down today," he said.

Deb gave him a tired smile.

"You say that every day."

"And every day you pretend to believe me."

She leaned against him briefly before straightening again.

Across the yard, Lucy was chasing Rosa and Marisol with the wooden spoon again.

Deb watched them for a moment.

Three small girls running through the sunlight like the world had never broken at all.

Marcus followed her gaze.

"Worth it," he said quietly.

Deb didn't answer.

But she didn't disagree either.

Chapter Thirty

Too Far

Jake slipped from his bed and out of the Lodge before the sun touched the ridge.

The Lodge remained tranquil at that hour. If you didn't want to cross paths with Jo, you had to leave very early.

Smoke drifted lazily from the banked fire in the kitchen, and the dew still clung to the grass.

He walked through the yard at a leisurely pace.

Sandy raised her head from the porch as Jake passed quietly through the yard.

Jake stopped briefly to give her a scratch behind the ears.

"You keep an eye on them," he whispered.

The old dog thumped her tail once against the boards.

Then Jake disappeared into the trees.

The trail rose steadily through the pines, eventually narrowing along the ridge. Jake navigated it for a spell before veering off into the underbrush.

He treaded carefully down toward the low hollow where the Harbinger camp sprawled beneath the trees.

The place had grown over the last few weeks.

More shelters filled the space.

More woodsmoke curled into the air.

More folks moved quietly between the structures.

From the thicket, he studied the camp.

The first thing anyone noticed about the Harbingers was how little sound they made.

Children moved through the clearing, their buckets clutched tightly.

Two boys were busy chopping wood next to a neatly stacked pile of logs.

A woman knelt at a row of small gardens, her hands working with a practiced precision to pull weeds.

No shouting.

No laughter.

No chitchat.

Just work.

Jake shifted a bit for a better look.

A group of children formed a rough half-circle at the far end of the clearing.

A man stood before them.

Not a teacher in the traditional sense.

More like a conductor leading a steady beat.

Jake struggled to catch the words at first.

Then the wind carried them closer.

"...order protects the whole."

The children echoed the phrase in unison.

Calm.

Steady.

"...order protects the whole."

Jake felt a weight settle in his chest.

No one spoke out of turn.

No one whispered.

No one moved restlessly.

They repeated the phrase once more.

"...order protects the whole."

Jake scanned the edge of the clearing.

Two armed men stood guard near the trees.

Not pacing, just standing.

Watching.

Jake leaned slightly back into the brush for cover.

He had seen enough. Yet the old curiosity tugged at him once more.

If he could only get a little closer—

He waited until a group moved across the clearing, baskets in hand, heading to one of the larger shelters. Then he made his move.

Slow.

Careful.

The ground dipped slightly here, offering him better concealment as he crept along the camp's outer edge.

From this vantage point, he could peek inside one of the larger structures.

Rows of narrow bunks.

Sleeping quarters.

Children's boots lined neatly against the wall.

Jake studied the scene intently.

Everything had its place.

Everything matched.

He shifted again, straining to see deeper inside.

That was when he spotted the books.

A stack of thin volumes rested on a small table by the door.

All identical.

Jake focused on the title stamped across the cover.

The wind shifted once more.

A page fluttered open.

A symbol filled the center.

A circle divided into four neat sections.

Jake recognized that mark.

On the Harbinger banners.

His heart started to race.

This was more than just a camp.

This was a school.

Jake eased back into the brush again.

If he could get one of those books back to the Lodge—

A twig cracked in the stillness behind him.

Jake froze.

The woods held their breath. He waited. No movement. No voices.

No cause for alarm.

After a long pause, he gradually turned his head.

Only the whisper of the wind.

Jake let out a quiet breath.

Probably just a squirrel.

He shifted his weight again, pressing on along the ridge.

If he veered wide enough, he could find a better view by the old rock outcrop.

From there, he could take in the whole camp.

The thought brought a smile to his face, unexpected as it was.

He was getting good at this.

Down below in the clearing, the children repeated their mantra.

"...order protects the whole."

Jake slipped further into the trees.

He never saw the man standing silently behind the trunk of a cedar, thirty yards away.

Ash observed him leave.

And remained silent.

CHAPTER THIRTY-ONE

THE RIDGE

Jake waited until midmorning this time.

If he left too early, the Harbinger camp stirred slowly.

If he waited too long, the paths filled with people moving between the shelters.

Midmorning felt safer.

Or at least, safe enough.

He slipped away from the Lodge while most were busy with chores. Buck was splitting kindling by the shed. Clare and Fiona were hauling water from the pump. Lucy chased after Rosa and Marisol through the grass, wooden spoon in hand, just like the day before.

Jake didn't linger.

If he paused too long, someone might notice.

Instead, he crossed the meadow at a relaxed pace and disappeared into the trees along the ridge.

The woods swallowed him almost immediately, cool and shady beneath the pines.

Jake moved with care.

He'd picked up a few lessons over the past weeks.

Never take the same route twice.

Never leave a straight trail behind.

And never let curiosity outrun patience.

Gus had shared that one during Jake's first winter at the Lodge.

He smiled faintly at the memory.

So far, he figured he was doing alright.

The ridge rose gradually before dropping into the shallow hollow where the Harbinger camp had taken hold.

Jake slowed as he neared the tree line.

Today felt different.

Not wrong, exactly.

Just... quieter.

He crouched low behind a fallen cedar, watching the clearing below.

The camp appeared much the same.

Shelters nestled among the trees.

Smoke drifted from cooking fires.

People moved steadily and silently between their tasks.

Children toted buckets of water to the gardens.

Two men split wood beside a stacked pile of logs.

Everything looked orderly.

Everything felt calm.

Yet, there were fewer folks near the camp's outer edges.

Jake narrowed his eyes.

The guards had shifted their posted spots.

Yesterday, two stood by the eastern tree line.

Now, one was nearer to the center of the clearing.

Another leaned against a post by the largest shelter.

Jake watched them for several minutes.

Neither moved much.

Neither spoke.

Just stood watch.

The wind carried soft voices across the clearing.

"...order protects the whole."

That familiar tightness gripped Jake's chest.

The children sat in their half-circle once more, repeating the phrase as the man spoke.

"...order protects the whole."

No laughter.

No whispers.

Just the steady cadence of voices in unison.

Jake shifted slightly for a better view.

The bunkhouse stood partly hidden between two tall spruces.

That was where he had seen the books yesterday.

If he circled wide enough...

Jake carefully backed into the brush.

Taking care not to snap any branches.

Then he began making his way along the ridge toward the old rock outcrop.

From there, he could see nearly the entire camp.

He had used that spot before.

So far, no one had noticed him.

At least, not that he could tell.

The outcrop emerged through the trees and Jake slowed his pace.

The ground sloped downward here, offering him a clearer view of the clearing below. Just right.

He crouched by the rocks and leaned in slightly. The bunkhouse door hung open. Inside, he caught sight of the small table again. The stack of books remained there. All identical.

Jake examined the symbol stamped on the cover. A circle split into four neat sections. The same mark he had noticed on the banners. If he could bring one of those books back to the Lodge—

A faint crunch came from somewhere behind him.

Jake froze.

Every muscle in his body tensed.

He listened.

The forest held its breath.

No birds.

No wind.

Only silence.

Jake slowly turned his head.

Nothing.

Just trees.

He lingered a few more seconds.

Still nothing.

Probably just another squirrel.

He let out a soft breath and shifted his weight.

Ten more minutes would do, then back home.

Just enough time to see if anyone entered that bunkhouse—

The branch snapped again.

Closer this time.

Jake turned quickly.

A shadow flitted between the trees.

Instinctively, Jake's hand moved toward the pocket knife at his belt.

Then something struck him from the side.

The world tilted sharply.

Leaves and dirt erupted as he hit the ground.

Jake twisted, trying to break free—

A rough hand gripped his shoulder.

Another hand covered his mouth.

A voice murmured in his ear.

"Curiosity," the voice said steadily. "Can be a dangerous habit."

The forest swallowed the rest.

A few leaves drifted slowly back to the forest floor.

Then the woods were quiet again.

Max stood staring across the meadow as the late afternoon sun caused the shadows from the ridge to stretch like fingers toward the Lodge.

Chores were almost done.

Dinner simmered on the stove.

The familiar stillness cloaked the Lodge as dusk approached.

Max stood at the edge of the yard, gazing at the ridge.

The trees stood dark green against the sinking sun, their shadows sprawling across the meadow.

Jake had wandered off in that direction earlier before Max had even gotten up that morning.

Max remembered exactly when — his mind had counted the minutes without him noticing.

Jake ought to have been back by now.

Max waited a little longer.
Then a little longer than that.
The ridge remained silent.
Something in Max's chest suddenly felt wrong.

Chapter Thirty-Two

The Missing

Max stood near the porch steps waiting for the dinner bell.

He had held on to the hope that Jake would return before that chime sounded.

When the bell finally rang, its echo rolled across the yard, bouncing off the trees along the ridge. Usually, Jake would appear somewhere between the last echo and the first bowls being placed on the table.

But the trail stayed empty.

Max lingered by the porch steps as everyone else filtered inside.

Lucy dashed past him, the wooden spoon she had carried all afternoon still gripped tightly in her little hand.

"Come on," she urged. "Mary made biscuits."

Max nodded but stayed rooted to the spot.

The ridge was already fading into shadow.

Jake ought to have been back long before this.

Something in Max's stomach twisted.

Inside the Lodge, the familiar sounds of supper filled the air.

Chairs scraped against the floor. Bowls exchanged hands.

Jo stepped onto the porch and called for Jake to come eat. Laughter erupted at something Buck mumbled from the end of the table.

Max sat quietly between Edwin and Lily, glancing often at the door.

Edwin caught on.

"You waitin' for someone?" he asked in a low voice.

Max hesitated.

"Have you seen Jake?"

Edwin's brow furrowed slightly. He glanced up and down the table, then into the great room.

"Not since this morning."

Max's grip tightened around his spoon.

"He went to the ridge."

Edwin tensed.

"When?"

"Early."

"How early?"

"Before breakfast."

Edwin set his spoon aside.

Across the table, Lily chatted with Fiona about the garden, oblivious to the boys' shift in mood.

Edwin leaned in closer.

"He didn't come back?"

Max shook his head.

"No."

Edwin looked towards the windows, noticing the darkening ridge.

"You sure?"

Max nodded once more.

"I watched."

Gin sensed something was off before anyone else noticed it.

She'd been sitting at the far end of the table with Franklin and Gus, listening more than talking, as was her habit.

When Edwin paused his meal and turned toward the door again, she caught the change instantly.

"What is it?" she asked.

Edwin hesitated.

Max spoke first.

"Jake hasn't come back from the ridge."

The atmosphere shifted, growing still.

Franklin placed his cup down softly.

"When did he leave?"

"This morning," Max replied.

Buck frowned.

"That boy goes wandering sometimes."

Edwin shook his head.

"Not this long. Not through dinner."

Gin rose to her feet.

"How long has it been?"

Max swallowed hard.

"All day."

The silence that followed felt heavier.

Franklin glanced toward the windows.

"Edwin."

"Yes sir."

“You saw him go?”

Edwin nodded.

“He headed through the meadow.”

Gin was already grabbing her jacket.

“I’ll go take a look.”

Franklin stood.

“I’ll join you.”

Gus pushed back his chair.

“Me too.”

Jo’s voice held them back.

“Take a lantern.”

Everyone turned to her.

Jo stood by the stove, her gaze calm but keen.

“Don’t make assumptions,” she said quietly.

“But don’t waste time either. The rest of us will search around here to be sure.”

Franklin nodded in agreement.

"Call Gunny. See if Yaz is around."

By the time they reached the meadow’s edge, the evening air had turned cooler.

Gin walked ahead, her lantern low, eyes scanning the ground.

Tracks were trickier to read in the dimming light, but not impossible.

She moved slowly along the beginning of the ridge trail.

After a moment, she crouched down.

Franklin stepped closer.

“What do you see?”

“Jake’s boots.”

“You’re certain?”

Gin nodded.

"Same tread."

She stood again and looked up the ridge.

"He came this way."

Gus examined the tree line.

"You think he ran into the Harbingers?"

Gin hesitated before lifting the lantern slightly and continuing along the path.

They hadn't gone far when she halted again.

This time, she crouched longer.

Franklin knelt beside her.

"What is it?"

Gin lightly ran her fingers over the disturbed dirt.

More than one set of prints.

She looked up slowly.

"He didn't leave alone."

Gus muttered a curse under his breath.

Franklin's jaw clenched.

"You're sure?"

Gin nodded once.

"Someone was waiting."

Back at the Lodge, Max stood on the porch steps. He watched the lantern light slowly working its way along the ridge trail.

Lily emerged from the shadows behind him.

"What are you doing out here?"

Max didn't turn his gaze.

"Jake's missing and it is your fault."

Lily blinked, her surprised expression evident.

“What?”

“He went to the ridge.”

“So?”

“He didn’t come back.”

Lily frowned.

“That doesn’t mean—”

Max turned toward her, the words coming out sharper than he meant.

“He was watching you.”

The tone caught Lily off guard.

“What are you talking about?”

Max shook his head, a tear running down his cheek, trying to gather his thoughts.

“He thought they were trying to pull you over there.”

Lily’s demeanor shifted, concern creeping in.

“Jake said that?”

Max remained silent, eyes fixed back on the ridge.

The lantern light had stilled.

And for the first time since dusk had settled, the Lodge felt all too small.

Chapter Thirty-Three

The Tracks

The lantern light swayed gently along the ridge trail.

Gin moved ahead, Franklin not far behind her, while Gus and Boone fanned out to either side. The forest had fallen into that hush it sometimes embraced after sunset, when the daytime creatures had settled in and the night ones had yet to emerge.

Crouching once more where the earth had been disturbed, Gin noticed clearer prints nearby.

Jake's boots.

She trailed them for a few more yards before halting again.

Franklin lowered the lantern.

"What is it?"

Gin studied the ground for a long moment.

"There's more of them now."

Gus stepped in closer.

"How many?"

"Two. Maybe three."

Franklin felt the tightness in his chest deepen.

"Harbingers?"

Gin didn't reply.

She rose slowly, scanning the trees.

"Someone was definitely waiting," she finally said.

They ascended the ridge further. The lantern's glow illuminated the old rock outcrop.

Gin halted once more. This time, she didn't crouch. She simply gazed at the earth. Franklin noticed it a heartbeat later.

The ground was disturbed. Leaves were strewn about. Boot prints were everywhere. A broken branch hung twisted above the disturbed ground.

Evidence of a struggle.

Gus knelt down and retrieved something from the soil.

Jake's little pocket knife.

Franklin felt the breath leave his body.

Gus turned the knife over in his hand.

"He wouldn't leave this behind," he murmured.

Gin shook her head.

"No. Never."

Franklin peered at the ground again.

"How many?"

"Three," Gin replied.

"Maybe four."

Gus swore softly.

"An ambush."

Franklin squeezed his eyes shut for just a moment.

Then he stood tall.

"We need Yaz."

The Lodge yard buzzed with activity upon their return.

Lanterns flickered along the porch and in the barn. Groups moved through the yard, their voices low and urgent.

Cole lingered near the steps with Marcus and Boone.

As Franklin stepped into the light, Cole caught the answer etched on his face.

"What happened?"

Franklin raised the knife.

Cole tensed.

"Where?"

"Ridge."

"How many?"

"Three. Maybe more."

Cole nodded once.

"Harbingers."

It wasn't a question.

Grace leaned against the porch rail, Gemma at her side.

Hunter perched on the lower fence rail for a better view.

Quinn emerged from the shadows.

"Do we know he's still—"

"No," Franklin interrupted.

"We don't know anything yet."

Yet the look in his eyes revealed more than words could say.

The uncommon sound of an engine broke the silence.

Everyone turned toward the road. Headlights bounced through the trees before the truck burst into the yard in a cloud of dust.

Gunny slammed the truck into park and climbed out before the engine even finished dying.

Yaz jumped down from the passenger side. Riley followed from the back.

Gunny looked around the yard once.

"What happened?"

Cole stepped forward.

"Jake's gone."

Gunny's jaw tightened.

"Where?"

"The ridge."

Yaz was already moving.

"Show me."

They arrived at the outcrop again in under twenty minutes.

Yaz squatted where Gin had indicated. He stayed quiet for a long while.

His gaze remained fixed on the ground.

Then he shifted a few feet to the left.

Then back to where he had been.

The lantern's light danced over the disturbed soil.

At last, he rose.

"Well?" Cole prompted.

Yaz gestured to the earth.

"Three men."

Franklin felt the heaviness of the words sink into him.

"Harbingers?"

Yaz nodded toward the prints.

"Boots match what we've tracked at Market."

Gunny crossed his arms.

"An ambush?"

Yaz affirmed with a nod.

"They were waiting for him."

A hush fell over the trees.

Franklin peered into the darkness beyond the ridge.

The Harbinger camp was hidden somewhere in those woods.

Waiting.

Back at the Lodge, the word spread swiftly. No one shouted. No one panicked.

But the atmosphere had shifted.

Grace was perched on the porch steps with Gemma at her side.

Hunter lingered by the barn doors, gazing into the dark as if he expected Jake to emerge from the shadows at any moment.

Father Tom moved quietly among small groups, speaking gently, offering a soothing presence wherever he could. His face held the stark fear he felt, even when his voice was steady.

Inside the Lodge, Lily sat at the table, her hands clenched tightly in her lap.

Max stood near the window, watching the lanterns flicker along the ridge.

Neither of them uttered a word.

Outside, the night enveloped the Lodge slowly.

And for the first time since the power failed— the Callahans grasped that their deepest fear had come to pass.

They had lost one of the children.

CHAPTER THIRTY-FOUR

THE DEBATE

The Lodge was quieter than usual, but not calm.

Lanterns burned along the long table and across the mantle. Boots tracked dirt across the floor as people came and went, voices low but urgent.

Outside, the ridge stood black against the night sky.

Inside, the Lodge gathered.

Cole stood near the end of the table with his arms folded, the old lawman's stance settling over him like a familiar coat. Gunny leaned against the wall beside him, Riley close by. Yaz sat quietly on the bench near the door, elbows on his knees, saying nothing.

Franklin stood at the head of the table.

No one had touched the food.

"They took him," Cole said finally.

The words hung in the room.

"We don't know that," Gus replied.

Cole turned.

"We found the knife."

"And tracks," Buck added from the far side of the room.

His voice was tight.

"They took him."

Gus met Cole's eyes.

"Maybe."

Cole's jaw tightened.

"You saw the ground."

"I saw enough to know rushing in blind could get him killed."

Buck slammed his palm against the table.

"They already took him!"

Everyone flinched.

Buck's face had gone red, his eyes bright with the same wild anger they had seen after Zeke disappeared.

"So we sit here?" Buck demanded.

"We do nothing?"

Cole stepped forward.

"We don't sit."

He looked around the room.

"We go up there tonight."

Several heads turned.

"With what?" Gus asked calmly.

"Every rifle we have."

Gunny gave a slow nod.

"Not the worst idea."

Gus stared at them.

"You start a shooting war with those people while they're holding the boy?"

Cole didn't hesitate.

"You think they'll let him go?"

"They might if we don't give them reason not to."

Buck laughed harshly.

"You think they're reasonable?"

Gus didn't answer immediately.

"They're organized," he said finally.

"And patient."

Cole shook his head.

"They ambushed a kid."

"They removed someone they saw as a threat," Gus said.

Buck shoved his chair back.

"He's ten years old!"

"And curious," Gus said quietly.

That landed harder than anyone expected.

The room fell silent.

Franklin rubbed his hand across his beard.

"What would you do?" he asked Gus.

Gus looked toward the dark windows.

"I'd wait."

Buck exploded.

"Wait?"

His voice cracked.

"We waited with Zeke!"

Silence enveloped them.

Buck's breath turned jagged.

"And what did that get us?" he demanded.

His gaze locked onto Lily.

"You."

The word cut through the air like broken glass.

Lily froze. Mary's head turned to him, face filled with shock.

Buck pointed at her.

"He was up there because of you."

Franklin stepped in.

"Buck—"

"He was watching her!" Buck shouted.

Max, who had been quietly observing from the end of the bench, now stood.

"He was."

The room shifted.

Max's voice trembled.

"He told me."

Lily's complexion went ashen.

Franklin focused intently on the boy.

"What did he say?"

Max swallowed hard.

"He said they were trying to pull Lily over there. He said that the adults were busy with important things. He said..."

Max sniffed, tears spilling down his cheeks.

"He said he wanted to help Franklin. "He said he was helping.

He said he loves this family."

Lily's chair scraped softly against the floor.

"I never—"

Buck turned sharply to Franklin.

"You knew!"

Franklin held his ground.

"I suspected."

Buck's expression crumbled.

"You let him go up there."

Franklin's tone remained steady.

"I didn't know."

Franklin felt the weight of every decision he had made settle on his shoulders.

Buck's fury broke apart.

The anger faded from his face, replaced by a heavy weariness.

"He's just a little boy," Buck murmured, his voice breaking.

Then the tears came.

Buck staggered back and sank into the nearest chair, his hands shielding his face.

"I can't bury another one," he said hoarsely.

The room fell into silence.

Father Tom stepped forward.

Buck didn't resist when the older man wrapped an arm around his shoulders.

The big woodsman collapsed into him like a man whose legs had finally given out. Buck's sobs filled the room.

Max stood frozen beside the table, tears running silently down his cheeks.

Across the room Lily stared at the floor, face white as a ghost.

Franklin closed his eyes.

Jo watched them all.

For a long moment she said nothing.

Then she spoke.

"We will bring him home."
Her voice was quiet.
But every person in the room heard it.
"We will do it wisely," she continued.
"Or we will lose more than Jake."
The room held its breath.
Outside, somewhere beyond the dark ridge—
the Harbingers waited.

Chapter Thirty-Five

The Quiet Ones

Jake stirred awake.

For a moment, he lay still.

His head throbbed, and the ground beneath him felt wrong—too even, too smooth for the forest floor. He opened his eyes. Wooden beams spanned the ceiling overhead.

A lantern flickered somewhere close.

The air carried a hint of smoke mixed with something medicinal.

Jake blinked, trying to clear his mind.

Fragments of memory returned.

The ridge.

The snap of a twig.

A shadow looming behind him.

The voice.

Curiosity can be dangerous.

Jake attempted to shift himself upright.

Pain shot through his shoulder, and he gasped.

"Easy there."

The voice came from his left.

Jake turned his head.

A woman sat on a stool by the wall, grinding something in a small stone bowl.

She met his eyes calmly.

"You hit the ground hard."

Jake's eyes scanned the room.

It resembled a bunkhouse.

Narrow beds lined the walls, each with neatly folded blankets.

Boots were arranged beneath each bunk in perfect order.

The woman observed him as he took it all in.

"You're quite observant," she noted.

Jake remained silent.

His throat felt parched.

"Where am I?"

"You know where you are."

Jake's stomach clenched.

"The camp."

The woman nodded once.

"You've been watching us long enough to know that."

Jake went still.

The words settled heavy in the air.

They knew.

"How long?" Jake asked quietly.

The woman shrugged slightly.

"Long enough."

Jake's eyes moved toward the door.

It stood open.

Beyond it he could see part of the clearing.

Children walked past carrying buckets of water.

Two boys stacked firewood in perfect, neat piles beside a chopping block.

No one shouted.

No one laughed.

Everything moved in quiet rhythm.

Jake swallowed.

"You took me."

The woman continued grinding herbs.

"You came to us."

Jake didn't respond.

After a moment she stood and crossed the room.

Up close he could see the gray streaks in her hair.

"You are Jake," she said calmly.

It wasn't a question.

Jake stared at her.

"How do you know that?"

She ignored the question.

"You live at the Lodge on the other side of the ridge."

Jake said nothing.

"You watch the girl."

That one hit harder.

Jake's chest tightened.

"I don't know what you're talking about."

The woman studied him for a long moment.

Then she smiled slightly.

"You are loyal," she said.

Jake didn't like the way she said it.

Not mocking.

Not angry.

Just... noting it.

"Loyalty is a powerful thing," she continued.

"But loyalty without understanding can be dangerous."

Jake pushed himself up, wincing against the pain.

"Where are the men who took me?"

"They're working."

Jake turned his gaze toward the door once more.

"You going to keep me here?"

The woman tilted her head slightly.

"You're not locked up."

He shot a glance at the wide-open doorway.

"You think I won't run?"

"You might try."

Jake met her gaze.

"And?"

"And you wouldn't get far."

She placed the bowl on a nearby table.

"Besides," she said softly, "we have questions."

Jake's stomach churned again.

"What kind of questions?"

She stepped toward the doorway.

"About your family."

Jake's jaw clenched.

"I'm not telling you anything."

She didn't seem offended.

In fact, she appeared almost satisfied.

"We expected that."

She stepped outside.

"Come," she said.

Jake hesitated.

Then he swung his legs off the bed.

His shoulder protested immediately but he ignored it.

The moment he stepped outside the bunkhouse the camp came into full view.

More people than he had realized before.

Gardens. Work tables. Smoke drifting from cooking fires.

Children moving through their chores with steady purpose.

The man who had been leading the children's lesson earlier stood across the clearing.

Several of the children were gathered around him again.

"...order protects the whole," they repeated together.

Jake felt a chill run down his back.

No one stared at him.

No one pointed.

But he could feel eyes on him.

Watching.

Measuring.

The woman spoke again.

“You are wondering why we brought you here.”

Jake looked at her.

“You ambushed me.”

She shook her head.

“We stopped someone who had been spying on our children.”

Jake didn’t answer.

She gestured toward the clearing.

“Look carefully.”

Jake did.

The camp was orderly.

Clean.

Disciplined.

Nothing like the raider camps Gus had described from the early days after the blackout.

“These people are building something,” she said quietly.

Jake looked back at her.

“What?”

“Stability.”

Jake’s voice hardened.

“You kidnapped a kid.”

The woman’s expression didn’t change.

“You are ten,” she said.

“Old enough to understand choices.”

Jake stared at her, how did she know that?

“We protect our community,” she continued.

“Just as your family protects theirs.”

Jake's mind raced.

If they knew about Lily...

If they knew about the Lodge...

He forced himself to stay calm.

"You're scared of them," Jake said suddenly.

The woman's eyebrow lifted slightly.

"Of who?"

"My family."

That earned a faint smile.

"No."

She looked toward the tree line beyond the clearing.

"We are not afraid of guns."

Jake followed her gaze.

"Then what?"

The woman turned back to him.

Her voice dropped slightly.

"We are afraid of people who make others think for themselves."

Jake let the weight of that settle slowly in his chest, quiet and heavy as river stone. It wasn't a sudden thing. It came the way cold did — creeping in at the edges first, then filling everything up until there was nothing left in him that wasn't touched by it.

Somewhere beyond the treeline, beyond the birch stands and the old logging trails and the long shadows that stretched between the pines, the Lodge was waiting for him. He could picture it without even trying — the low golden light in the windows, the smell of woodsmoke curling up from the chimney, his Jo's voice somewhere in the background, his Gus's boots on the porch boards. Everything he loved in one place. Everything that mattered.

And then it hit him, and it hit him hard. Something far worse than that settled over him like ice water — a knowing that sat in his gut and refused to move.

They already knew.

They already knew about the Lodge. They knew who was there, how many, and exactly where to find them. Every single person he loved was sitting inside those walls right now, warm and unsuspecting, and the Harbingers had already done the counting.

Chapter Thirty-Six

The Measure of a Boy

The camp had a rhythm.

It began before the sun broke over the treetops.

People moved early.

Quietly.

No bells. No shouting.

Just motion.

Jake perched on the edge of the bunkhouse steps, observing.

Children fetched water from the hand pump in the middle of the clearing. Two older boys swung axes with practiced efficiency, splitting wood. A woman stirred a heavy pot over a low flame.

There was no wasted movement.

No arguments.

No laughter.

It unsettled Jake.

At the Lodge, mornings erupted with noise.

Lucy chasing after chickens.

Buck calling for someone to close the barn door.

Jo summoning everyone for breakfast, clanging her bell.

Life had a cadence.

This place had order.

The woman who had spoken to him earlier was nearby, sorting bundles of dried herbs.

She glanced at him from time to time but stayed silent.

Jake wondered if she was watching over him.

Or simply observing.

He guessed it was the latter.

Then a man crossed the clearing.

Jake recognized him right away.

Ash.

The same man who had stood among the trees the day before.

Ash halted near the bunkhouse steps and looked down at Jake.

"You sleep?"

Jake shrugged.

"Some."

Ash regarded him for a moment longer before nodding once.

"He'll want to see you."

Jake's stomach knotted.

"Who?"

Ash paused before answering.

He turned toward the largest structure in the camp.

The one Jake had noticed earlier.

The one no children dared approach.

"The Oracle."

The name hung in the clearing like a gathering shadow.

Jake rose to his feet, his shoulder still throbbing.

Ash took note of him.

"You run?"

Jake shook his head.

"No."

Ash seemed content.

"Good."

****

The building was larger than the others, not grand but purposeful. The walls were made of squared timber instead of rough logs, and the windows were narrow, covered by wooden shutters.

Ash opened the door and stepped aside.

Jake hesitated just a moment before crossing the threshold.

Inside, the faint scent of paper and oil filled the air.

Shelves lined the walls, loaded with books—more than Jake had seen in one spot since before the blackout.

A man sat at a wooden table near the far wall, older than Ash but not quite old; his hair had turned mostly gray.

He looked up as Jake entered, his eyes keen—not angry, just observing.

"So," the man said softly.

"This is the boy."

Jake felt Ash move in behind him, and the door closed gently.

The man stood.

He was taller than Jake expected.

Not broad like Buck or Franklin.

Lean.

Controlled.

The Oracle walked slowly around the table.

"You've been very curious," he said.

Jake crossed his arms.

"You grabbed me."

The Oracle smiled faintly.

"You were spying on our children."

Jake didn't answer.

The Oracle studied him for a moment.

"You are Jake."

Again not a question.

Jake kept his face still.

The Oracle stepped closer.

"You call Augustus Callahan your grandfather."

Jake's stomach tightened.

"He is a builder," the Oracle continued.

"A farmer. A man people listen to."

Jake stayed silent.

The Oracle tilted his head slightly.

"The woman you call grandmother," he said. "Jolene."

That one made Jake's pulse jump.

The Oracle noticed.

"She speaks often at the Market now," he said.

"People gather around her."

Jake's jaw tightened.

"You keep track of everyone, huh?"

The Oracle ignored the tone.

"Influence is important," he said calmly.

He began to pace slowly.

"Some lead through fear."

He shot a brief glance at Ash.

"Some lead through strength."

Then he turned his attention back to Jake.

"And some lead through trust."

Jake stayed silent.

The Oracle halted in front of him.

"Your grandmother is one of those people."

Jake's gaze dropped to the floor.

"And you," the Oracle said quietly, "ventured into the woods alone because you thought you were protecting her family."

Jake looked up.

The Oracle's eyes met his.

"You're just ten," the man continued.

"And already willing to put yourself at risk for others."

Jake remained quiet.

The Oracle nodded slightly.

"Yes," he said gently.

"I can see why they put their faith in you."

Jake's heart started to race.

"Why am I here?" he asked.

The Oracle regarded him for a long moment.

Then he answered.

"Because boys willing to sacrifice for their people often become men that others will choose to follow."

Jake wasn't sure he liked where this was heading.

"And men like that," the Oracle went on, "shape the future."

The room seemed to shrink around him.

Jake swallowed hard.

"You're not going to let me go, are you?"

The Oracle paused before responding.

He picked up one of the slender books Jake recognized and turned it slowly in his hands.

Then he focused back on the boy.

"That," the Oracle said with a measured calm,

"depends on the kind of future you choose."

Jake felt the weight of those words settle over him.

Outside the window, he could hear the familiar hum of the camp carrying on.

Work.

Order.

And somewhere deep in the woods—

the Lodge awaited.

But for the first time since waking, Jake saw things with clarity.

The Harbingers hadn't taken him by chance.

They had taken him because of who he might become.

Chapter Thirty-Seven

The Plan

The Lodge had not slept.

Not truly.

Lanterns had burned low through the hours before dawn, the kitchen table still cluttered with coffee cups and papers nobody had bothered to clear. The pot had been brewed three times before first light. Boots crossed the porch boards and came back again. Doors opened and shut with the careful quiet of people who knew the difference between rest and sleep.

The ridge stood gray in the early morning.

Franklin leaned over the long table with both hands braced against the wood, studying the rough map spread out before him. Cole stood opposite, arms folded. Gin sat at the corner of the table, working the bolt of her rifle with slow, practiced strokes. Yaz crouched near the edge of the map, reading it the way he had studied the ground. Gunny sat back in his chair, boots planted wide, saying nothing.

Nobody spoke for some time.

Cole broke it first.

"We go in."

Gus exhaled slowly.

"You say that like it's a door we can just kick open."

Cole pointed to the ridge on the map.

"They took him from here."

"No," Yaz said quietly.

Everyone looked at him.

"They took him after here."

Franklin straightened slightly.

"You're sure?"

Yaz nodded once.

"The ambush was planned."

Gin set the bolt aside.

Yaz tapped the map with two fingers.

"They knew he was coming."

No one spoke.

Cole frowned.

"How?"

No one answered.

Near the window, Jo sat with Odin settled beside her chair, his broad head resting against her knee. She had been quiet most of the morning, watching, listening.

Now she looked up.

"They've been watching us."

The words settled over the room like cold water.

Franklin dragged a hand across his dark beard.

"The Market."

Jo nodded.

"They learn who people trust there."

Cole glanced toward her.

"You think they knew Jake?"

"No." Jo's voice was quiet but certain. "They knew us."

The whole room felt that one.

Gunny leaned forward, elbows on his knees.

"So the kid walked right into something they already had waiting."

Gus nodded slowly.

"I think so. The market is where they got Zeke"

Cole's jaw went tight.

"All the more reason we move fast."

Gin shook her head.

"With what?"

Cole gestured around the room.

"We have rifles."

"They have Jake," Gus said, "and they have a camp full of children, Cole."

The room went quiet again.

Yaz spoke without looking up.

"They did not kill him."

Franklin lifted his eyes.

"You sure about that?"

One slow nod.

"If they wanted him dead, they would have left him where he fell."

Gunny grunted low in his throat.

"Means they want something."

Franklin's gaze dropped back to the map spread across the table.

"Or someone."

Nobody filled the silence after that.

Across the room, Lily sat at the edge of the bench, still as carved wood. She hadn't said more than a handful of words since the night before. Max sat beside her, swinging his feet in slow, listless arcs beneath the seat. Neither one looked up.

Buck stood near the door with his gaze fixed on the ridge. His eyes were red, but dry now, and whatever storm had passed through him had left something harder in its wake.

"Then we take him back," he said. The words came out rough, like gravel underfoot.

Franklin looked at him. "How?"

Buck turned from the window. "With guns."

Marcus shook his head. "You start shooting up that camp and the first thing they do is put a bullet in the boy. Would you be able to live with yourself if one of your bullets found a child?"

Buck's hands pulled into fists at his sides. "Then what do we do?"

Silence settled over the room like woodsmoke.

Jo spoke. "We think."

Every head turned toward her.

"The Harbingers believe they are the only ones capable of patience," she said quietly. "They are wrong."

Franklin held her gaze. "You're saying we wait."

"I'm saying we learn." She gestured toward Yaz,

"You've already started."

He gave a single, slow nod.

Yaz rose to his feet.

"I can follow them."

Cole leaned forward.

"How far?"

"Far enough."

Gunny rubbed his chin. "We need to get eyes on that camp, then we can plan something smarter."

Franklin looked around the table. Cole. Gin. Yaz. Gunny. Gus. Every one of them waiting. The weight of it settled onto his shoulders the way a pack does when you know the trail ahead is long.

"We find him first," he said finally. "Then we bring him home."

Across the room, Max looked up for the first time.

"You promise?"

The question cut through everything.

Franklin held the boy's gaze. Eight years old and carrying something no child should have to. He nodded.

"Yes."

Max studied his face a moment longer, then gave one small nod of his own.

Outside, the ridge stood quiet beneath the early sun, the tree line still and indifferent. But somewhere beyond those trees, Jake was waiting.

And the Lodge had finally begun to move.

Chapter Thirty-Eight

The Trail

They left before sunrise.

No speeches. No goodbyes.

Just quiet movement through the gray edge of morning.

Yaz led. Gin followed a few steps behind, rifle slung across her back. Cole came next, then Franklin, Boone and Marcus. Gunny brought up the rear, boots careful on the damp forest floor.

The woods were still half asleep.

Mist pooled in the low ground and the air carried pine and cold earth, the kind of smell that meant the night hadn't fully let go yet.

Nobody spoke.

Yaz didn't look back. He simply moved, steady and unhurried, the way a man moves when he trusts the ground to do the talking.

They reached the ridge not long after the sun began burning off the darkness.

The place where they'd found Jake's knife looked different in daylight. Less threatening, maybe. But no less plain.

Yaz crouched beside the disturbed earth. The others held their positions and waited while he read the ground the way some men read a page, slow and deliberate.

"Three men."

Cole moved closer. "Same as last night?"

"Same."

Franklin's eyes cut toward the tree line. "They carried him?"

"No."

That pulled everyone's focus.

Yaz pressed two fingers into a deep scuff in the dirt. "He walked here."

Gin's brow creased. "With them?"

"Yes."

Gunny grunted low in his chest. "Kid's tougher than he looks."

Franklin felt something tighten behind his ribs, pride and dread wound together so tight he couldn't separate them. Jake had stayed on his feet. Which meant he'd still been alive when they left this ridge.

Yaz stood and turned toward the trees.

"They went this way."

He stepped into the shadows without waiting.

The trail wound deeper into the forest than Franklin had expected.

Yaz slowed.

Every few yards he stopped to read something the rest of them couldn't see. Broken moss. Bent grass. A faint scuff in the pine needles where no wind had passed.

Gin caught the pattern first.

"They're careful."

Yaz nodded.

"Trained."

Cole looked between them.

"Military?"

Gunny shook his head.

“Maybe. But I doubt it.” He pointed toward the ground. "Military leaves security behind them."

Yaz crouched low again, fingers hovering just above the earth.

"These men trust their perimeter."

Franklin studied the tree line.

"How far?"

Yaz rose slowly.

"Closer now."

Nobody spoke after that. The forest thickened as the ground fell away toward a shallow hollow, the trees pressing in tighter with every step downhill.

Then the air shifted.

Woodsmoke. Faint, but there.

Yaz stopped dead, his hand rising.

Everyone froze.

He raised one hand.

Gin slowly unslung her rifle.

Cole's hand drifted toward the pistol at his belt.

Gunny leaned forward.

Franklin's pulse climbed.

Yaz turned slowly and dropped his voice to almost nothing.

"Camp."

Nobody moved.

The trees ahead grew dense, the ground falling away in a long, gentle slope into a wide depression below.

Smoke threaded between the trunks.

They moved forward another ten yards. Then five more.

Yaz crouched behind a fallen cedar and waved the others down beside him.

Franklin eased forward and parted the branches with two fingers.

The clearing spread out beneath them.

There it was.

The Harbinger camp.

More than he'd expected. More buildings, more order. Gardens laid out in careful rows. Wood stacked in cords along a low wall. Cook fires sending thin grey ribbons into the canopy above.

People moved through the clearing with a quiet, practised purpose. Children hauling water buckets. Two men working a splitting maul in steady rhythm. A woman bent low over something near the garden edge.

No shouting. No chaos.

Just work.

Gin leaned in close.

"How many?"

Yaz studied the movement below for a long moment.

"Forty."

Cole let out a slow breath.

"More than I hoped."

Gunny's eyes tracked the clearing.

"They're very organized."

Franklin kept searching the far edges, the shadows between buildings.

"Do you see him?"

Yaz shook his head.

"Not yet."

Franklin stayed on the scope.

Then something near the far tree line pulled his eye. A small figure moving alongside a woman, keeping pace with her slow, unhurried steps.

Jake.

The boy moved stiffly, but he was upright.

Alive.

Franklin felt the air go out of him.

Gin saw him next.

"There."

Cole leaned forward. Gunny followed his gaze.

Nobody spoke.

Jake crossed the clearing in slow, careful steps. The woman beside him said something Franklin couldn't catch from this distance. Jake looked up at her, then turned his head toward the trees. Toward the ridge.

Toward home.

Franklin froze, his heart clenching.

The boy's eyes moved along the tree line. Searching, maybe. Or maybe just looking at nothing. Then he turned away and followed the woman toward one of the larger buildings. The clearing took him in and gave nothing back.

Cole let out a long breath.

"He's alive."

Franklin nodded.

"Yes."

Gunny swept his gaze across the camp one more time, jaw working slow and quiet.

"Now comes the hard part."

Franklin kept his eyes on the place where Jake had gone.

"How do we get him out?"

No one answered.

Below them the Harbinger camp continued its quiet rhythm.

Order.

Discipline.

Patience.

And somewhere inside that clearing—

Jake waited.

CHAPTER THIRTY-NINE

ON THE RIDGE

No one moved for a long time. Eyes scanning, watching silently.

Below them, the camp kept its rhythm. Children lugged water buckets. A woman worked a garden row with a hoe, turning soil in long, patient strokes. Two men split firewood with the slow, deliberate swing of men who'd done it a thousand times before.

It looked almost peaceful.

Franklin hated that most of all.

Cole finally let out a long breath. "Well," he muttered. "That answers that."

Gunny kept his binoculars trained on the clearing. "Forty, give or take. Probably a few more we haven't laid eyes on yet."

Boone shifted beside Franklin. "How many fighters?"

"Half, maybe." Gunny lowered the binoculars a fraction. "Hard to know for certain. Looks like a lot of women. Hard to say who's a fighter."

Cole shook his head. "Too many."

Buck had been crouched behind a pine a few yards back, staring down at the camp with burning, restless eyes. He turned sharply. "So we shoot the men first."

Cole looked at him. "And the kids standing next to them? The chaos that follows?"

Buck had no answer for that.

Gin lay flat behind a fallen cedar, rifle resting across her forearms, eye to the scope. Her voice came out tight and controlled. "I could drop three before they knew where it came from."

Gunny glanced at her. "And the fourth puts a knife in Jake before the second body hits the ground."

Gin didn't argue. She just kept looking through the glass.

Franklin knew what she was thinking. He'd been there himself, just a moment ago. For one wild second the idea had blazed through him clean as lightning.

Then reality followed.

Jake was down there. So were a lot of other children.

Marcus finally spoke.

"This isn't a battlefield."

The words came out quiet, but they landed hard. Everyone on the ridge went still.

He had his forearms resting across his knees, eyes fixed on the camp below where cook fires flickered between the tents and lean-tos. A woman moved past one of them carrying a child on her hip.

"There are women and children everywhere down there."

Buck snorted. "They took our kid."

"Yes." Marcus didn't look away from the camp. "But we start shooting, we kill theirs."

The silence that followed had weight to it.

Gus nodded once, slow and deliberate. "That's the truth of it."

Buck turned on him, jaw set hard. "So we just leave him?"

"No." Gus's voice was flat and certain. "We bring him home."

Buck stared at him a long moment, the muscle in his jaw working.

"Then say how."

Gus kept his eyes on the camp below.

"We learn first."

Cole dragged a hand down his face.

"I hate to say it, but he's right."

Buck stared at him.

"You too?"

Cole pointed toward the clearing.

"You think we can charge forty people with rifles and not get Jake or the other kids killed?"

Buck had no answer for that.

Cole's voice dropped a register.

"This isn't a bar fight, Buck."

Franklin watched the camp without a word. Jake had disappeared into the large building near the center. The one with the narrow windows.

"Yaz." He kept his voice low.

The tracker shifted beside him.

"Yes."

"How hard would it be to get one man in there?"

Yaz studied the clearing for a long moment.

"Hard."

Gunny let out a quiet chuckle.

"That's Yaz language for very hard."

Yaz kept watching the movement below.

"Night is better."

Gin lifted her head from the rifle.

"Security?"

"Light," Yaz said. "Rotating patrol."

Marcus nodded slowly.

"They trust the perimeter."

Gunny leaned forward.

"That means they expect people to be stupid."

Cole looked at him.

"Meaning?"

Gunny's smile was thin and did not reach his eyes.

"They expect a fight."

The idea formed slowly in the back of Franklin's mind, turning over like an engine finding its timing.

"So we don't give them one."

Gin sat up.

"You're thinking infiltration."

Franklin nodded.

"One person in. Find Jake. Get him out."

Buck shook his head hard.

"That's insane."

Cole glanced at him.

"Less insane than charging that camp."

Buck looked back down at the clearing.

Somewhere inside those buildings, Jake was waiting.

"So who goes?" Buck asked quietly.

The question hung in the air like smoke.

Everyone knew the answer. Nobody said it.

Yaz spoke first.

"I can."

Gin shook her head.

"No."

Yaz looked at her.

"You shoot better," he said. "You stay here."

Gunny leaned back against the tree behind him, arms folded.

"Tracker sneaks in. Sniper watches the perimeter." He nodded toward Gin. "Not the worst plan."

Marcus looked between them. "Still dangerous."

Gus let out a slow breath. "Everything from here on out is. Life's dangerous these days."

Franklin studied the camp one last time, then turned back to the group. "We wait until late."

Buck hadn't moved. His fists were clenched so tight the knuckles had gone bone-white. A long moment passed before he gave a single nod.

"Fine." His voice came out rough, scraped thin. "But if they hurt that boy..."

He left it there.

He didn't need to finish it.

Below them, the Harbinger camp went about its quiet, disciplined work, unhurried and unaware.

They didn't know the Lodge was watching from the trees.

They didn't know that come nightfall, someone would be coming for Jake.

Chapter Forty

Nightfall

The forest changed when the sun went down. The sounds shifted first.

Day birds faded into silence. Night insects filled the gap. Somewhere deeper in the trees, an owl called once, then again, its low hollow note drifting through the dark like smoke.

On the ridge above the Harbinger camp, the Lodge waited.

Nobody spoke.

They had spent the afternoon watching. Learning. Counting movement, counting heads, counting the slow rhythm of patrols circling the outer edge of the clearing.

Now the sky had gone black.

Only thin ribbons of firelight bled between the trees below.

Yaz checked the straps on his pack one last time. Nothing heavy. Nothing that would snag on a branch or make a sound. Just a small knife, a coil of thin cord, and a narrow flashlight wrapped in cloth to kill the beam.

Gin lay prone beside a fallen cedar, rifle resting across her pack, scope trained on the far side of the camp.

Franklin crouched at her back.

Cole and Marcus watched the lower ridge.

Gunny sat with his back against a pine, working dirt from beneath his fingernails with the tip of his knife like he had nowhere better to be.

Buck stood a little apart from the rest. His eyes never left the clearing.

Yaz leaned close to Franklin.

"Patrol passes every twelve minutes."

Franklin nodded. "You're sure?"

"Yes."

"Window?"

"Four minutes."

Franklin studied the camp. It seemed impossible that a man could slip through that many bodies and not be seen.

But Yaz didn't look worried.

He looked ready.

Franklin lowered his voice.

"You find him."

"Yes."

"If anything goes wrong—"

Yaz shook his head once.

"Then I do not get caught."

Franklin held his gaze a moment. He understood what that meant, and he didn't like it, but he understood it.

"Bring him home."

Yaz said nothing.

He turned, and the darkness took him.

The woods swallowed him almost immediately.

Yaz moved low and slow, each foot placed before his weight followed. The ground ran soft with pine needles, which helped. But dry sticks were scattered everywhere, and he threaded between them the way water finds its way around stone.

Patient.

Quiet.

He reached the edge of the slope overlooking the camp and went still.

Below, the clearing spread open under the moonlight. Firelight glowed between the buildings. Voices floated up now and then, loose and unhurried. The Harbingers did not sound like people bracing for anything.

Yaz waited.

A man crossed the clearing with an armful of split wood. Another moved along the far edge of the gardens, a lantern swinging at his side.

The patrol.

Yaz counted seconds. When the lantern swept past the tree line, he moved.

Down the slope. One step at a time.

The camp grew around him.

Closer.

Voices sharper.

Someone laughed softly near one of the fires. The smell of cooking beans hung in the warm air.

He slipped behind a woodpile and held still.

The patrol passed within twenty yards. The lantern light dragged across the ground, then moved on.

Thirty more seconds.

Then he crossed the shadow between two buildings and moved toward the larger structure near the center. The one Franklin had pointed out.

The one Jake had walked into.

A low murmur of voices came from inside.

Yaz pressed flat against the outer wall and listened. Footsteps. Two people, maybe three. He circled around toward the back of the building.

There.

A narrow window, no glass. Just shutters pushed open to let in the night air.

He rose slowly, just enough to see over the sill.

A lantern hung from a ceiling beam inside, casting amber light across shelves of books. More books than he'd seen in years, stacked floor to ceiling on every wall. A table sat in the center of the room. Two men faced each other across it.

And on the far side, on a bench against the wall, sat Jake.

Hands on his knees. Back straight. Alive.

Yaz let out the breath he hadn't known he was holding.

Then one of the men shifted, and the lantern caught the angle of his face.

Yaz knew that face.

The Oracle.

He eased himself back below the window and pressed his shoulders against the rough wood.

The mission had just gotten harder.

Somewhere above him on the ridge, the Lodge waited in the dark.

Act 2

CHAPTER FORTY-ONE

QUESTIONS

Inside the building, the air smelled of lamp oil and old paper.

Jake sat on the bench with his hands resting on his knees, the way Gus had always told him to sit when grown men were talking.

Still.

Quiet.

Listening.

The lantern above the table threw a thin, shifting light as a breeze moved through the open window at his back.

Across the table, the Oracle turned a page in the slim book in front of him. Ash stood off to the side with his arms folded, watching Jake with the easy patience of a man who had nowhere better to be.

Jake didn't look at him.

He watched the Oracle.

The man closed the book.

"You're very quiet tonight," he said.

Jake shrugged. "Not much to say."

The Oracle smiled, just barely. "That is rarely true." He folded his hands on the table. "You come from a family that speaks often."

Jake said nothing.

The Oracle studied him for a long moment. "Your grandmother," he continued, "has quite a gift for it."

Jake kept his face still.

"She speaks at the Market now. People gather when she talks."

Jake stared at the floor.

The Oracle leaned back. "Most people believe leadership comes from strength." He tapped the cover of the book. "But strength fades."

Jake glanced up.

"Your grandfather understands that," the Oracle said. "He builds things."

Jake's jaw tightened. "He fixes things."

The Oracle nodded slowly. "Yes. That too."

Ash shifted near the wall. Jake caught it in the corner of his eye but didn't turn his head.

"You came to our camp alone," the Oracle said. "That shows courage."

Jake shrugged again. "Or stupidity."

The Oracle's smile widened just a fraction. "Sometimes those two things look very similar."

Jake leaned forward. "You going to keep me here?"

The Oracle tilted his head. "That depends."

"On what?"

The Oracle's eyes settled on him, unhurried.

"On whether you learn something from being here."

Jake frowned.

"What kind of something?"

The Oracle gestured slowly toward the window.

"Look around our camp."

Jake didn't move.

"Order," the Oracle continued. "Purpose. No chaos."

Jake's voice hardened.

"You kidnapped a kid."

Ash's head turned slightly toward him.

The Oracle didn't flinch. He simply watched Jake with quiet interest.

"We stopped someone who was spying on our children."

Jake crossed his arms.

"Same thing."

For the first time, the Oracle's eyes narrowed, just a fraction.

"You care about your family."

Jake said nothing.

"And they care about you."

Something shifted in Jake's chest before he could stop it, quick and involuntary as a held breath.

The Oracle caught it.

"Yes," he said softly. "They do."

Outside, Yaz listened.

Every word carried faintly through the open window.

He held himself flat against the wall, breathing slow and shallow, a man made of patience.

The Oracle's voice drifted out again.

"Do you believe they will come for you?"

Jake answered without hesitation.

"Yes."

Yaz nearly smiled.

Inside, the Oracle chuckled softly.

"That kind of faith is rare."

Jake leaned forward.

"They always come."

Silence followed. Yaz counted the seconds against his pulse.

Thirty.

Forty.

A chair scraped lightly against the floor.

Ash moved toward the door.

Yaz dropped below the window sill.

Footsteps crossed the room. The door opened, then closed.

Only two voices remained.

He raised his head just enough to see.

Ash was gone.

The Oracle stood near the shelves now, moving slowly along the rows of books as though he had all the time in the world.

"Your family has influence," he said.

Jake said nothing.

"People listen to them."

The Oracle turned slightly.

"That makes them dangerous."

Jake's hands curled into fists at his sides.

"They're not dangerous."

The Oracle studied him with quiet curiosity, the kind that felt more like a trap than a thought.

"Every person who teaches others to think becomes dangerous to someone."

Yaz watched them both in the lantern light. The room had gone still in the way rooms do before something changes.

The patrol outside would circle back soon.

The window was open. The drop to the floor inside was barely four feet.

He measured the shadows. Counted the timing.

Then he moved.

Silent as breath.

One hand on the sill.

Inside, Jake turned his head toward the soft sound.

Their eyes met.

The boy went rigid.

Yaz raised one finger to his lips.

Jake blinked once. Then gave a slow, deliberate nod.

Behind him the Oracle reached for another book, his back turned, unhurried.

Unaware that the rescue had already begun.

Chapter Forty-Two

The Window

Yaz pulled himself through the window.

Slow.

Controlled.

One hand braced on the sill, one foot feeling for the floor below.

Four feet, maybe less. But boots on bare wood could carry a long way when the night was quiet enough.

He let himself down the last few inches.

Touched the floor.

Nothing.

The Oracle stood across the room with his back turned, running his gaze along the shelves like a man with all the time in the world.

Jake sat on the bench.

Still.

Watching.

Yaz raised one hand.

Wait.

Jake didn't move.

The lantern above the table breathed a soft, unsteady light.

Outside, beyond the wall, a voice drifted through the dark.

The patrol.

Yaz moved.

Two steps, no sound, and he was behind the boy.

He crouched beside the bench.

"Slow," he breathed.

Jake gave a single nod.

Up close he seemed smaller than he remembered. Younger looking, too. But the eyes told a different story. There was a steadiness in them that had no business being in a ten-year-old's face.

Yaz pressed the coiled rope into Jake's hands.

"Window," he whispered.

Jake eased off the bench.

The wood creaked.

Across the room, the Oracle's head tilted.

Yaz went still.

The man stood with one hand resting on the spine of a book.

A breath passed.

Then he moved on down the shelf.

Yaz let out a slow breath.

Jake took one careful step toward the window.

Then another.

The night air drifted in through the open shutters, warm and thick with summer insects.

The patrol's lantern threw a faint wash of gold across the far wall.

Yaz crouched low beside the bench, weight forward, ready.

Jake reached the window and turned back.

Yaz gave a single nod.

Go.

The boy climbed onto the sill. He hung there for a moment, caught between the room and the dark.

Then he slipped through and was gone.

Yaz rose without a sound and moved toward the window.

One more step—

"Interesting."

The voice came from behind him, quiet and unhurried.

Yaz went still.

He turned slowly.

The Oracle stood near the shelves, one hand resting lightly against the wood.

His eyes were on the window.

Then they moved to Yaz.

Calm. Curious. Not surprised.

"You must be the tracker," the Oracle said.

Yaz didn't answer.

The two men studied each other across the length of the room, the silence between them deliberate on both sides.

Outside, the patrol lantern drifted closer.

The Oracle glanced briefly toward the door. Then back at Yaz.

"You came alone," he said.

Yaz remained still.

"Yes." The Oracle's voice stayed quiet, unhurried. "That makes sense."

Yaz stepped backward toward the window.

The Oracle didn't move.

"Go, take him," the man said.

Yaz stopped.

Those weren't the words he'd expected.

The Oracle tilted his head slightly. “Children belong with the families who chose them.”

Yaz didn't trust it. He kept backing toward the window, slow and steady, eyes never leaving the man.

Outside, the lantern light grew brighter.

Ash's voice drifted faintly through the dark. The patrol was returning.

The Oracle watched him.

"You will tell them something for me," he said.

Yaz stopped.

"Tell Jolene Callahan..." The man smiled, just barely. "...that I would like to speak with her."

Yaz said nothing.

The lantern light reached the door.

He stepped onto the sill and dropped silently into the darkness below.

Inside, the Oracle returned to the shelves and picked up another book.

By the time Ash pushed open the door, the room was empty.

Chapter Forty-Three

The Treeline

Jake dropped from the window and hit the dirt hard.

The ground came up faster than he expected. His knees buckled and he caught himself on one hand before he went down face-first.

Yaz landed beside him a moment later.

The man's hand closed around the back of Jake's collar. Gentle. Firm.

"Stay low," he breathed.

Jake nodded.

Outside the building the night smelled different. Smoke. Damp earth. Cooking beans drifting over from the fire near the center of the clearing.

Voices moved through the camp, soft and unhurried. People winding down, finishing the day.

Nobody sounded alarmed.

Not yet.

Yaz crouched against the wall and studied the nearest buildings. Two lanterns burned out by the gardens. Another flickered beside the cook fire. The patrol's light dragged along the far edge of the clearing.

Closer than before.

Yaz leaned down until his mouth nearly touched Jake's ear.

"Follow where I step."

Jake swallowed. Nodded.

Yaz moved. One quiet step into the shadow behind the building.

Jake followed. His boots settled softly into packed dirt as they slid along the wall toward the corner.

Yaz stopped.

Jake went still beside him.

Across the clearing a man spoke. Another voice answered. The patrol lantern swung lazy arcs through the trees beyond camp.

Yaz watched it. Counting.

When the light disappeared behind the smokehouse, he went.

Open ground now. Five steps. Ten.

Jake's heart was hammering so hard he was certain somebody would hear it.

They reached the shadow of a stacked woodpile and Yaz pulled him down beside it.

The patrol lantern swung back into the clearing.

Jake pressed himself flat against the dirt, cheek against the cool ground.

Boots crunched nearby. Two men moved past, no more than thirty feet out, voices low and careless.

"...morning watch again."

"...fine by me."

The lantern glow swept across the woodpile and Jake stopped breathing. The light kept moving. Drifted on.

Yaz waited. Ten seconds. Twenty. Then a hand found Jake's shoulder.

Move.

They slipped between two smaller buildings and came out along the garden rows. The soil was worked loose here, soft under their feet. Jake's boot caught the edge of a furrow.

The sound was nothing. A whisper.

But Yaz went stone-still.

Across the clearing, a figure turned.

Ash.

Jake recognized him even in the thin light, standing near the cook fire, head up and scanning. The guard's gaze drifted toward the gardens and held there.

Jake didn't move. Didn't breathe. Didn't blink.

For a long moment he was sure the man could see straight through the dark, straight through him.

Then someone called Ash's name from across the camp.

He turned back toward the fire.

Yaz moved without hesitation, threading through the last row of corn toward the treeline with Jake so close behind he nearly clipped the man's heels.

Branches caught his shoulders, then gave way.

Trees. Dark. Dense. Safe.

They pushed another twenty yards into the forest before Yaz finally stopped and crouched, studying the camp through a gap in the branches. The patrol lantern continued its slow arc along the clearing's edge, unhurried and unaware.

No alarm. No shouting.

Jake bent at the waist, hands on his knees, lungs burning from the effort of keeping quiet and moving slow when every instinct had screamed at him to run.

Yaz glanced down at him. "You did well."

Jake tried to answer. His throat wasn't ready yet.

"They're going to know," he managed after a moment.

Yaz gave a single nod. "Yes."

Jake looked back through the trees toward the faint smear of light bleeding from the camp. "Are we safe?"

Yaz went still, listening to the forest the way a man does when he knows it has something to say. Then he shook his head.

"Not yet."

Somewhere deeper in the dark, an owl called.

And high above them on the ridge, the Lodge was waiting.

Chapter Forty-Four

Home

Yaz stopped at the base of the ridge and listened.

The forest had gone quiet again.

Just insects and the far-off hiss of wind through the high pines.

He crouched beside Jake and set a hand briefly on the boy's shoulder.

"Stay behind me."

Jake nodded.

They climbed slow.

The slope came up steep under the trees, pine needles soft and silent beneath their boots. Yaz picked his way with care, eyes tracking the shadows pooled between the trunks.

Halfway up, a low whistle drifted through the dark.

Two short notes.

Gin.

Yaz answered with a soft click of his tongue.

A shape pulled itself out of the shadows ahead.

Gin came forward first, rifle already slung across her back. Her eyes went straight to Jake.

"Well I'll be damned," she breathed.

Jake managed a tired half-smile.

Behind her, the others took shape one by one.

Cole.

Marcus.

Gunny.

And Buck.

The mountain man went still the moment he saw the boy.

He stood there like something carved from the hillside itself.

Then he crossed the distance in two strides.

"Jake."

The boy barely got a breath in before Buck's arms came around him and lifted him clean off his feet. The hug was the kind that cracked ribs and didn't apologize for it. Buck pressed his face into the top of Jake's head, and when he spoke, his voice had gone to gravel.

"Don't you ever," he growled, "ever scare me like that again."

Jake held on, both arms locked around Buck's neck. "I'm okay."

Buck kept him there a beat longer before he set him down. When he stepped back, his eyes were bright and he didn't try to hide it.

Gunny laid a hand on Yaz's shoulder. "Nice work and thank you."

Yaz nodded once.

Franklin hadn't moved. He stood a few feet off, watching Jake the way a man watches something he nearly lost and still can't quite believe is standing in front of him.

Jake looked over and found him.

"Franklin..."

Franklin closed the distance in two quick steps and pulled the boy into a tight embrace.

Jake stiffened for a moment, surprised.

Franklin's voice came low near his ear.

"You stupid, brave kid."

Jake swallowed.

"I was trying to help. I was watching Lily."

Franklin stiffened but Jake kept talking.

"They were trying to talk to her at the Market. I thought maybe they were trying to pull her over there."

Franklin slowly leaned back.

"You did that for her?"

Jake shrugged slightly.

"And you."

Franklin swallowed hard.

For a moment he couldn't speak.

Then he pulled Jake into another quick hug.

"Thank you," he said quietly.

Jake blinked.

"No one had ever said that to him before for something like this.

For a second his hand rested on the back of Jake's neck the same way Gus used to do when someone had done something both admirable and reckless.

"You should've told me," Franklin said quietly.

Jake looked down.

"I thought you'd make me stop."

Franklin almost smiled.

“Yeah. Next time,” he said, “you let the adults do the dangerous stuff.”

Jake nodded.

“Okay.”

Behind them Buck snorted.

“Good luck with that.”

The tension on the ridge eased just a little.

But Yaz’s voice cut through it.

“We need to move.”

Everyone turned.

“The patrol will notice soon,” he said.

Gunny nodded.

"Let's go."

They moved back through the trees without another word.

Jake fell in beside Yaz at first, but within a few minutes he drifted closer to Franklin, the way a kid will when something is sitting heavy on him.

"Franklin?"

"Yeah?"

"The Oracle said something."

That sucked the air right out of the group.

"What?" Cole asked, his voice low.

Jake hesitated.

"He knew about the Lodge."

Silence.

"He knew a lot about Jo and Gus," Jake said. "and he knew you'd come."

Franklin felt it land somewhere deep in his chest.

"What exactly did he say?"

Jake glanced back toward the dark wall of trees behind them.

"He said to tell Jolene Callahan that he'd like to speak with her."

Even Buck stopped walking.

Marcus spoke first. "That wasn't a threat."

"No." Gus's voice came from the back of the group, quiet and certain. "It was an invitation."

Franklin looked toward the distant glow of light where the Harbinger camp sat beyond the treeline.

One thought settled in and wouldn't move.

"He knew we were there."

Yaz gave a single nod. "Yes."

Franklin let out a slow breath. "And he let you leave."

Nobody argued with that.

Ahead, the warm glow of the Lodge's lanterns began bleeding through the trees.

Jake saw it first. His pace quickened before he even knew it had.

Home.

Behind them, somewhere back in the dark and the deep timber, the Oracle was already thinking about his next move.

Chapter Forty-Five

The Return

He broke through the trees and the Lodge came into view.

His feet slowed without him meaning them to.

He stood there a moment, just looking. The big house. The barn. The garden rows pale and quiet under the moon. All of it exactly as he'd left it, and yet somehow that made it stranger, not easier. Something in his chest loosened without him realizing it had ever been tight.

He hadn't truly believed he'd see it again.

Yaz let him have the moment, then said quietly, "Go on."

Jake went.

The front door swung open before he'd even reached the steps.

Max came through it like he'd been fired from something.

He pulled up short at the edge of the porch, chest heaving, staring down at his best friend and 'brother' the way you stare at something that doesn't quite fit the shape of what you expected.

Then he screamed it.

"JAKE!"

He launched himself off the steps and crossed the yard at a dead run and hit Jake square in the chest, both arms locking around his waist, the force of it enough to rock them both sideways.

Jake laughed. He couldn't help it.

"You're alive!"

"I told you I was."

Max only squeezed harder, face buried against Jake's ribs.

"I knew they'd bring you back."

Behind him, the porch steps filled fast.

Father Tom came down them two at a time.

He didn't slow when he reached Jake. He grabbed the boy by both shoulders and pulled him into a tight embrace.

"Thank you, God," he said quietly.

His voice shook despite the smile on his face.

Jake hugged him back.

"I'm okay, Father."

Father Tom held him a beat longer before stepping back and studying his face, tears in his eyes.

"You had us worried."

Jake glanced around the yard. People stood everywhere now. Clare. Beth. Ellie. Mary. The younger kids clustered near the porch steps. Ruth and Ian stared wide-eyed. Marisol clutched Rosa's hand. Edwin stood a little apart, his expression tight with relief he was working hard not to show.

But Jake's eyes stopped on one person.

Lily.

She stood at the edge of the porch light. Very still. Arms wrapped around herself like she was holding something in.

Their eyes met.

Something was wrong. He knew it the way you know weather before it turns.

Lily looked away.

Max was still talking, words spilling out faster than Jake could sort them.

"We looked everywhere. Gin said Yaz would find you. Buck said if they hurt you he was gonna--"

"Max."

Franklin's voice was quiet but it landed clean. The boy stopped and looked up.

Franklin rested a hand on Jake's shoulder.

"Let the kid breathe."

Max nodded and fell quiet, but stayed pressed close to Jake's side.

Jake's eyes drifted back toward the porch.

Lily hadn't moved.

The look on her face did something to his chest he couldn't name.

He pulled free of Max and moved toward the steps.

Lily tried to turn away.

"Hey."

She stopped. Jake stepped up beside her.

"You okay?"

Lily shook her head. When she spoke, her voice came out thin as thread.

"This is my fault."

Jake frowned.

"No it isn't."

"Yes it is."

She looked up at him, eyes bright and wet.

"They were talking to me at the Market."

Jake nodded.

"I know."

"That's why you went out there."

Jake shrugged one shoulder.

"Maybe."

"You could have died."

He leaned against the porch post, arms loose at his sides.

"You could have gone with them."

Lily stared at him.

"I almost did."

The words settled heavy between them. Jake held her gaze.

"I was making sure you didn't."

She didn't speak for a long moment. Then she stepped forward and wrapped both arms around him, hard and a little desperate, the way people hold on when they've just understood how close they came to losing something. She drew a shuddering breath when Jake hugged her back.

"You idiot," she whispered into his shoulder.

He smiled just slightly.

"Yeah."

Behind them, the Lodge yard hummed with quiet relief.

Voices carried across the gravel. Laughter broke the still summer air. Boots shuffled and scraped as people moved without urgency for the first time in days.

Jake sighed, the sounds of love and laughter washing over him.

Father Tom stood near the porch steps, watching the two of them with a tired smile worn thin by too many prayers and not enough sleep.

Max hovered close to Jake's side, the way only a kid could hover, close enough to be a nuisance, far enough to look casual about it. He wasn't letting Jake out of his sight again. Not today.

Across the yard, Jo stood beside Gus. Her hand rested lightly on his arm, her eyes finding Jake the way a mother's eyes always do, checking him over without saying a word, reading what she could from that distance.

Then her gaze shifted to Franklin.

He held it for a moment, then gave one slow nod.

She understood. There was more to tell. There always was.

The Oracle. The message. The invitation.

All of it would come, in the quiet of the evening when the little ones were put to bed and the fire burned low and there was space enough for hard things.

But right now, Jake was standing in the yard with mud on his boots and the bright, dawn sun rising on his face.

And that was enough.

Chapter Forty-Six

The Kitchen Table

The Lodge settled into itself as the evening wore on.

The younger children were ushered inside first, the nervous excitement of Jake's return having finally burned through them. Ruth and Ian hovered close to him until Mary shooed them toward the kitchen with promises of hot bread and stew.

Max refused to move.

He stayed planted beside Jake like a small guard dog, arms crossed, eyes daring anyone to suggest Jake might disappear again.

Father Tom rested a hand on the boy's shoulder.

"He's not going anywhere tonight," he said gently.

Max thought about that.

Then nodded once.

"Good."

Inside, the kitchen lamps threw warm light across the long wooden table. Jo stood at the stove, stirring slowly, the motion steady and familiar as breathing. Gus leaned against the counter nearby, watching Jake the way a man watches a fence line after a storm — checking what held, looking for what didn't.

Jake sat at the table with a mug of tea cradled in both hands, clothes still dusty from the woods.

Jo finally turned from the stove.

"Come here, boy."

Jake didn't hesitate. He crossed the kitchen in two steps.

She pulled him close without ceremony, wrapping both arms around him and holding on. Her cheek came to rest against the top of his head, the same as it had since the day Father Tom first brought him through the Lodge door.

She didn't say anything for a moment.

"You scared us," she murmured.

Jake swallowed. "I'm sorry."

Jo pulled back just enough to read his face, her sharp eyes moving carefully over him.

"You hurt?"

"No."

"You hungry?"

He nodded.

"That's a good sign," Gus said.

He stepped forward then and pulled Jake into a rough hug that smelled of wood smoke and worn leather.

"You did a foolish thing," he said quietly, his voice low against the boy's ear.

Jake nodded against his shoulder. "I know."

Gus stepped back and gripped the back of his neck, firm and steady.

"But it was a brave one too."

Jake didn't have an answer for that. He looked down at the table instead.

The door opened behind them and people drifted in. Franklin. Cole. Marcus. Gin. Gunny. Hunter Maddox came in last, ducking slightly through the frame. He caught Jake's eye and gave a single nod.

"Glad you're back, kid."

Jake nodded back.

Near the far wall, Gemma stood beside Grace and Quinn. Grace had one hand tucked through Quinn's arm, the way she often did since the accident earlier that year. Quinn gave Jake a quiet look.

"Nice work not dying."

Jake managed a faint smile. "I tried."

Gemma stepped forward and gave him a quick hug. "We were about ready to drag Hunter out there whether he wanted to go or not."

Hunter raised an eyebrow. "Pretty sure I was already going."

A few tired smiles moved around the room.

Jo set a bowl of stew in front of Jake.

"Eat."

He obeyed without a word.

Marcus rested both forearms on the table.

"Deb's still over at the school," he said quietly to Jo. "She stayed to help Zara with a few of the kids and see Doc for her checkup."

Jo nodded. "She'll be glad to hear Jake's home."

Franklin leaned back in his chair. "She's due in October. She doesn't need this kind of stress."

Jo's expression softened. "None of us do."

Silence settled over the kitchen for a moment.

Then Gus looked at Jake. "Okay son, tell us about the Oracle."

The room went very still.

Jake swallowed a bite of stew and wiped his mouth. "He knew about the Lodge."

Cole frowned. "How much?"

Jake hesitated. "A lot. He knew about lots of things." He glanced toward Jo. "He knew about you."

Jo didn't look surprised. "What did he say?"

Jake shifted in his chair. The memory of the man's calm voice made the room feel colder somehow. "He said to tell Jolene Callahan that he would like to speak with her."

No one spoke for several seconds.

Gunny leaned back slowly.

Marcus folded his arms. "It is bold."

Franklin rubbed a hand across his jaw. "He also knew we were coming." His voice was quiet. Flat.

Jake nodded. "Yes, I think he did."

Yaz spoke from the doorway where he'd been standing. "He let us leave."

Every head turned toward him.

Jo rested both hands flat on the table. "That means he wants something."

"Yes," Gus said.

"What?" Cole asked.

Jo looked toward the dark window above the sink. "Influence. Men like that don't fear guns, they fear people who make others think."

The word settled into the room like a stone dropped in still water.

Hunter shifted slightly. "You think he wants to talk?"

Jo nodded once. "Oh yes." Her eyes moved slowly across the faces around the table. "He wants to see who leads this place."

The kitchen went quiet again.

Outside, the summer night hummed warm and soft around the Lodge. Inside, the long wooden table had become what it always became in hard moments. The center of the family.

And somewhere beyond the ridge, in the dark tangle of the woods, the Oracle was waiting.

Chapter Forty-Seven

What Jake Saw

The kitchen had gone quiet.

Most of the younger children had drifted off to bed, worn out from the excitement of Jake's return. The lamps burned low over the long table, throwing warm light across the worn wood.

Outside, the night hummed with crickets.

Inside, everyone listened.

Jake sat with both hands wrapped around his mug, staring down into the steam before he spoke.

"It was quiet there."

Cole leaned forward slightly.

"What do you mean?"

Jake shrugged.

"Just quiet. Not like here."

He gestured around the room.

"At the Lodge people talk. Kids argue. Somebody's always laughing or fixing something."

A faint smile tugged at the corner of Gus's mouth.

"That's accurate."

Jake looked back down at the table.

"There wasn't any of that. No laughing. No playing at all."

No one interrupted.

"The kids didn't joke around," Jake continued. "They didn't run or shove each other or anything."

Edwin frowned.

"What did they do?"

Jake thought for a moment.

"They listened."

He looked up, trying to explain it the way it had felt.

"They sit in rows sometimes while the Oracle talks. Or one of the adults teaches. And the kids answer questions."

Gin tilted her head.

"Like school?"

Jake shook his head slowly.

"No."

"What's different?" Clare asked gently.

Jake hesitated.

"They already know the answers."

The room went still.

"What kind of questions?" Father Tom asked.

Jake's brow furrowed as he tried to remember.

"Things like... why confusion hurts people."

Franklin's eyes narrowed.

Jake continued slowly.

"One of the kids said something wrong once. Just a little wrong."

"What happened?" Buck asked.

"They corrected him."

"Who?" Marcus asked.

"The other kids."

Jake's voice had gone softer.

"They all said the right answer together."

Max shifted uneasily beside him.

"What was the right answer?" the younger boy asked.

Jake swallowed.

"That confusion is cruelty."

The words settled like cold ash.

Jo's fingers stilled against the edge of the table.

Jake went on.

"The Oracle said people who create confusion hurt everyone around them."

Cole leaned back in his chair.

"And what counts as confusion?"

Jake hesitated.

"Questions."

Nobody spoke. The kitchen held the silence like it was something fragile.

Outside, a night breeze moved through the trees, slow and easy, indifferent to all of it.

After a time, Gus spoke.

"Did you hear them talk about anyone from around here?"

Jake frowned, working through his memory.

"Maybe."

Everyone leaned forward slightly.

"One of the kids asked about an old man."

Buck's head came up.

Jake didn't notice.

"They said he used to come to Market. Talk to people."

Nobody moved.

"What did they say about him?" Jo asked quietly.

Jake stared at the table.

"They said he made people doubt things."

Buck's chair scraped softly against the floor.

Jake kept on, his voice slow and careful.

"One of the older boys said the Teacher told them that men like that cause confusion."

"Teacher?" Father Tom asked.

"The Oracle." Jake nodded, "That is what the kids call him.

"And what did the Oracle say about the man?" Gus asked.

Jake's voice had dropped to just above a whisper.

"He said when someone keeps making others question things... it harms the whole community."

The kitchen felt colder without anything changing.

"What happens to people like that?" Gin asked.

Jake swallowed hard.

"They said... those people have to be removed."

Silence settled over the room like a held breath.

Jake's eyes moved slowly around the table.

Only now was he beginning to understand why everyone looked the way they did. The reason why every face at that table looked carved from stone.

"I think they meant Zeke."

Buck stood so fast his chair cracked against the floor behind him.

"No."

The word came out rough, scraped raw.

"They didn't say his name," Jake said quickly.

"They didn't have to," Cole said quietly.

Buck stood there staring at the table, jaw working, a vein ticking at his temple. For a moment it seemed like words were building up behind his teeth.

They never came.

He turned and walked out onto the porch. The screen door whispered shut behind him.

Nobody in the kitchen moved.

Jo unfolded her hands and laid them flat on the table. "What else did you see?" she asked Jake, her voice careful and low.

Jake thought for a moment. "They write things down."

"What kind of things?" Marcus asked.

"Who talks to who at Market. What people say."

Franklin's head came up sharp. "They're studying us."

Jake nodded. "The Oracle said people who lead others are the most dangerous."

A slow understanding moved through the room like a cold draft under the door.

Jo didn't react. She already knew.

Jake continued quietly.

"He knew who you were."

Her eyes met his.

"I gathered that."

Jake hesitated.

"He called you... important."

Cole frowned.

"That can't be good."

Jo leaned back slightly in her chair.

"No," she said calmly. "It usually isn't."

Silence settled again like woodsmoke after the fire dies down.

Finally Marcus spoke.

"So what do we do about it?"

Jo looked toward the dark window over the sink. Beyond it, the forest stretched black and endless, the tree line swallowed whole by the summer night. Somewhere past those trees sat the Harbinger camp. And the man who had built it.

"He invited a conversation," she said.

Franklin shifted in his seat.

"You're not actually considering that."

Jo turned her gaze back to the table.

"Yes."

Cole shook his head.

"That's a trap."

"Of course it is," Jo said.

Buck's footsteps creaked slow and steady on the porch outside.

Gus studied his wife for a long moment, reading her the way a man reads weather.

"You've already made up your mind."

Jo gave the faintest smile.

"Not completely."

"What are you waiting for?" Gin asked.

Jo's eyes moved slowly around the table, resting briefly on each face.

"For him to make the next move."

The room went quiet. Across the table, Jake stared down into his mug. Somewhere deep in the woods beyond the ridge, a man had his eyes on the Lodge.

But now the Lodge had its eyes on him.

CHAPTER FORTY-EIGHT

IN THE QUIET

The Lodge had settled into the deep quiet that only came after the last person finally gave up and went to bed.

The lamps downstairs had been blown out. The dishes were dried and stacked. Somewhere down the hall a floorboard groaned softly as the old house breathed against the night air.

Jo lay on her back, staring at the ceiling.

The window beside the bed sat cracked open, pulling in the smell of pine and cool mountain air. Crickets sang their steady song out beyond the ridge.

Beside her, Gus shifted onto one elbow.

"You're thinking too loud."

Jo smiled faintly.

"Didn't realize I was making noise."

"You always do."

He studied her in the dim light. Forty years and he could still read her face better than anyone living.

"Oracle," he said.

Jo didn't answer right away.

"Yes."

Gus exhaled and leaned back against the headboard.

"You're considering it."

"Yes."

"Meeting him."

"Yes."

He rubbed a slow hand over his beard.

Neither of them spoke for a moment.

Outside, the wind moved softly through the trees.

Finally he said, "Then I'm going with you."

Jo turned her head on the pillow.

"No."

The word came easy. Certain.

Gus gave her a look.

"Jo--"

"You barely go to Market anymore," she said quietly. "He hasn't noticed you."

"That doesn't mean--"

"It means exactly that."

She rolled onto her side to face him.

"The only reason he's paying attention to me is because I've been there so often since Zeke."

Gus didn't argue with that. They both knew it was true.

"You come with me," she continued, "and suddenly he's studying you too."

He stared at the dark window for a moment.

"I don't much like the idea of you meeting a man who had Zeke killed."

Jo's expression softened slightly.

"Neither do I."

That earned a small snort.

"Well. At least we agree on something."

She reached over and took his hand. His fingers closed around hers without thinking.

"You know why he's interested," she said.

Gus nodded slowly.

"He thinks you lead this place."

Jo lifted one shoulder.

"I do, sometimes."

“Most of the time you do.”

She smiled faintly.

"People listen to you too."

"Not the same way."

She didn't argue. They both knew the truth of that.

After a moment Gus spoke again.

"You know who he's not worried about?"

"Gunny."

"Exactly."

Jo nodded.

"The Oracle understands soldiers."

Gus raised an eyebrow.

"How so?"

"Soldiers follow orders."

He waited.

Jo's voice dropped a little.

"But people follow influence."

The room went quiet.

Gus watched her carefully.

"That's what he's afraid of."

Jo nodded once.

"Zeke made people think for themselves."

Gus stared at the ceiling for a long moment, jaw working slowly, the way it did when something sat heavy with him.

"He always did."

Silence settled between them like woodsmoke.

Finally Gus looked back at her.

"You're still not meeting him alone."

Jo sighed softly, the sound more tired than argued.

"One of us has to stay safe."

"Jo—"

"I'm serious."

Her tone had shifted. Not hard, but final.

"If something happens to me, the Lodge will listen to you."

Gus frowned. "They listen to you because you're right."

"That's not why."

"Then why?"

"Because I say things out loud that everyone else is already thinking."

That pulled a quiet chuckle out of him.

"That sounds about right."

She squeezed his hand and kissed his fingertips.

"If he takes both of us off the board, the Lodge loses its center."

Gus studied her face in the thin dark. The soft lines. The steadiness behind her eyes.

"You've been thinking about this a lot."

"Yes."

He exhaled slowly. "I don't like it."

"I know."

A quiet moment stretched between them.

Then Gus said, "You remember the first time we met Zeke?"

Jo smiled into the darkness. "He told you your fence was crooked."

"It was crooked."

"You didn't like hearing that."

"I still don't."

She laughed softly, and the sound loosened something in the room.

Gus spoke again, his voice lower now. "If the Oracle had met Zeke before the world fell apart, he would've been terrified of him."

Jo nodded. "He was anyway."

Gus turned his head toward her. "What do you mean?"

Her eyes were distant, thoughtful. Zeke talked to everyone. Asked questions. And people trusted him. Long before the world fell apart, he was already beloved. Think of the old Farmers Market he and EmmaJean ran. He knew everyone, and I can't think of a time I heard a bad word about him."

Gus understood without needing it spelled out. "That's why he was dangerous."

Jo nodded slowly.

Outside, wind moved through the pines, long and low.

After a moment, Gus squeezed her hand. "If you do meet him..."

Jo looked at him.

"...you don't let him think he's the smartest person in the room."

Jo smiled faintly. "That might be difficult."

"For him," Gus said as he gave her hand a gentle squeeze.

The room settled back into quiet.

The crickets kept on outside, steady as a pulse.

After a while, Gus spoke again.

“That boy was ready to walk into that place alone.”

"He learned that from all of us."

"If that man looks you in the eye and says something clever about leadership..."

Jo raised an eyebrow.

"...what do you think he'll say?"

A hint of amusement rose in her voice. Gus turned it over in his mind. Smiled. Then he answered.

"He'll say soldiers follow orders."

Jo waited, eyebrow raised.

"And people follow you."

She nodded, slow and certain.

"Yes, exactly."

Beyond the Lodge walls, the forest ran dark and deep beneath a scatter of stars. And somewhere past the ridge, a man was readying himself for a conversation he had been shaping in his mind for a very long time.

Chapter Forty-Nine

Under the Pine

The afternoon sun filtered through the branches of the old pine near the edge of the Lodge yard.

Marisol sat cross-legged in the shade with a book open across her knees. The breeze shifted the pages now and then, carrying the warm scent of cut grass and pine needles.

A few yards away, Gin sat on a low stool beside the shed, a length of paracord looped between her hands as she braided it slowly into a thicker line. Tools and small parts lay scattered across the wooden workbench beside her.

The rhythm of her fingers never stopped moving.

Marisol chuckled softly at something in the book.

Gin glanced over.

Marisol held the page up slightly.

"Someone tried to cook soup with shoe leather," she said.

Gin snorted.

"Wouldn't be the worst thing we've eaten since the lights went out."

Marisol smiled and went back to reading.

For a while the yard was quiet except for the scrape of rope fibers sliding against Gin's hands and the distant sound of someone hammering in the barn.

Then footsteps approached slowly across the grass.

Marisol noticed the shadow first.

She looked up.

Willow stood a few feet away, her hands clasped behind her back.

The Harbinger girl hesitated like she wasn't sure she should come any closer.

Gin's eyes flicked up from the rope.

She studied the girl for a second.

Then she gave the smallest nod toward Marisol.

Safe enough.

For now.

Willow settled herself onto the ground beside Marisol, tucking her legs beneath her. She set a small cloth bundle in her lap and drew out strips of fiber, working them between her fingers into a thin braided cord.

Neither girl spoke for a while.

Marisol read. Willow braided.

Finally, Willow glanced at the book. "What is it?"

Marisol tilted the cover toward her. "Stories."

"What kind?"

"Funny ones."

Willow considered it the way you study a word in a language you almost understand.

"Why?"

"Why what?"

"Why do you read funny things?"

"Because they make me laugh."

"You all laugh a lot."

"We do.

Willow's brow creased. Not annoyed. Genuinely puzzled.

“We’re not supposed to.”

Marisol studied her for a second and realized the girl wasn't being difficult. She just didn't know.

"You don't have funny stories?"

Willow shook her head. "No."

Marisol let that sit. "That's kind of sad."

Willow didn't answer. Her fingers kept moving through the fiber.

After a moment, she asked, "Why did you laugh?"

Marisol held up the page. "The man in the story tried to make soup from an old shoe."

"That's funny?"

"Yeah."

Willow looked at her as if she were trying to work out a problem that kept coming up wrong.

"Teacher says laughing makes people careless."

"No, it doesn't."

Willow dropped her gaze back to the rope. Something shifted in her expression, brief and hard to name.

Then, quietly: "Do your parents let you ask questions?"

"Of course. We all ask questions."

"Any questions?"

"Mostly."

Willow twisted another strand into the braid. "We are told questions cause confusion."

Across the porch, Gin had gone still. She wasn't looking at them, but she wasn't not listening either.

Marisol looked back at Willow. "Questions help you understand things."

Willow's hands slowed. "That's not what Teacher says."

Marisol turned a page. "My grandma says if someone doesn't want questions, it's probably because they don't like the answers."

Willow went quiet for a long moment.

Finally, she spoke again.

"Teacher says people who make others question things hurt the community."

A cold knot settled in Marisol's stomach.

She thought of the whispers about Zeke. She thought of the way everyone at the table had gone quiet when Jake told them what he'd heard.

Willow kept braiding the rope.

"Sometimes Teacher removes people who cause confusion."

Marisol's eyes lifted slowly.

"What do you mean?"

Willow's shoulder moved in a small shrug.

"They go away."

The breeze pushed through the branches overhead.

Gin's chair creaked as she shifted her weight.

Marisol dropped her voice.

"Willow."

The other girl looked up.

"Do you want to stay there?"

Willow didn't answer. Her fingers tightened around the rope.

Then, very quietly: "I asked too many questions last week."

Marisol's chest went tight.

"What happened?"

"Teacher said curiosity can become dangerous." Willow's eyes fell again. "I am trying not to ask questions now."

Neither girl spoke.

Across the yard, Gin rose slowly from her chair and carried the finished length of rope toward the shed. As she passed behind them, she set a hand briefly on Marisol's shoulder.

Just a hand, a small squeeze. Just a moment.

Marisol understood.

Be careful.

Willow looked up suddenly.

"Do you ever feel scared asking questions?"

Marisol thought about it honestly.

"Sometimes."

"Why do you still do it?"

"Because it's how you learn things."

Willow studied her the way she sometimes did, like she was trying to grasp something she couldn't quite reach.

"Do you think questions can hurt people?"

Marisol closed her book.

"No," she said quietly. "I think they make people smart, people who can think."

Willow looked down at the rope coiled in her hands. Then she whispered it, so soft Marisol nearly missed it.

"Teacher says people who spread curiosity must be corrected."

The cold knot pulled tighter.

Across the yard, Gin had stopped walking. She turned back toward the girls, slow and deliberate.

The afternoon light shifted through the pines.

The wind moved through the high branches, and for a long moment that was the only sound.

But somewhere, past the treeline, past the long summer quiet of the Lodge, someone was watching.

Patient.

Waiting.

Chapter Fifty

What Marisol Heard

The next morning came warm and bright.

Market days always started early.

By the time the wagons were loaded and the horses hitched, the sun had just begun shouldering its way over the eastern ridge. Mist curled low across the fields as the Lodge wagons rolled toward town.

Marisol sat beside Ruth on the wagon bench, her book tucked under one arm.

She wasn't really reading it anyway.

Her thoughts kept pulling her back to Willow. The way the girl had asked her questions. The way her voice had gone quiet when she said she was trying not to.

That feeling hadn't left her.

By the time they reached the Market, the square was already breathing with quiet movement. Stalls opened. Tables unfolded. Voices carried across the green as neighbors called to one another.

Marisol climbed down from the wagon and drifted toward the far edge of the square where the old maples cast long shadows over the grass. She liked it there. It was easier to think.

She settled against one of the trunks and opened her book.

Across the square, Gin was helping someone unload baskets of vegetables. Father Tom stood near the bread table, deep in conversation with two older women, his hands folded in front of him the way they always were when he was listening hard.

Everything looked easy. Normal.

Marisol tried to read.

The words wouldn't hold.

After a few minutes, she closed the book and leaned her head back against the bark.

Voices drifted from the other side of the tree.

Two men.

She could see the gray scarves at the edge of her vision without turning her head.

Harbingers.

Marisol went still.

She wasn't trying to listen.

But they were close, and the words came anyway.

"...been watching her."

"Teacher noticed."

A pause.

Her stomach pulled tight.

"She asks too many questions."

The other man made a low sound in his throat.

"Curiosity spreads."

"Exactly."

Marisol's fingers tightened around the edge of her book.

The breeze moved through the leaves above her head, a soft sound that didn't match the words beneath it.

One of the men spoke again.

"Teacher says it's time."

"Soon?"

"Very."

The cold feeling returned to Marisol's chest.

She knew that word now. Had learned its different shapes.

Removed. Corrected. Gone.

The voices dropped lower.

"We'll move her before the next Market day."

"Cleaner that way."

Boots shifted on gravel. For a moment, she was certain they'd come around the tree. Instead, their voices drifted toward the far side of the square, fading the way bad dreams sometimes did — just far enough that you could almost pretend they weren't real.

Marisol didn't move.

Her heart knocked hard against her ribs. She stared down at the book in her lap, but the words on the page meant nothing.

I asked too many questions.

Willow's voice. Clear as a bell.

Marisol swallowed against the knot in her throat.

Last time she'd heard whispers like these, she'd told herself she'd misunderstood. That she was wrong. That it wasn't her business.

Then Zeke disappeared.

The knot pulled tighter.

Across the Market, Father Tom stood near the bread table, laughing at something one of the vendors had said. Gin was a little farther off, stacking crates like she had nothing more pressing on her mind than getting the work done.

Everything looked ordinary.

Marisol pushed herself to her feet. Her legs felt strange beneath her, like they belonged to someone else. She hesitated a moment, the doubt creeping back in.

What if she was wrong? What if those men hadn't been talking about Willow at all? What if she stirred up trouble over nothing?

The knot in her stomach pulled tighter.

Then she remembered Willow under the pine tree. That small, careful voice.

Teacher says curiosity can become dangerous.

Marisol closed her book and didn't wait any longer.

She crossed the square at a near-run. Father Tom saw her coming and smiled.

"Good morning, Marisol."

She stopped beside him, her voice coming out smaller than she'd meant it to.

"I need to tell you something."

His expression shifted at once. He knelt so his eyes were level with hers.

"What is it?"

Marisol glanced around. Gin had already clocked her and was walking over, unhurried but deliberate.

Marisol dropped her voice low.

"Willow is in trouble."

Gin stepped in beside them. "What kind of trouble?"

"I heard two Harbingers talking." Marisol's fingers curled tight around the spine of her book. "They said she asks too many questions." She swallowed. "They said Teacher is going to move her before the next Market day."

Father Tom and Gin traded a look over her head.

"You're sure that's what you heard?" Father Tom asked. His voice was steady, almost too steady.

"I didn't understand all of it. But I think they meant Willow."

Gin's eyes went distant the way they did when her mind was already three steps ahead. After a moment, she gave a single nod.

"You did the right thing telling us."

Some of the tightness left Marisol's chest.

Father Tom rested a hand gently on her shoulder. "Exactly what you were supposed to do."

Gin turned and looked toward the far end of the square, where the Harbinger camp road cut between the trees.

"How long until the next wagon leaves for the Lodge?" Gin asked quietly.

Her jaw was set, her eyes flat and thinking.

"Looks like we've got work to do."

The morning sun climbed above the treeline, warm and indifferent. And somewhere beyond that ridge, a girl who asked too many questions was running out of time.

Chapter Fifty-One

The Plea

By the time the wagons rolled back from Market, the Lodge yard had already begun its slow surrender to evening.

The sun hung low behind the western ridge, throwing long amber light across the grass. Chickens scratched lazily near the fence. Somewhere near the barn, the steady crack of splitting kindling marked the evening.

But inside the Lodge kitchen, the air had gone tight.

Word traveled fast.

Jo sat at the head of the long table, her cane propped against the chair beside her. Gus stood near the window, arms folded, watching the last wagon creak into the yard. Gin leaned against the counter without a word. Father Tom had taken the chair beside Marisol. Franklin and Marcus stood near the doorway, speaking low with Yaz and Riley.

Marisol hadn't moved.

Her book sat on the table in front of her, closed. She hadn't touched it.

The words she'd overheard were still turning in her head.

Jo broke the silence.

"Tell us exactly what you heard."

Marisol swallowed. "They said Willow asks too many questions." She paused, her fingers finding the edge of the table. "They said curiosity spreads and Teacher noticed."

Nobody spoke.

"They said they're going to move her. Before the next Market day."

The quiet that followed had weight to it.

Gus looked toward Gin.

Gin gave a single nod. "Sounds like a removal."

The word settled over the room like a stone dropped into still water.

Marisol felt the knot in her chest pull tighter.

"They can't do that," she said suddenly.

Her voice came out louder than she intended.

Everyone looked at her.

Marisol's eyes filled before she could stop them.

"She didn't do anything wrong."

The words started spilling out of her.

"She was just asking questions. She wanted to know why we laugh. She wanted to know why we read stories."

Her hands moved in front of her, helpless.

"She didn't sound bad. She sounded... curious."

The room went very quiet.

Marisol looked at Jo.

"They're going to take her away just because she asked questions."

Her voice caught.

"That's not fair."

Jo watched her carefully.

Marisol swiped at her eyes, annoyed with herself for crying.

"She's just being a kid."

That broke something loose.

"If someone had told me not to ask questions when I was little, I would've asked even more."

A few quiet smiles moved through the room.

Marisol didn't stop.

"Willow isn't trying to hurt anyone." Her voice shook. "She just wants to understand things."

For a moment, she couldn't get any more words out.

Then she looked straight at Jo.

"Please help her."

The kitchen held its breath.

Jo rose slowly from her chair, the soft tap of her cane marking each step across the wooden floor until she stood beside the girl.

She didn't say anything at first.

She simply wrapped one arm around Marisol and drew her close.

Marisol pressed her face against Jo's shoulder, her breath ragged and small.

Jo's voice was barely above a whisper.

"Of course we will."

Marisol pulled back, blinking fast.

Jo brushed a strand of hair from the girl's face.

"Curiosity is not a crime here, sweetheart."

She glanced toward Gin, who stood leaning against the counter. The corner of Gin's mouth twitched.

Jo straightened and looked at the others.

"Marcus."

The colonel came to attention without thinking about it.

"Yes, ma'am."

"Looks like we're going to need a quiet trip into the woods."

He nodded once. No questions.

Franklin uncrossed his arms.

"Extraction?"

Gin pushed off the counter.

"That's the idea."

Yaz spoke from the doorway, quiet and steady as a man who already knew the terrain.

"I can track the camp again."

Gus looked at Jo the way he'd looked at her for forty years, searching her face for doubt and finding none.

"You're sure about this?"

She held his gaze.

"If we allow someone to punish a child for asking questions...and we could stop it," Her voice didn't waver. "Then we're not the people we think we are."

Nobody argued.

Across the table, Marisol wiped her eyes with the back of her wrist.

The knot that had lived in her chest since morning loosened, just a little.

Gin reached up and pulled the map from the wall.

"Well." She smoothed it flat on the table. "Let's go get ourselves a curious kid."

Outside, the last of the daylight bled away behind the pines.

Somewhere beyond the ridge, a girl who asked too many questions was about to find out she wasn't alone.

CHAPTER FIFTY-TWO

THE MAP

The map covered nearly half the kitchen table.

Gin had pinned the corners down with a mug, a compass, a box of cartridges, and Gus's old folding knife.

The paper was crowded with lines—ridges, creeks, logging trails, and narrow deer paths that never appeared on official charts.

Yaz stood beside the table, one finger tracing a narrow draw that cut through the forest east of the ridge.

"The camp sits here," he said quietly.

Everyone leaned in.

Marcus folded his arms. "How many people?"

"Hard to say." Yaz lifted his eyes. "Twenty men, maybe. More women and a lot of kids."

Franklin nodded slowly. "Guards?"

"A few."

Gin spoke from the far side of the table. "They're not soldiers."

Riley, standing near the window, shook her head. "Doesn't mean they aren't dangerous."

Cole rested both hands flat on the map. "We're also talking about civilians."

Gin gave him a flat look. "They're planning to disappear a child."

Cole didn't flinch. "I know."

Deb leaned forward beside him. "But we still need to think about how this looks afterward."

Franklin glanced between them. "This isn't a courtroom."

"No," Deb said quietly. "But it might be someday."

That slowed the room down to nothing.

Marcus finally spoke.

"Explain."

Deb tapped the map with one finger.

"If we go in like a raid and someone gets hurt, the Harbingers will claim we attacked them."

Cole nodded slowly.

"We police officers have some experience with accusations like that. They're already watching us. Already studying how we operate."

Riley shifted against the wall.

"So what's the alternative?"

Deb met her eyes.

"Witnesses."

That pulled everyone's attention to her.

"From town," she continued. "People who can see firsthand what the Harbingers are doing."

Gin's frown was slight but clear.

"You want civilians standing in the middle of a potential conflict."

"I want accountability. Plus, we don't know how many of those newer families have someone with real experience. But I'd wager Zara knows someone who does."

Boone's voice came from the doorway.

"And if the Harbingers decide to fight anyway?"

Heads turned.

He stepped into the room, Owen and Tobias moving in behind him. He leaned over the map, finger pressed to the tree line marking the camp's eastern edge.

"These woods don't forgive mistakes."

Owen's voice was quiet.

"Especially not at night."

Tobias unfolded his arms just long enough to set both palms on the table.

"And there are children inside that camp."

The room went still once again, all eyes on the map.

Gus was the first to break the silence.

"We are not going in there looking for a fight."

Gin gave a single nod.

"We're going in quiet."

Yaz tapped the map again, his finger settling on a thin blue line threading across the page.

"There's a creek bed here. Dry this time of year." He traced it slowly. "Good cover."

Franklin leaned in.

"How close does it get us?"

"Within fifty yards of the outer cabins."

Riley's eyes narrowed.

"That's close."

"Close enough," Gin said.

Cole looked at Deb.

"If we bring witnesses, they stay well back."

"No argument there."

Marcus studied the map a moment longer.

"Team size."

Heads turned toward him.

"Too many people and we make noise." He tapped the page. "Too few and we risk getting pinned."

"Five," Gin said.

Marcus looked up. "Five?"

"Tracker. Two shooters. One extraction. One overwatch."

Riley raised her hand, just slightly.

"I'll take overwatch."

Nobody pushed back.

Yaz gave a single nod. "I track."

Franklin glanced toward Marcus.

"You or me?"

Marcus didn't hesitate. "You."

Gin leaned back in her chair.

"I go."

Cole's frown cut across his face. "You're the Lodge's gunsmith."

She met his eyes. "Exactly."

That settled it.

Marcus looked around the room.

"That's four."

No one spoke for a while.

Riley broke it first.

"We should bring a medic."

Tobias stepped forward before the words finished landing.

"I'll go."

Gin shook her head.

"You're not tactical."

"No." Tobias kept his voice even. "But I can keep a child alive if something goes wrong. I am also a dead shot."

Marcus held him in a long, steady look.

Then he gave one short nod.

"Fair point."

Deb spoke from the corner, quiet but certain.

"I'll coordinate the witnesses."

Cole glanced over. "You sure about that?"

She gave him the kind of look that didn't need words.

"I'm the sheriff's deputy."

Cole's mouth tugged sideways. "Fair enough."

Jo had said nothing through all of it. She'd just listened, her hands wrapped around her mug.

Now she set it down and said a single word.

"Timing."

Every head turned.

Yaz answered first. "Night."

Gin nodded. "After midnight."

Franklin kept his eyes on the map. "Most people sleep deepest around two."

Marcus scanned the table one last time.

"Objective."

Franklin didn't hesitate. "Get Willow out."

"No confrontation unless necessary."

"Silent if possible," Gin added.

Riley reached out and checked the rifle leaning against the wall. "And if they try to stop us?"

The room went still as everyone held their breath.

Marcus met her eyes.

"We leave with the girl."

Gus had been standing back near the doorway the whole time. Now he pushed off the frame.

"Just remember something."

Everyone looked at him.

"These people aren't afraid of guns."

Jo finished it without looking up.

"They're afraid of influence."

Marcus folded the map slowly and deliberately.

"Let's make sure they remember that. I'll stay here with Gus and coordinate if things go wrong."

Outside, the forest lay dark under a rising moon, the tree line holding its silence. Somewhere past the ridge, a girl slept, unaware she was almost out of time.

The Lodge was coming.

Chapter Fifty-Three

The Approach

The moon hadn't quite cleared the ridge when the team slipped out of the Lodge.

Five figures melted into the tree line without a word.

Yaz went first.

He moved through the forest the way water moves through stone — quiet, steady, almost effortless. Every few steps he paused just long enough to listen before pressing on along the narrow deer trail threading between the pines.

Franklin followed close behind.

Then Gin.

Tobias came next, a small medical pack riding one shoulder.

Riley held the rear.

She carried her rifle low, eyes working the dark tree line in steady sweeps.

The forest breathed around them. Wind stirring the high branches. An owl calling somewhere across the valley. Pine needles soft beneath careful boots

Nobody spoke.

After the better part of an hour, Yaz raised a fist.

The line froze.

He crouched at the edge of a shallow, dry creek bed and pointed ahead.

Franklin moved up beside him.

The ground fell away into the narrow channel, its rocky floor winding through the trees like a pale scar in the moonlight.

"Here," Yaz murmured.

Franklin gave a single nod.

They dropped into the creek bed one at a time. The walls barely reached their waists, but that was enough to break their silhouettes as they moved.

For several minutes, the only sound was the faint scrape of boot leather on gravel.

Then Yaz went still again.

He knelt and pressed two fingers to the dirt beside the creek.

Franklin crouched next to him. "Tracks?"

"Recent."

Franklin studied the marks. Two sets of boots, both heading toward the camp.

He lifted his eyes. "How close?"

Yaz glanced toward the dark ridge above them. "Two hundred yards."

Behind them, Gin adjusted her rifle sling. Tobias rolled the tension out of his shoulder beneath the weight of the pack.

Riley scaled the creek bank in a slow, careful pull and put her eye to the scope. She held there a full minute before sliding back down.

"Cabins," she said.

"How many?"

"Four."

Franklin nodded.

Yaz kept moving.

The creek bent hard after another hundred yards.

He stopped again, but this time he didn't kneel. He just went still and listened.

The others followed his lead.

At first, Franklin heard nothing but the water and the wind working through the pines. Then voices reached them, faint and shapeless, carried down through the trees like smoke.

Gin tilted her head toward the sound. "More than a few people awake."

Franklin's jaw tightened. "They shouldn't be."

Riley scaled the bank and eased her rifle up to the ridgeline. She held there. Five seconds. Ten. Twenty.

When she came back down, something had shifted behind her eyes.

"What?" Franklin asked.

"Lanterns."

"How many?"

"Three."

Yaz kept his voice low. "They're gathering."

Gin's eyes narrowed. "For what?"

Nobody answered, because nobody needed to.

A voice drifted down through the trees. Calm. Unhurried. Clear enough to carry even at that distance.

Franklin felt the hair rise on the back of his neck.

The Oracle.

Riley looked toward the others.

"Sounds like a ceremony."

Franklin's stomach dropped.

A faint bitter smell drifted down the ridge.

Franklin recognized it immediately as medicinal tea.

So did Tobias. They shared a look that spoke volumes.

Yaz's voice was barely a breath.

"We're too late."

Nobody moved. A beat of dead silence.

Then Franklin spoke.

"No."

He checked his rifle.

"Not yet."

Above them, lantern light shifted between the trees like something restless. And somewhere just past the ridge, a child who asked too many questions was about to learn what happened when you did.

Chapter Fifty-Four

The Ceremony

The ridge rose gently above the creek bed.

Yaz moved first.

He climbed the slope in careful silence, using roots and rocks for handholds as he worked his way toward the tree line. The others followed, spreading out as they crested the rise.

Franklin dropped to one knee beside a thick stand of brush.

The camp lay just beyond.

Lantern light flickered between the cabins.

Three buildings stood around a small clearing. Beyond them, a larger structure, more barn than house, sat with its doors thrown open to the night.

People had gathered in the clearing.

Franklin counted quickly.

Fifteen.

Maybe more.

Men, women, and a handful of children.

They stood in a loose circle around a small wooden table. At the center stood the Oracle. Even at this distance, he was unmistakable.

Tall.

Still.

Franklin couldn't catch every word, but the tone carried easily across the night air. Measured. Certain. The voice of a man who had never doubted he would be obeyed.

Gin slid in beside him.

"What do you see?"

Franklin kept his eyes on the clearing.

"A ceremony."

Riley's voice whispered through the radio earpiece.

"Overwatch set."

Franklin shifted slightly to open her line of sight.

"Anyone armed?"

"Two men. Rifles."

"Positions?"

"North edge of the clearing."

Yaz moved beside them and pointed without a word.

Franklin followed the direction of his finger.

A small wooden chair sat near the table.

Willow.

She was slumped against the back of it, her head drooped forward, her small frame gone slack. A woman stood beside her holding a cup.

Gin's voice dropped.

"Already dosed."

Franklin's jaw tightened.

Then the smell reached them.

Herbs in the cool night air. Sharp and green and wrong.

Belladonna. Foxglove. Something else underneath he couldn't name.

Tobias leaned close.

"Sedative first," he whispered.

"How long?"

Tobias studied Willow's posture for a moment.

"Not long."

The Oracle lifted his hands.

The circle went quiet as stone.

His voice carried across the clearing without effort.

"Peace comes when confusion ends."

Several voices murmured the words back to him.

"This child has been troubled by questions."

Willow stirred weakly in the chair.

The woman beside her lifted the cup.

Franklin's pulse hammered at his temples.

"Final dose," Tobias whispered.

Gin glanced at Franklin.

Willow stirred in the chair and murmured something no one could hear.

"Now."

Franklin exhaled once.

Then he stood up out of the brush.

"Hey!"

The word cracked across the clearing like a hammer on stone.

Every head turned.

For half a heartbeat, the entire camp froze solid.

Franklin stepped fully into the lantern light.

Gin moved up beside him. Yaz appeared to his left. Behind them, Tobias broke forward at a run toward Willow.

On the ridge above, Riley's rifle tracked.

The Oracle didn't move. He simply watched.

"Step away from the child," Franklin said.

The woman holding the cup hesitated.

One of the armed men swung his rifle up.

Riley's voice came sharp from above.

"Don't."

The laser dot settled on the man's chest.

He froze.

Gin reached the chair first. She knocked the cup from the woman's hand before it reached Willow's lips. It hit the ground, and the liquid soaked into the dirt

Tobias dropped to his knees beside the girl and pressed two fingers to her throat.

"Alive."

Willow's eyelids fluttered, barely.

Franklin turned back toward the Oracle.

The man's expression hadn't shifted. Not a muscle.

"You misunderstand," the Oracle said, his voice almost tender. "This is a sacred ceremony."

Franklin didn't blink.

"You were about to poison a child."

The Oracle tilted his head, unhurried, like a man correcting a neighbor over a fence line.

"Medicine," he said. "Correction."

Behind Franklin, Tobias lifted Willow carefully from the chair. The girl barely stirred, her head lolling against his shoulder. Gin stepped in close beside them, hand resting on her sidearm.

"We're leaving."

The Oracle's gaze swept across the clearing. Some of the Harbingers looked confused. Others had gone hard around the eyes. But not one of them moved.

His attention drifted back to Franklin.

"You believe you're saving her."

Franklin held his gaze steady.

"I know we are."

Neither man spoke for a long moment. Then the Oracle smiled, just barely.

"You've only made the division deeper."

Franklin didn't answer. He turned toward the tree line.

"Let's move."

They slipped back into the darkness the same way they'd come, quiet and quick, swallowed by the woods.

Behind them, lantern light trembled across the clearing. The Oracle stood watching the tree line long after the last sound faded. When he finally spoke, his voice was low and deliberate, shaped for every ear around him.

"The Lodge has taken one of our children."

And with those seven words, everything shifted.

Chapter Fifty-Five

The Withdrawal

They moved fast once they reached the trees.

Franklin didn't look back.

Yaz took point again, threading through the forest with the same quiet certainty he'd carried on the way in. The deer trail reappeared under the moonlight, winding through dark stands of pine and spruce.

Behind him, Tobias carried Willow.

The girl hung limp against his shoulder, one small arm swaying with each stride. Her breathing came slow and steady, but she hadn't woken.

Gin stayed close beside them.

Every few yards, she cut a glance back toward the ridge.

Franklin settled into step behind Yaz.

"Any movement?" he murmured.

Riley's voice came soft through the earpiece.

"Negative."

Still on overwatch.

A few seconds stretched out.

Then: "They're not following."

Franklin's jaw tightened.

"They should be."

Behind him, Tobias shifted the girl carefully against his shoulder.

"She's light," he said, low. "Too light."

Gin glanced over.

"Pulse?"

"Strong."

Franklin eased his pace just enough to see Willow's face in the moonlight.

Her eyelids fluttered once. Then went still.

"The sedative's still working," Tobias said.

Franklin gave a single nod.

They covered another hundred yards before Riley's voice came again.

"I'm moving."

She appeared from the tree line behind them seconds later, sliding into place at the rear of the line.

"No pursuit," she said quietly.

Yaz stopped just long enough to listen.

The forest behind them was silent.

Entirely too silent.

Franklin turned slowly. He should hear shouts, or commotion of some kind.

The ridge had disappeared behind the wall of trees. The lantern light couldn't reach that far anymore.

"Why didn't they come after us?" Gin said.

Nobody answered right away.

Tobias spoke first.

"Because he didn't want them to."

Franklin looked at him.

"You're sure about that?"

Tobias shifted Willow slightly against his shoulder.

"That man never lost control of that crowd."

Franklin thought back to the clearing. The Oracle hadn't shouted. Hadn't raised his voice even once. He'd simply watched them go. Let them walk right out of it.

Franklin let out a slow breath.

"He already has a plan."

Yaz started moving again. "We should keep going."

The creek bed reappeared ahead, pale and shallow in the moonlight. They dropped into it one by one, and the narrow walls swallowed them whole.

They walked without talking for a while.

Then Willow stirred.

Tobias stopped immediately. Her eyes fluttered partway open. She blinked, slow and confused, looking up at the dark shapes of the trees.

"Marisol?" she murmured.

Gin crouched beside her. "You're safe."

Willow's brow creased slightly. "Teacher said..."

Her voice trailed off.

"What did he say?" Franklin asked, keeping his voice easy.

The girl's eyes drifted toward the canopy above them. "That questions make people sick."

Something tightened in Franklin's chest.

Gin touched the girl's shoulder gently. "Not here."

Willow blinked once more, then her eyes closed.

Tobias nodded. "She'll sleep a while longer."

Yaz pulled himself up the far bank and paused, scanning the woods ahead. The eastern sky had begun to soften, that first gray whisper of dawn bleeding through the dark.

"Two miles," he said quietly.

Franklin looked back toward the ridge one last time. Nothing moved. But the stillness felt off, the way a held breath feels off.

He turned away.

"Let's get her home."

Behind them, somewhere beyond the tree line, the Harbinger camp had already begun telling a different story. And by the time the sun cleared the valley, that story would already be spreading.

Chapter Fifty-Six

A Different Kind of Quiet

Morning had settled softly over the Lodge.

Sunlight came through the tall windows in the common room in long slanted bars, warming the wide plank floors and the long wooden table where breakfast dishes still waited to be cleared.

The house had already found its rhythm again.

Someone was working in the garden. A hammer tapped steadily from the barn. Children's voices drifted in and out from somewhere outside.

But in the small guest room at the end of the hall, everything stayed quiet.

Marisol sat cross-legged on the floor beside the bed, a book open across her knees. She'd been there nearly an hour.

Willow lay beneath the quilt, still and pale against the pillow. The herbal sedative had worn off slowly, leaving her breathing deeper, but her body heavy with exhaustion sleep alone couldn't fix.

Jo had checked on her twice. Tobias once. Each time, the same answer.

Let her sleep.

So Marisol waited. And read.

Her voice was soft and steady.

"Dorothy lived in the midst of the great Kansas prairies..."

The words drifted quietly through the room. Marisol turned the page and had just begun the next paragraph when the quilt shifted.

She stopped reading.

Willow's eyes opened.

For a moment, the girl just stared at the ceiling.

Then her gaze moved slowly around the room, touching each thing like she was cataloging it. The wooden dresser. The window. The chair.

Finally, she found Marisol.

Her body went rigid.

She pushed herself upright too fast, and the fear on her face was plain as daylight.

"Where am I?"

Her voice came out raw, scraped thin.

"It's okay," Marisol said quickly.

Willow pressed herself back against the headboard like the wood might swallow her.

"You took me."

"We helped you."

Willow's breathing picked up. "Teacher said strangers would try to take us away."

Marisol lifted the book a little. "I won't hurt you. I'm just reading."

Willow stared at it like it might bite her

"What is it?"

"A story."

The girl's frown deepened. "You read stories."

"Yeah."

Willow glanced toward the door, watching it like she was waiting for someone else to come through.

"Teacher will be angry."

Marisol held her voice steady. "No one here is going to hurt you."

Willow studied her face for a long moment. Then her eyes drifted back to the book.

"What story?"

Marisol turned the cover toward her. "The Wizard of Oz."

Willow tilted her head. "Is it about medicine?"

Marisol laughed softly. "No."

Willow blinked. "Then what's it about?"

Marisol thought for a second. "Mostly about finding your way home."

Willow seemed to turn that over in her mind.

"I don't know where my home is," she whispered.

The room went still.

Marisol looked down at the open book.

"Do you want me to keep reading?"

Willow hesitated, then gave a small nod.

"The cyclone had set the house down very gently..."

The words settled into the quiet like woodsmoke.

A few minutes passed before the door eased open and Jo stepped inside, carrying a tray. A bowl of oatmeal. A slice of bread. A cup of tea, still steaming.

She stopped when she saw Willow's eyes open and watching.

"Well," Jo said, her voice warm and unhurried. "Looks like someone decided to join us."

Willow's shoulders drew in.

Jo set the tray on the bedside table and lowered herself into the chair beside the bed, her cane hooked over the arm.

"Good morning."

The girl said nothing.

"You must be hungry."

Willow stared at the bowl. "What is it?"

"Oatmeal with brown sugar and some dried apples."

A flicker of suspicion crossed her face. "Is it medicine?"

Jo smiled, though the word medicine landed heavier than the girl realized.

"No."

Willow watched her with those careful, measuring eyes. Jo picked up the spoon and took a bite herself, unhurried, easy.

"See?"

Something loosened in the girl's expression. She took the spoon slowly, tasted it, then took another bite without being asked.

Jo let her eat. Waited until the rhythm of it settled before she spoke again.

"Do you have parents, sweetheart?"

Willow shook her head.

"No parents at the camp either?"

"Some kids do." She swallowed another spoonful. "Not me."

"Where did you come from?"

Willow shrugged. "I don't remember."

Marisol had stopped reading. The book lay open in her lap, forgotten.

Jo kept her voice even. "Are there many children like you there?"

"Some."

"Who looks after you?"

"Teacher."

Jo nodded, her face giving nothing away. "And they told you that you were special?"

Willow looked down at the bowl. "They said we were chosen."

The quiet that followed had weight to it.

Marisol watched Jo the way a child watches an adult, trying very hard to stay calm.

Jo leaned forward and tucked the quilt a little closer around Willow's shoulders.

"You're safe here now."

Willow's brow creased. "Teacher says safety comes from obedience."

Jo settled her hands in her lap. "That's one way of looking at it."

Willow studied her face for a long moment. "What do you think?"

"I think safety comes from people who care about you."

Willow didn't answer. She scraped the last of the oatmeal from the bowl and set the spoon down quietly.

Across the room, Marisol turned the page and began to read again.

Chapter Fifty-Seven

Whispers at the Market

The morning air carried the first hint of fall.

Not cold yet, but cooler than August's thick heat. The kind of crispness that sharpened everything — hills smelling of pine and dry leaves. The scent of woodsmoke threaded faintly through the valley from somewhere up the ridge.

Market days always started early.

By the time Gus guided the wagon into the field beside the school, several vendors had already claimed their spots and gotten to work. Tables unfolded and canvas awnings snapped up against the pale sky.

He would only stay long enough to help Jo set up. Boone and Beth were coming down from the Lodge later to take over the table. Gin was pulling up with Gemma, Hunter, and various children who had lessons.

The fewer times he and Jo appeared together in town these days, the better. The Market was busy today. Crates of vegetables moved hand over hand from the backs of trucks and wagons, and somewhere nearby, someone was already frying onions.

Jo breathed it in and smiled.

"September," she said.

Gus squinted at the tree line where the maples were just beginning to turn.

"Best month there is."

They worked the way people do after forty years together, without needing to say much. Gus dropped the tailgate while Jo set her cane against the wagon wheel and started unloading baskets. Mary's blackberry jam, each jar sealed tight and labeled in her careful hand. Bundles of dried herbs tied with twine. A small crate of late tomatoes, still warm-looking even in the morning cool.

Across the field, children were already threading between the tables while their parents worked. Market mornings had always felt something like a small, unhurried festival.

But today sat differently.

Jo felt it before she could name it.

A woman she recognized from town slowed near their table. She gave Jo a short nod, and then moved on a little faster than was natural.

A man passed on the far side, glanced once at Gus, and looked away. His jaw was set.

Jo kept her hands moving, straightening the jam jars.

"You feel that?" she asked quietly.

Gus didn't look up from the crate he was lifting.

"Yep."

A pair of younger men stopped about twenty feet off.

They weren't shopping.

They were watching.

One leaned toward the other and said something low. The second man's eyes cut to Jo.

Then they walked away.

Jo straightened slowly.

"Word travels fast."

Gus wiped his hands on his jeans.

"Usually not this fast. We don't even have phones anymore, Jo."

More people filtered in, but the easy back-and-forth the Lodge folk normally got at market wasn't there. The air had a different weight to it. Some people still waved. Others found somewhere else to look. A woman picked up a jar of jam and studied the label like she was working out a math problem, then set it back down without a word.

Jo shifted slightly closer to Gus.

"That man there."

"Which one?"

"Blue jacket."

Gus let his gaze drift over, unhurried.

The man was looking straight at them. When Gus's eyes met his, he turned away fast.

"Yeah," Gus said quietly. "I see him."

A familiar voice cut through the market noise a few minutes later.

"Morning."

Jo turned.

Zara Malard stood a few feet back, arms folded loosely across her chest. Rita beside her. Both women wore the same expression — the kind that didn't come with good news.

Jo rested her hand on her cane.

"Well," she said. "That doesn't look like a friendly visit."

Zara stepped closer. "We need to talk."

Gus gestured toward the empty chair behind their table. "Pull up some shade."

Zara didn't sit. Instead, she glanced across the market field. Several people were still watching.

"That story's been spreading since yesterday afternoon."

Jo felt something tighten low in her stomach. "What story?"

Rita answered. "That the Lodge kidnapped a child."

The words settled over them like smoke.

Gus exhaled slowly. "Didn't take him long."

Zara nodded. "The Harbingers came through town yesterday evening." She paused. "Told people you interrupted a religious ceremony."

Rita added quietly, "They said the girl wanted to stay."

Jo didn't react right away. She reached out and adjusted the position of one of the jars on the table, just slightly.

Gus glanced toward the road leading back toward the Lodge.

Boone and Beth should have been here by now. He would not leave Jo until they arrived now.

"How many people believe it?"

Zara sighed. "Some don't."

"Some do," Rita said.

Gus leaned his forearms on the table. "Newer folks?"

"Mostly."

Jo nodded slowly. That tracked. The families who'd known the Lodge for years weren't easily rattled. But newcomers only knew what they'd been told — and they'd been told first.

Zara lowered her voice. "The Oracle was very calm when he told it."

Jo almost smiled. "I imagine he was."

Rita glanced toward the far edge of the field. "They're here today too."

Jo didn't turn immediately.

She already knew where to look.

She turned her gaze across the Market. Two Harbinger women stood near the cider stall. Not selling anything. Not browsing. Just watching. One of them caught Jo's eye and offered a small, polite smile before turning back to the crowd.

Jo kept both hands on her cane.

"Well," she said quietly. "That didn't take long."

Zara studied her. "What really happened out there?"

Jo met her eyes without blinking. "They were about to poison a child."

Zara didn't flinch. Rita gave a single nod.

"Yeah. That tracks."

A ripple moved through the nearest cluster of shoppers — low voices, quick glances. Jo could feel it spreading across the field the way wind moves through tall grass, bending everything it touches.

The Oracle had told his version. Now the town would weigh it.

Jo straightened the last jar on the table and turned toward the next customer stepping forward.

"Morning," she said warmly. "What can I get you today?"

Behind her, the whispers kept moving.

Chapter Fifty-Eight

Learning the Sound of Laughter

The afternoon sun hung warm over the meadow behind the Lodge.

September had taken the edge off the heat. The air carried the dry sweetness of late grass and something faintly apple-sweet drifting up from the orchard down the hill.

Willow sat on the edge of the porch steps, bare feet resting in the dust, watching the yard.

She had been watching for nearly an hour.

Children were everywhere.

Running. Arguing. Laughing.

It made no sense to her.

Near the fence, Max and Ruth crouched over a tangle of sticks and twine, working at something with the serious focus of engineers.

"What are you doing?" Lucy demanded.

"I told you," Max said patiently. "It's a trap."

"For what?"

Max hesitated.

"Something."

Lucy frowned. "That's not a plan."

Behind them, Ian was chasing Rosa across the grass with a long stick he had declared to be a sword.

"Stop!" Rosa shrieked.

"I'm the dragon!"

"You're not a dragon!"

"I am!"

"You're too small to be a dragon!"

Ian stopped running and drew himself up with great dignity. "That's not how dragons work."

Rosa considered this for a moment.

Then she tackled him anyway.

They hit the grass together in a heap of limbs and laughter.

Willow blinked.

At the camp, children spoke softly. They stayed where they were put. They didn't interrupt the adults, and they certainly didn't tackle each other into the dirt.

She had never seen children behave like this.

She wasn't sure what to make of it.

Across the yard, Marisol sat on a wooden bench beside the garden, working a length of rope into a braid.

Edwin was sprawled in the grass nearby, a small radio set open in front of him.

"You're going to break it again," Marisol warned.

"I fixed it last time."

"You fixed it wrong."

"That's still fixing."

Willow watched all of it. The arguing. The laughter. The easy way the children moved around each other, like water finding its level. No one seemed afraid.

Then Lucy came running past the porch with something cupped in both hands.

A frog.

"Look!" she shouted.

Max groaned. "Oh no."

Lucy thrust the frog proudly toward the others. "It's my friend."

"That's not your friend," Ruth said.

"It is."

"You just met it."

"That's how friends start."

Max leaned in to inspect it. The frog jumped. Lucy shrieked. It landed square on Max's shirt, and for one stunned second, nobody moved.

Then Max shouted. Lucy screamed. Ruth went down in the grass laughing so hard she couldn't breathe. Ian declared it the best thing that had happened all day, possibly all week.

And before Willow could stop herself, she laughed.

It burst out of her like something that had been waiting a long time. Loud. Bright. Real. She slapped a hand over her mouth, eyes wide.

The children turned.

Lucy stared at her. "You laughed."

Willow felt the heat climb her face. "I didn't mean to."

Max frowned. "Why not?"

She hesitated. "Teacher says laughing too much makes people careless."

The children looked at one another. Ruth snorted. "That's dumb."

"Ruth," Marisol said, glancing up from the rope.

"What?" Ruth said. "It is."

Lucy climbed up onto the porch step beside Willow. "You can laugh here."

Willow looked down at her. "Why?"

Lucy shrugged. "Because it's fun."

Willow sat very still. She could feel the echo of it yet, that strange warmth still humming somewhere behind her ribs.

It had come so easily. Too easily.

She wasn't sure that was allowed.

Jo came through the screen door with a tray balanced in both hands, her cane hooked over her forearm. A small plate of cookies, two glasses of milk. She slowed when she spotted Willow standing at the porch rail, watching the children tear up the yard.

She crossed to her without a word and set the tray on the rail.

"Thought you might want to try something."

Willow looked down at the plate. "What is it?"

"Cookies."

A small crease formed between the girl's brows. "I don't remember having those."

"Well." Jo kept her voice easy. "That seems like something we ought to fix."

Willow picked one up, like it might be a trick. It smelled of butter and sugar and something warm she had no word for. She took a careful bite.

Her eyes went wide.

Jo looked out at the yard.

"Good?" she asked.

Willow nodded and took another bite. Then a third.

Across the grass, Lucy's voice cut through the noise. "Told you."

Max was now sprinting after the frog. Ruth was hollering instructions nobody was following. Ian had planted himself between the frog and everyone else, arms spread wide, solemn as a little judge.

The racket rose and fell like wind moving through the pines.

Willow took another bite of the cookie.

And she laughed. Not the small startled sound from before. This one she meant.

Chapter Fifty-Nine

What They Call Burdens

Evening settled slowly across the Lodge.

The sky above the ridge had gone that soft amber color, the kind that lingers just before the sun drops behind the tree line for good. The smell of supper drifted out through the open kitchen windows and hung in the warm summer air.

Inside, the long table had filled again.

Not with food this time.

With people.

Gus sat at the head of it, forearms resting flat on the wood. Marcus had pulled his chair back a few inches, arms crossed, doing more listening than talking. Cole had spread a folded map across the table, though nobody was paying it much attention.

Gin stood near the window.

Franklin paced.

"It's spreading faster than I expected," Cole said.

Franklin stopped.

"How bad?"

Cole shrugged.

"Depends who you talk to."

Marcus kept his voice low.

"The Oracle's version?"

Cole nodded.

"That we interrupted a religious ceremony and took a child who wanted to stay."

Franklin shook his head slowly.

"Anyone who saw that clearing knows that's nonsense."

Marcus lifted one eyebrow.

"Not everyone saw it."

The room held its quiet for a beat.

Gin spoke without turning from the window.

"He's not trying to convince everyone."

They all looked at her.

"He only needs to convince enough."

Gus nodded slowly.

"That's how influence works."

Cole leaned back slightly.

"Zara says most of the older families aren't buying it."

Franklin crossed his arms.

"The new ones might."

Marcus tapped one finger against the table.

"New people don't know the Lodge."

"They know the story they heard first," Cole said.

Silence settled over the room.

Outside, the last light of day dragged long shadows across the yard.

In the hallway just beyond the kitchen door, Willow had gone still.

She hadn't meant to listen. She'd only been moving quietly through the house, learning its corners and sounds the way she'd learned to learn everything -- carefully, without being noticed.

But the voices had carried.

She recognized certain words the way you recognize a scar.

Lodge. Market. Oracle.

And one other.

Burden.

Willow didn't move.

Inside the kitchen, Franklin was still talking.

"The Harbingers believe some people weaken the group."

Gin nodded once.

"They remove what they call burdens."

Something cold moved through Willow's stomach.

Her eyes tracked slowly toward the kitchen doorway. She could see them at the table -- four men, talking low and even, the way men talked when the thing they were discussing was ugly but familiar.

Marcus spoke again.

"Old. Sick. Disabled."

The words dropped into the room without drama.

"Influential," Gus added quietly.

Cole nodded.

"Anyone who threatens the Oracle."

Willow's gaze drifted toward the living room.

Jo sat in her chair near the fireplace, cane leaning against the armrest, Odin stretched across her feet like a warm rug.

Willow had noticed the cane the first day.

Teacher would have called that a burden.

The breath in her chest went tight and thin.

Before she even realized she'd moved, Willow was standing in the kitchen doorway.

Every head turned.

The conversation died.

"Am I a burden?"

Her voice was barely above a whisper. The question settled over the room the way the first cold rain of autumn settles into dry ground — quiet, and impossible to ignore.

Nobody spoke.

Then Jo stood.

She crossed the room, her cane tapping a soft, steady rhythm against the floorboards. When she reached Willow, she lowered herself down until they were eye to eye, her knees protesting the way they always did.

"Where'd you hear that word?" she asked.

Willow's gaze dropped to the floor. "Teacher says some people are burdens."

Jo studied her for a long moment. Then she laid one hand gently on the girl's shoulder.

"That word doesn't mean the same thing here," she said. "Not at the Lodge."

Willow looked up.

Jo's smile was slow and certain. "We don't throw people away because they're different or weak."

"But what if they make things harder?"

"Then we help them."

Willow's eyes drifted to the kitchen table. None of the adults had moved. They were all watching, still and quiet as hearthstone.

Jo followed her gaze. "Family does that," she said.

Outside, the evening wind moved through the trees, lifting the leaves in a long, gentle shudder.

Willow stood very still.

Something in her chest, wound tight for longer than she could name, loosened just enough to let a little light in.

Chapter Sixty

The Story Spreads

The market had grown louder as the morning stretched toward midday.

More wagons had rolled in. The smell of cider and fried bread drifted on the warm air. Children cut between tables while their parents haggled over jars of jam or honey and bundles of dried herbs.

On the surface, it looked like any other summer market day.

But something had shifted in the conversations.

Near the cider stall, two Harbinger women stood beneath a canvas awning. They weren't selling anything. They weren't hurrying. They were simply talking — patient, unhurried — the way people talk when they know exactly what they're doing.

One of them held a small basket of apples and spoke quietly with a gray-haired man Jo recognized from town.

"We don't blame the Lodge," the woman was saying. "They were misled."

The man's brow creased. "Misled how?"

"The ceremony was misunderstood."

"What ceremony?"

The woman's smile was gentle, almost sorrowful. "A blessing ceremony."

The man glanced across the field toward the Lodge table. "They said it was poison."

The second woman shook her head slowly. Her voice never rose above a murmur. "No. It was medicine."

The first one nodded. "All of our children go through it."

The man rubbed the back of his neck. "Then why did they take the girl?"

The two women exchanged the briefest of looks.

"Fear," the first one said finally. The word settled like ash. "Fear makes good people do strange things."

Across the field, Gus had stopped pretending to tend the table. He leaned against the wagon wheel, arms folded loosely over his chest, watching.

Jo stood behind the table, arranging jars. She hadn't missed a word of it either.

"They're good at it," Gus said quietly.

Jo nodded. "Very."

At the far edge of the market, Zara stood speaking with two other vendors, her expression tight. Rita moved slowly through the crowd nearby, listening more than talking.

The Harbinger women continued their conversation.

"We pray for the Lodge," one of them said gently. "That girl will need guidance now."

The gray-haired man frowned. "Guidance?"

The second woman's smile never wavered. "She's been taken from her community, her family."

The man shifted his weight. "I've known Jo Callahan a long time."

"We have too," the first woman said, her voice soft with something that almost sounded like grief. "That's why this is so sad."

The man glanced back toward the Lodge table, and his doubt sat right there on his face for anyone to read.

That was enough.

Across the field, Jo exhaled slowly. "They don't argue," she said. "They sympathize."

Gus nodded. "Harder to fight that."

A woman approached their table carrying a basket of eggs. She hesitated a beat before speaking. "Morning."

Jo smiled warmly. "Morning."

The woman studied the jars on the table, then lowered her voice. "That story about the girl..."

Jo met her eyes without flinching. "Yes?"

The woman shifted her basket from one hand to the other. "I just wanted to hear your side."

Jo nodded once.

“Fair enough.”

She reached for one of the jars and set it gently in front of the woman.

Across the market, the Harbinger women had already moved on to another cluster of shoppers. Their voices carried just far enough to be heard. Just soft enough to sound reasonable.

One conversation at a time, the story kept spreading.

Chapter Sixty-One

First Market

Willow stood at the kitchen doorway and watched the morning move without her.

Market days had their own particular energy. People cut through the room with baskets and crates, boots loud against the floorboards, the smell of coffee and frying eggs drifting through it all. From somewhere inside the pantry, Beth's voice carried out a string of instructions that nobody seemed to be following.

The whole house was in motion.

Willow studied it for a while.

Then she said, "Can I go?"

The room didn't exactly go quiet, but it slowed.

Jo looked up from the bundle of herbs she was tying off with twine. "Go where?"

"The Market."

Nobody answered right away.

Gus leaned back in his chair. "You sure about that?"

Willow lifted one shoulder. "I want to see it again."

Marisol didn't hesitate. "I'll stay with her."

Lily nodded from across the table. "Same."

Fiona set down her pencil. "I can show her where everything is."

Jo pressed both hands flat on the table and let her eyes move from one girl to the next, unhurried. Then she looked at Gus.

"What do you think?"

He scratched at his beard. "Crowded."

"Yep."

"Harbingers will likely be there."

"That too."

Gin spoke up from the doorway. "I'll go."

Hunter, leaning against the frame beside her, shrugged. "Same."

Marcus lowered the paper he'd been reading. "That's four armed escorts."

Gunny Jennings made a quiet sound from his chair near the stove. "I'll walk the market."

Jo lifted one eyebrow. "You were already planning that."

Gunny's mouth curved just slightly. "Habit."

The room eased.

Jo looked back at Willow. "You understand something going in?"

Willow nodded carefully. "People will talk."

"They might."

"Teacher said outsiders would try to confuse us."

Jo tilted her head. "And do you feel confused?"

Willow thought about it honestly. "A little."

"That's okay," Jo said.

Across the table, Lily pushed back her chair.

Willow blinked. "Where are we going?"

"We need to fix your clothes first."

Upstairs, the girls spread a small pile across the bed.

Shirts. Jeans. A pair of boots.

Marisol held up a green sweater.

"This one."

Fiona shook her head. "Too big."

Lily tossed a flannel shirt toward Willow. "Try that."

Willow stood in the middle of the room while they worked around her, uncertain where to put her hands. Back at the camp, everyone wore the same plain clothes. Same colors. Same cuts. Nothing that marked one person from another.

Here everything looked different. Brighter. Softer.

Marisol held out a pair of jeans. "Those should fit."

Willow changed slowly. When she stepped back in, the three girls looked her over the way only girls that age could, thorough and unselfconscious.

Lily nodded. "Better."

Fiona grinned. "You look normal now."

Willow frowned slightly. "I didn't look normal before?"

Marisol smiled and shrugged. "You looked like you needed friends."

Willow had no answer for that.

By midmorning the wagons were rolling toward town.

Willow sat between Marisol and Lily, her hands folded tight in her lap as the road wound down the hill.

The valley opened up ahead of them.

Colorful tents. Tables. People were moving in every direction.

The market seemed bigger and brighter than she remembered. Louder too. It was like looking at everything through a new pair of glasses. Voices carried on the warm air like sparrows flushed from tall grass. Somewhere past the first row of stalls, music was playing.

The wagon slowed near the edge of the field.

Gin climbed down first. Hunter followed. Gunny was already walking the perimeter with slow, deliberate steps, nodding to folks as he passed like a man taking stock of inventory.

"Stay close," Gin said, not loud, not sharp. Just said it.

"We will," Marisol promised.

Gemma dropped down from the wagon beside them and smoothed her shirt. "I'll track down Doc before it gets too thick out there."

Hunter tipped his hat in her direction. "Try not to adopt any more patients."

"No promises."

The girls moved together through the first row of tables. Willow's head turned constantly. Wooden crates stacked with vegetables. Jars of honey catching the sunlight like amber glass. Fresh bread piled in baskets, still warm enough to smell.

Some people smiled as they passed. Some didn't.

Near the cider stall, Willow stopped.

Across the field, two Harbinger women stood beneath a canvas awning. Still. Quiet. Watching. When they saw her, one tilted her head just slightly. The other leaned in and whispered something. A few nearby shoppers turned to look.

The way they watched her made her stomach tighten.

The market noise rolled on around them, unchanged.

But something had shifted.

Marisol slipped her hand into Willow's.

"You're okay," she said softly.

Willow didn't answer. She kept her eyes on the women across the field.

And slowly understood that it wasn't just them.

The whole town was watching.

Chapter Sixty-Two

Words in the Air

The market noise closed back in the moment Willow started walking again.

It was easy to get swept up in it.

Tables filled the field in uneven rows, and people moved steadily between them, trading jars, vegetables, tools, and news. The smell of cider and fresh bread drifted through the warm September air.

For a moment, Willow almost forgot about the Harbinger women studying her.

Almost.

Marisol kept hold of her hand as they moved slowly past the first few stalls.

"Bread first," Lily said. "Always."

"That's not a rule," Fiona replied.

"It is for me."

The baker's table stood near the center of the market beneath a wide canvas shade. Loaves of dark bread and round rolls were stacked in neat rows.

The baker smiled when he saw the girls.

"Morning."

"Morning," Lily said brightly.

Willow watched the easy exchange. People here spoke differently. At the camp, conversations were quiet and careful, words chosen like tools. Here they were loose. Friendly. Sometimes loud.

The baker handed Lily a loaf wrapped in cloth.

"Fresh out of the oven."

Lily inhaled deeply. "Worth waking up for."

The baker laughed.

Then he noticed Willow.

His smile didn't disappear exactly. It just thinned at the edges.

"You must be the girl."

The words weren't unkind. But they weren't warm either.

Marisol answered before Willow could. "This is Willow."

The baker nodded once.

"Well," he said slowly. "Welcome, I suppose."

The pause sat heavier than the words on either side of it.

The girls thanked him and moved on.

Willow didn't ask about it.

But she filed it away.

They passed a table crowded with honey jars, the amber light catching in the glass like trapped summer.

A woman leaned close to another shopper and dropped her voice. Both of them looked at Willow.

The conversation died the moment Marisol glanced over.

Fiona touched Willow's elbow. "Try the cider."

The stall was simple enough — a small wooden barrel, cups stacked beside it. Fiona poured three and passed them around without ceremony.

Willow lifted hers and took a careful sip.

Sweet. Cold. Bright as a bitten apple.

She blinked at the cup.

"That's good," she said quietly.

Fiona grinned. "Told you."

Two men stood talking beside a wagon not far off. They didn't bother to lower their voices much.

"That's the girl."

"From the ceremony?"

"Yeah."

One of them frowned, arms crossed. "They said the Lodge took her."

"They said a lot of things."

The first man's eyes drifted toward the cluster of Harbinger women standing at the far edge of the field. "They looked pretty upset about it."

Marisol's hand tightened around Willow's, small fingers pressing firm.

"Let's go see the goats," she said quickly.

They turned away together.

But the words stayed.

They moved past another row of stalls. Handmade soap and candles sat stacked in baskets, neat and cheerful. The market noise rose around them again.

Laughter. Music. The back-and-forth of haggling.

But underneath it all, Willow still heard the other words.

Taken. Ceremony.

She glanced back. The Harbinger women were still there beneath the awning. One of them caught her eye.

Then smiled.

Not warm. Not cruel. Just like she knew something.

Willow turned away.

"Are they mad?" she asked quietly.

Marisol didn't answer right away.

"No," Lily said.

"Then why do they keep watching me?"

Fiona's voice came softly. "Because you left."

"I didn't leave."

The three girls traded a look between them.None of them corrected her.

Marisol squeezed her hand. "You came somewhere better."

Willow gave a slow nod.

But as they pushed deeper into the crowd, she felt it still, the pressure of those eyes sitting between her shoulder blades like a stone. And above the laughter, above the music, above all of it, the whispers came with her.

Chapter Sixty-Three

The Oracle's Message

The market had thickened by late morning.

Voices layered over one another across the field as people moved between the stalls, unhurried. The smell of cider and warm bread drifted on the summer air, and somewhere nearby a fiddle was being coaxed into tune.

Willow stayed close to the others.

Marisol still held her hand. Neither of them mentioned it.

They were passing the goat pen when Willow slowed without meaning to.

Across the narrow lane between tables, a familiar figure stepped into the open.

Devotion.

Willow went still.

The woman moved through the crowd the way a stone sits in a current, unhurried and unmoved. Her long gray dress brushed the grass as she passed between the stalls. People drifted aside for her without seeming to notice they'd done it.

She wasn't looking at anyone else.

Only Willow.

The fear came fast and settled deep, the way cold water does.

Marisol felt the hand in hers go tight.

"What is it?"

Willow didn't answer.

Devotion stopped a few feet away.

Up close, her face was exactly as Willow remembered it.

Serene.

Certain.

"Hello, Willow."

Her voice was low enough that only the girls caught it.

Marisol eased herself forward, putting her shoulder in front of Willow's.

Lily and Fiona drew closer without a word between them.

Devotion noticed.

She didn't let on.

"I was hoping to see you."

Willow's throat worked.

Devotion tilted her head, patient as still water.

"The Oracle asked me to deliver something."

She held out a small cloth bundle.

Willow stared at it. The smell reached her first — dried herbs, faint and sweet, bleeding through the weave of the fabric.

"It's for your new grandmother," Devotion said.

The words settled over them like a stone dropped in a well.

Marisol's frown cut deep.

Willow didn't move.

Another figure stepped into the edge of the firelight.

Gin.

She'd come up quietly enough that none of them had caught her approach. She stood beside the girls now, arms folded loosely across her chest.

"You done?" she asked.

Her voice was mild.

Devotion glanced at her. "Yes." Then she turned her attention back to Willow. "The Oracle believes your new grandmother will understand the meaning of these."

Willow hesitated. Then slowly she took the bundle. It felt heavier than it looked.

Devotion's gaze lingered on her. "You look well."

Willow said nothing.

For a moment, the noise of the market seemed to pull back around them, like a tide going out.

Then Devotion smiled. Not warmly. Not cruelly. The smile of someone who'd already gotten what they came for.

"Tell Jolene Callahan the Oracle wishes her good health and awaits their meeting."

And just like that, she stepped back into the crowd and was gone.

Marisol let out a slow breath. "Well that was creepy."

Gin reached down and took the bundle from Willow. She untied the cloth carefully, peeling it back.

Inside lay several small packets of dried herbs. Gin recognized them without having to think about it.

Foxglove. Belladonna. St. John's wort.

A thin square of folded paper rested among them. Gin opened it. The handwriting was neat, almost deliberate.

She read it once. Then held it out to Willow.

"Take that to Jo."

Jo stood behind the table when Willow reached her, the girls staying close at her back.

She studied Willow's face for a moment before speaking.

"What happened?"

Willow held out the folded paper, then the cloth bundle.

Jo opened the bundle first. Her eyes moved over the herbs, recognition settling in before she'd touched half of them. Then she unfolded the note.

It was short.

Jolene Callahan,

You and I share an understanding of the natural world. These plants can heal or harm depending on the wisdom of the one who holds them.

Leadership carries the same burden.

I hope we will speak soon.

— The Oracle

She read it twice, then folded it along the same creases.

Gus had appeared at her shoulder, quiet enough that Willow hadn't noticed him move.

"What is it?"

Jo passed him the note and watched his face while he read. The change was subtle — a tightening around the jaw, something cooling in his eyes.

"He's inviting you to a conversation."

"Or a challenge," Jo said.

Gin reached over and retied the cloth bundle without being asked.

"What do you want to do with these?"

Jo looked at the herbs a moment longer.

"Take them home."

The ride back to the Lodge was quieter.

Wagon wheels creaked along the dirt road as the hills rose slowly around them again, the tree line thickening on both sides until the sky narrowed to a pale strip overhead.

Marisol and Lily talked softly about something Willow didn't quite follow. She sat still, watching the trees scroll past, thinking.

When the wagon crested the final ridge, the Lodge came into view below. Smoke drifted from the chimney. Chickens wandered the yard. Everything looked exactly the same as they'd left it.

But Jo saw them the moment the wagon rolled through the gate.

Marcus stood on the porch. Deb sat beside him, one hand resting against the curve of her belly.

Jo climbed down before the wheels had fully stopped.

"You alright?"

Deb smiled, a little sheepish. "Probably nothing."

Marcus looked less convinced.

"She's been having contractions."

Deb waved a hand. "Braxton-Hicks."

Jo glanced at Marcus, then back at Deb. "How long?"

"About an hour."

Jo nodded slowly. "Well," she said, her voice steady. "Let's keep an eye on things."

Behind them the wagon groaned to a stop. Inside the cloth bundle, the Oracle's herbs shifted softly against each other.

And somewhere far down the valley, the man who had sent them waited.

Chapter Sixty-Four

Early

The Lodge had just settled into the quiet rhythm of evening when Deb felt the first one.

She stopped halfway across the kitchen.

Her hand moved instinctively to her stomach.

The tightening lasted only a few seconds, then faded like a held breath released.

Deb frowned.

Beth noticed immediately.

"You okay?"

"Probably."

"What kind of probably?"

Deb shifted her weight.

"It just... tightened."

Beth's eyebrows lifted.

"Again?"

Deb blinked.

"You mean that wasn't the first one?"

Beth's expression said everything before her mouth did.

"Oh honey."

Across the room, Marcus was sharpening a knife at the counter. The steady draw of steel against stone stopped dead.

"What?"

Deb offered him a small smile.

"It's probably nothing."

Marcus set the knife down and straightened.

"What kind of nothing?"

Beth folded her arms.

"The kind that might be labor."

The room went still. Marcus didn't move, didn't speak. He just stood there, and something shifted behind his eyes.

Then, very carefully, he said, "That seems like something we should be certain about."

Deb laughed softly.

"That's what I said."

Beth wrapped a hand around Deb's wrist and steered her toward the nearest kitchen chair. Gemma entered with her medical bag and a huge smile.

"Sit."

Deb sat.

Marcus was already pacing.

"How far apart?"

Beth looked at Deb.

"Have there been more?"

Deb thought a moment.

"Maybe."

Marcus stopped pacing.

"Maybe?"

"They weren't very strong."

"That is not reassuring."

Jo stepped in from the hallway just then, her cane tapping twice on the hardwood before she stopped.

"How are we doing? What's going on?"

Beth answered without looking up.

"Possibly labor."

Marcus pointed at Deb.

"She said maybe."

Jo looked at Deb.

Deb lifted one shoulder.

"They're not bad."

Jo nodded slowly.

"When was the first one?"

"About an hour ago."

Marcus made a noise that sounded suspiciously like distress.

Jo ignored him.

"Alright," she said. "Let's not panic yet."

Marcus opened his mouth.

Jo lifted one finger without looking at him.

"Marcus."

He closed his mouth.

Across the table, Gemma pressed her hand to Deb's stomach again. Another contraction rolled through, and Deb's fingers went white around the edge of the chair.

"That one," she admitted quietly.

Gemma looked up.

"That one's real."

The color left Marcus's face and he swore under his breath.

Jo nodded once.

"Alright." She turned toward the door. "Someone get Gunny."

Marcus was already halfway across the room.

"I'll go."

Jo caught his sleeve.

"No, you won't."

Marcus blinked.

"Why not?"

"Because if this is labor," Jo said calmly, "your job is to stay right here."

He looked deeply unhappy about that.

Hunter appeared in the doorway a moment later, one hand braced on the frame.

"What's going on?"

Jo pointed toward the road.

"Ride to the school. Get Doc Ramirez."

Hunter didn't hesitate.

"On it."

He was gone before the door finished swinging.

Marcus resumed pacing. Faster this time.

Deb watched him for a moment.

"Marcus."

He stopped instantly.

"Yes."

"You're making me nervous."

He sat down without a word.

Jo hid a small smile.

Beth checked Deb again.

"How strong?"

Deb took a slow breath.

"Manageable."

"Good."

Marcus leaned forward.

"How early is this?"

Deb shrugged helplessly.

"I told you I don't know."

Jo rested a hand on Marcus's shoulder.

"Babies come when they come."

He looked at her.

"That is not helpful."

"It's true, though."

Outside, the hoofbeats faded down the road.

Inside the Lodge, things began to shift. Quietly. Purposefully. Water started heating. Clean blankets appeared. The older children were steered, gently but firmly, toward the far end of the house.

Deb leaned back and breathed through another tightening, her jaw set, her eyes steady.

Marcus took her hand and held it.

"This is happening," he said.

Deb smiled at him.

"Looks like."

He shook his head slowly.

"I was more prepared for firefights."

Deb laughed softly at that.

"Me too."

Jo glanced toward the window. The last light of the day was pulling back behind the ridge, slow and final, the way it did up here in summer when the world felt both enormous and close all at once.

"Let's get ready," she said.

Because whether they were ready or not—

a new life was already on the way.

Chapter Sixty-Five

The Long Night Begins

The truck came up the road faster than anyone at the Lodge usually drove. Headlights swept hard across the treeline as it crested the last rise toward the gate. The engine cut before the dust had a chance to settle, and the driver's door swung open in the same motion.

Hunter hit the ground first.

Doc Ramirez came around from the passenger side with his medical bag already in hand.

"How long?" he asked, crossing the yard at a clip.

Marcus met him halfway.

"Couple hours. Maybe."

Doc nodded once.

"Contractions?"

"Getting stronger."

Doc didn't break stride.

"Good."

Marcus blinked.

"That's good?"

"Means things are moving."

Hunter was already pulling a second bag from the truck bed when Jo appeared on the porch, cane in hand, Odin pressing close to her side.

"Kitchen," she said.

Doc dipped his head and went straight in.

Hunter paused just long enough to land a quick clap on Marcus's shoulder.

"You're gonna do great."

Marcus looked at him.

"I am not doing anything."

Hunter grinned.

"Exactly."

Inside the Lodge, something had shifted.

Not panic. Not chaos.

Purpose.

Beth and Jo had already claimed the large bedroom at the end of the hall. Folded blankets sat in a neat stack near the foot of the bed, and a heavy pot of water murmured on the stove, sending thin ribbons of steam toward the ceiling.

Doc stepped through the doorway and swept the room with a practiced eye.

"Good setup."

Gemma stood beside the bed, sleeves rolled to the elbow. Tobias held his place against the wall, arms folded, wearing that particular calm of his that never seemed to waver.

Doc set his bag on the table and snapped it open.

"Let's see where we are."

Deb sat propped against the pillows, hair pulled back from her face. Her cheeks were flushed, but her eyes were steady.

Doc checked her pulse first. Then the baby. A small Doppler hummed to life, and for a moment the room held its breath before the quick, galloping rhythm of a heartbeat filled the silence.

Doc nodded.

"Strong."

Marcus closed his eyes briefly.

Deb let out a long breath. "Good."

He moved on to contraction timing. "How far apart?"

"About six minutes," Gemma said.

He nodded once, unhurried. His gaze moved around the room.

"This is going to take a while."

Beth smiled. "We figured."

Downstairs, the Lodge reorganized itself around the quiet urgency of what was happening upstairs.

Hunter stepped into the kitchen and clapped his hands once.

"Alright, children."

A dozen eyes swung toward him.

He regretted it immediately.

Cole leaned against the doorway, arms crossed.

"You sure you want to lead with that?"

Hunter pointed at him.

"You're helping."

Boone materialized beside them with a stack of plates tucked under one arm.

"What's the plan?"

Hunter gestured toward the living room.

"Food. Games. Keep them busy."

Cole tipped his chin toward the staircase.

"And quiet."

Gus moved into the room then, unhurried, and the children settled just by his presence. His eyes swept once across the gathered faces.

"Your Uncle Marcus needs a little peace right now."

Max's brow creased.

"Is the baby coming?"

Gus smiled, small and steady.

"Working on it."

Lucy caught a fistful of his sleeve.

"Can I see it?"

"Not yet, little bug."

Ruth frowned, practical as always.

"How long does it take?"

Hunter rubbed the back of his neck.

"Uh..."

Cole stepped in cleanly.

"Sometimes a while."

"How long is a while?" Fiona pressed.

Hunter pointed toward the shelf along the far wall, lined with battered board game boxes.

"Long enough for three rounds of Monopoly."

A collective groan rose from the room.

Upstairs, another contraction rolled through, and Deb's knuckles went white on the bed frame.

Marcus sat close beside her, holding her hand like he could anchor her to something steady.

He looked like a man white-knuckling his way through a firefight.

"You're doing great," he said.

Deb raised an eyebrow.

"Marcus."

"Yes?"

"You're crushing my fingers."

He let go like he'd touched a hot stove.

"Sorry."

Jo stood near the window, working a small blend of herbs in the mortar, the pestle making a soft, rhythmic scrape against the stone.

Doc glanced over.

"What's that?"

"Red raspberry leaf and chamomile."

He gave a small nod.

"Good."

He checked on Deb again, quiet and unhurried.

"Progress is steady."

Gemma pressed a cool cloth to Deb's forehead.

"Drink some water."

Deb obeyed without argument, which said plenty about how she was feeling.

The next contraction built slow and mean. Marcus pulled a sharp breath through his nose.

Doc pointed at him without looking up.

"You breathe too."

Marcus blinked.

"Oh."

He tried.

Deb laughed, weak and breathless between contractions.

"You're worse than me."

Tobias smothered a chuckle from his spot against the wall.

Outside, the last light slipped behind the ridge. Inside the Lodge, the lamps came on one by one, soft and steady, pushing back the dark room by room.

The old house settled into the long wait.

Upstairs, slowly and on its own stubborn schedule, a new life was finding its way in.

CHAPTER SIXTY-SIX

THE WAITING HOUSE

The Lodge didn't sleep that night.

It breathed.

From the outside, it looked quiet enough. Lamplight pushed soft and amber through the windows, and smoke rose steadily from the chimney into the cool dark that had settled across the ridge.

Inside, every room held its own kind of waiting.

Downstairs

Hunter had never supervised this many children in his life.

He stood in the middle of the living room holding a stack of blankets like they were tactical equipment, turning a slow circle as if a threat assessment might help.

"Alright," he said.

Nobody listened.

Lucy and Rosa had curled together on the rug, whispering with the intense focus of small conspirators. Max and Ruth argued in low voices over a board game, moving pieces with suspicious authority. Fiona and Lily had claimed the couch, with Leah wedged between them as if she'd always belonged there. Marisol sat beside Willow, braiding rags into ropes for a rug.

Near the kitchen doorway, Quinn sat with one arm draped over the back of his chair, easy as a man twice his age.

Declan and Donovan had posted up nearby, watching him the way barn cats watch something move under the floorboards.

Hunter noticed.

"You two planning something?"

Declan straightened up fast.

"No."

Donovan crossed his arms.

"We're helping."

Quinn grinned at that.

"Are you?"

"Yeah."

Hunter thrust a stack of cups at them.

"Then help by filling those with water."

They were gone before he finished the sentence.

He cut a glance at Quinn.

"You're enjoying this."

Quinn lifted one shoulder.

"Little bit."

On the far side of the room, Jake sat cross-legged beside Edwin and Ian, the three of them deep in conversation that had clearly taken a turn.

Ian looked like he'd swallowed something wrong.

"So the baby just comes out?"

Jake nodded with the confidence of someone who had no idea what he was talking about.

"Pretty much."

Edwin's eyes narrowed.

"That can't be the whole story."

Ian made a face like he'd smelled something bad.

"That's disgusting."

Jake shrugged.

"Babies are messy."

Ian groaned and buried his face in both hands.

Across the room, Lily was doing her level best to be responsible.

"Lucy, you have to be quiet."

Lucy whispered back at full volume.

"I am quiet."

Fiona didn't look up.

"That's not how quiet works."

Leah leaned in like she was sharing classified information.

"I heard babies cry right away."

Lucy's eyes went wide.

"Why?"

"Because they're mad."

Max turned this over carefully, like a stone he wasn't sure about.

"That makes sense."

The Kitchen

Mary and Ellie moved between the stove and the counter in the easy rhythm of women who'd cooked together through harder nights than this one.

Soup rolled in a slow simmer. Clare worked a mound of dough at the table, her hands pressing and folding with the kind of steadiness that didn't come from calm so much as practice.

Grace sat beside her, shaping small rounds with careful fingers.

"Doc will need food eventually," Mary said.

Clare nodded. "And Marcus."

Ellie laughed softly. "He's not eating anything tonight."

Grace glanced toward the staircase.

"Do you think Deb's scared?"

Clare wiped flour from her hands, taking a moment before she answered.

"Probably."

Mary nodded, not looking up from the pot. "But she's tough."

Upstairs

The contraction hit hard and fast.

Deb's knuckles went white on the bed rail.

"Okay," she breathed.

Doc watched from the foot of the bed, arms loose at his sides. "Good."

Marcus looked like he'd taken a hit. "That did not look good."

Gemma checked her again, steady and efficient. "Five minutes now."

Doc nodded. "Progress."

Jo appeared at Deb's side with a warm cup, pressing it gently into her hands. "Small sips."

Deb obeyed without argument.

Marcus had drifted to the corner, then back toward the window, then halfway to the door.

Beth caught his arm on the return trip. "Sit."

"I'm fine."

"You're pacing again."

He looked down at his feet like they'd betrayed him.

He sat.

Then stood again before the chair had time to warm.

Tobias pressed his lips together to keep from laughing and failed. "You're doing great."

Marcus cut him a look that could have stripped bark. "I hate all of you."

Gemma didn't glance up from her work. "That's normal."

Downstairs

The Monopoly game had collapsed into chaos.

The game had devolved into a full courtroom drama, with Hunter planted between Max and Ruth like a reluctant judge.

"You can't charge rent if you're in jail," Max insisted.

"That's not the rule," Ruth said flatly.

"It should be."

Hunter pinched the bridge of his nose.

The twins had drifted back from their water run and settled near Quinn, drawn to him the way younger kids always seemed to be drawn to someone who didn't talk down to them.

Quinn tilted his head slightly in their direction.

"Rule one."

They leaned in.

"What?"

"Stay out of the way."

Both boys nodded with the gravity of recruits receiving orders.

On the far side of the room, Jake had resumed his whispered campaign on Edwin, and whatever he was saying had finally reached Ian's ears.

Ian's face twisted, and he gagged. "Stop talking."

"Why?"

"Because I know what you're talking about now and it's nasty."

Jake laughed, which was answer enough.

Upstairs

Deb curled forward through the contraction, jaw tight, breath coming in slow, deliberate pulls.

Doc watched her a moment, then gave a short nod. "That's it."

Gemma pressed a damp cloth to her forehead. "You're doing great."

Marcus held her hand carefully this time, like he'd learned his lesson. The color hadn't fully returned to his face.

Deb caught him looking and managed a weak smile. "You look worse than I do."

"I would rather fight ten men." He dragged a hand through his hair. "You are unbelievably strong."

Jo let out a low chuckle from the corner. "That's why women run this part of the world."

The next contraction rolled in before the last one had fully passed. Doc repositioned, checked, and when he looked up his expression had changed -- focused, certain.

"Alright." A beat. "Now we're getting somewhere."

The night settled in deep and quiet.

Children had given up the fight against sleep, tangled together across the living room floor in a heap of quilts and slow breath.

Hunter and Quinn moved through the space in easy rotation, keeping watch over the comfortable disorder.

In the kitchen, Clare finally slid the bread into the oven. Mary poured tea without being asked. Ellie stacked bowls with the practiced calm of a woman who needed something useful to do with her hands.

Grace kept glancing toward the staircase.

Upstairs, the rhythm of labor went on.

Slow. Steady.

The kind of force that doesn't hurry for anyone.

And somewhere between one contraction and the next, the Lodge held its breath together, waiting for the moment that would change everything...again.

Chapter Sixty-Seven

Jacqueline Jean

The night had stretched long past the point where time made much sense.

Somewhere downstairs a floorboard creaked.

Someone laughed softly.

Then the house went quiet again.

Upstairs, Deb gripped the bedrail as another contraction crested and broke through her.

Theo watched carefully from the foot of the bed.

"Alright," he said. "That's the one."

Gemma leaned closer.

"You're doing great."

Deb didn't answer. She was too busy breathing.

Marcus stood beside her, pale and rigid, one hand locked around hers. The knuckles of his free hand had gone white where he gripped the bedpost.

"Marcus," Jo said gently.

He blinked. "Yes."

"You're going to break the furniture."

He let go immediately. "Sorry."

Beth chuckled softly from the other side of the bed.

Theo checked again, then gave a single nod.

"Okay."

He said it quietly, but something in his voice changed the air in the room.

"It's time."

Marcus went still as stone.

Deb closed her eyes and let out a slow, steady breath.

"Good," she whispered.

Downstairs, the house had gone quiet in the way old houses do after midnight, settling into itself.

The children slept in loose piles across the living room floor, quilts tangled, small faces slack with the kind of sleep only the young could manage.

Quinn sat in the chair nearest the hearth, his eyes half-open, watching the room the way his father had taught him. The stump of his wrist rested across his knee.

Hunter leaned against the wall beside the staircase, arms folded, boots still on.

Cole and Boone had drifted in and out through the night, checking doors and windows out of habit more than any real sense of threat. Something to do with their hands. Something to do with the waiting. Franklin held a book open, attempting to read and not getting anywhere.

Gus sat at the kitchen table with a cup of coffee that had gone cold an hour ago. He hadn't touched it in a while. Just sat there, turning it slowly between his palms.

The floor above creaked. Sharp. Deliberate.

He looked up.

Hunter's eyes went to the ceiling.

"Sounded different."

Gus set the cup down.

"Yeah."

Neither of them moved.

Upstairs, the room had pulled tight around the moment.

"Alright, Deb," Doc said. "You know what to do."

Deb nodded, pale and damp-haired against the pillow.

Another contraction rolled through her.

"Now," Doc said.

She pushed.

Marcus looked like a man standing at the edge of a cliff he hadn't meant to find. Jo eased a chair quietly behind him.

"Sit."

"I'm fine."

"You're swaying."

He sat.

Tobias leaned against the wall with his arms crossed and a small smile he wasn't trying very hard to hide. Gemma hadn't taken her eyes off Deb.

"You're doing great," she said.

Another push. Doc's voice stayed level and sure.

"That's it. Come on."

Deb gasped. Pushed again.

The room held its breath like the whole house was waiting.

Then a cry split the silence. Sharp and strong and full of pure, indignant life.

Marcus went utterly still.

He stood frozen for a long moment, then covered his face with both hands.

Doc lifted the baby with the careful ease of a man who'd done this before, and held her up just long enough for everyone to see.

"Well," he said. "There she is."

Gemma let out a laugh that sounded more like a sob. Beth turned away just long enough to wipe her eyes. Jo stepped closer to the bed.

Deb leaned back into the pillows, spent and smiling. "Is she okay?"

"Perfect," Doc said, and meant it. He wrapped the baby snugly and placed her into Deb's arms.

The crying stopped almost at once.

Marcus lowered his hands slowly. He stared at that small bundle the way a man stares at something he's afraid to believe in.

"She's real."

Marcus sounded surprised by his own words.

Deb laughed softly. "Very."

He leaned in close, his voice barely a whisper. "Hi."

The baby opened one tiny fist. Marcus touched it with a single finger, and she grabbed on.

He inhaled sharply. "Oh."

Jo smiled at that.

"What's her name?"

Deb looked at Marcus. He swallowed once.

"We talked about a few," he said. "But there was one we kept coming back to."

Deb nodded. "One we both liked."

Marcus took a slow breath. "Jacqueline."

"Jean," Deb added softly.

Jo's smile spread. "Jacqueline Jean Callahan."

"But," Marcus said, and the corner of his mouth moved.

Deb grinned. "We're calling her Jax."

Jo chuckled low. "That suits her just fine."

Doc finished his checks, quiet and efficient, then stepped back and tilted his head toward the door.

"Go tell them."

Marcus blinked. "Tell who?"

Jo laughed outright. "The entire Lodge."

Marcus stepped into the hallway.

The door creaked behind him.

Hunter looked up from the staircase.

"Well?"

Marcus opened his mouth. Then stopped. Whatever he'd planned to say caught somewhere in his chest. Emotion hit him like a freight train.

Hunter grinned. "That good, huh?"

Marcus nodded once, quick and tight. Wiped his eyes with the back of his hand.

"A girl."

Boots hit the stairs before the words were fully out. Gus was already halfway up, one hand on the rail.

"How's Deb?"

Marcus smiled. First time in hours. "She's perfect."

Gus let out a slow breath and nodded, the kind of nod that carries more weight than words.

"And the baby? She got a name?"

Marcus glanced back toward the bedroom door, then turned with something quiet and proud in his face.

"Jacqueline Jean."

Hunter tilted his head. "That's a mouthful."

"We're calling her Jax."

Downstairs, Quinn was already on his feet. The younger kids stirred as voices carried through the Lodge. Lucy blinked up from the couch, hair mussed, eyes still heavy with sleep.

"Is the baby here?"

Max grinned. "Yep."

One by one, the Lodge came back to life. Lamps flickered on. Feet padded across old floorboards.

After a long night of waiting, a new Callahan had arrived.

Chapter Sixty-Eight

Morning at the Lodge

Morning came gently to the Lodge.

The first light slipped through the tall windows and stretched across the worn wooden floors. Outside, the ridge glowed soft gold under the rising sun while mist still clung to the low places between the trees.

Inside, the house stirred slowly back to life.

The smell of coffee came first.

Then bread.

Someone moved quietly through the kitchen, setting pans on the stove and opening the oven door.

A floorboard creaked upstairs.

Another downstairs.

The Lodge woke the way it always did—piece by piece.

Clare stood at the stove working through a stack of pancakes while Mary moved along the counter filling a row of mismatched mugs with coffee and tea. Ellie slid a tray of biscuits onto the table and stepped back to make room.

Grace hovered near the doorway, still searching for something useful to do.

"Did anyone sleep?" she asked.

Mary laughed, quiet and tired.

"A little."

Clare glanced toward the staircase.

"How's Deb?"

"Resting."

Grace leaned in.

"And the baby?"

Mary's smile came easily this time.

"Perfect."

Gus sat at the table with a fresh cup of coffee, looking more human than he had in hours. He'd aged a year overnight and shed it just as fast.

Lucy shuffled in from the hallway, rubbing one eye with her fist.

"Where's the baby?"

Gus chuckled.

"Good morning to you too."

She climbed into the chair beside him without ceremony.

"Can I see her?"

"Soon."

Max materialized behind her a moment later, hair sticking up, already curious.

"Is her name really Jax?"

Gus nodded.

"Sure is."

Max grinned wide.

"That's so cool."

Hunter stepped carefully over a pile of sleeping children.

Quinn was already awake, sitting in the chair by the window.

"You sleep at all?" Hunter asked.

Quinn shrugged.

"Little."

Declan and Donovan were still asleep nearby, one blanket pulled halfway over both of them.

Jake sat cross-legged on the floor whispering to Edwin.

Ian was listening again with a look of horror.

"So she's really here?" Ian asked.

"Yep," Jake said proudly.

"Did you see her?"

"Not yet."

Ian considered this.

"Do babies have teeth?"

Jake stared at him.

"No."

"Oh."

The bedroom door swung open slow and quiet.

Marcus stepped out into the hallway, blinking against the light. He had the look of a man who hadn't slept a wink and couldn't have cared less about it.

Hunter spotted him before he'd taken two steps.

"Well?"

Marcus smiled. It was the kind that started at the corners and took over everything.

"They're both doing great."

Hunter gave a single nod.

"Good."

Marcus turned toward the stairs. Made it about three steps before he stopped cold.

"Actually—"

Hunter raised an eyebrow.

"Yeah?"

Marcus turned back around and leaned in slightly, as though delivering classified information.

"We're limiting visitors."

Hunter burst out laughing, the sound carrying down the empty hallway.

"You lasted six hours."

Marcus crossed his arms over his chest.

"She's very small."

Hunter's grin spread wide.

"They all are. They're babies."

Deb lay propped against a heap of pillows, the morning light falling soft and unhurried across the bed. The baby slept curled against her chest, small as a secret.

Jo sat in the chair by the window, both hands wrapped around a mug of tea, watching.

Gemma leaned in and checked the baby with practiced care, her fingers gentle, her face giving nothing away until it did.

"Still perfect," she said.

Deb smiled, the kind of smile that only comes after a body has been wrung completely out. "She's so tiny."

Jo took a slow sip of her tea. "Most miracles start that way."

The baby stirred, a soft twitch of her fist, then settled back into the deep, boneless sleep of the newly born.

Jo studied her for a long moment. The little face. The rise and fall of that impossibly small chest.

"Jax," she said, her voice barely above a whisper.

Deb looked down at her daughter. Something settled in her expression, quiet and certain.

"Jax."

Marcus hit the bottom stair just as the kitchen erupted.

The children swarmed in from every direction, voices tumbling over each other before he'd even cleared the newel post.

"Can we see the baby?"

"What does she look like?"

"Is she loud?"

"Is she small?"

He raised both hands like a man stopping traffic.

"Alright."

The room settled, more or less.

"Everyone will get to meet her."

A cheer went up immediately.

He lifted one finger.

"But not all at once."

Max was already leaning forward, practically vibrating.

"Can I go first?"

Lucy had bypassed Marcus entirely and gone straight for Gus, tugging his sleeve with both fists.

"Me too."

Gus laughed low in his chest, the sound rolling out of him like distant thunder.

Marcus exhaled slowly. Then the corner of his mouth gave way.

"Okay," he said. "Let's go meet Jax."

The house erupted into motion.

And one by one, in something that only loosely resembled a line, the Lodge began making its way upstairs to welcome the newest Callahan into the world.

Chapter Sixty-Nine

The Circle Widens

By midmorning, the Lodge was no longer quiet.

Word had spread faster than anyone expected.

Boots sounded on the porch. Voices drifted in through the open kitchen window. The screen door swung open and shut often enough that Lucy finally stationed herself nearby to watch who came next.

The Lodge had a new baby.

And everyone wanted to see her.

Clare was still cooking.

Pancakes had given way to eggs, eggs to bacon, bacon to another round of pancakes as more people filtered in. Mary kept the coffee moving in a steady circuit around the table. Ellie had long since abandoned any attempt at organizing seating and was simply pressing plates into whatever hands reached for them. Grace drifted between rooms with clean blankets and cups of tea, quiet and unhurried, as though she'd been doing it her whole life.

At the far end of the table, Gus leaned back in his chair and watched the whole beautiful mess with something close to satisfaction.

Franklin came through the door first, dragging a rag across his knuckles.

"I hear we got a new Callahan."

Gus grinned.

"Sure did."

Franklin glanced toward the stairs.

See, I step out for a few hours to fix the axle on the wagon and miss it. How's Deb?"

"Tired."

"And Marcus?"

Gus chuckled.

"Terrified."

Franklin laughed.

"That sounds right."

Owen arrived next with Merryn perched on his hip.

“Is the baby awake?” Merryn asked immediately.

“Sometimes,” Owen said.

Luke slept in a sling across his chest, unaware of the excitement.

Cole followed behind him.

He took one look at the number of people gathered inside and shook his head.

“This house just got louder.”

Boone clapped him on the shoulder.

"You should hear the upstairs."

Cole glanced toward the stairs.

"Marcus guarding the door?"

"Pretty much."

Marcus was, in fact, guarding the door.

He stood in the hallway with his arms crossed, and Tobias leaned against the wall nearby, doing nothing to hide his amusement.

"You know they're all coming up eventually," Tobias said.

Marcus nodded. "In small groups."

Tobias smiled.

"You've been a father for all of six hours."

Marcus didn't answer. He just eased the bedroom door open and looked inside.

Deb rested against the pillows. Jax slept in her arms.

He pulled the door shut again with the kind of care a man gives to something he can't afford to break.

Tobias shook his head. "You're going to be impossible."

Marcus shrugged. "Probably."

Lucy went first.

Of course she did.

Max followed close behind, chin lifted, doing his best impression of someone at least two years older than he was.

Rosa and Marisol came next, nudging each other softly as they climbed the stairs. Willow brought up the rear, hanging back just enough to keep the others between herself and whatever waited in that room.

They gathered around the bed in a loose, careful cluster, the way children do when they sense something fragile and sacred in the air.

Deb smiled at them. "This is Jax."

Lucy leaned in, eyes round as coins. "She's tiny."

"Most babies are," Gemma said.

Max studied the newborn with the grave attention of a boy who considered himself an authority on most things. "She looks mad."

Jo's laugh was low and quiet. "She'll grow out of that."

Marisol reached out and touched the edge of the blanket, just the corner of it. "She's warm."

Willow didn't move closer. She stood a few feet back, watching the whole of it — the softness, the leaning in, the easy way these people occupied the same space without fear.

No rigid order. No enforced quiet.

Just people who loved each other, plain and simple, and didn't think twice about showing it.

Boots hit the porch again.

Heavier this time.

Buck came through the door first, hat already in his hand before he'd cleared the threshold. Gin stepped in behind him. Gunny Jennings filled the doorway a moment later, with Doc Ramirez coming up from the truck. Kosinski and Morales filed in after.

The kitchen swelled with bodies and noise.

"Well?" Gunny asked.

Gus pushed up from his chair.

"Healthy girl."

Gunny gave one slow nod. "Good."

Buck hadn't moved far from the door. He stood there quietly, turning the brim of his hat in his hands.

"Can I see her?" he asked, his voice barely above a murmur.

Gus reached over and clapped him on the shoulder.

"Course you can. You all can. If you can get past Marcus that is."

Buck stepped into the room first, moving slower than anyone had seen him move in a long time. He stood beside the bed, hat still in his hands, studying the tiny bundle in Deb's arms like he was trying to memorize something.

"Well now," he said softly, his voice rough at the edges. "Ain't you something."

Deb tilted the baby slightly so he could see better. Buck's weathered face went somewhere else for a moment, softer and older and younger all at once.

"She's got a strong set to her," he murmured. "Zeke would've liked that."

Gin came next, quiet as always. She leaned slightly over Jo's shoulder and studied the baby with the same careful attention she usually gave a rifle she was pulling apart and putting back together.

"Looks solid," she said after a moment.

Marcus blinked.

Gin shrugged.

"All the important parts are there."

Gemma laughed under her breath.

Gunny Jennings filled the doorway behind her. He paused just long enough to read the room, then stepped closer and looked down at the baby. He nodded once, slow and deliberate.

"Well," he said, his voice like gravel on a tin roof. "Smallest recruit I've seen in a good while."

Marcus frowned.

Gunny glanced up at him.

"Relax, Colonel. She outranks all of us already."

Father Tom stepped forward last, hands folded loosely as he looked down at the sleeping baby.

“Every child is a gift,” he said softly.

Jo met his eyes across the room.

“A reminder that God and the world hasn’t given up on us yet. Sometimes the world needs reminding.”

Willow hadn't stopped watching the baby.

Jax stirred in Deb's arms, and one tiny fist uncurled, fingers reaching for nothing in particular.

Lucy sucked in a sharp breath. "She moved!"

Soft laughter rolled through the room like woodsmoke.

But Willow didn't laugh. She tracked that small hand with her eyes, then looked at Jo, then at the cane resting against the side of Jo's chair.

Something shifted in the girl's face. Not fear. Not quite curiosity either.

A thought.

A question.

She didn't speak.

Not yet.

Outside the Lodge, the early Autumn sun climbed higher above the ridge.

Inside the house the newest Callahan slept peacefully in her mother's arms.

And slowly, one by one, the people of the Lodge gathered around her.

Chapter Seventy

A Question

The Lodge slowly settled again as the morning stretched toward afternoon.

Visitors drifted back downstairs after meeting the baby, their voices quieter now, their movements slower. The excitement had softened into something calmer.

Deb slept.

Jax slept too, curled against her mother like a small warm stone.

Marcus had finally allowed the door to remain open.

Within reason.

The kitchen had become the center of the house again.

Clare wiped down the counter while Mary rinsed dishes beside her. Ellie stacked plates, and Grace passed out fresh mugs of coffee to anyone who looked like they needed one. Beth swept under the table.

Hunter, Quinn, and Boone had stepped outside to split wood.

Cole and Owen talked quietly near the porch about repairing the chicken fence before winter.

Franklin leaned against the table, listening with half an ear while Ian and Ruth argued about something deeply important involving a checkerboard.

Gus sat in his usual chair watching it all.

The Lodge felt full.

Safe.

Alive.

Willow sat cross-legged on the hallway floor outside Deb's room, her back against the wall.

Marisol settled in beside her.

From inside came a small, soft sound — the baby stirring.

Both girls looked up at the same instant.

"She does that a lot," Marisol whispered.

Willow nodded slowly. "Babies make noises."

Marisol tilted her head. "You've never been around one before?"

"No."

Willow's eyes drifted toward the staircase at the end of the hall, where grown-up voices floated up from below, warm and indistinct.

"People here like babies."

Marisol smiled. "Of course they do."

Willow turned that over in her mind a moment.

"At the camp," she said carefully, "Teacher said babies were important too."

Marisol waited.

"But only the strong ones."

The words settled between them like something dropped and left there.

Marisol's brow creased. "What does that mean?"

"I don't know exactly." Willow glanced back toward the bedroom door. "They watch them, though."

"Who does?"

"The elders."

The smile had gone quiet on Marisol's face. "Watch for what?"

Willow found a loose thread on the rug and pulled at it gently.

"For burdens."

Jo sat in the chair near the bed with a book open in her lap.

She hadn't turned the page in several minutes.

She had heard every word.

Across the room, Father Tom leaned quietly against the window frame.

He had heard it too.

Neither of them spoke.

Not yet.

Marisol looked confused.

"Babies aren't burdens. They can't be, they're babies."

Willow shrugged again.

"That's what Teacher said."

"What happens if they are?"

Willow answered simply.

"They return them to the earth."

Marisol stared at her.

"What does that mean?"

Willow didn't answer right away. Her gaze had drifted back toward the bedroom door. Toward Deb. Toward the tiny bundle sleeping against her chest.

Then her eyes moved, just slightly, to Jo's cane resting against the chair.

She was quiet for a long moment. When she finally spoke, the words came out slow and careful, like she was testing the weight of them before she let them go.

"Would Jax be one?"

The hallway went still.

Inside the bedroom, Jo closed her book. Gently. Without a sound.

By the window, Father Tom straightened.

Neither of them spoke. Neither of them had to.

The question hung in the air like woodsmoke, and the Lodge held its breath around it.

Chapter Seventy-One

What Doc Sees

The Lodge settled into itself as afternoon leaned toward evening.

The visitors had drifted back to their chores, and someone had finally managed to push the younger children outside, where their noise and energy could spend themselves against open sky.

In the bedroom, the light had gone amber and soft.

Deb rested against the pillows, her blonde hair loose around her shoulders, Jax sleeping against her chest in that boneless, fathomless way of newborns. Each breath was slow. Each breath was steady. Each breath seemed almost too small for the world it was entering.

Marcus sat beside the bed, one hand resting lightly on the blanket. He hadn't moved much in the last half hour.

Doc Ramirez stood at the foot of the bed and reached for his medical bag again.

"Mind if I take another look?" he asked.

"Of course," Deb said.

Marcus leaned forward immediately. "Is something wrong?"

Doc shook his head. "No. I just like to check newborns again after the first few hours and then again in a day or two. It's habit."

Marcus eased back. "Right."

Gemma stood at Doc's elbow, ready.

"Alright, little one. Let me take a look at you." Doc lifted Jax gently from Deb's arms and laid her on the blanket beside them. The baby stretched, her tiny fists opening and closing as if testing the air.

Doc worked slowly, his hands practiced and unhurried. He checked her breathing first, then pressed the small stethoscope to her chest.

Strong. Steady.

He nodded once. "Heart sounds good. Very good."

Deb exhaled.

Doc moved to the baby's hands next, opening the tiny fingers with care. Gemma watched closely. He turned the palm upward, his eyes settling there for a moment before moving to the other hand.

Marcus caught the pause. "What is it?"

Doc didn't answer right away. He lifted one of Jax's feet, studied her toes, then ran his fingers gently along her arms. The baby moved slowly, her muscles loose and relaxed. He wrapped her again and set her back down.

The room had gone very quiet.

Deb watched his face. "Doc?"

He pulled a chair close to the bed and sat.

"First," he said, "she's healthy."

Marcus let out a long breath.

Doc folded his hands. "But there are a few things I'm noticing."

Deb's voice held. "What kind of things?"

Doc glanced briefly at Gemma, then back to both of them. "Some babies are born with physical features that suggest a genetic condition. It's called Down syndrome. You may also hear it called trisomy twenty-one."

Marcus blinked. "I've heard of it."

Deb looked down at her daughter. "She doesn't look sick."

"She isn't," Doc said gently. "Most children with Down syndrome are healthy and happy, though they can face certain medical challenges down the road."

Marcus frowned. "You said suggest."

"That word matters," Doc said. He leaned forward slightly. "Normally we'd confirm something like this with a blood test, a look at the chromosomes."

Marcus gave a quiet, humorless laugh. "We don't exactly have a lab anymore."

"No," Doc said. "So we can't confirm it." He gestured toward the baby. "What I can tell you is that Jax has a few physical signs that sometimes appear in babies with Down syndrome."

Deb studied her daughter. "What signs?"

"Low muscle tone, for one. That's why she feels so relaxed when you hold her." He paused. "And there's a crease across her palm that we sometimes see."

Marcus looked at the small hand. "She's just a baby."

"Yes," Doc said softly. "And she's a beautiful one."

Deb looked up. "Could you be wrong?"

Doc smiled. "Absolutely. Some babies have one or two of these features and grow up completely typical." He glanced between the two of them. "There's also something called Mosaic Down syndrome, where only some of the body's cells carry the extra chromosome. When that's the case, the effects tend to be milder."

Marcus rubbed the back of his neck. "And if you're not wrong?"

Doc took his time with the words. "Then Jax may grow a little differently than other children. Some people with Down syndrome live very independent lives. Some need more support. It varies widely, and we won't know more until she shows us."

Deb's arms tightened around the baby.

Not fear. Just instinct.

Marcus leaned forward slowly. "So what do we do?"

Doc's smile was quiet and unhurried. "Exactly what you were already planning."

"Which is?"

Doc nodded toward Deb. "Raise your daughter."

The room held that for a moment.

Jo's voice came from the chair near the window. "Sounds like a good plan to me."

Father Tom smiled and said nothing.

Marcus looked down at Jax's tiny hand, the fingers curled loosely around his own. He was quiet for a long moment.

Then he nodded once.

"Yeah," he said softly. "That sounds about right."

Chapter Seventy-Two

No Burden

Evening settled slowly over the Lodge.

The last of the sunlight slipped behind the ridge, leaving the old building wrapped in that soft gray quiet that came just before the lanterns were lit.

The bedroom was warm and still.

Deb rested against the pillows, Jax curled against her chest, the baby's tiny mouth making small, dreaming motions.

Marcus sat beside the bed, one hand resting near the baby's back. Not hovering. Just there. As though his presence alone could hold the world at a safe distance.

Doc snapped his medical bag shut.

"She looks good," he said again.

Deb nodded.

Marcus didn't move.

Theo paused at the bedside, his eyes moving once more over mother and child before he turned toward the door.

"Get some rest," he said. "Both of you."

"We will," Deb said.

He nodded once and stepped out into the hallway.

The hallway wasn't empty.

Willow and Marisol sat cross-legged on the floor a few feet back, a book spread open between them. They'd gone still as fence posts.

Doc caught Marisol's face first. Then Willow's. He gave them both a smile, quiet nod, and moved on down the stairs.

Jo pulled the bedroom door most of the way shut behind her.

Father Tom stayed near the window, hands loosely folded. Deb's eyes had gone back to Jax.

"She seems so small."

"All babies do," Jo said gently.

Marcus ran his thumb slowly across the edge of the baby's blanket. Doc's words still hung in the air between them, unhurried, the way truth tends to settle.

Deb spoke first. "Do you think he's right?"

Jo didn't rush her answer. "I think Doc sees things clearly."

Marcus nodded, slow and sure.

"We'll figure it out."

Jo leaned forward just slightly. "You will."

The bedroom door creaked open a few inches.

Jo looked up.

Willow stood in the doorway, and behind her, Marisol hovered with that particular uncertainty of a child who wasn't sure if she'd done something wrong.

"Sorry," Marisol said quickly. "We didn't mean to listen."

Jo waved a hand.

"Come in, girls."

The girls stepped inside. Willow's eyes went straight to the baby.

"Is she okay?"

Deb smiled softly. "She's perfect."

Willow hesitated. "I heard what the doctor said."

The room settled into quiet. Marcus watched her carefully. She looked confused more than anything, working through something she hadn't been given the right tools to sort out.

"At the camp," she said slowly, "Teacher said sometimes babies are born wrong." Deb's arms tightened around Jax without thinking. Willow looked down at the floor. "They said if someone was a burden... they returned them to the earth."

The words just sat there.

Marisol shifted beside her. "But she's not a burden," she said quickly.

Willow looked up. Her eyes moved from the baby to Jo, to the cane leaning against the chair, then back to the baby.

"Is she going to be?"

It was a small question. It landed like a stone dropped into still water.

Marcus straightened. Deb drew the baby closer. Father Tom said nothing.

Jo rose slowly from her chair and crossed the room. She stopped beside Willow and looked for a moment at the child sleeping in Deb's arms. Then she looked back at the girl.

"No," she said.

Willow waited.

Jo rested one hand on the back of her cane. "In this house, we don't measure people by what they can do for us."

Willow's brow creased. "Then how do you know if someone matters?"

Jo smiled. "We don't decide that." She gestured toward the baby. "Every person is born already mattering."

Willow turned that over in her mind. "But what if someone needs help forever?"

"Then we help them."

"Doesn't that make them a burden?"

Jo's voice stayed easy and steady. "No." She leaned a little closer. "That makes them family."

The room went quiet.

Willow looked back at Jax. The baby stretched one tiny fist and made a soft sound in her sleep. Marisol smiled. Willow watched the movement the way you watch something you don't fully trust yet but want to.

"Even if she grows different?"

"Especially then."

Willow stood there a long moment. Something in her face shifted, not full understanding, but the first hairline crack in everything she'd been taught to believe.

Father Tom spoke quietly from across the room. "Sometimes the strongest thing a community can do is take care of the people who need it most."

Willow nodded slowly. She looked at Jax one more time.

And for the first time since she'd come to the Lodge, she smiled a soft genuine smile.

Chapter Seventy-Three

How Do You Play?

The afternoon sun had done its work on the morning chill, burning it off clean by the time the kids spilled out behind the Lodge.

The grass had gone warm underfoot, the air carrying pine and the faint green smell of lake water drifting up from the valley below.

It started the way most Lodge chaos did.

Boredom.

Jake made it outside first, Edwin and Max close behind, the twins a half-step after. Fiona and Lily followed with a laundry basket Clare had pressed on them, firm instructions about the clothesline attached.

They managed three shirts before Lucy found the water pump.

That was all it took.

Max worked the handle while Lucy held her hands under the cold stream, shrieking the moment the water hit her warm skin.

"It's freezing!"

"That's the point," Jake said.

Edwin leaned against the fence post, arms crossed. "What point?"

Jake's grin came slow and deliberate. "You'll see."

He grabbed the empty bucket sitting by the garden. Max pumped faster. Water splashed off Lucy's hands and darkened the dry dirt around the pump, and she giggled like she couldn't help it. Merryn joined her and the two girls giggled until they could barely breathe.

Jake filled the bucket halfway, lifted it with exaggerated care, walked toward Edwin with his eyes straight ahead like he was carrying communion wine.

Then dumped it over Edwin's head.

Edwin stood there. Dripping. Blinking. The yard went churchyard quiet.

He dragged a hand down his face and wiped the water from his eyes.

"Oh," he said.

And then all hell broke loose.

Within seconds, the yard had gone to war.

Buckets. Tin cups. A watering can liberated from the garden.

Max tore across the grass shrieking, Lucy hot on his heels with a cup she had no intention of wasting. Declan and Donovan had chosen sides before the first splash hit dirt, and they were taking it with the kind of dead seriousness that only thirteen-year-olds can bring to something completely ridiculous.

Fiona held her ground at the edge of it all, arms crossed, staying dry through sheer force of will.

She lasted thirty seconds.

Lily caught a full splash square across the back and spun around, dripping.

"Jake!"

Jake ran.

Ruth jumped from the porch step and ran into the fray.

The pump handle clanged in a wild, frantic rhythm as someone worked it without mercy. Water arced and scattered and soaked everything it touched.

Laughter rolled off the side of the Lodge and into the early Autumn trees.

Willow stood near the edge of the yard, watching.

Marisol stood beside her.

"They're fighting," Willow said.

Marisol shook her head. "No they're not."

Willow watched Jake dump another bucket over Max, who collapsed into the grass laughing.

"That looks like fighting."

Marisol smiled. "That's playing."

Willow frowned slightly. "What's the difference?"

Marisol thought about it, then shrugged. "I don't know."

Another splash arced past them. Lucy ran by squealing, soaking wet and not caring even a little.

Willow studied the other children. No one seemed angry. No one seemed afraid. They were shouting, running, laughing, getting drenched, and doing it all over again.

She looked at Marisol. "How do you play?"

"You just... do."

"That's not very clear."

Marisol laughed. "You want to try?"

Willow hesitated.

Jake spotted them. His grin spread like something he couldn't help. "Oh no."

Marisol sighed. "Too late."

Jake filled a cup and started walking toward them with the unhurried confidence of someone who already knew how this was going to go.

Willow stiffened. "What is he doing?"

"Recruiting."

Jake stopped a few feet away. "You two look dry."

Willow stared at the cup. "You're going to throw that water."

"That's the game."

"Why?"

He shrugged. "Because it's fun."

Willow considered that carefully, the way she considered most things. Then she asked, dead serious, "Am I allowed to throw water back?"

Jake's grin stretched wider. "Oh yeah."

She nodded once. "Alright."

He tossed the cup. It splashed harmlessly against her shoulder. She blinked, then turned and slowly lifted the empty bucket sitting beside the pump.

Max saw it coming. "Oh no."

Willow filled it halfway, carried it carefully across the wet grass while Jake backed away.

"You don't have to go that big right away."

She tipped the bucket. Water came down over Jake from crown to boot heel. The yard erupted. Edwin's cheers rang the loudest.

Jake stood there dripping, blinking water out of his eyes.

Willow watched him. "Did I do it right?"

He wiped his face with the back of his hand. "Perfect," he said.

And for the second time that day, Willow laughed.

Chapter Seventy-Four

Whispers at Market

Even after the power failed.

Even after the world shrank down to the handful of communities still willing to trade with one another.

People still came to the Market.

Wagons creaked down the old road before sunup. Horses stamped in the cool morning air while tables were unfolded and crates stacked. The smells hadn't changed much.

Fresh bread. Apples. Leather. Smoke.

For a few hours each week, you could almost forget what had been lost.

Almost.

Jo stepped down carefully from the wagon beside the long wooden table that had slowly become the Lodge's place at the Market.

Gus handed her the cane before lifting the first crate of vegetables.

"You alright?"

Jo nodded.

“Just stiff.”

Gus studied her for a moment.

“You say the word and we head home.”

Jo smiled faintly.

“I will. You need to get back. “You need to get back. Ty can take me home if I need to leave later.”

Gus grunted and reached for another crate that was full of onions and garlic.

They began setting up their usual spread.

Tomatoes.

Fermented Pickles.

A basket of late raspberries.

Mary’s jars of preserves.

Herbal remedies.

Across the square other vendors were doing the same.

Beth and Boone arrived a few minutes later with another wagon.

Boone set a crate down beside the table and stretched his back.

“Looks busy today.”

Jo glanced across the Market.

It did.

But something about it felt different.

Quieter.

Not in the usual way.

More like a room where people had stopped talking when someone walked in.

Beth noticed it too.

“People are staring.”

Gus followed her gaze.

Several small clusters of people stood near the well.

They weren't shouting.

They weren't arguing.

They were watching.

Zara Malard crossed the square from the far side, moving fast, her expression pulled tight.

Jo straightened.

"Well, that's not a social visit."

Zara reached the table and dropped her voice.

"I thought you should hear this first."

Gus shifted his weight against the wagon wheel.

"Hear what?"

Zara glanced around the square before she spoke.

"The rumor mill is in overdrive."

Something tightened in Jo's chest. Old and familiar.

"What do you mean?"

Zara exhaled slowly.

"The Harbingers are still telling people the Lodge kidnapped one of their children."

Beth scoffed.

"That's ridiculous. People saw Willow just a week or two ago when she was here."

"Most people here know that, Beth." Zara's voice dropped further. "But some of the newer families..."

Gus finished it quietly.

"Don't."

Zara shook her head.

"The Oracle's saying Willow was taken during a religious ceremony."

Beth crossed her arms.

"What ceremony?"

Zara's expression darkened.

"One where the child was supposed to return to the earth."

The words landed like cold water on bare skin.

Gus didn't move. Neither did Boone.

After a moment, Gus spoke.

"So he's admitting it."

"Not directly."

"Of course not."

"He's calling it symbolic."

Beth let out a short, hard laugh.

"Symbolic murder."

"He's also saying the Lodge interfered with something sacred. That you all are trying to be a dictator or a prophet. Nonsense."

Jo looked out across the square. People were still glancing toward their table. Still whispering. Still pretending they weren't.

"Anything else?"

Zara hesitated.

"Yes."

Gus looked at her.

"What?"

Zara's voice dropped again, nearly beneath the noise of the market.

"He's started using your name."

Jo turned slowly.

"Mine."

"He's telling people the Lodge is led by a woman who believes she has the right to decide what lives and what dies."

Beth stared at her.

"That's the exact opposite of what happened."

Zara spread her hands.

"I know."

Gus kept his voice even.

"What else?"

Zara met Jo's eyes.

"That you've become dangerous."

Nobody spoke for a long moment.

The market moved around them anyway. Voices. Trade. A pair of children sprinting past the well like the world hadn't changed at all.

Jo rested both hands flat on the edge of the table.

"Well," she said quietly. "That's inconvenient."

Gus studied her face.

"You alright?"

"Yes."

"Maybe I should just take you home now, Jo."

She looked back across the square at the watching faces.

"He's afraid."

Boone frowned.

"Of what?"

Jo answered without hesitation.

"Of people thinking for themselves."

Gus gave a slow nod.

"Zeke used to say the same thing."

Jo's gaze drifted briefly toward the ridgeline beyond town.

"Yes," she said softly. "He did."

And across the market, the whispers went on.

Chapter Seventy-Five

Watching the Edges

The wagon rolled slowly back up the ridge road toward the Lodge.

Late afternoon light filtered through the tall pines, laying long bars of gold across the dirt track. The horses moved at an easy pace, wheels crunching steadily over gravel and pine needles.

For a while, nobody spoke.

Jo sat beside Gus on the wagon bench, her cane resting across her knees. Beth and Boone rode in the back alongside the empty crates.

The Market had ended the way it always did.

Quietly.

But something in the air had shifted, and they all felt it.

Beth broke the silence first.

"Well," she said, "that was cheerful."

Boone snorted.

"Could've been worse."

Beth raised an eyebrow.

"How?"

He thought about it a moment.

"They could've been throwing rocks."

The corner of Jo's mouth lifted.

"Give them time."

They reached the clearing just before the Lodge came into view, the roofline appearing first through the breaks in the timber. Then the garden rows. Then the broad yard, loud with the afternoon.

Max and Jake were at it across the grass, brandishing sticks that had long since become swords in their minds. Lucy churned along behind them, arms pumping, determined to be part of whatever it was whether they wanted her or not.

Near the porch, Quinn and Hunter were working through a cord of wood. The maul rose and fell in its steady rhythm, each crack rolling clean across the clearing.

Gus eased the wagon to a stop and sat a moment, just taking it in.

"Home."

Inside the Lodge, the evening routine had already taken hold.

The kitchen smelled of onions and venison, warm and close against the cooling air outside.

Mary and Ellie stood shoulder to shoulder at the stove while Clare worked the cutting board, her knife moving steady through a pile of root vegetables. Grace carried a basket of bread to the table without being asked.

The noise level climbed the moment the wagon door swung open.

"How was Market?" Fiona called from the hallway.

Beth set the first crate down on the table with a thud.

"Interesting."

One word. That was enough.

The room filled within minutes. Franklin appeared in the doorway, wiping his hands on a shop rag. Cole came in from outside a moment later, Riley Brenner a half-step behind him. Gunny was last through the door, hauling a small crate of ammunition he'd been counting out in the barn. He set it down and looked around at the gathered faces.

"Why does everybody look like someone kicked the dog?"

Boone answered first. "Oracle's stirring the pot."

Gunny nodded once. "Figured."

Jo eased into her chair near the head of the table. "He's telling people we kidnapped Willow again."

Riley's eyes narrowed just slightly. "Not surprising."

Cole folded his arms. "What exactly is he saying?"

Beth repeated Zara's warning word for word. When she finished, the only sounds were the simmer of the pot and the fire settling in the hearth.

Gunny scratched his jaw. "So he's framing it as a religious dispute."

"Looks that way," Gus said.

Cole nodded slowly. "That's smart."

Beth looked at him. "You're admiring him now?"

"No." Cole's voice stayed even. "I'm recognizing the tactic."

He moved to the window and stood looking out toward the ridge. "If he makes it about belief instead of violence, people hesitate."

"Especially people who weren't there," Riley said.

Jo watched them both carefully. "What comes next, do you think?"

Gunny didn't hesitate. "Pressure."

Franklin frowned. "What kind?"

"Social first." Gunny's voice was flat, matter-of-fact. "Whispers. Doubt. People pulling away from you a little at a time."

Riley nodded. "Maybe a few concerned conversations."

"Then he waits," Cole added quietly, "to see who sides with who."

Boone shifted against the table. "You think it'll go that far?"

Cole looked at his brother. "It already has."

Outside, the children's laughter drifted through the open window.

Willow stood near the fence watching Max and Jake argue loudly over the rules of whatever game they had invented. Marisol tried to explain something to both of them at once. Lucy ignored all of it and ran straight through the middle of the argument, holding a stick above her head like a battle flag.

Willow laughed softly.

Inside the Lodge, the adults had gone quiet.

Jo listened to the voices outside for a moment, the way you might hold your hands near a fire before stepping back out into the cold.

Then she looked at the people gathered around her kitchen.

"Well," she said. "We'll just have to keep being who we are."

Gunny nodded once.

"That tends to annoy the wrong people."

Jo smiled faintly.

"Yes," she said. "I've noticed."

Outside, the children kept shouting. Inside, the adults began quietly making ready for the trouble they all knew was coming.

Chapter Seventy-Six

Missing

Market morning came cool and bright.

The early frost that had touched the fields the week before had pulled back, leaving the valley wrapped in that last, borrowed warmth the mountains sometimes offered before winter made up its mind. It wouldn't last. It never did.

Wagons rolled in along the road. Voices carried across the square. The smell of bread and chicory coffee cut through the cold air like something worth holding onto.

From a distance, it looked like any other market day.

Up close, it didn't.

Jo noticed it straight off. People still came to the Lodge table. Still bought vegetables, still thanked Beth for the preserves and Mary for the bread. But the conversations had grown short and clipped, the easy back-and-forth of neighbors replaced by something careful. Eyes moved faster than they used to. More than once, Jo caught someone glance toward the Harbinger stalls before they spoke, like they were checking which way the wind was blowing.

Gus noticed it too. He leaned in close while setting out the baskets of tomatoes.

"They're measuring their words."

Jo nodded slowly.

"People always do when they think someone is listening."

Across the square, the Harbinger tables were already laid out. Simple cloth. Dried herbs stacked in neat bundles. Several baskets of apples. Devotion moved among them without hurry, speaking with the quiet confidence of a woman who believed the ground beneath her feet already belonged to her.

Willow stood beside Marisol near the Lodge wagon, watching the Market with the quiet attention of a child who had learned early that watching kept you alive.

Her eyes drifted toward the Harbinger tables. Then her brow creased.

"That's wrong."

Marisol looked up from the basket she was sorting. "What is?"

Willow pointed without pointing, just a tilt of her chin. "That woman."

Jo followed the direction of it.

One of the Harbinger stalls was being managed by a younger woman she didn't recognize, standing stiffly behind the table, arranging bundles of dried herbs with movements that were a little too careful, a little too deliberate.

"What about her?" Jo asked.

Willow hesitated. "That's not who runs that table."

Marisol squinted across the square. "Are you sure?"

"Very sure."

Jo turned slightly, keeping her voice easy. "Who usually does?"

Willow studied the stall a moment. "Constance. She's older." A pause. "She coughs a lot."

"Maybe she's just sick," Marisol offered.

Willow shook her head. "She was sick before. She still came."

Jo watched the younger woman move behind the table. "Did you know her well?"

Willow shrugged one shoulder. "She was nice. When I was small she used to give me extra bread." Her voice stayed flat, but something behind it didn't. "She said children shouldn't be hungry."

Marisol softened. "That sounds like a good woman."

Willow nodded once.

Jo glanced back across the square. "Have you seen her lately?"

"No."

A few seconds settled between them.

"She never misses Market," Willow said quietly.

Across the square, Devotion finished speaking with a farmer and turned briefly toward the Lodge table.

Her eyes moved across the group.

Past Jo.

Past Gus.

Then they settled on Willow.

Her smile never wavered.

But she didn't wave.

Jo felt something cold pass through her chest, quiet as a draft under a door.

She turned back to Willow.

"When was the last time you saw Constance?"

Willow took her time with it.

"Before the ceremony."

"What ceremony?"

No hesitation.

"The one where they returned someone to the earth."

The words came out soft. Almost gentle.

The weight behind them was anything but.

Jo set her hand flat on the table. Steadying herself without meaning to.

"If you were with us, how did you know when the ceremony happened?" Jo asked gently.

"After the ceremony, everyone wears their sash on the opposite side for three days as a remembrance."

Jo looked across the crowd and saw every Harbinger had their sash on the left today.

Across the square, Devotion had already moved on, leaning toward another customer, easy and pleasant as a summer afternoon.

The market carried on around them. Bartering hands and raised voices. Children cutting past the well in a knot of noise and laughter. The whole ordinary machinery of a Tuesday morning.

Jo looked toward Gus.

His jaw had gone still. He'd heard it.

Neither of them spoke.

Not yet.

But the thought that had taken root in the back of Jo's mind was already spreading, slow and sure, like frost working its way under a windowsill.

It didn't feel like coincidence.

It didn't feel like coincidence at all.

CHAPTER SEVENTY-SEVEN

SIGNS IN THE WOODS

The woods behind the Market were quiet in the late afternoon.

Most people never wandered far past the last stalls and wagons. A narrow deer trail slipped away through the trees toward the ridge, disappearing into the thick pine and maple that crowded the hills above town.

Cole stood just inside the tree line, studying the ground.

Behind him Riley crouched beside a patch of disturbed soil while Yaz moved slowly through the brush ten yards away, reading the forest floor the way other people read a book.

Gunny leaned against a tree with his arms folded.

Gin knelt beside Riley, brushing loose dirt aside with careful fingers.

No one had spoken in a few minutes.

The woods carried sound differently.

Better to listen.

After a while Gunny broke the silence.

"So."

Cole didn't look up.

"So."

Gunny nodded toward the trail.

"This where she usually walked?"

"According to Willow."

Riley lifted a small broken twig between her fingers.

"Someone came through here recently."

Yaz spoke from the brush.

"Two people."

Everyone turned slightly toward him.

He pointed to the soft patch of soil near the roots of a maple.

"One set older. Slow steps."

Then he gestured to a second track.

"The other younger."

Gin leaned closer.

"Helping her walk."

Yaz nodded.

"Or guiding."

Cole frowned.

"Guiding where?"

Yaz straightened and looked farther up the slope.

"That way."

The trail narrowed as it climbed the ridge.

Leaves had been disturbed recently.

Just enough to notice if you knew what you were looking for.

Riley stood and followed Yaz a few steps.

"You think they carried her part of the way?"

Yaz shook his head.

"No drag marks."

Gunny pushed away from the tree.

"So she walked."

"Looks that way."

Cole rubbed his chin.

"That doesn't sound like someone being forced."

Gin brushed more dirt away beside the roots.

"Not necessarily."

She held something up between her fingers.

A small bundle of dried leaves tied loosely with twine.

Gunny stepped closer.

"What's that?"

Gin sniffed it lightly.

"Herbs."

"Medicinal?"

Gin shook her head slowly.

"Some."

Cole stepped over to look. He had learned a lot from his mother over the years.

She pointed to a darker leaf near the center.

"But not all." Cole said, recognizing the leaf.

Riley crouched beside Gin.

"What kind?"

Gin spoke quietly.

"Foxglove."

Cole frowned.

"That's poison."

"In the right dose."

Gin studied the small bundle again.

"Or the wrong one."

No one spoke for a moment.

Yaz moved farther up the trail.

A few seconds later he stopped.

"Here."

The others joined him.

The ground dipped slightly near a fallen log.

Leaves had been disturbed recently.

But not by animals.

By feet.

Several of them.

Cole crouched and brushed the dirt aside.

The soil beneath was darker.

Fresh.

Riley looked at the shape of the disturbed ground.

"Not a grave."

Yaz shook his head.

"No."

Gunny studied the trees around them.

"How many people you think were here?"

Yaz answered immediately.

"Five."

Cole looked up.

"Witnesses."

Cole nodded slowly.

"Ceremony."

Gunny's jaw tightened.

"So she didn't die here."

"No," Yaz said.

He pointed deeper into the trees.

"They carried her after."

Cole followed the direction of his hand.

"Where?"

Yaz's eyes moved slowly across the forest.

"Farther than we should go today."

Gunny gave a short nod.

"Harbinger territory."

Gin stood and brushed dirt from her hands.

"They didn't kill her here."

Cole looked down at the disturbed earth again.

"No."

Riley's voice was quiet.

"They said they returned her to the earth."

Gin shook her head.

"No."

She looked at the small bundle of herbs still resting in her palm.

"They put her to sleep first."

The woods fell quiet again.

Somewhere deeper in the forest a crow called once and then went silent.

Gunny looked toward the ridge where the Harbinger camp sat somewhere beyond the trees.

"Well," he said.

"That answers one question."

Cole stood slowly.

"Which one?"

Gunny's voice stayed calm.

"They're not just talking about it."

No one disagreed.

And for the first time since Willow had mentioned the missing woman—

the suspicion had turned into something closer to proof.

Chapter Seventy-Eight

What it Means

The sun had already slipped behind the ridge by the time they reached the Lodge.

Evening came down over the clearing the way it always did in the mountains, slow and heavy, pressing the treeline in close and stretching the shadows long across the yard. Lantern light glowed warm in the windows. The last of the children's voices faded toward bedtime.

Cole stepped down from the truck first.

Gunny followed.

Gin and Riley climbed out of the back. Yaz moved off without a word toward the barn, leading the borrowed horses back into the dark.

Nobody had talked much on the drive in.

There wasn't much worth saying.

Inside, the smell of supper still lingered. Franklin sat at the far end of the table working on a lantern, his tools spread in a neat row beside him. Tobias and Boone moved quietly between the table and the basin, clearing the last of the dishes. Father Tom stood near the stove with a towel in his hands.

They all looked up at once.

Boone read their faces before anyone opened their mouth.

"Well," he said slowly. "That doesn't look good."

Cole pulled out a chair and sat down. "No."

Gin set the small bundle of herbs on the table.

Gunny closed the door behind them.

"What'd you find?" Franklin asked.

Cole nodded toward the bundle. "Start there."

Tobias leaned forward. "Foxglove."

Gin nodded. "And more besides."

Boone frowned. "Medicinal herbs?"

"Some." Gin pointed to a darker cluster near the center. "Not those."

Franklin looked between them. "So what are we talking about?"

Gunny answered. "They walked her into the woods."

The room went still.

Cole continued. "Five people. Maybe six."

"A ceremony, like with Willow." Riley added.

Father Tom lowered the towel slowly. "And afterward?"

Cole exhaled. "They carried her deeper into the ridge."

Boone leaned back. "So they buried her somewhere."

Gin tapped the herbs. "They poisoned her."

The words settled over the room like smoke.

Franklin stared at the bundle on the table.

Father Tom's voice dropped to almost nothing. "Peaceful."

Gunny snorted. "Convenient."

Cole leaned forward, elbows on the table.

"They didn't hide it."

Boone frowned.

"What?"

"They wanted witnesses."

Riley nodded.

"That clearing was prepared."

Franklin shook his head slowly.

"Why?"

Cole answered without hesitation.

"To make it normal. To hide the reality from his brainwashed followers. Make it look like something ceremonial to outsiders."

Silence settled over the room.

Outside, they heard Grace laugh somewhere near the barn, Quinn's teasing tone answered. The sound felt like it belonged to a different world.

The door opened.

Buck stepped in. His eyes swept the room once, taking in the dried herbs on the table, the set of every face. He didn't need it spelled out.

"They killed another one."

Nobody corrected him.

He walked to the table. His jaw worked before he spoke again.

"Who?"

Gin nodded. "An elderly Harbinger woman."

Buck let out a long breath through his nose.

"How many now?"

Cole answered quietly.

"Enough."

Buck's eyes hardened.

"Then what are we waiting for?"

Gunny met his stare.

"Careful."

Buck rounded on him.

"Careful?" His voice climbed. "They killed Zeke." He pointed toward the tree line beyond the window. "And now they're killing their own people."

Nobody spoke.

Buck's palm hit the table.

"You gonna tell me we just sit here and watch?"

Gunny didn't raise his voice.

"That's exactly what I'm telling you."

Buck's eyes flashed.

Gunny leaned forward slightly.

"You start a war with believers, Buck, you better be ready to fight every man, woman, and child who thinks they're doing God's work."

Buck stared at him.

"You think that scares me?"

"No."

Gunny's voice stayed level.

"But it should."

The air in the room pulled tight.

Jo's voice came quietly from the doorway.

"That's enough, gentlemen."

Everyone turned.

She stood with one hand resting on her cane, Gus a half-step behind her. Neither of them looked surprised.

She moved slowly to the table, her eyes traveling across each face before settling on the herbs laid out between them.

"They used tea again," she said.

Gin nodded.

Jo looked back up. "And they had witnesses."

"Yes," Cole said quietly.

She let that sit for a moment.

"They want it to look peaceful."

Father Tom gave a single nod. "Ritual."

Jo exhaled softly, then turned toward Buck.

"I understand why you're angry."

Buck said nothing.

"But anger is exactly what he wants."

Buck's brow creased. "Who?"

"The Oracle."

The room went quiet.

Jo set both hands flat on the table. "We go into those woods with guns blazing, we become every story he's been telling about us."

Gunny dipped his chin once.

Buck turned toward the dark window, jaw working.

"So we watch," Jo said.

Cole picked it up immediately. "We gather proof."

Yaz stepped back in from the porch, moving quiet as smoke. "And we learn their pattern."

Jo nodded. "Yes." She looked around the table. "Because when we stop him, we stop him in the daylight."

Outside, a soft wind moved through the pines. Inside the Lodge, no one argued.

But the weight of what they'd just named settled over the room like the first pressure of a coming storm.

Chapter Seventy-Nine

What Children Hear

The afternoon lay warm and unhurried over the Lodge.

Whatever tension had coiled through the night before seemed to loosen in the heat, dissolving into the ordinary pulse of the place. Laundry snapped between two pines, pushed by a lazy breeze. Someone had left the pump running again, and a thin ribbon of water traced its way down the dirt path toward the garden beds.

The children had claimed the far edge of the yard, where the mown grass gave way to the treeline.

A game had taken shape out there, though nobody could have said exactly when it started.

Max and Jake were arguing about the rules.

Again.

"You can't be the sheriff every single time," Max said.

Jake crossed his arms. "I'm older."

"That's not a rule!"

"Should be."

A little ways off, Fiona and Lily had settled onto a high flat limestone outcropping that held the warmth of the sun, braiding long strips of grass into something that might turn into a crown or a rope, depending on how their patience held out. Marisol sat beside them with a book spread open across her knees. The girls liked this perch because they could see the whole yard and all the way down the meadow to the treeline that led to the Ridge and a bit of the road that led to the Market.

Willow had positioned herself nearby, watching the boys with the careful attention of someone still learning the grammar of other children. Every few seconds her eyes moved between them, tracking the argument.

"They fight a lot," she said quietly.

"They're not fighting," Fiona said, not looking up.

Willow watched Jake give Max a shove. Max answered with a harder one.

"That looks like fighting."

Lily smiled. "If it were real, somebody'd be crying by now."

As if the yard had been listening, Lucy wandered straight into the middle of them and caught her foot on a stick. She went down hard into the grass.

A beat of silence.

Then Lucy erupted into tears of considerable feeling.

Max forgot the sheriff argument on the spot. He dropped into a crouch beside her. "You okay?"

Lucy sniffled. "Yes." She climbed to her feet and ran off.

The game picked back up.

Willow blinked. "That was fast."

Marisol turned a page. "You get used to it."

The yard filled again with the noise children make when no one is watching them too closely. Running feet. Disputed rules. Laughter rising and falling like the breeze in the pines.

Willow's attention drifted toward the road that wound down to the Market.

Three Harbinger children were making their way up the road at a slow, unhurried pace. They turned and followed the fence line, heading toward the ridge.

They didn't come close to the Lodge. They almost never did, preferring the tree line when they moved toward the ridge.

But today they stopped near the fence.

One of the boys leaned toward the other and said something low.

Another cut a glance toward the house.

The third looked directly at Willow.

Then they put their heads together again.

Their voices carried farther than they knew.

"...shouldn't be here..."

"...Teacher said..."

"...they steal people..."

Willow went still.

Marisol noticed right away.

"What is it?"

Willow didn't answer.

She was listening.

The Harbinger children moved on, their voices swallowed by the trees.

But the words had already taken root.

Marisol nudged her shoulder.

"What did they say?"

Willow's brow creased.

"They think the Lodge steals people."

Lily looked up from her grass braids.

"What?"

Willow gave a slow nod.

"They said we steal children."

Fiona snorted.

"That's ridiculous."

Marisol closed her book.

"That's what the Oracle is telling people at the Market."

Willow kept her eyes on the empty road where the others had gone.

"And they believe him."

The girls fell quiet.

Across the yard, Jake had finally won the sheriff argument and was loudly laying out the new rules to Max.

Lucy tore through the middle of them again, stick raised like a battle standard.

Willow watched.

The noise. The laughter. The ordinary, sprawling chaos of it.

Then she spoke.

"They think this place is dangerous."

Marisol looked around the clearing. At the Lodge. At the figures moving along the porch and near the barn. At the sound of Gus laughing somewhere by the woodpile, low and easy as rolling thunder.

She shrugged. "Maybe dangerous for the wrong people."

Willow didn't smile. Her eyes stayed on the road.

"They're going to tell more people."

Marisol nodded slowly. "Yes."

Neither girl spoke for a moment.

Then Willow asked quietly, "Does Jo know?"

Marisol considered that. She closed her book.

"She does, I am sure."

Near the porch steps, Jo stood with Gus and Cole, the three of them talking in low voices. From where the girls sat, the words didn't carry. But Willow watched Jo for a long moment. The way she stood. The set of her shoulders.

"They're afraid of her," Willow said. It didn't sound like a question.

Marisol followed her gaze. "Yes."

Willow nodded once.

At the Harbinger camp, fear meant someone was a threat. Here at the Lodge, she was still working out what it meant.

But something was coming clear to her, slow and certain as a morning frost.

Sometimes the person people feared most was simply the one telling the truth.

Chapter Eighty

The Meaning of Burden

The afternoon eased toward evening the way it did in early autumn, unhurried and quiet, the shadows stretching long across the yard and deepening the grass to a richer green where the sun slipped behind the ridge. Even small sounds carried farther than they should have. A woodpecker somewhere in the tree line. The distant thunk of Gus stacking cord wood near the barn.

The girls had found their way back to the limestone outcropping.

They always did, eventually. From that flat shelf of rock they could see the yard, the road down toward the Market, and the far edge of the meadow where the tree line began its slow, dark rise.

Marisol sat cross-legged with her book open across her knees. Fiona and Lily had their shoulders pressed against the warm stone, still working at the long braid of grass they'd started earlier. Willow sat nearby with her knees drawn up, watching the road the way she always did, like she was waiting for something she couldn't name.

Nobody spoke for a while.

Then Marisol looked up.

"You're thinking about something."

Willow blinked. "What?"

"You get that look."

"What look?"

"The thinking one."

Willow considered that a moment. "I was thinking about what the boys said earlier."

"The Harbinger kids?"

She nodded. "They said the Lodge steals people."

Fiona snorted. "That's ridiculous."

Willow didn't smile. "They believe it."

Lily twisted the grass braid tighter between her fingers. "Because the Oracle told them to."

"Yes." Willow paused. "In the camp they say something else, too."

Marisol closed her book.

"They say the Lodge protects burdens."

The girls looked at her.

"What does that mean?" Lily asked.

Willow answered as if the meaning were plain. "People who make the world heavy."

Marisol tilted her head. "I still don't understand."

Willow looked toward the barn where Gus moved steadily between the woodpile and the stack, unhurried and sure. "In the camp, they say every community has to stay strong."

"That sounds normal enough."

"Yes." She let a beat pass. "But they say some people make a community weak."

Fiona frowned. "Like who?"

"People who can't work." A small shrug. "People who are sick."

Marisol's expression shifted. "Like Constance."

Willow nodded.

Lily stared at her. "They killed her because she was sick?"

Willow didn't answer that directly. She looked down at her hands instead, then back at the road, and when she finally spoke her voice was low and even, the way someone speaks a thing they've heard so many times it no longer surprises them.

"They say a burden steals strength from everyone else."

The girls went very still.

Behind them, a voice cut through.

"That's stupid."

All four girls turned.

Edwin stood a few feet away, a small radio part pinched in one hand. He'd been there long enough. That much was plain.

Willow's expression flickered.

"That's what Teacher says."

Edwin stepped closer.

"What else counts as a burden?"

Willow hesitated.

"Sometimes old people."

Marisol's eyes went wide. "Like Zeke?"

Willow looked down at the rock beneath her feet.

"Yes."

Nobody said anything for a moment.

When Edwin spoke again, his voice had dropped.

"What about children?"

Willow shook her head. "Children are supposed to grow strong."

"And if they don't?"

She didn't answer right away. Her gaze drifted toward the Lodge, toward the windows where lantern light had begun to push back the dark.

"Then they might become a burden."

The words settled over the rock like something heavy and cold.

Edwin stared at her a long moment. Then he turned and walked toward the house.

"Where are you going?" Marisol called after him.

"To tell Gin."

Gin had the rifle's action stripped down on the long workbench, a patch of bore cleaner working through the channel while she ran a rod through with the careful rhythm of someone who'd done it a thousand times.

Edwin didn't slow when he came through the barn door.

"Gin?"

She glanced up without setting the rod down.

"What's wrong?"

"Maybe nothing." He hesitated, turning his cap in his hands. "But Willow just told me something."

Gin set the rifle down then.

"What kind of something?"

He repeated the conversation as carefully as he could, word for word, the way he'd learned to do with anything that mattered. The way he took messages on the radio. When he finished, the barn was quiet except for the swallows shifting in the rafters.

Gin's face had gone very still.

"Where are they now?"

"By the rock."

She was already moving.

"Come on."

The girls settled around the big kitchen table, and the room drew itself quiet.

Jo was there, and so were Gus, Cole, Riley, Father Tom, and Gunny. Nobody had said much getting to their seats.

Gin sat close to Willow, close enough that their shoulders nearly touched.

"No one is in trouble," she said. "We just want to understand."

Willow gave a small nod. Marisol found her hand beneath the table and held it.

Jo leaned forward slightly. "You said the Harbingers talk about burdens. What kinds of people do they mean?"

Willow took a slow breath. "People who cannot work." Her eyes moved briefly to Jo's cane where it rested against the table's edge, then pulled away. "People who are sick. People who make others doubt."

Cole glanced at Riley. Jo caught it.

"And what happens to those people?" Jo asked.

Willow's voice dropped to nearly nothing. "They return to the earth."

The silence that followed had weight to it.

"Who decides if someone is a burden?" Jo asked.

Willow looked up. "Teacher."

Across the table, Gunny's jaw went tight. Cole leaned back in his chair, slow and deliberate. Riley turned her gaze toward the dark window. Father Tom dropped his eyes to the table.

Jo nodded once. "Thank you for telling us."

Willow's brow creased. "Did I do something wrong?"

"No." Jo reached across and laid her hand gently over Willow's. "We ask questions because we want to understand. You helped us with that, thank you."

The girl's shoulders eased a little.

At the Lodge, questions weren't something you got punished for. That wasn't how things worked here.

But the answers Willow had given them tonight sat heavy in every chest in that room. The Harbingers weren't simply casting people out. They had woven a whole belief around it, shaped it into doctrine, and taught it to children as though it were gospel. They had built an entire belief system to justify their actions.

Chapter Eighty-One

What Makes a Community Strong

The kitchen held its quiet long after Willow stopped speaking.

The lantern above the table burned steady, throwing soft yellow light across the walls and the faces gathered beneath it.

Outside, wind moved through the pines in a low, restless murmur.

Inside, no one rushed to fill the silence.

Willow sat very still, hands folded in her lap. Marisol pressed close beside her. Jo's hand rested over Willow's, unmoving and warm.

Gunny leaned back in his chair. Cole worked his jaw slowly, rubbing his chin. Riley had fixed her eyes on the dark window above the sink, seeing nothing in the glass but her own reflection.

Father Tom broke it.

"They believe weakness spreads."

Willow nodded. "Yes."

"And they think removing someone stops that." Jo's voice was even, measured.

"Yes."

The word settled over the room like ash.

Gin crossed her arms. "That's not strength."

"That's fear," Cole said.

Willow's brow creased. "But Teacher says helping people who cannot help themselves makes everyone weaker."

From across the table, Buck let out a slow breath through his nose. He leaned forward, setting his elbows on the wood.

"I ever tell you about my brother?"

The room turned toward him.

Buck didn't look at anyone in particular. He studied the grain of the table a moment before he spoke.

"Born with a bad leg. Couldn't walk right, couldn't run with the rest of us boys." He paused. "Couldn't climb a tree worth a damn."

A faint shrug.

"But he could fix anything." He glanced at Gin. "Kept our whole farm running half the time."

Willow's frown deepened. "But if he couldn't work—"

"He worked." Buck tapped the table once, flat and final. "Just different."

The room stayed quiet until Gus spoke.

"When a storm hit our valley when I was a boy, the strongest man I knew lost half his strength in one winter."

Willow looked at him.

"Was he a burden?"

Gus smiled, just a little. "No."

"Why not?"

"Because the rest of us carried him until he got it back."

Willow looked down at the table, turning that over somewhere behind her eyes.

Gin leaned forward. "You know what happens when people help each other?"

Willow shook her head.

"They get stronger."

Gunny nodded slowly. "Units work the same way."

Willow blinked. "Units?"

"Soldiers."

He folded his hands on the table, his knuckles scarred and thick. "Strongest teams I ever served with weren't made of perfect people." He shrugged. "They were made of people who didn't leave each other behind."

The quiet settled back over the room.

Willow's eyes moved around the table. Jo's cane leaning against her chair. Buck's scarred hands resting flat on the wood. Cole. Gin. Each face steady, unhurried.

"So helping someone," she said softly, "makes you stronger?"

Jo squeezed her hand. "Yes."

Willow sat with that for a long moment.

Then she looked toward the living room where the soft sound of a baby stirred.

Jax made a small, sleepy noise.

Everyone in the room heard it.

Willow's eyes moved back to Jo.

"She's not a burden."

Jo smiled.

"No."

Willow nodded once.

At the Harbinger camp, strength had always meant cutting away weakness. Here at the Lodge, she was learning something different. Strength sometimes meant carrying someone who couldn't walk alone.

Across the table, Cole leaned back slowly.

"Well," he said quietly. "Now we know."

Gunny looked at him. "Know what?"

Cole's voice stayed even. "The Oracle isn't just killing people." He glanced toward Willow. "He's building a world where anyone can be declared a burden."

No one argued.

Outside, the wind moved softly through the pines.

Inside, the realization settled over the room the way cold air seeps under a door -- quiet, and impossible to ignore.

This wasn't just a cult.

It was an ideology.

And it was already spreading.

Chapter Eighty-Two

The Watching

Market morning came gray and cool.

Low clouds pressed down over the valley, draining the sunlight to something thin and silver. Wagons rolled slowly into the square, their wheels grinding over packed dirt, and the smell of fresh bread and woodsmoke threaded through the open air as vendors shook out tablecloths and set down their baskets.

From a distance, it looked like any other market day.

Up close, it didn't.

Jo felt it before she even climbed down from the wagon.

Eyes that stayed a beat too long. Voices that dropped when she passed.

Nothing hostile. Nothing she could point a finger at.

Just a careful distance that hadn't been there a few months ago.

Gus handed down the crate of squash and set it beside her without a word.

"You feel that?" he asked quietly.

Jo nodded once.

"The wind's changed."

Boone and Beth pulled in a few minutes later with the rest of the Lodge goods. Mary's preserves. The herb bundles from Jo's garden. Two baskets of late apples, heavy and fragrant.

The table filled quickly.

Customers came slowly.

Some still talked easy, the way they always had. Others kept it short and transactional, eyes sliding away before the conversation had really finished.

Across the square, the Harbinger tables were already set up and busy. Simple cloths. Bundles of tied herbs. A row of honey jars catching what little light the clouds allowed.

Devotion moved among her people with that unhurried calm she carried everywhere, her pale gray coat neat against the morning chill, dark hair tied back at the nape of her neck. She spoke to each person in turn, her expression settled and certain. Like someone who already knew how every conversation would end before it began.

Jo noticed the exact moment Devotion saw her.

The woman paused mid-sentence with a customer. Her gaze drifted across the square and found Jo's face with quiet precision.

It held for only a moment.

Then she turned back to her customer and finished what she was saying, as smooth as if nothing had interrupted her at all.

Gus had caught it too.

"She's been doing that all morning."

"I know."

Jo straightened a basket on the table, turning it just so.

"Let her look."

Chapter Eighty-Three

The Pattern

Night settled slowly over the Lodge.

The last of younger the children had been sent to bed, though the older ones still moved quietly through the house finishing chores. Somewhere upstairs a floorboard creaked. The faint murmur of voices drifted down through the stairwell before fading into nothing.

Downstairs, the kitchen table had filled once more.

Cole spread a rough map across the wood surface. It wasn't a proper map. Just a sheet of butcher paper covered in pencil marks showing the ridge, the Market, The School, the road to town, and the narrow deer trails Yaz had traced through the surrounding woods.

Gin leaned forward beside him. Riley stood near the window with her arms folded. Gunny rested against the wall by the stove. Yaz stayed near the door, quiet as timber.

Jo and Gus sat at the far end of the table.

For a while, nobody spoke.

Cole tapped the pencil against the paper. "Zeke disappeared here." He marked a spot near the road that ran between the Market and the ridge.

"Constance's ceremony was here. This is where we rescued Willow from her ceremony." Another mark, slightly farther up the slope.

Yaz stepped closer. "There are two more places like that."

Cole glanced up. "You're sure?"

"I saw signs weeks ago."

Riley turned from the window. "Why didn't you say something?"

Yaz shrugged slightly. "At the time it looked like animal disturbance."

Gin frowned. "And now?"

"Now it looks organized."

Cole leaned back slowly in his chair. "That's because it is." He drew a loose circle around the ridge. "They aren't reacting to problems."

Gunny nodded. "They're selecting them."

Jo had been watching the map without a word. "Influence," she said quietly.

Cole nodded. "Yes."

Gin crossed her arms.

"Constance wasn't influential."

Cole shook his head.

"No."

Riley broke the quiet, her voice low.

"She was considered a burden."

The word settled over the room like ash.

Gunny rubbed the back of his neck.

"So we've got two lists."

Cole looked up.

"Exactly."

"Influence."

He tapped the paper.

"And burden."

Jo studied the map, her fingers tracing the ridge lines.

"And who decides which list someone belongs on?"

Yaz answered from the doorway.

"The Oracle."

Silence moved through the room like a draft.

Cole spoke carefully.

"That's the real danger."

Gin looked at him.

"How so?"

"If one man decides who's useful and who isn't--"

He let it hang there.

Gunny picked it up without hesitation.

"Then everyone's expendable."

Jo nodded once.

"Yes."

She pressed both hands flat on the table.

"Which means this doesn't end with the Harbingers."

Riley frowned.

"What do you mean?"

Jo gestured toward the road that wound down to town.

"He's already planting the idea."

Nobody needed to say it out loud. They were all thinking about the whispers at Market. The rumors. The way people had started keeping a careful distance from one another, like they were already measuring each other's worth.

Cole exhaled.

"You're saying he wants the town thinking the same way he does."

Jo met his eyes.

"I think some of them already do."

No one argued with her.

Outside, the wind moved soft and easy through the pines. Inside, the map lay spread across the table, small pencil marks dotting the ridge like a rash of quiet warnings. The longer you looked at it, the harder it was to pretend it meant nothing.

This wasn't random.

It was a system. And systems had architects.

The Oracle wasn't just removing people. He was reordering the world to suit himself, one quiet decision at a time.

Chapter Eighty-Four

What We Carry

The Lodge had gone quiet.

Night had settled full over the clearing, the windows throwing warm light against the dark wall of trees beyond the yard. Most of the family was relaxing. The older kids had finished their chores and were hanging out in the great room, and somewhere down the hall the younger ones were still at it — whispering, shifting, putting off sleep the way children always do.

Upstairs, a small lantern burned low in the room Marcus and Deb shared.

Marcus sat on the edge of the bed, one elbow on his knee, his large hand pressed against his forehead like he was trying to hold something in place.

Deb sat across the room in the rocking chair.

Jax slept in her arms.

The baby made a small sound — soft and contented — and her slow, even breathing filled the quiet between them.

Neither spoke for a long while.

Finally Deb said, "My goodness your brain is loud."

Marcus lowered his hand. "Sorry."

She smiled faintly. "You've been apologizing for two days."

He rubbed the back of his neck. "I just —"

He stopped.

Deb waited.

Marcus looked down at the tiny bundle cradled against her chest.

"I don't know how to protect her from everything."

Deb's expression softened. "You can't."

He shook his head slowly. "I've spent my whole life solving problems."

"I know."

"And this one —" He exhaled. "This one I can't fix."

Deb looked down at Jax. "You're not supposed to fix her."

He frowned. "What do you mean?"

"She isn't broken."

The words settled between them like snow on still water.

Marcus leaned back on the bed. "I know that."

"Do you?"

He met her eyes. Held them. Then nodded. "Yes."

"She's perfect," Deb said quietly.

Marcus looked at the baby again. "She is, isn't she. She might have a harder road."

"Yes."

"I hate that."

"I know."

The rocking chair creaked as Deb shifted her weight. After a moment she said, "But she's not walking it alone."

Marcus looked up at her.

"Not ever."

A soft knock came at the door.

Marcus stood and opened it.

Willow hovered in the hallway, her expression unreadable, somewhere between wanting to come in and wanting to disappear.

"Is it okay that I knocked?"

Deb smiled. "Yes, come in."

Willow stepped inside. Her eyes went straight to the baby, the way a compass needle finds north.

"Jax is sleeping."

"Oh."

She drifted closer to the chair, drawn without seeming to mean it.

"She's very small."

Marcus chuckled quietly. "That's how babies start."

Willow stood still for a moment. Then, carefully, like she was choosing each word before she let it out:

"May I hold her?"

Deb glanced at Marcus. He nodded. Marcus pulled a chair over and WIllow sat.

Deb rose and settled Jax into Willow's arms. The girl went rigid, shoulders climbing toward her ears, as if breathing too hard might break something.

"Support her head," Deb said gently.

Willow adjusted. Jax made a small sound, a soft creak of noise, and stilled again.

Willow stared down at her.

"She's warm."

"Yes."

Willow began to rock, slow and unconscious, the way bodies seem to know things the mind hasn't caught up to yet.

After a moment, her voice dropped.

"At the camp... babies like her..."

She didn't finish.

Marcus watched her. "What about them?"

Willow swallowed. "They said sometimes they return to the earth early."

The room went quiet in a way that had weight to it.

Deb didn't flinch. She simply reached out and rested her hand on Willow's shoulder.

"That doesn't happen here."

Willow looked up. "No?"

"No."

She looked back down at the baby. Something was shifting behind her eyes, slow and cautious, like ice going soft at the edges.

"She's not a burden."

"No," Deb said softly.

"She will learn things."

"Yes."

"And people will help her."

"Yes."

Willow was quiet for a moment. "Good. I like her. Helping her makes the community stronger?"

Marcus smiled. It was the first real one all evening.

"Exactly."

Willow kept rocking. Jax slept on, warm and unhurried, tucked against a girl who was only just beginning to understand that some lives were worth fighting for, not ending early.

Downstairs, the kitchen lantern still burned.

Jo sat at the table with both hands wrapped around a mug of tea. Across from her, Gus had his chair tipped back, arms folded, watching her the way he'd watched her for forty years — steady, patient, reading every small thing she didn't say out loud.

The house around them had finally gone quiet.

Jo stared into the steam curling up from her cup.

"You heard what Devotion said today."

"Hard to miss."

She took a slow sip.

"He's watching."

"Yes."

The fire settled in the stove. A log shifted. Neither of them spoke for a moment.

Then Gus asked the question he'd been sitting on all evening.

"You're going soon, aren't you?"

Jo didn't answer right away. Her eyes moved to the dark window, to the black shape of the ridge rising somewhere beyond the treeline.

"Yes."

Gus nodded slowly. "I figured."

She set the mug down on the table. "If we're going to stop him, I need to understand him."

Gus studied her face. "You sure that's safe?"

Jo smiled, just barely. "No."

He chuckled low in his throat. "Well. That's reassuring."

"You know I'm going anyway."

He exhaled through his nose and leaned forward, reaching for the pot. "Yes." He poured himself more tea. "So when?"

Jo's gaze drifted back toward the ridge.

"Soon. I have something to take care of first."

The lantern flame dipped and steadied. Outside, the wind moved through the pines in long, slow passes.

Somewhere out beyond the valley, in whatever dark hollow he'd claimed as his own, the man who called himself the Oracle was waiting.

One way or another, that waiting was going to end.

Chapter Eighty-Five

The Invitation

Morning came pale and cold.

A thin frost had settled over the valley in the night, whitening the grass and the old wagon tracks that wound down toward the road. The sun hadn't yet cleared the ridge, and the Lodge sat deep in the long gray shadow of the pines.

Jo came down off the porch one step at a time, her cane finding solid ground before she trusted her weight to it.

Odin stayed close, the big dog's breath rising in small clouds around her legs.

Gus was at the wagon, working a strap over one of the crates, cinching it down with the practiced ease of a man who had loaded wagons most of his life. He glanced up when he heard her coming.

"You sure you want to go today?"

Jo smiled faintly.

"It's Market day."

"That wasn't the question."

She pulled herself up onto the wagon seat without asking for help.

Gus watched her for a moment, something working behind his eyes. Then he shook his head and climbed up beside her.

"Well," he muttered. "Too late to pretend I didn't know the answer."

The market square was already humming when they pulled in.

Wagons sat in loose rows along the road, tables unfolded beside them, piled with bundles of herbs and baskets of apples and jars of preserves catching the morning light. The smell of woodsmoke and fresh bread drifted through the crowd. The murmur of trading and talk filled the air, and for a moment it almost felt like none of it had happened. Like the world was still whole.

Then people noticed Jo.

Conversations didn't stop. Nobody pointed or whispered loud enough to hear. It was quieter than that. A shift in the air, the way eyes followed her as she stepped down from the wagon. A watchful stillness that had been growing stronger every market day.

Beth and Boone arrived a few minutes later with the rest of the Lodge goods. Mary began arranging the preserve jars along the table edge, her hands quick and sure. Jo laid out the herb bundles from her garden, smoothing the twine on each one.

Across the square, the Harbinger stalls stood in their usual neat rows.

Devotion moved among them, her pale coat easy to spot against the darker clothing of the crowd. Jo saw the exact moment the woman's eyes found her. A pause, barely a beat, and then Devotion was walking toward them.

Gus leaned slightly toward Jo. "Well."

Jo didn't look at him. "Let's not keep her waiting."

Devotion stopped at the Lodge table. "Mrs. Callahan."

"Devotion."

The woman's face stayed composed, pleasant as carved stone. "Teacher was wondering if you'd given any thought to his invitation."

Jo reached into the pocket of her apron. The envelope was folded neat, sealed with a small press of wax. She held it out.

"For him."

Devotion took it without hesitation. "May I ask what it says?"

Jo rested both hands on the head of her cane. "You may."

Devotion waited.

Jo met her eyes. "Tell him I accept."

Something moved across Devotion's face, not surprise exactly. Closer to satisfaction, the look of a woman whose expectations had been confirmed.

"I thought he might appreciate that."

Jo gave a single nod. Devotion tucked the envelope inside her coat, inclined her head politely, and walked back toward the Harbinger stalls without another word.

The market noise filled back in around them.

Gus let out a slow breath. "That seemed important."

Jo watched Devotion disappear into the crowd. Then she climbed back up to the wagon seat. Gus gathered the reins.

"So what was that about?" he asked.

Jo glanced toward the ridge rising at the far end of the valley, dark against the summer sky.

Then she smiled, small and unhurried.

"I think it's time we met the neighbors."

ABOUT THE AUTHOR

KELLY SCHWEIGER lives tucked among the hills, fields, and trees of upstate NY, where stories grow wild and the seasons write their own poetry. A lifelong lover of

quiet places and fierce characters, she writes fiction that explores resilience, family, and the unbreakable thread between land and heart. When not writing, Kelly can be found relaxing with her loving husband, Fred, playing with her grandchildren, foraging for 'lawn salad', reading, or drinking too much coffee with her cats curled at her feet. This is her debut novel, although she has published several cookbooks and children's books in the past.

www.ingramcontent.com/pod-product-compliance
Lightning Source LLC
LaVergne TN
LVHW100500110826
845146LV00002B/464

9798999099877